MW01124649

Cascading Sunsets on Sandy Island
Natlie Bartholomew Pitt

With all my

heart

Copyright © 2021 Natlie Pitt

All rights reserved. No part of this book may be reproduced or transmitted in any form or by any means, electronic or mechanical, including photocopying, recording or by any information storage and retrieval system without permission in writing from the publisher.

Roaring Seas Press—Big Bear Lake, CA
ISBN: 978-1-7369938-9-7
Library of Congress Control Number: 2021906901
Title: *Cascading Sunsets on Sandy Island*
Author: Natlie B Pitt
Digital distribution | 2021
Paperback | 2021

This is a work of fiction. The characters, names, incidents, places, and dialogue are products of the author's imagination, and are not to be construed as real.

Dedication

This book is dedicated to my Sister-in-Law Susan to always remember that Love is the journey of an ever unfolding rose...

Chapter 1

T he sound of seagulls awakens the morning as the sunrise casts its glistening rays upon the surf. It was almost summer, and Faith knew it would never be the same. It seems the months had flown by since her marriage ended, leaving her life in a state of uncertainty. Faith had to be strong, for her seven-year-old daughter Katherine; her only blessing from a deceitful marriage.

"Mommy, Mommy you're awake," Katherine said, climbing onto her mom's bed embracing her tightly.

"Fain please come quickly; mommy's awake."

The assistant came hurrying toward the main bedroom. He knew that her mother did not want her to see her like this and had requested for him to keep her at bay for now.

"Katherine, sweetheart, come so that your mommy can have her rest," he called. But Faith motioned to him that it was alright. He exhaled a sigh of relief to see mother and daughter in a tight embrace. The two were almost identical with large green eyes and sandy blond hair. She had spent the entire winter and spring months indoors and he was beginning to worry about her. Unknown to her, there were times he'd pressed his ear against her bedroom door and heard her sobbing quietly, wishing there was something he could do to ease the pain she'd endured from her emotionally, abusive, husband Eric. But he was gone now, and to him, whether she had realized it or not, it was the best thing that could have happened to her. The only pain he felt was that she had genuinely loved him and that was worthy of grief; however long it took.

A few hours later, Faith wandered into her kitchen. For some reason, something about her home appeared different than she had remembered. She could tell that Fain had done an excellent job managing things. He had also rearranged some furniture and new paintings hung on the walls in the living room, dining room and kitchen. She liked the changes he'd made and thought that maybe it would be the beginning of a new life for her and Katherine. She sipped on the cup of coffee she'd poured and stepped onto the balcony overlooking the ocean. She was greeted by the warm sunrise on her face and for the first time in months, she felt like she was coming back to life.

She had invested her entire life into being the perfect wife for him. He was everything to her: having agreed to move to this Island to build a life with him. Far away from any memory of her tainted life in Germany. Nothing could have prepared her for this. Not even the many evenings he had come home unusually late. As she reflects on the past six months, she no longer wishes to search for answers. Maybe there were none and if there were any answers at all, she no longer needed them. She'd found her answers in the absence of words, in the depths of her being, she reached for that last ounce of strength, sufficient to step forward into the unknown. As she glanced upon the rough waters below; it was almost as though there was a message depicted in the angry tides. For even the roughness eventually came to a calm; instilling sudden hope that the roughness of her life will surely arrive at a place of rest.

She must have fallen asleep on the balcony and awoke to the sound of an engine as a small fishing boat sped across the surf. She looked closely realizing it was Fain and Katherine. Katherine was wearing an orange safety jacket and was clinging onto Fain as he cut water on the open surf. A sudden panic came over her. What was he thinking? This is no water for a boat ride with a seven-year-old child. She sprang up and ran toward the beach, waving her hands to grab his attention, with no luck. She then removed the white scarf from around her neck and waved it anxiously to get Fain's attention, but it was no use. As she approached the surf, she missed her footing on a slippery rock and fell backwards; her head barely missing a large piece of driftwood. He'd crossed the line and regardless of how much help he's been, he had a lot of explaining to do, including where in the world he'd gotten that boat from? She lay on the soft white sand where she had fallen, staring up at the clear blue sky. She then glanced to her side and noticed a graceful, white Seagull approaching her cautiously, carrying a small fish in its mouth. It was almost unreal. As this beautiful winged being continued to approach her, she looked on in disbelief as the fearless creature placed the fish next to her. Then just as she had a chance to believe what she'd seen; the Seagull flew off. Something must have startled him and as sure

2

as her thoughts, she looked in time to see Fain and Katherine running toward her.

"Faith are you alright?" he panicked.

Seeing him this concerned caused all anger toward him to subside. Instead she laughed and stood up in time to avoid being wet by the gliding surf.

"Mommy, are you feeling better?" Katherine asked, looking up at her with hopeful eyes. Faith looked at them both and began chuckling softly. Still unsure why she was laying in the sand, Fain joined in the laughter. As they walked back to the beach house, Katherine held both her Mother's and Fain's hand. For now, they were the only people in the world that mattered to her and that is the way she'd hope it stayed forever.

Later, as they sat admiring the sunset, Fain reminded her that he was nearing the end of his contract. He'd been with the French family an entire year and would love to have his contract renewed, for at least another year; especially now that Eric was out of the picture and Faith and Katherine needed him. She didn't respond to his inquiry regarding his contract, but he wasn't concerned.

"Where did you get that fishing yacht from, Fain Collins?" Surprised, he looked over at her.

"Oh, I rented it from your neighbor, about ten boat slips down the surf.

"Neighbors, we have neighbors?"

"The Hutton family, they moved shortly after..." He wanted to say shortly after the divorce, but he didn't want to remind her.

"Shortly after Eric left?" she asked, finishing his sentence.

He was surprised that she was able to even mention his name. He swore it would have taken her at least a decade to get past the bitterness Eric had put her through. But she did and he knew that Faith had arrived at a good place-a place that may one day lead to complete happiness for her.

"Yes," he replied."

"I'm surprised that we have neighbors this time of year. It's been at least five years since anyone's occupied that Bungalow. I've also heard that it needed a lot of repairs."

"I guess that would explain all the activity there during the early spring months," Fain said.

"What else have I missed Fain Collins?" she asked, now sitting up from her lounge chair smiling at him. Considering everything, she looked remarkable.

"Faith Elizabeth French, I can ask you the same question, you look so different."

"Hmm?" she mumbled, grabbing a small mirror and holding it up to her face. He giggled when he realized what she had thought.

"No, I meant you look like a brand-new dish from the store." She laughed at his odd description.

"I'm happy that you're here Fain. I wouldn't have gotten this far without you; especially for my darling Katherine." He took this as a sign that he had an excellent chance of getting his contract renewed and didn't feel the need to mention it again. He was here for now, and that is all that mattered-at least to his new Bff Katherine. Who at such a tender age already understood the meaning of friendship; something he'd always hoped to have, regardless of how all their lives turned out.

Faith stared at her image in the mirror. She had lost at least twenty pounds and her pale complexion seems almost transparent from being indoors all these months. She felt stronger than she could remember; at least more alive than before. She was ready to embark on a journey, one that would erase all memory of him. She could hardly believe how she now felt, even though only six months before, she thought that it would be sane to plummet deep beneath the ocean. Nothing could have prepared her for the newness she now felt; energy, that only a miracle could explain.

Faith dug through her dresser drawers searching for the final divorce decree that she'd received from Eric French. How silly she'd been to have not seen this as a blessing in disguise. It was like a gift from a thief; a thief who'd stolen her life. The thief that had the audacity to set her free; how is it she couldn't see the blessing in all of this? It was perfect and now she was free to be her, free to find truth. She had lived, died and has now resurrected into the butterfly that she didn't realize she wanted to be. Free from all duty to an undeserving 'Brat' who dared to call himself a man. The only sorrow she now felt is for the next woman that would dare to call him 'Husband.' Nevertheless, she'd forgiven him, in complete love, and adoration of all that is possible.

4

The days ahead beaconed, calling her to embark on a journey that have been prolonged by an enmity that prohibited and limited her to walls and roads that led nowhere. All of which created within her a desire for adventure. As she sat thinking of these things; her doorbell rang. She waited for Fain to answer it. But the bell rang again, then she heard keys jingle and then the door swung open.

"Uncle Calvin," said Katherine, running and jumping into her uncle's arms.

"Eric?" said Fain in disbelief.

"You must be Fain. I'm Calvin, Eric's twin brother. Pleased to finally meet you."

"I had no idea Eric had a twin brother, it's a pleasure to meet you," Fain said, still surprised by the strange encounter.

"Katherine, darling, you haven't grown an inch in years," Calvin joked.

"Oh uncle Calvin, you're hilarious, you haven't changed for one bit, but wait a minute, you've got yourself a little tummy there," Katherine teased. Both men laughed.

Fain was impressed how well Katherine was able to distinguish between her uncle Calvin and her dad, the fact that they looked identical. He was unsure of the reason for Calvin's surprise visit and wondered if it was Faith that had invited him.

"Where's Faith?" he asked looking over at Fain. At that moment, Faith joined them in the Kitchen.

"Mommy, look it's Uncle Calvin," said Katherine excitedly.

"Calvin, when did you get in?" said Faith looking puzzled.

"I didn't expect to see you around here this time of year."

"Oops, pardon my manners. Calvin, I want you to meet my assistant Fain," she said proudly.

"Yes, we met earlier. How have you been?" said Calvin quickly changing the topic.

"I've been great," she said now realizing why he'd come.

"Calvin, I wished you'd inform us of your visit," said Faith looking away from him. He reminded her so much of Eric, yet they were complete opposites, as night and day.

"I didn't realize you've had such a devoted assistant and so I've come to offer my support after learning what happened." At that Faith nodded for Fain and Katherine to leave the room.

"I know he never deserved you," Calvin said angrily. Faith smiled and walked toward the balcony. Calvin stared at her from the hallway; the wind stirred her hair and clothing. She always looked beautiful but there was something new in her eyes and she appeared more confident than he'd remembered. As he joined Faith, she turned to face him.

"Calvin Jonathan French, what are you doing here, and what can I do for you?"

"Faith Elizabeth, I know that I don't have the most popular look around, but you

know that I can at least check on my niece and favorite sister-in-law. I've just talked Eric out of a lot of nonsense."

"Meaning?" Her eyes narrowed.

Calvin knew that he was getting nowhere and he knew that he had very little time to change the conversation.

"Calvin I'm terribly sorry, please pardon my aggression. I think it's awfully sweet that you've dropped by to check on Katherine and I. Your resemblance to Eric is not your fault at all and I'm truly over it," she laughed. I've made up my mind that it was truly a moment of grace when he'd finally freed me and I've come to a place of acceptance in my life-I'm truly over him, Calvin," she said confidently.

Overjoyed by her new confession, he embraced her tightly. As she embraced him, she noticed a small hydroplane anchored near the surf.

"Are you and Kat ready for a little adventure?"

"Nope, no way," she laughed. "The last time you said it was a little adventure, we crash landed on a strange Island and Eric almost killed you. Worst, I was pregnant with Katherine. You're crazy Calvin, not this time, I've retired from little so-called adventures," she said pushing him gently. She was almost back to her old self and he believed her when she said that she was over it all.

Calvin's visit was a refreshing change, yet a reminder that she was ready to embrace her new life. It was almost as though fate was the reason. It almost angered her that he resembled her Ex so much, yet he was so different in so many ways. As she looked at her image in the mirror, she knew that change was the only answer to her question. After all, she felt nothing. Nothing but a refreshing change that beckoned her to move forward to the unknown-something she couldn't wait to experience.

Chapter 2

Fain stared at little Katherine as she played with her new Barbie doll house that had just arrived. She was the smartest, most resilient first grader he'd ever seen. The fact that her father had been out of the picture for almost six months, she seemed to have adjusted well. Yet, with each passing day, he grew more concerned for his favorite employer. Although he enjoyed his position as Faith's Assistant, at times he felt out of place with the French family. Was he in over his head?

"Fain, would you like to help me with my dolls? They all need to get into their evening dresses. We are going out to tea," said Katherine in a lady-like expression.

"Sure sweetheart," he called.

"What do you think of my new doll house?" Katherine asked optimistically.

"I think it needs new paint. It's pink, and you hate pink," Fain scolded in a pretentious tone.

"I knew you'd agree," Katherine said happily. As they headed down the stairs to the Garage to find new paint, the doorbell rang.

"Don't answer it Fain, if it's important, they will call again," said Katherine. Fain smiled at her mature expression; no one ever calls this time of year anyway, he thought. Faith was surprised that neither Katherine nor Fain had answered the door and she thought that they had somehow gotten locked out. She hurried out of the shower and wrapped her bathrobe around her. She was surprised when she'd opened the front door that there was no one there. The bell rang again and this time she realized that it was coming from the back. Why in the world would anyone ring the doorbell from the back balcony? She thought. As she swung the door open, she was surprised to see a tall gentleman who appears to be in his mid-forties. Surprised, she shut the door. She then spoke to him through the barely opened window.

"Who are you and what do you want?" she called.

"Sorry for the unexpected call, but I'm looking for Chance, I just saw her ran up your stairwell."

"Oh, who's Chance?" Faith asked puzzled.

"My daughter's dog, I knew that bringing her with us would be a lot of work, she's a bit of a handful," he replied.

"Are you sure she came this way?"

"Yes, just a minute ago," he replied.

Faith was a bit reluctant but she allowed him to check the balcony. While he searched, Faith hurried inside to get dressed. She came out as he was carrying an adorable brown Lab puppy down the stairwell.

"You found her?"

"Yes, my daughter is very determined to have her back," he admitted.

"How old is your daughter, and what's her name?"

"Sydney, she took seven this April."

"She's about the same age as my Katherine; she'll be seven in a couple of months. By the way I'm Faith," she said, the wind stirring her long white backless summer dress.

"I'm Hank, I'm going through a divorce, and my daughter and I are here for the summer. It's refreshing to know that we have neighbors," he said.

"You speak for us both," she smiled.

"Alright then it was nice meeting you, maybe we can arrange for the girls to get together sometime," she said, turning to leave.

"Yes, Syd would be excited to know that she isn't the only kid on this Island," he said patting Chance's ear. Faith looked at him as he left. There was sadness in his eyes, and she wondered what else might have brought him to Sandy Island.

Later that day after Fain and Katherine finished repainting her doll house, he went for a jog on the beach. It was the perfect day and not a wave could be seen out for miles. This is one of the reasons he loves Sandy island; so secluded and private, not a care in the world. He was living his dream and wasn't sure if he'd ever return to France. At times he thought of his ex-girlfriend whom he'd sworn to spend the rest of his life with. Only now he could see how wrong such a commitment would have been. He remembered how hurt she was when he'd told her of his decision to accept this job offer. After leaving France, they hadn't spoken for an entire year. He was determined to prove to her that he'd made the right decision. After months of refusing to speak with him, she'd finally agree to hear his reasoning. It was then she'd revealed to him in an email that she'd submitted a video audition and had gotten a part in a Feature Film in Los Angeles. He couldn't believe it. Unknown to him, she'd been in Los Angeles the last four months filming. This has been her dream for a very long time and he was excited for her. Despite how she feels, he plans to visit her in the coming weeks. Just as soon as he was certain that Faith would be fine without him for a little while.

Calvin was surprised when the combination lock to his Mother's home didn't work. She'd just downsized from her six-bedroom Marina home in the Marina District to a smaller three-bedroom Italianate Victorian home in the Presidio Heights. Calvin and his brother Eric thought it was a great decision. He thought that maybe she was more motivated to downsize since the loss of their father five years before. After entering the combination code a second time, he rang the doorbell. A few moments later a woman that appears to be in her late twenties swung the door open.

"Hello, I'm Rachael..." Before he introduced himself, Eric came into the room.

"Calvin, when did you get in?"

"Eric, what are you doing here?" he asked. Hearing her son's voice, Elizabeth came hurrying.

"Oh how wonderful, Calvin, you're home!" She said embracing her son excitedly. Of both sons' Calvin was the baby by one minute and has always won his mother's affection.

"Mother, you look well," he said embracing her almost to a lift.

"Calvin, I would like you to meet my fiancée Rachael." Eric said in a hesitating tone. Calvin responded under his breath.

"Pleasure to meet you." At the same time wondering what in the world was Eric thinking bringing this woman to their Mother's house, this soon.

"How long will you be in town?" he asked.

"About a week," he responded following their mom to the kitchen.

"Mother I'm starved, what's cooking?" said Calvin going through the kitchen. Rachael giggled at the expression. Despite their similarities, she noticed the immediate difference in their personalities. As they all sat around the dinner table, Calvin mentioned his short visit with Faith and Katherine.

"We landed on Sandy Island to refuel. It was the closest encounter to landing in the middle of the ocean I've ever had in my twenty years as a Pilot. Of course, this is a new Aircraft and we've had to make an unexpected stop in New York which may have been the cause. Nonetheless, it was great to see my little niece. She's grown tremendously since my visit a year ago.

"How's my granddaughter and her mother?" Elizabeth asked smiling broadly.

"They both look well. Katherine and Faith looked surprisingly well."

"That sounds like my granddaughter." Both Rachael and Eric seemed uncomfortable with the conversation and remained silent throughout. With Eric smiling every now and then when Katherine's name is mentioned.

"I've never really understood why she hired a male Nanny and all the way from France."

I have to admit it was a bit surprising, but he seems like a nice guy and very passionate about what he does. I had a chance to look at his resume and this appears to be all he's ever done since high school. Maybe it's something he truly loves.

"Maybe so, but however, there has to be something more to this male Nanny," said Elizabeth pouring herself more wine.

After dinner, Calvin stepped out on the porch where Eric and Rachael were in an embrace.

"Excuse me folks," he said and was about to leave.

"Calvin, can I see you for a minute?" When they were alone, Eric's soft appearance became stern.

"What were you thinking? I already told you to stay out of my business." He said in a fiery tone. How dare you bring up my family at the dinner table?"

"Don't make this about me, Eric. I can ask you the same question. How dare you bring this woman to our Mothers house? You are shaming this family. So, don't you dare make this about me. You never deserved her, you bastard!"

"Wow, where is this coming from?" said Eric surprised. Calvin left the balcony without responding.

Faith tossed and turned all night, by dawn she'd fallen into a deep sleep and didn't wake until late afternoon. She awoke to a delicious familiar scent and just as she was about to inquire, Fain entered her bedroom carrying a tray of her favorite Armenian pastry; Nazook, which she renamed (Nanook) and piping hot coffee.

"For you, my dear just the way you like," said Fain placing the tray next to her.

"You're up to something Fain. You never make my favorite morning snack unless you're thinking of something very expensive in return."

"*Pas du tout*," he replied with a wink.

She smiled at his nonchalant response. He'd make a fine actor, she thought. As she sipped on her coffee, Katherine stood in her doorway, wearing a tiny chef's apron and hat. Her face almost entirely covered in flour.

"Fain said I could help, but I did the entire work mommy, I made your favorite pastry all by myself. What do you think mommy?" Before Faith could respond, she broke into laughter. But her very serious seven-year-old daughter folded her hands and waited for a response. Faith choked back laughter trying her best to appear as serious as possible.

"These are your best yet sweetheart. You've outdone yourself, they're amazing." Her flour covered cheeks went from serious to a broad grin.

"Glad you like 'em mommy," she said and skipped down the hallway.

Later, Fain and Katherine presented Faith with a set of goggles, Fins and an oxygen tank.

"No way, not in a million years," she laughed.

"Maybe this will change your mind," said Fain leading her to the balcony. Hank and Sydney were standing on the surf next to a large fishing boat with the name 'Sandy Babe' written on the stern.

"I thought this would be a great way to introduce the girls," called Hank.

"That's quite the intro," said Faith looking in time to see Katherine running down toward Hank and Sydney.

"Get your fanny down here mommy, this looks like a lot of fun!" Faith narrowed her eyes at Fain.

"Did you teach my daughter English?" Fain scratched his head.

"She said she'll be right there," said Fain answering for Faith.

"Alright, that's great," said Hank, escorting both girls to the boat.

12

"Fain Collins, you are in so much trouble," Faith said, eyes narrowed.

"Take another look at my resume, maybe there's something you might have missed," he laughed taking her handbag.

"And besides, you've barely been out of the Bungalow, we missed you like crazy. Here's the deal, I help bring you back to life and then you're free to kill me after," he laughed.

"Ahh, fantastic proposal, this will be so much fun. So, would you throw me off the boat or bury me behind your Bungalow?"

"Take your best guess," she said wickedly, eyes narrowed. Fain laughed heartily. As they neared the surf…

"This is a huge boat," said Faith climbing onto the narrow stairwell, leading to the deck. As they stepped onboard, Katherine and Sydney came running toward them.

"Mommy, Fain, this is Sydney, my new friend and we are sharing a room on deck," she said excitedly.

"What about me, who am I sharing with," said Fain pretentiously. Katherine and Syd laughed.

"You're funny," said Sydney introducing herself. "My dad and I just bought this old Bungalow over there," she said pointing. "I was really excited when he told me about Katherine and I suggested to him that we meet this way. I hope it's alright," she said.

"Sydney, I'm Katherine's mom Faith, you are a beautiful girl, thanks for inviting us."

"You are very welcome," she said and then ran off. As the girls ran about excitedly, Hank joined them on deck carrying three glasses of Champagne.

"What's the occasion?" Faith asked. Hank stared blankly for a moment.

"How about the craziest summer ever?" All laughed.

"Well this is truly surprising, maybe you might live after all," said Katherine looking over at Fain, already relaxed on a lounge chair on deck, sunglasses in place and legs crossed. Hank laughed at Katherine's mature expression.

"Mind if I show you around," ask Hank.

"Not at all," said Faith.

"Fain, I'm going to have a look around, want to join us?" She called.

"Enjoy, I will keep an eye on the girls," he called.

"Thanks Fain," Hank called. As they looked around; this is a beautiful boat, large enough to cater a major event. This is right up Fain's ally with a fully stocked bar," Faith said.

"I can hear you," Fain Called.

"Glad you like it. I thought it was a mistake choosing the boat over the house, but I'm starting to think I got the better end of it," Hank said excitedly. As they neared the Captain's quarters…"Would you like to steer for a little?"

"Umm, why not, after all I do know my way around better than you," she boasted.

"Ha, and to my benefit. Let's give you and Sydney a tour of Sandy Island."

I'm in," he says lifting the anchor onto the Deck.

Girl's we are going to take a tour of the Island" Fain called. Where are you?" Syd and Katherine stood on the edge of the deck and on the count of three, both girls jumped legs first into the water. Fain heard a splash but had no idea which side of the boat it came from. As he searched, he realized that the boat had begun to move. The girls, not realizing, splashed about the water fully geared in their divers outfit. Fain searched frantically, he tried not to panic. As he neared the Stern of the boat, he noticed the girls flip flops and bath towels. As he looked up from his discovery, he noticed that both girls were at least a mile away from the boat.

"Katherine! Sydney! What in the name of Fain are you thinking?" Both girls laughed and waved.

"Jeez, calm down Mr. Fain. It's summer." Hank heard noises and came hurrying.

"Sydney, you are so grounded young lady!" he called.

Faith followed shortly after.

"Katherine Elizabeth French, you are toast." Both girls looked at each other and Sydney whispered in Katherine's ear.

"They're pretending." Hank knew what Sydney had whispered to Katherine and realized that he would have to get wet in order to get the girls back onto the boat. Unnoticed, Fain walked toward the back of the boat and dove underwater then surfaced an inch away from the girls. Both screamed in terror and began to climb onto Fain's shoulder.

"I have to agree, this water feels great," Fain called. Hank shook his head and looked at Faith.

14

"This water beats, come on guys lighten up." Syd called. Just as she was about to scream at Fain, Hank jumped into the water and back stroked toward Fain and the girls. Faith looked on at the group and after removing her sunglasses, downed the remainder of her Champagne, she spread her towel on a lounge chair and stretched out on deck.

"Better yet, the sun thanks you for your nice pale complexion in which to dine?" said Fain.

"I've changed my mind Fain, I will have your head," Faith promised. Hank laughed. Earlier, he wondered what their relationship was, but it was clear that it was either business or possibly the best friendship he's ever seen.

"Fain, I heard you're the perfect host. Sydney and I would love to try one of your French Entrees."

"Consider it done," said Fain proudly. After lunch, the new found friends cancelled the tour for another time and relaxed on deck. At Fain's request, Hank swung his fishing line into the water in the hopes of a fresh catch for dinner. Faith relaxed with the girls and Sydney painted Faith's nails in pink and silver. Katherine could tell that Sydney liked having her mom around but she understood. Her mom is beautiful and kind. There's a hidden strength about her, one that shone on her face, defining her elegance. She was glad that her mom had agreed to this; it was refreshing and unexpected. As the ladies enjoyed each other's company, they heard a sudden...

"You stubborn bastard, I got you," said Hank reeling in what looked like a large catch. "Look what we have we here?" Hank said admiring his catch.

"Based on the looks of this, dinner looks great," said Fain folding his arms. Katherine and Sydney looked on in disgust.

"That's dinner?" Sydney growled.

"Oh, my word, look at its grinding bones," said Katherine.

"No thanks, I'll have a steak," said Sydney, taking Katherine by the hand and walking away.

"More for us," Hank called.

"Largest catch I've ever seen. Fain maybe we can try your *Pasta Nicoise*," Faith suggested.

"Exactly what I had in mind," he replied. Hank lifted his proud catch and placed it on the scale. He whistled loudly.

"This baby weighs almost forty pounds. I swear my luck has been a lot better on Sandy Island." Faith smiled at his sense of humor. He seemed like a happy, free spirited guy who knew what he wanted. There's no denying that he was long over his previous relationship. Well, at least it appears that way.

After dinner, Sydney approached Fain. "I thought you were making Salmon for dinner." All including Katherine who's had Fain's *Pasta Nicoise* before laughed heartily.

"We've just kissed that Salmon goodbye, Hun. I thought you wanted a steak," her father played. All except Katherine laughed.

"You mean that was Salmon? What happened to its heads and tails? What about the bones?"

"I'll take that as a complement. Glad you've enjoyed my famous *Pasta Nicoise*," Fain said proudly.

"Fain you rock, you're the first guy to make all heads and tails and bones disappear. How do we say awesome in French?" Sydney asked.

"*Impressionnant,*" said Fain, closing his thumb and index to indicate perfection.

"I like you Fain."

"But what about your old dad; I'm the one that caught the Fish, and removed the head, bones and tail."

"Oh dad, that's gross, and you work too hard."

"But, but, but," her dad said, pretentiously.

"Be sure to lather up dad, or you'll smell like fishy and I won't want to come near you," Sydney said looking scornful.

Everyone laughed as Hank glared at his daughter eyes narrowed. Later, the girls got into the Jacuzzi on deck. Sydney admitted that this was the most fun she's had in a long time. They'd spend almost the entire day onboard Sandy Babe. It was already almost 7:00pm and the twilight sky appeared sun kissed; displaying an orange pinkish display. There were still a few white fluffy clouds that were slowly fading grey, as the sun slowly descended onto the horizon. Despite being only ten miles offshore, Faith felt like she was on a tiny vacation; one she hoped would last more than a day. As she gazed at the fading evening, the sound of a jet ski got louder as it approached the boat. As the watercraft neared, Faith noticed there was a young couple holding on tightly as they sped off. A short moment later, a small coast guard followed the couple, demanding

16

that they pull their craft over. Hank took the stairs to the second deck where Faith stood overlooking the banisters.

"Well, that's what I called the end of a quiet evening," said Hank. Faith turned to face him and smiled.

"Hank, I would like to extend my deepest thanks to you and Sydney for a lovely evening," she said, removing her sunglasses.

"It is I that should thank you for sharing your family and best of all, your French Chef," he said, his eyes expressing genuine gratitude.

As they neared the surf, Faith helped Katherine down the stairwell, onto the boardwalk. Both girls were sleepy and had argued that they spent the night on deck, but even as convinced as Sydney was that it was a great idea, all three adults agreed that it was an evening well spent. Possibly the most relaxing and quiet, since the summer brings in the crowds from every corner of the Bay. Before parting, the girls hugged each other and agreed to get together the following day. Hank shook Fain's hand and thanked him for dinner. Faith smiled as she held her hands out to Hank'. He embraced her instead and placed a soft kiss on her face. It was unexpected but felt good. As Hank and Sydney drove Sandy Babe toward the boat slip in front of their home, Faith and Hank looked over their shoulders at the same time. Something about that evening made her want to spend more time with him and Sydney, sometime soon, she hoped.

Chapter 3

It's been two weeks since Katherine met Sydney and the two were now inseparable. They'd had several sleepovers and had discussed some of the things they shared in common. Although Sydney was only almost seven, the way she folded her arms and discusses her parent's divorce made her appear much older. She'd mentioned to Katherine that she'd hoped that this summer would never end. It was almost as night and day the person she becomes when at play and when discussing grown up things. Katherine only listened. She wanted to be the stronger of the two; the one that listened. She admitted that her dad was much happier here on the Island and hopes that he remains this way after they returned to New York.

"My mom says that most times it's for the best. Let's look at the bright side of things. After all we're friends, we would have never met if none of this had happened," said Katherine taking a bite from the Sandwich that Fain had made for them. Sydney laughed the way Katherine narrowed her forehead to make her point.

"You can always borrow my mom when you need the best hug that anyone on this Island can get," said Katherine, sipping on her lemonade. By then Sydney was feeling herself again and made an excitable suggestion.

"Let's go collect seashells, I'd like to make a necklace for your mom," she said, putting on her flip flops.

"That's a great idea, maybe we should ask Fain to go with us, he knows all the best places to find the prettiest shells," said Katherine. But Sydney suggested that they keep it a surprise and Katherine agreed. Faith awoke from a nap to Fain's voice calling for the girls.

"Katherine, Syd? Girls this is not the time for hide and go seek. Forecast warns of a mild storm heading this way. Katherine?" Faith hurried out of her bedroom. She knew by the sound of Fain's voice that he was growing more concerned about the girls.

"Have you checked all the rooms?" ask Faith, throwing on her white broad rim hat and boots.

"I've checked everywhere, they seemed to have disappeared," he said, searching more frantically.

"I'll put in a call to Hank," said Faith hurrying. The phone rang continuously then the voicemail answered. Faith thought that Hank might have taken the girls somewhere. Even if that were the case, he would have said something to her or Fain before taking Katherine. Then as she returned the handset, her phone rang.

"Faith, sorry I was letting down the storm shutters over the windows. Heard about the storm heading this way right?"

"Hank?"

"Yes Faith."

"Have you seen the girls?"

"They're not with you?"

"No, we can't seem to find them anywhere…I thought maybe they got bored and went to your house. Hank kept Faith on the line as he frantically searched the Bungalow.

"Sydney? Katherine? Girls are you in here? Faith, they're not here. We need to find them before the storm sets in."

"Faith, I have an idea," said Fain pointing to a pair of footprints in the sand leading toward the Coral.

"Hank, we think they might have taken a walk down the coast."

"You're kidding." Hank said grabbing his coat, boots and hat and headed over to Faith's.

"Fain, please grab a flashlight and umbrellas, in case," said Faith. Hank joined the three and they followed in the direction of the tiny flip flop footprints down the coast. There were small spills of seashells that followed the footprints and Hank confirmed that this was the girls. They knew that they had extraordinarily little time to find the girls as strong winds were already in effect. What started as a beautiful sunny afternoon quickly vanished, as storm clouds hastened across the sky, causing it to appear much later than 11:00am.

"Katherine…Sydney?" Faith called. Hank formed an arch with his index and thumb, placed it in his mouth and whistled loudly: something that he and Syd had created as part of a game. It was so loud that Fain covered his ear.

"Wow, that was almost deafening," said Faith. As the beach curved, Fain looked in the distance and saw Katherine and Sydney's towels hanging on the branches of wild sea grapes that grew on the coast.

"Look!" said Fain running ahead.

"Girls?!" Hank called for the hundredth time. As they neared the Sand Corals, they heard someone scream. Panicked, Faith took off with lightning speed calling Katherine and Sydney at the top of her lungs.

"Katherine! Sydney!" By then, it had started to rain a light drizzle. Lightning flashed against the abandoned Coral rocks and thunder clapped against the sky.

"Sydney, Katherine, where are you," called Fain.

"Over here said Katherine, come quickly, Sydney's in trouble," she cried. Fain climbed over the Corals and hurried toward Katherine. Her elbows and knees were covered in scrapes.

"Katherine, what happened?" Fain looked in time to see Sydney slipped and almost fell into the water. The storm was now in effect with waves rummaging angrily against the rocks, splashing them with cold sprinkles. Just then, Hank and Faith caught up to them.

"Sydney!" he screamed and followed after Fain to help pull her to safety. She was hanging against a rock and one of her feet was caught between two narrow reefs.

"Please, help me daddy, please don't let me fall," she cried.

"No sweetheart, don't worry, daddy's got you," he said laying flat against the rock attempting to pull her up.

"Ouch," she cried. Her feet were jammed between the rocks and it would take a little more effort in order to free her. The waves are becoming angrier by the minute and both Hank and Sydney was soaking wet.

"Fain, come quickly, I'm going to need to climb over to the other side to remove her feet.

"I'm so sorry daddy, please help me," she cried. Faith and Katherine hugged tightly, and looked on fearfully as both men tried to free Sydney.

"Oh mommy, I'm so sorry, we wanted to get to the prettier shells."

"It's okay baby, everything's going to be okay," said Faith, holding the umbrella over them. All signs of daylight had disappeared and what was expected to be a mild storm had eloped into a full-blown tempest. Katherine and Faith looked up to see Hank free Sydney's feet leaving her sandals stuck between the rocks and Fain pulling her upward to safety.

The trees bend and swayed by the strength of the ravaging winds, as the party of five made their way up the beach, with Sydney's arms hugging tightly around her father's shoulders. Despite her minor scrapes, Katherine was determined to walk, but Fain hugged her tightly in his arms as Faith tagged closely behind. As they neared home, Hank agreed to take Sydney to Faith's house. Faith hurried inside and came back with a large first aid kit. Both girls sobbed quietly assuming that they were both in a lot of trouble. There was no doubt in Sydney's mind that her dad was going to cut their trip short, and that she would be in New York by morning. But that was the last thing on Hanks mind. He was simply happy that the girls were safe and that they had located them in time.

Sydney sustained a sprained ankle from the incident and Hank and Faith drove her to the hospital the morning after the storm. Faith accompanied him to the Emergency Room. She thought it was the fair thing to do since Sydney was in her care while all this happened.

"You are a very lucky young lady," said Doctor Benjamin with a broad smile, gently wrapping Sydney's ankle.

"The X-ray revealed a tiny fracture in Sydney's right ankle. She'll have to stay off her feet for at least 2 weeks to ensure the fracture properly heals," he said, gently tapping Sydney's nose. She smiled for the first time in an entire day, but her smile quickly faded at the thought of not being able to play with Katherine for two whole weeks.

"Daddy, it was all my fault," she cried. "I saw those pretty seashells above the corals and I wanted to get to them. I wanted to make the prettiest necklace for Faith but I couldn't get to them. Katherine told me that we should be heading back but I told her to wait. I wanted to make her mommy happy and nothing was going to stop me from getting to those shells. I wish they weren't so pretty, darn it," she fretted. Hank looked at Faith. She was in tears.

"Hunny, I can't believe that you went through all this for me. You are amazing. I've only met you two weeks ago, but you are more devoted than any friend that I've ever known," she cried. She lay on Sydney's bed and hugged her tightly. Hank looked at them and realized that Sydney had never grown close to her mother who's always away on business trips or too busy to make time for her. And that maybe why she thought that making Faith a bracelet with Seashells was her way of connecting with her; hoping that she would stay. There was no doubt that his daughter was getting closer to the French Family. He wasn't sure how he felt about it but for the first time in almost forever, his daughter looked happy; even if it were for a moment, he would allow it. Whether Faith is a friend or a familiar neighbor, nothing could rearrange the joy he feels to see his only daughter embraced in the arms of a beautiful stranger.

Chapter 4

Fain packed a duffel bag while glancing at the Roman clock on the wall. It was almost 9:00am and he was catching the 10:00am flight out of Sandy Island to Los Angeles, to surprise his ex-girlfriend Camille. Despite how things ended with them, he was determined to meet with her. The last time they'd spoken, she'd mention that she would be at the Ambian Café,' filming, later that afternoon. He wanted her to see that it was for the best that he'd left. He could tell that she was still very angry with him for the way he'd left things, with little explanation. He knew that she had expected him to propose, but like his Father told him, he was a wandering spirit who needed the heart of an incredibly unique woman to help him settle down. Besides, he had just turned twenty-eight and Camille was only twenty-two. Within his family, it was custom for young men and women to be wedded by at least twenty, but he was a different kind of kid; and maybe it would take a long line of tiny Fain Collins to change this stubborn tradition.

It was a little after 11:00am when Fain arrived in Los Angeles. There was a small film crew wrapping things up at the Café'. He'd rented a midsize SUV, one that he was certain could survive L.A traffic. As he looked at the Ambian Café' from across the street, he noticed a tall Brunette speaking with one of the crew members. It was when she'd entered her convertible coupe parked across the street, he realized that it was Camille. She looked almost unrecognizable, and taller than he remembered. As she pulled out of the lot, he followed her a short distance to a small diner. It was his first time driving through Los Angeles but he loved it. He didn't do much driving on Sandy Island but when he did, there was almost no traffic. Fain entered the small diner and sat in the chair opposite Camille. Her face slowly lit up as she held back the sudden joy she felt.

"Fain…what are you doing here?" He stood up and they embraced each other tightly.

23

"Camille April Sanders, a lady should never dine alone," he said, releasing her.

"You look well. I almost didn't recognize you as a brunette with the shorter hair."

"Yes, I had to wear shorter hair and lose a bit of weight for this role."

"I see. I still can't believe that you got the part and you're here in Los Angeles. Camille Sanders, when did you get to be so hot? You remind me of an FBI agent in that tight black outfit."

"Are you saying I was never hot?"

"Yes, I'm still the high school jerk," he said pulling his beret over his eyes.

"I'm on a 30-minute lunch break. I'll be shooting a few stunts later today," she said excitedly.

"Fascinating," said Fain staring at her seductively as she sipped on a virgin summer splash.

"I see some things never change," he said remembering this was her favorite summer drink since high school. She laughed.

"Fain, you still haven't answered my question. What are you doing in Los Angeles?"

"It's obvious though, isn't it?" he said. She laughed.

"But you left. We broke things off the day you left me in tears. I hate you; you know that. I still haven't forgiven you," she smiled.

"Then if not, why did you come to the States?"

"My word, you already sound like them."

"Marriage is not for everyone Camille, and besides, we were much too young," he admitted. Camille looked at her wrist.

"I should be heading back. I'm meeting the crew at the Santa Monica Peer in ten minutes to jump out of a Helicopter. I'll invite you except the Set isn't open to the public."

"I'm really proud of you, Camille for following your heart. I know at some point you will agree that it was for the best. Maybe," she said walking out of the diner to her parked car.

"I'll be staying at the Ritz Carlton on Rodeo Drive, room 222. Let's have dinner later."

"Maybe," she said, for a second time. She looked at Fain one more time before speeding off.

After checking into his hotel room, he phoned Faith to let her know that he'd arrived safely. This was the first time he'd been away

24

from her and Katherine and he knew that this would be good for her. He knew that she needed some time to think about the next chapter. He didn't want to influence any decision that she needed to make for herself and her daughter. After all, he is only in their life for professional reasons; and at some point, sooner or later he would have to figure out his next move: hopefully, later rather than sooner. He enjoyed his position as Faith's Assistant. Despite their professional relationship, Faith and Katherine were more like family to him. He spoke to Faith for about an hour. She'd mention that Katherine's grandmother had called earlier and asked for her to spend a few days with her up in the Marinas. He told her that it was an excellent idea because Kat was missing Sydney and the fact that he would be in Los Angeles for the next ten days would be somewhat boring for her. As he thought of his conversation with Faith, he realized that it was after five and Camille hadn't shown. She did say maybe…he smiled.

Katherine was overjoyed that she was visiting her Grandma for the next two weeks. But she didn't like the idea of leaving her mommy alone for this long.

"Mom, I don't want to leave you, maybe we can both visit with Grandma," she suggested. Faith wanted to tell Katherine that her dad and his Fiancé' Rachael was the reason she couldn't be there but she didn't want to set a negative tone over why it would be best that she goes to visit Elizabeth alone. She's never met Eric's Fiancé' Rachael, but she knew that it was important that Katherine formed her own opinion of her.

"Sweetheart, I would love too, but Grandma has a few important events planned just for the two of you and it wouldn't be fair for mommy to ask her to adjust those plans to include her." Katherine still hoped that her mom would change her mind but she understood. A few hours later Elizabeth and Eric pulled into Faith's driveway, next to the small sailboat still attached to the Truck where Fain had left it a few weeks earlier.

"Dad, Grandma Liz," Katherine shouted excitedly, running toward them.

"Careful honey," said Elizabeth opening her arms just as excited to see her Granddaughter. "My goodness, sweetheart, you're almost as tall as your mom," she said embracing her. Eric snapped a few photos of Katherine and Elizabeth. He knew that with all the changes taking place, that there would likely be very little moments like this left. Faith walked slowly toward them, carrying Katherine's tiny luggage. She was wearing a white silk blouse over a long white skirt that almost swept the ground. Eric thought she looked great.

"Faith, you look well," said Elizabeth embracing her. Eric looked at them from in front of his black 2016 Land Rover.

"I can say the same," said Faith, removing her sunglasses.

"It's been my intention to have Katherine over since I returned from Italy, but it's still a bit untidy at the new place, since my move earlier this year, and as you know, I don't like unpacking that much. It's not like me to live out of boxes," Elizabeth joked.

"I've always enjoyed your unexpected sense of humor Liz. I have to say, you looking nothing short of stunning. I couldn't tell whether you've just pulled this dazzling summer dress out of a box," Faith joked. Both women laughed.

"I heard you just got neighbors," Elizabeth said looking over at Hank and Sydney's bungalow.

"Oh yes, but I'd rather let Katherine fill you in on this one," said Faith looking over at her daughter playfully punching her dad in the stomach.

"Ouch, Ouch," Eric said pretentiously. Elizabeth laughed.

"You deserve it Eric."

"But, mom…?" Both women laughed.

"He misses you Faith. I know him. I hope it's alright to say this. I think my son has made a terrible mistake. You're the woman he's meant to be with Faith darling. I knew it the first time he came home with that stupid look on his face. The first time he's ever stood up to me. I thought he was high on something, but it was a side of Eric I didn't know existed. I never knew he had a backbone until I asked him what the rush was to marry," Elizabeth admitted.

Faith laughed.

"You've never told me that one before, love you Liz," she said, trying to hide the joy she felt.

"You know I love you too honey. Know that I'm still only a speed dial away, should you need someone to share a gossip."

"Thanks mom," said Faith blowing her a kiss.

Katherine ran toward her mom and hugged her tightly.

"It's still not too late mom. You can still come," Katherine grinned broadly.

"My baby, my one and only, pwease, pwease, pwease come home safely, okay. You'll have lots of fun at grandma's new house. Uncle Calvin is building a cave for you too on the third floor loft. Oops that was supposed to be a surprise," said Faith covering her mouth.

"Ah ha, I knew Uncle Calvin was up to something last time we spoke," she grinned, revealing her two missing front teeth. "I love you mommy. If you miss me I'm only a pink phone call away," she said climbing onto the truck. Eric beeped loudly and everyone waved enthusiastically. Faith noticed Eric glanced at her a few times in his mirror as they drove away from Sandy Island.

Chapter 5

A lone for the first time in forever, Faith relaxed on her sofa in her entertainment room and reached for the remote control from the coffee table and flicked through the channels. She's never found the time to watch television while married to Eric. She spent most of her time preparing him for his business trips and being a mother to their only joy, Katherine. Throughout her marriage, she felt more like his Personal Assistant rather than his wife. As she skipped through the channels, she avoided everything that had anything to do with the news, especially current events. Her home always felt more like the Senators office; the fact that Eric always watched the news or if not the news the crazy stock market numbers that never made any sense to her. Every room in their home was broadcasting something of his interest. She wanted to exist under her own conditions, ones that were unique to her and did not remind her of him.

Later that week, as Faith prepared dinner, she realized that she hadn't heard from her daughter. It's been two days since she's been away but it felt more like a month. Her daughter is the life of their home. As much as she enjoyed the quiet, she knew that she couldn't go more than an hour without her darling Katherine, but she had to try. She reminded her so much of herself that one would believe that Eric had nothing to do with her existence. As she reached for her mobile to dial Elizabeth, her phone began to buzz in this very unusual tone. What in the world she thought? It was a new phone and Fain had put it together for her since she has no interest in cell phones other than to make or receive calls. By the time she had figured how to answer, it had stopped ringing. The missed call showed up red on the call list and as she observed it, she realized it was from Fain. She was still mystified by his sudden plans to visit Los Angeles, but she realized that he needed the time away. After all, he's been with her and Katherine an entire year and didn't take any time off. He's earned his time away, but she hoped that that's all it was, as she wasn't ready to lose him too. He's an excellent assistant, more like a life saver, she thought. She dialed his number and Fain answered on the first ring; laughing out of control. The sound of his laughter echoed through the phone and she didn't say a word until he'd stopped laughing. Finally, he spoke.

"Faith, you won't believe this."

"Try me," she said.

"I just got shot in the ass. Mistaken for a pizza thief wearing a grey shirt and blue pants…"

"Fain, that's not very funny. Are you really okay?" she asked, still puzzled as to why being shot in the ass is funny. She then heard female voices and she thought that maybe Fain was having one of his French parties; the ones he told her that he threw in his Father's house in France just to piss him off. Then Faith heard gunshots. This time a woman screamed and sirens blared.

"Drop the gun and step away from it," someone shouted. Faith could hardly believe what she was hearing. Was Fain in trouble? A thousand thoughts raced through her mind.

"Fain!" she called but the line had gone silent. She waited a few moments then she heard a blood curdling scream and she screamed in response. When she'd stopped, the line went silent again. Then she heard someone say…

"Cut." Then the sound of applause could be heard.

"Well done Faith, I knew you would pull it off. Thanks so much for calling me back, you helped save the life of a major production," Fain said, almost out of breath.

"Fain, please tell me, are you okay, what are you talking about? Someone should call an ambulance," she said shaking.

"Faith, you will receive payment within a week for your time. I will explain in a few days when I get home. Love you, see you soon," he replied before hanging up. What in the world just happened? she thought. Oh well, he sounded like he was having fun and that is all that mattered to her.

After dinner, Faith called Elizabeth. They had just returned from their trip into town and Katherine had fallen asleep. Elizabeth told her some of the things that she and Katherine did together, and it almost made her jealous. She wasn't surprised when she explained that Katherine showed great interest in the artworks displayed in some of the galleries they'd visited in downtown San Francisco.

Overall, she was overjoyed that Katherine and Elizabeth had enjoyed their day and she was even more thankful for the time she had to herself.

Hank lay in his hammock thinking of how comfortable Sydney looked as Faith hugged her at Sandy Island hospital. It was the best moment he's remembered sharing with anyone outside of his relationship with Cassandra; his ex, who's never really been around. The woman he thought he'd loved, who never supported any of his dreams as an Author. The more he thought of Cassandra, the more he remembered the word 'never.' The one that prevented him from finishing almost everything he'd started. The word that even when not spoken became a part of their lives and prevented almost everything he's ever dreamed of from happening. If only she'd loved him enough to trust that he's always had her best interest at heart; they would have still been married. But she never trusted him. He's often wondered if maybe it was their age difference. He was 22 and Cas was 34 when they were married. To him, Cas has never trusted him to be an equal lead in their home. She was naturally dominant yet complained when she believed he's failed her. To him, she's never given him the chance to show her how much he truly loved her. She simply gave up... having voluntarily taken the lead out of a lack of trust in his ability to love her. He's always supported her. There are no words to describe what a brilliant woman she truly is. She's the definition of a strong intelligent woman, worthy of much praise. Yet he yearned to be there for her only if she would accept his truth and allow it.

"Daddy, where are you daddy? Mom's on the phone," said Sydney.

"Okay hunny, I got it," he said, reaching for his old-fashioned handset that Sydney had complained about numerous times. Cassy was calling with questions regarding Sydney's hospital visit because her insurance company had called with questions. He was waiting a few more days to tell her about the incident on the beach and was slightly annoyed that she'd learned this way. He told her about Syd's new friend and what had happened. Of course, she blamed him for not keeping a better eye on their daughter and even more for trusting her with his neighbors who she pointed out were merely strangers. She didn't care that they'd become friends with the French family. She was the same as always. He listened to her grueling arguments without interruption until she finally called him unworthy and immature. He was tired of her accusations and was visiting Sandy Island for reflection. He didn't need to hear all of this and was basically the only parent who's mostly present in Sydney's life. His career choice despite being highly criticized by her for its late debut, allowed him to be there for their only child. He was not going to listen to her continue this way and as she was about to attack his integrity once more, he simply hung her up. In response to her many insults, he sent her an email that he would no longer take her phone calls and that if she needed to contact him, she would have to do so in writing. It's been three years since their divorce, and he had no more tolerance for her insults. In his email, he'd indicated specifically that her emails needed to be insult free or this mode of communication to would also be restricted.

Sydney knew by the look on her dad's face that her parents had been fighting. He didn't have to tell her what happened. His silence was much louder than any amount of shouting. Suddenly she wished Katherine were here. It's only been a week since she left but it felt like an eternity. Then she thought of Faith. She felt closer to her at the hospital, but she feared that she might pull away if she showed her how much she really liked being around her.

"Syd, your dinner's ready," said Hank standing at the bottom of the stair with an apron tied around his hips.

"Dad, is that a new apron?" she giggled.

"Are you making fun of me?" he said placing his hands on his hips and stepping in a ladylike manner. Despite how boring her day had been, he'd managed to make her laugh.

"Oh, dad, you're silly," she said sitting at their table. As they dined, Sydney saw her dad glanced over at Faith's house often. He hadn't mentioned her since their last visit to the hospital a week ago. Despite being only seven, she knew her dad better than any person alive. She knew there was something on his mind but she said nothing as they ate but stared at him continuously. Hank finally looked up from his steak dinner and said, "I know that look sweetheart. But daddy has nothing to hide.

"Daddy is not thinking about Faith." She laughed loudly.

"Daddy, you just gave yourself away."

"No I didn't," he said keeping a straight face, pretending to be serious.

31

"You are to."

"No I'm not."

"Yes you are daddy, I know you like her. I saw that look on your face when she climbed onto our Yacht that first time." He hadn't seen anyone since his divorce. He thought about dating after two years but Sydney and his second Novel was enough to keep him occupied.

Another beautiful evening had dawned and Faith gazed upon the surf, admiring the glistening sunset. Although it was early June it was still slightly cool outside. She was enjoying every bit of it as Sandy Island was not as fortunate as her mother, San Francisco which maintained almost the same temperature year-round. The soft wind shuffled her clothing and hair and almost blew her scarf from around her neck. Despite the unexpected events that had shadowed her life in previous months, she felt a wind of change had arrived. She was looking forward to what it had brought this year, as each summer, Sandy Island sailed like a ship on her own unique journey. As she pondered these thoughts, her mobile phone buzzed another strange somber. She fiddled with the large device until she remembered how to answer it.

"This is Faith," she answered. Surprised by the tiny voice, she almost laughed at how excited Katherine sounded.

"Hello baby, how are you honey? You are? That's great honey." She was having a blast with her uncle Calvin who apparently was chasing her around her girl cave in the attic wearing his usual clown outfit. Katherine tolerated everything except that giant red nose which made everyone else laugh but made her both laugh and scream. Hearing Katherine's laughter echoed that even the winds danced at the sound of her voice. She was happy, and she knew that this was all she needed to help her enjoy the conclusion of twilight as the sun disappeared beyond the horizon.

She must have fallen asleep for the hundredth time on the balcony and was awakened by a soft male voice…

"Faith." As she awoke and her vision became clearer... she noticed it was Fain. A duffel bag at his feet, his white shirt unbuttoned revealing his toned chest and torso. Surprised by his sudden appearance, she sat up quickly.

"Fain, what are you doing here, I didn't expect you back till Thursday."

32

"It's Thursday," he replied, reaching for her hands and lifting her up slowly. Before she uttered another word, he covered her lips with his, polishing all memories of the boy she met the year before. He was no longer the nervous crazy eyed French boy she'd flown in from France. Suddenly, he appeared manlier than she remembered. As she looked in his clear grey eyes, lost for thought and unable to resist, she sunk in his arms and submitted to their newest desires.

Fain awoke around five am and looked over at Faith. She was sleeping more sound than a well fed newborn and a sudden chill ran through him. Despite his attraction to Faith, she'd never expressed romantic interest in him. He wondered if everything, including his job would disappear when Faith's eyelids finally blinked to an open. Her pale skin revealed a slight tan. She looked more beautiful and much stronger than he remembered. He knew everything that she's been through and was there for her, every step of the way. He's helped carry her through storms that he didn't believe anyone else could have possibly survived. As he remembered the past few months, Faith sat up quickly startling Fain causing him to tumble headfirst off the bed. She had forgotten and thought that maybe she'd spent the entire night on the balcony. As she rubbed her eyes, she noticed a pair of eyes staring at her from the edge of the bed. She screamed and threw a pillow at him.

"Fain, what are you doing?" she screamed and laughed at the same time. As her laughing subsided, she remembered the night they'd shared and he watched as his fears were slowly confirmed.

"Faith, please don't say it was a mistake. Please," he said climbing onto the bed next to her. As he got closer, she held the linen up to her face.

"I could be your mom," she laughed. "Fain Collins, you've crossed the line," she said trying to maintain a professional stance, but it was too late. Fain slid beneath the sheets and began to tickle her. She screamed playfully and tried to get away from him, but she was only an inch away from his longing eyes. She threw another cushion at him, but he had caught it with his teeth. She laughed at his silliness.

"You've changed. What's gotten into you Fain Collins?"

"Los Angeles Traffic," he said kissing her toned shoulders. She laughed.

"Come here," he said. At the sound of his voice, a fire kindled within her.

"*No way, Fain Collins*," she said softly, as his lips touched her soft skin, awakening her former lifeless body into an ocean of bliss.

A few hours later, Hank phoned Faith and asked if she wanted to join them for breakfast.

"Please, Faith Please," said an anxious Sydney in the background. It was after nine in the morning and she was snuggled in Fain's strong arms after the most unexpected night she'd remembered. She stared at his handsome shaven face as his chest rose and fell in a deep sleep. She knew he would want to make them breakfast but couldn't refuse Sydney and Hank's enticing invitation. A few moments later as Fain slept, she sneaked out of her Malibu Style beach house and stepped onto the brick layered path way through the morning mist onto the sandy front lawn of Hank's bungalow. Sydney had swung the door open even before Faith had the chance to knock.

"Hi Sydney, I see that you are no longer wearing your cast."

That's right Mrs. French. I'm much too stubborn to lay around feeling sorry for myself in a cast. Please join us. Daddy is in the kitchen getting a fresh baked apple pie out of the oven."

"Thank you, sweetie," said Faith looking around the room.

"Something smells delicious."

"I did it all by myself. The only thing is that daddy's new apron was too big for me, so that's why I'm covered in powdered sugar," she laughed.

"Sounds like you've done a great job, sweetie." Sydney smiled proudly.

"Hi there," said Hank, removing his mittens walking briskly toward Faith.

"Hank, why does it feel like I haven't seen you in forever, we're supposed to be neighbors," said Faith leaning forward to accept a hug and smooch on the cheek.

"I thought I'd chased you away," he said looking curiously at Faith.

"Maybe you did, but not my new Bff," she said winking at Syd. Hank laughed at Faith's honesty and Sydney blushed for the second time today. She was overjoyed that Faith agreed to do breakfast with them.

After breakfast with her neighbors, Hank showed Faith around their home. Faith had been to the Bungalow before, but the recent construction completely transformed the interior.

"This is beautiful Hank! This makes me feel a bit outdated. Maybe it's time I make some changes to my place," she said.

Did anyone ever tell you that you were funny?" he asked looking at Faith halfway up the stairwell.

"Who me?"

"No, the ghost I just spotted leaping out that window. Yes you," he joked. Faith smiled.

"You find me funny? You're a natural."

"Maybe it's true that funny people don't know they're funny."

"You must be crazy Hank."

I've been called studious, straight forward, no fun, staunch, even a pain in the ass. Funny is definitely a surprise."

Well, there's always a first time for everything. And whoever called you those things, never knew you."

"It doesn't take very long for anyone to see that you're a very sweet, gentle, angel. You're the type of person that's easy to love." Faith listens as Hank continues to associate her with these amazing attributes. No one has really complemented her like this before and when he looked over at her, he noticed that she was standing a few feet from him down the hallway.

"Hey, I promise you, I'm not full of shit," he said grinning. He looked exactly like Sydney, they were almost identical. She then busted out laughing. Her laughing echoed throughout the second floor. He laughed.

"Yes you're funny, you're very funny Faith."

"Oh, is that a good thing?"

"Ask me again," he said, taking her hands and leading her to the balcony.

"Your view is crazy beautiful Hank."

"Thanks, and yes, you're exquisitely beautiful," he said removing a piece of white paint from her forehead. His eyes met hers and before he said another word she'd kissed him. She then pulled away and quickly apologized. Hank was surprised but only because he was thinking of kissing her first the minute she'd walked through his door. Seeing that he had no reaction, she thought it was not what he'd expected.

"Oh, I'm sorry, I didn't mean it," she said and hurried away from him.

"Wait!" he called hurrying toward her. "Faith, please wait," he called after her. But she was fast and he had to pick up a slight pace to catch up to her.

"Faith?"

I'm sorry Hank. I'll call you later," she called walking away briskly. He watched as she entered her house and shut the door behind her.

About an hour later, the doorbell to the front door rang and noticing it was Faith, Hank answered quickly.

"Hank, I'm sorry. You were being sweet and I got more out of it," she said.

"I forgot my purse. And I also forgot to thank you and Sydney for breakfast" she said looking embarrassed.

"I forgive you Faith," called Sydney.

"Syd? Okay daddy, I promise I didn't hear anything. Faith smiled at Sydney peeking at her from the kitchen. She then stretched her hand out to Sydney and she ran to her. The two hugged each other like best friends.

"Thanks again honey."

"You're very, very welcome," she said and ran off.

"Let me make you dinner sometime. How does this Wednesday sound?"

"Sounds perfect," Syd said excitedly. After grabbing her purse the two embraced tightly. Hank looked at her intensely. She smiled.

"I'll see you Wednesday?"

"Can't wait," he replied.

As Faith entered the door of the beach house she was greeted by the smell of coffee and a hint of cinnamon.

"Someone ran away without saying good morning," Fain said, handing her a cup of coffee. She was about to admit that she already had breakfast but she wasn't ready to explain why.

"Someone's been busy," she said, removing her sandals.

"Seriously, where were you?" he said smiling curiously. She smiled without responding. Somehow, the night they shared made her feel the need to explain her whereabouts to him but didn't.

"Fain Collins, I do not owe you an explanation," she replied, placing her hands in her pockets.

"Is that so?" said Fain, removing his baker's hat and apron.

"Is that the thanks I get for making you breakfast?" he said approaching her, his hands folded.

"Stop it," she laughed.

"Fain Collins?"

Yes Faith." How may I help you today Faith Adonna Winters French."

"You know I don't like when I'm called by my full name," she laughed and backed away from Fain as he approached her.

"Fain, you're really starting to creep me out. Exactly what happened to you in Los Angeles? What have you been smoking?" she said laughing and without looking in time she toppled landing on a recliner. Fain laughed at her awkward facial appearance. He looked at her for a moment as she laid there.

"Fain, please come here. I need to speak with you."

Sounds serious," he said sitting next to her. As she turned to face him. Fain unable to contain himself took her in his arms and kissed her aggressively. Faith wanted to stop him but didn't. It felt like forever since she felt alive and nothing, not even her sharp, stubborn, professional mindset could stop him. Fain's warmth aroused her like warm cinnamon and she basked in joy as he removed his shirt.

"Fain?"

"Yes Faith?"

"I need to speak with you," she reminded him.

"I'm listening baby." But his strong arms drew her closer to him. As she spoke his soft lips met hers restoring life to her.

Chapter 6

F aith cranked the outboard engine of the small boat that Fain rented from Hank. As she cranked it a fourth time, the engine danced into play and sped forward into nowhere. She had no idea where she was going, but she was leaving Sandy Island and no one could stop her. She and Fain had a fight earlier. He'd discovered that she had dinner with Hank and was about to quit his position as her Assistant. She was not ready to lose him and as a last resort he would have to prove to her that he was truly finished. She knew how selfish she was being by getting in that boat, having no idea how to operate it. As the boat sped ahead, she hoped that she had gotten Fain and Hank's attention.

Fain was about to take the outboard for a spin around the Island when he noticed that it was no longer attached to the truck. He panicked because he remembered that Faith had never driven a boat before. Something was different about her since he came back from Los Angeles and he wondered if he was the only reason. Katherine was coming home in only two days and he wasn't prepared for her to meet her mom this way. He knew that Faith would never take the boat alone. He knew that she was upset and that he had little time to get to her. He ran next door and pounded on Hank's front door.

"Hank, please open up," he yelled. Sydney opened the door.

"Sydney, please ask who it is before opening," Hank called from upstairs.

"It's Fain daddy and he's only wearing underpants," Sydney called.

"What's the matter Fain and where's your shirt?" Sydney asked, staring at him angrily.

"I said, what do you want Fain and where's your shirt?" Fain almost laughed but he had Faith on his mind.

"Hank, where the hell are you? Faith's gone!" he called.

"Fain, what do you mean she was just here an hour ago? We just had dinner," he called. He was about to have an argument with

38

Hank. But there was no time. "Maybe she forgot to mention that she had somewhere to be.

"No, I know her, I know her schedule. Trust me I would have known," said Fain leaving.

"Can I borrow one of your boats?"

"My boat?" Before he approved, Fain jumped into one of the smaller boats and pulled on the engine cord.

"Wait, why the boat!"

"Daddy, let's get in the gad dam boat. I think it's obvious," Sydney called.

"Wait!" called Hank. After grabbing Sydney's life jacket, they both climbed into the small outboard and sped ahead.

"Which direction do you think she went?" Hank asked.

"Look," said Fain pointing to the smooth apparition that Faith's boat made on the water.

"It looks like she's headed to the cove," said Fain picking up speed.

"Oh no, I really hope Faith's okay. Daddy, do you think she's mad at me? Is that why she took off?" ask Sydney close to tears.

"No Hunny, don't worry, daddy will explain later."

"Oh, it's grown up stuff. Daddy I'm seven now, you know you can talk to me. I'm not too little and you know it. Not now sweetheart. Daddy will explain after we find Faith, okay."

"Okay daddy," she said folding her hands and making a mad face.

"You're adorable," said Fain looking over at her.

"Look, over there," said Sydney pointing toward the cove. Faith had pulled into the cove and was sitting in clear view; her hands wrapped around her knees. She glanced as they approached but said nothing.

"Fain, do you mind if I go speak with her first?" Hank asked climbing out of the boat onto the cliffs. Fain shook his head in approval. He wanted to speak with her first, but Hank seemed more determined.

As Hank spoke with Faith, a siren was heard, and a patrol boat pulled up next to Fain.

"Hello there folks, did you realize how fast you were going. There are specific rules for these waters, especially so close to the shorelines.

"My apologies officer, we had somewhat of an emergency situation," said Fain standing. The officer noticed Fain's French accent and realized that maybe he wasn't aware of the rules.

"How long have you been in Sandy Island? A little over a year sir," he replied; trying his best to avoid being ticketed.

"Officer, can I get a ride in your Patrol boat?" Sydney asked, hugging onto a towel.

"Hi there, I can't give you a ride, but you can climb on for a bit sweetie," the officer said sounding more relaxed. Fain was relieved as Sydney chatted with the officer. After Sydney's short visit with the Patrolman, he appeared much friendlier and let Fain off with a warning.

"I really appreciate this sir, I promise it won't happen again," he called as the officer sped away.

Sydney looked Fain up and down.

"You're lucky Fain. Patrol George has a reputation for handing out more than a thousand tickets a month, even on less crowded days. Now that I got you off the hook, you owe me big," she said looking at him crossed.

"And why do I get the feeling that would be expensive?"

"What do you think?" she asked, eyeing his Rolex. That's got to help pay off my dad's mortgage. Fain laughed.

"Syd, this isn't actually what you think. It's an imitation Rolex. If you sell it, you might owe the person you sell it to," he said. As Fain and Sydney chatted, he looked in time to see Hank embracing Faith. He realized that Hank was getting closer to Faith and he shrugged it off. A few minutes later, they climbed onto Faith's escape boat. After Hank's thumbs up, the small rescue headed home.

As they approached the shorelines, Fain realized that he had forgotten to discuss with Faith that his ex-girlfriend was coming to visit him in only three days. Sydney had fallen asleep on the way back from the chase. Faith had barely looked at him and he feared that there was more going on that he may not be aware off. Suddenly, he couldn't wait to be alone with her. He realized that all that was happening may have been a result of all the changes, especially her new adjustment to single life. Maybe she'd forgotten how to be single. He couldn't imagine all that was happening to her and a shadow of guilt swept across him. Maybe all that had happened was simply too much for her and he understood. He was trying his best to not be selfish about their recent encounter, but he had no choice. It was obvious that Hank's motives were clear. He didn't know Faith the way he did. He was merely a stranger with a huge boat that Fain didn't care to ride again, and he didn't give a dam how Hank felt, he was out of place…. clearly out of place.

As they neared the shore, Fain grew tense. His fist was wrung to a clench and he was growing livid. He's seen Faith through impossible terrain the past year and nothing was going to get between them, and the way he now felt about her.

"You look pissed," said Sydney looking at Fain through sleepy eyes.

"What do you mean?" he said glancing at her while steering the boat.

"You bastard, you look mad. After everything I've done for you. How could you be so ungrateful? What do you mean?" Fain said looking at Sydney who was now sitting up.

"Oh, innocent. You think that because you're French, you're innocent." She walked toward Fain and stared him to the face.

"You're weird. I don't care if you're French, Fain Collins, you're really weird."

"Sydney, that's enough," said Fain steering the boat to a stop. As they neared the surf…

"I know why you're mad. You want to quit being Katherine's best friend because she's away and I won't allow it," she said climbing out of the boat onto the boardwalk.

"Sydney wait!" said Fain hurrying after her. She took off toward the pier and Fain picked up a light pace. Faith and Hank looked at them from a distance.

"I wonder what's going on. They look like an illegal couple having the final fight that determines whether they will stay together," said Faith. At Faith's statement, the two broke into laughter.

"Sydney, you've got it all wrong. Fain Collins do you think that I was born yesterday."

"Well, sort of," he said with a teasing smile on his face.

"Grrrrr, grrrrr."

"Sydney, please calm down."

"So you think you're mad."

41

"Well, it's my turn Mr. Collins!" Hank and Faith looked in time to see Sydney plunge toward Fain with both her fist wrung to a ball.

"Faith, will you be alright? It looks like my little tiger is on the loose," said Hank turning to leave. Faith laughed and hugged Hank. She then watched as he took off after Sydney, scooped her up and tossed her over his shoulders.

"I got you tiger," he said. He then waved at Fain and Faith, with Sydney kicking and screaming, trying her best to get off his shoulders.

"Thank you, sorry about all the trouble. I'll call you later," Faith called.

As he was about to mention Camille, Fain's cell phone rang. It was Camille. Faith looked at his expression went from exciting to disappointing.

"Are you sure? I can be there as soon as next week, just say the word. Please, I think you'd really like Sandy Island. Oh okay, I'll help with the search and let you know what I find. You're most welcome. Okay, thanks."

"Who was that?" ask Faith.

"I was going to mention her, but it slipped," said Fain leading the way up the balcony stairwell. Faith said nothing hoping that he would continue explaining why he appeared like a schoolboy in trouble. When they were finally inside, Fain hurried to his quarters and locked the door. Surprised, Faith stared at his door then entered her own quarters. After a long shower, she looked at her laptop computer and turned it on for the first time in almost an entire year. It was still brand new with little company stickers labeled near the keyboard. As she thought of all the events the past few weeks, she realized that she needed a new distraction: at least until Katherine gets home. As she browsed the web searching random items, she noticed that a few dating sites popped up in her results. Hmmm, that's the last thing I need, she thought. It's how she'd met Eric. The fact that they'd lasted more than fifteen years, she has to admit that it was more than a successful match. Hmmm, maybe, why not? After exploring a few sites, she decided on SandyMatch: a very attractive site boasting singles with almost or beyond Millionaire status. She didn't care about the Millionaire status, she liked how organized yet how bold and beautiful the site appears. There was a sense of security with each step involved, which encouraged her to continue.

A few moments later, she could hardly believe it. She'd actually filled out her details and uploaded a recent pic: one from her boat ride with Hank and Sydney. Almost instantly, after verifying her email, she received an email from the admin. Suddenly, she felt excited and didn't want to stop. After adjusting her age preference, she noticed that she's already received more than fifty views in only half an hour. Her excitement escalated. She felt like a schoolgirl, and then suddenly she felt like hiding her profile. There was a button under profile settings that allowed her to hide her entire profile. Her profile views went from fifty to over a hundred views in less than an hour. As she viewed the profiles of men who viewed her, she noticed a local profile. One from Sandy Island and her heart raced. She hesitated, but as she opened the profile, she noticed that the person had no profile pic and she quickly closed the page. As new thoughts ran through her mind, there was a soft knock on her door which startled her.

"Fain? Please come in," she called closing the browser.

"What is it?" she asked with her eyes searching for him. He handed her a large envelope labeled with Ascott Productions logo. "looks fishy," she said tearing open the thick envelope. As she removed the document, she looked over at Fain, who was now smiling.

"Thank you for filling in for us, you were awesome."

"For what?" she called. But he hurried off. Please read the document!" He called, shutting the door behind him. Dear Faith, on behalf of Ascott Productions, we would like to thank you for your excellent impromptu display. This was most unexpected, but your assistant was beyond convinced that you could pull this off and we quite agree. Please find enclosed a disc with your performance and payment for your participation as well as a nondisclosure agreement for your records. By the way, you were great. ~~~AP~~~

Puzzled, yet stunned by the letter, Faith realized that she was part of a production that she was completely unaware of. She had never been away from Sandy Island in over a year but had managed to be part of a production. This is awesome, she thought, but why was Fain suddenly so distant? She then realized that maybe it was her attempt to flee earlier this week. She'd forgotten to thank him for being there for her. Hank had completely taken over and had distracted her. Faith was hardly thinking. Her recent encounter with

Fain had left her confused and distracted. She was also developing feelings for Hank which was the reason she'd fled in the first place. She was hardly ready to face that fact and still didn't know how to approach him. This explains why he's become suddenly distant, and she panicked.

She opened her bedroom door and looked at his room across the hall. She tipped her way to his door and was about to knock but didn't. He was on his mobile and sounded like he was having a heated argument with someone. She was eavesdropping on her assistant and it felt like she was caught up in the middle of the worst breakup anyone could possibly imagine. Why in the world was he so angry? She thought. She then sat beside the door and leaned her ears against it. She could smack herself for being this nosy, but she's never seen him this upset... As she pressed her ears harder against the door, her mobile rang. Fain was no longer arguing, and she wondered if he'd heard her. As she reached into her pocket to remove her phone, he continued arguing. It was Elizabeth.

"Hi Liz, how's everything? "She asked trying to sound like herself.

"Of course she misses Sydney." Liz was taking Kat to another Art festival next weekend which means that she would only be back for a week before leaving again. Faith loved the time that Kat spent with Elizabeth, but she didn't want the girls to miss out on spending summer together.

"But Liz, there's another Art Festival the following week, maybe you can take Katherine to this one instead.

"But I just bought the tickets today and my friend from Australia will also be attending this particular event. I wish that I could cancel, but would prefer not to," said Liz sounding hopeful.

. "Oh, okay then, that should be alright. I'll see you both in the a.m. Love you too Liz." As she was about to replace her mobile into her pocket, she looked and was met with Fain's angry stare.

"Fain, how long have you been standing there?"

"I can ask you the same thing," he said his stare narrows.

"Who was that you were arguing with?"

"Oh I wish it was any of your business," he said walking away.

"Fain, I need to speak with you."

"Not now Faith. Why don't you ask your boyfriend across the way, he seems to have all the answers?"

"Fain that is not fair," she said following him. Fain ran to the beach and took off full speed ahead. He was in excellent shape and looked like an Olympian as he disappeared down the beach.

"Maybe he's fast, but one thing is certain, he will surely return," she said and returned to her room. Checking on her dating profile, she had ten new emails and an additional fifty views. Wow, she thought. As she was about to read her emails, a red chat balloon suddenly popped out on the screen causing her to flinch backwards. She tried to grab onto the drawer handle but missed, falling backwards onto a pile of pillows. She laid there for a while then laughed at how silly she felt. She stared at the ceiling and realized that this was too much excitement. She needed to enter the dating world more gracefully. But from her experience so far, she wondered if she was even know the meaning of the word. Maybe I needed a new distraction, she thought.

As she thought of what she might consider taking up, she heard Fain enter his room and locked the door behind him.

"Fain, wait. Who is this envelope from, and why didn't you tell me about this?" she called.

"Fain, please whatever I did, I'm sorry, please I need to speak with you.

"Faith, go away."

"I wish I could do that, but fortunately, I'm in my house," she said adamantly.

"Right, well, I'm on vacation. I'm taking my leave now. And from what it looks like, I believe that I have another fourteen days. I can stay in here and order in for the next two weeks if I so choose," he said sounding entitled.

"Fain this is ridiculous. Open the door or else you're...."

Go on, finish. You know you're nothing without me Faith Adonna French."

"Oh is that what you think? Well, screw you Fain Collins. I can make my own breakfast and do my own shopping. And pay my own bills."

"You've forgotten one thing."

"And what's that? I'm Katherine's Bff and I intend to keep that contract."

"You have a contract with my daughter?"

"Got that right. I suggest you do your research. It's a legal binding contract, not even the parents could terminate it. Only the original parties involved."

"What?"

A few seconds later she heard loud fictitious snores coming from Fain's room. She demanded that he come out of his room, but he refused. About an hour later, exhausted, and slightly bored she tumbled into her overly large kitchen to prepare dinner.

Katherine hurried up the stairs of her home and reached over the porch lamp for the spare key. She's only been gone two weeks, but it felt a lot longer. She hadn't heard from Fain since she'd left, and she couldn't wait to see him and her mom. Elizabeth watched as Katherine opened the door and when she was certain that she was safe inside, she drove off. She couldn't visit with them due to a doctor's appointment she has at 10:00a.m. Katherine is her only grandchild. She'd doubted that any of her sons would give her a grandbaby and was overjoyed when she learned of Katherine. She was like an unexpected miracle born and adorned on the finest spring day. She feared that things may get rocky between Eric and Faith that would affect her relationship with Katherine. Regardless, she was thankful that things between her and Faith remained positive, despite all the changes. Her friends had questioned her decision to keep Faith close but she knew that not everything could be left up to decision. Some decisions are made on their own, regardless of logic. A relationship such as hers and Faith was built on much more than lawful relation; their bond was outside of decisions, it was meant. Elizabeth was almost always the only one present in Faith's life when she had lost her mother, her only surviving parent. Katherine was only an infant at the time and Elizabeth thought that Faith would never see the light of day again; losing her mother was possibly the darkest hour she'd ever endured. Her divorce to Eric without a doubt took second place. Faith had seen many dark days; some she thought would consume her daughter-in-law. With Eric's schedule, she was almost always the only one there, catering simultaneously to young Katherine and her mother. They'd grown much closer than Eric had realized. And regardless of what he decides, she would always be there for her girls. She still hopes that they would consider getting back together, but she knew that this was more than a long shot.

As Elizabeth parked her car into the parking lot of Kenterfield and Klein's Medical Plaza, her left hand suddenly felt numb and a sharp pain shot across her chest. Luckily, there was a young couple that pulled up and parked right next to her.

"Help, please dial 911," she cried. Surprised by the sudden request, the gentleman hurried out of his car, while his wife dialed 911.

"Maam, maam, can you hear me?" he called. The gentleman tried all four doors, but Elizabeth was now unconscious and he had no way to get to her.

"Paramedics are on their way. Great but all the doors are locked and I can't get to her," he called.

"I have an idea. Here try this," his wife called, handing him an old wire clothing hanger.

"Genius," he called folding the hanger into a wired hook which he inserted into the small opening on the driver side of Elizabeth's Cadillac. After a few tries, the lock popped open and the stranger pulled the door open and placed his index finger on Elizabeth's upper neck.

"I can barely feel her pulse," he called.

"I know CPR, let me help," his wife called. The woman hurried toward Elizabeth and after reclining her chair and laying her flat, she began mouth to mouth resuscitation. A few moments later, Paramedics arrived.

"I think we should follow," the woman said. She was alone and we saw what happened."

"But we're going to be late for our appointment," he called. The woman was already in their vehicle and had taken the driver seat.

"Get in Sam, or I'll go without you."

"No you won't," he said almost jumping into the car head first. The couple followed the ambulance to the ER of Presidio Hope Memorial. As they were about to get past the authorized personnel only door, they were stopped by a feisty redhead nurse that appeared in her late fifties. She cleared her throat.

"Where do you two think that you are going? Are you family?"

"Umm, yep," she lied. The nurse eyed them suspiciously.

"Why don't I believe you?"

"Okay, we're not, we were the only ones that saw what happened and wanted to help."

"Hmm, I see. Okay, wait here, and I will check with the Doctor." Just then, the nurse and Doctor Weiss; Elizabeth's Primary care physician appeared in the hallway. After the couple explained the incident, Dr. Weiss realized that Elizabeth's family was unaware of what had happened, and he phoned her sons immediately.

Katherine had just arrived and was about to knock on her mom's door when the phone rang. She picked up the handset. Fain heard her on the phone and opened his door.

"Fain, mom, it's grandma, she's in the hospital."

"Katherine, when did you get in?" they asked almost at the same time.

"Mom, did you hear me, I said grandma was just rushed to the hospital."

"But she just dropped you off, when did all this happen?"

"Katherine, this isn't the time for games."

"Mom, do I look like I'm kidding? Please go put on your lipstick and Fain, please grab mom's coat, you know how easily she gets cold and please let's go." A few seconds later still in doubt, all three sped off Sand Island Blvd, toward the Golden Gate bridge. A few minutes later Fain made a sharp right turn off Golden Gate Blvd onto Hope way. As soon as they were parked, Faith and Katherine sped into the Emergency room. There was a Security guard who stood up as Faith approached the reception with questions. The guard directed them to Elizabeth's nurse.

"Oh, yes come this way," said the red headed nurse and pointed them to Elizabeth's room. Katherine ran toward Elizabeth.

"Grandma, I just left you a few minutes ago and you already got yourself in trouble?"

Elizabeth, who was fully alert and sitting up in bed, laughed at Katherine's remark.

"I missed you hunny," she said hugging her tightly.

"Love you Lizzy," said Faith, taking Elizabeth's hands and hugging her tightly. Shortly after they arrived, Eric and Calvin arrived together. They were both in wet suits and covered in sand.

"Mom, are you okay? What happened?"

"I'm great! My late husband didn't call me Elizabeth Thunderbird for nothing."

"But mom…" Just then Dr. Weiss arrived and explained that their mom suffered a mild atrial flutter which was likely triggered by stress.

"See, I told you boys I'm good to go," she chuckled. Dr. Weiss smiled at her response.

"Elizabeth, I'm glad you're in good spirits, but I'm afraid you would have to stay overnight for observation." After I review your tests, we will make a determination by morning whether you can go home.

As soon as Dr. Weiss left the room, Elizabeth jumped out of bed and despite the pleadings of her family, hurried out of Hope Hospital. Faith, Katherine, Fain, Calvin and Eric hurried after her. When they got to the parking lot, they saw Elizabeth searching frantically for her vehicle.

"Where's my car?" she said, becoming more upset by the minute. Everyone looked at each other confused.

"Wait a minute? Where's the couple that was with you when you had the incident?" Faith asked.

"What couple?" Elizabeth asked. The couple that saved your life?" Calvin and Eric looked at each other.

"Oh, that's right, I'm sorry I can't remember their names. But I do remember that I was on my way to a doctor's appointment.

"Who mom, was it Dr. Norris? " Eric asked.

"Oh, that's right; my car must have been left in the parking lot of Dr. Norris's office.

"I'm glad you are all here. But is that what it takes to have my family together?" Calvin and Fain laughed.

Faith and Eric glanced at each other and as Eric was about to speak, they were distracted by loud honking noise coming from Faith's Rover.

"Get in Grandma, I'll get you home. You don't have to worry about these rascals. Ummm, except mom. Get in grandma and I'll drive you home!" Katherine yelled.

The men laughed but couldn't believe when Elizabeth and Faith got into the vehicle and drove off the Emergency room lot onto the Golden Gate Blvd.

"Wait a minute, who's driving?" asked Eric looking at both men.

Fain and Calvin laughed loudly.

"Sorry Eric, that's my girl," said Fain proudly.

"Nice one Fain, but her mother was driving," Eric replied.

Calvin looks at both men staring at each other.

"Did you really go to college to be a Nanny?" asked Eric in a sarcastic tone.

"Glad I did Eric, because now I get to spend time with your lovely Ex," Fain said smugly.

Eric rung his fist and approached Fain, but Calvin got between them. Then all three men turned around at the sound of someone clearing their throat; to see a Sheriff leaning up against his vehicle with his hands folded. Fain hailed a Cab that had just pulled into the lot and the twins followed. The cab driver laughed silently. He wondered why Eric and Calvin were standing there dressed in yellow and blue wetsuits in a Hospital lot.

Chapter 7

Hank punched the keys of his new Apple computer, rushing to meet the new deadline set by his anxious publisher. His debut Novel was a major hit and his publisher had no choice but to cut the four months they had originally given him in half to accommodate his growing audience. He had less than twenty-four hours to wrap up the almost hundred thousand words Romance Mystery and it terrified him. With more than four thousand words to complete, he was determined to stay awake the remainder of the night to complete what he believes to be his best piece yet. It was a long day with Syd as she was dreading having to return to New York for the weekend to visit with her mom. He wished that there was more that he could have done to prevent his daughter from such torture, but he had no say in the matter. He hated to see his daughter this upset, but it was just the weekend. He had promised to have her in New York this weekend and that's just what he did.

It was already past midnight and although it was perfectly quiet at the bungalow, with Sydney away, he didn't feel as inspired. But he's learned to write in the absence of inspiration, when the words are only a deafening silence away, he would write his way into the deafening silence of noisy words that lay millions of miles away. As he typed a million miles a minute, he thought of Faith. Her deep mysterious green eyes played on his mind like a green emerald lost deep within the clear waters of Sandy Island. She was all the inspiration he needed to climb his way from the depth of four thousand words, deep within the ocean toward the surface. It was almost four am, barely awake; he punched in his final thought, defining the previous thousands, as the sound of the Sandy night surf sweeps the dawn to shore.

The sound of an electric saw became even more pronounced as its noise plummeted its way through the stillness. At its highest peak, when imminent danger is at its best, deafening sounds ripped its way through the deafness, alarming the peace of calmness, finally making its way to the stillness of sleep. Slowly but surely unwinding the gravity of chide, viciously ripping its way to a final climax....

"What the heck is this!" said Hand awaking from a deep sleep. He looked around confused. His office phone rang and removed his last ounce of confusion. Reaching for the handset, he answered in a revolting

"Yesss?

"Hank, it's Phyllis."

"Phyllis?"

"Yes Hank, we need the manuscript in less than five minutes. Please tell me that you have it, remember, we love you, but it's about the audience now."

"Nope it's not, it's about Phyllis now."

"What's that?"

"It's nothing, consider it done."

"Excellent," she said and hung up. Unedited, unprepared, he attached the one hundred and one-thousand-word manuscript to Phyllis Camden and emailed it off to New York.

It was only 7:15 am, but the island already promised to be a beautiful day. For the first time in forever, he didn't have to prepare breakfast and all he wanted to do was spend the evening with a beautiful woman. Hank does not remember the last time he did something spontaneous and he was ready to go crazy for the right reasons. He had a completely clean slate, a finished work, and an entire weekend to have his way. Did he say, his way? That felt good. It's been a while, but he refused to feel badly about it. Maybe he didn't realize how much he's missed taking time to self. This was a first and he realized that it was now or never... After pouring himself a cup of Joe, Hank contemplated his plan. Maybe it was time he got out of the state of perfection that promised nothing but the joy of the unknown. He was doing this and nothing in his past or current state of mind was going to stop him. It was now or never.

Showered, clean and unsure, Hank stride briskly toward Faith's house and knocked softly on her window. He thought that maybe he should have simply called, but he knew that this was a long shot and phones were out of the question. He needed this to happen, and nothing was going to remove this impossible barrier from experiencing the unknown. It was already an eternity, as he tried the back door to Faith's bedroom, entering her private domain in the hopes that she was alone. Bold, hopeful, and certain, he walked toward her bed. His heart racing, eyes determined, he lifted her covers unfolding his deepest desire. Still asleep, his Sandy Island Beauty had no idea that she was being carried out of her abode. As he carried her out into the soft morning air, she stirred in a mysterious way. Without hesitation, he carried her in his strong arms toward his nest with plans of passion.

Faith, still asleep snuggled with the softness of a sudden change. Hank stared at the beauty he dreamt would be in his bed for weeks; enjoying the sight of what was now possible. She was like a sleeping ocean in his bed. A glistening fountain of passion; a rare treasure. With all that could be true, he climbed into bed with the Sandy Island Faith, removing the wings of the morning, souring to heights and depths that only true love can beacon. Her silken appearance renews all lost hope of love, rewriting his heart to be endowed with the truth he most desired.

As the morning danced into play, Hank hardly cared about the hour. His true companion lay in complete adoration, in his arms, where his true heart basked in the harmony of desire. Maybe within seconds it would all go away. Maybe in a matter of minutes, the beautiful horror would take effect revealing the truth of the Mystery he had created. But one chance remains. That she too felt the miracle of what it takes to bring about the unexpected, in the most magical way. Faith stirred, sensing change, she looked around in slow realization.

"Where am I?" she asked staring sternly at the rugged writer.

"I had to steal you. There was no other way," he chuckled.

"You what?"

"Oh baby, don't be mad, I needed you."

"You're always with him. There has to be something very wrong with you Hank Hutton."

"I will have you arrested," she said hurrying out of his bed and heading for the door."

"Faith, wait a minute, nothing happened."

"I thought you were Fain."

"Fain? You're sleeping with Fain! Faith please wait!" he said stopping her as she was about to leave. As she turned to face him, his heart raced. Her green eyes appeared less angry and he pulled her into his arms.

53

"Hank, not to be frank but I hardly know you," she said now more relaxed.

"I know you," he replied covering her mouth before she spoke another word, kissing her softly; her soft lips basked in joy with each touch of affection.

As Faith was about to submerge into a heated moment with Hank, she resisted.

"Hank, I have to go. Kat's headed back to San Francisco to be with her grandmother."

"Have dinner with me," he said.

Her eyes narrowed.

"Hank, I can't, I have company."

"Your assistant, or is there a new title in the works?"

"Nope, just assistant," Faith said slipping on Hank's Jacket over her nightwear and heading out the door.

"I'll have dinner ready," he called.

She looked over her shoulder at him and smiled.

"You'll be wasting your time," she called.

"Well, I'll be prepared in the event," he called, his hands folded. She shook her head and hurried inside. She hoped that Kat and Fain did not realize that she was gone. Luckily, everyone was still asleep.

"Now, where was I?" she said slipping back into her unmade bed and falling into a deep sleep. A few hours later, she was awakened by Katherine hauling her tiny luggage on the hardwood floor. She sat up in bed and noticed Elizabeth's convertible pulled into the driveway. She wondered why Katherine was carrying three pieces of luggage. She thought that Fain might have helped her get ready, but noticed that he was still asleep due to loud snores coming from his room across the hall.

Faith hurried outside to greet Elizabeth but was surprised to see Eric standing on the balcony.

"Oh, Eric, where's Liz?"

"She had an early appointment and asked me to swing by to get Katherine. She wanted her to be ready because they were going out shortly after her appointment. I also thought it would be a great idea to spend a few hours with Kat before heading back to New York in the morning."

"I see, I had no idea you were out here. Were you going to take Katherine without letting me know?"

"C'mon, you're overacting," he laughed.

"Mom, you're up. Great! Don't worry I'm all packed and made myself a sandwich."

"You did, why didn't you get me up to help you hunny?"

"Don't be silly mom, you know I can manage."

"You are growing up much too fast darling." Eric giggled at his daughter's independent attitude.

"You know, she's exactly like you. Oh I highly doubt that," Faith said in an argumentative tone.

"Well hun, I'm going to miss you. I've hardly seen you in weeks."

"They hugged each other tightly. Mommy, I've been a really big help for Lizzy, she needs me. I've been helping her with lots of small projects. I promise I won't stay away too long."

"I'm so proud of you hun, and I love you."

"I love you too mommy."

"I'll see you in a week, okay." Eric carried the suitcases and Kat's overly stuffed luggage to the car. After embracing her mommy tightly, she took off down the stairs. Faith was glad that she was happy. She always believed that time was a gift, and that every moment should be cherished. Eric honked as they pulled out of the driveway. There was a distant sadness in his eyes, that she almost asked him about Rachael, but didn't. They were living separate lives and she was determined to exist in the world that she longed for, for so many years. Not even that least bit of care exerted by Eric's somewhat caring display would gain her interest. She wanted change, and with each passing day, she was determined to accomplish, just that.

Faith stretched out on a lounge chair enjoying her favorite view of the ocean. Sometimes it almost felt like she had a relationship with the tides-the fact that each day it sent her messages, ones that seem to reflect her current state of being. Today, it reflected a much deeper blue than the day before and there was stillness about it, with a slight ripple. It almost appeared solved, but deep within its calmness is a mystery, waiting to be solved.

"Good Morning," Fain said handing Faith a cup of pepping hot coffee.

"I should smack you," she said reaching for the cup of coffee from his firm grasp. He giggled.

"What were you thinking about so deeply?" he asked jokingly.

"None of your business," she snapped.

"My, my are we fickle today."

"Where's my Bff this morning?"

"You just missed her. She's already left for Liz's."

"I see. It's been different around here without her."

"I agree, she's the life of this place. But I thought about it and it's a good idea for now. Our new neighbor's daughter Sydney also left for New York a few days ago. It would have been a bit of an adjustment for her.

"Not with her handsome French Chef around," Fain joked. Faith smiled at his boyish sense of humor.

"With Katherine away, I feel like you don't have much use for me these days. What's new?" As Fain lingered closer toward Faith in the hope for an answer, she walked away from him. She needed a moment alone. Maybe it was everything that had happened. Maybe it was Hank's bold early morning capture, and the slight feeling that her daughter was slowly slipping away, created a new feeling of distrust and uncertainty. Whatever it was, it was happening at a mile a minute and she was slowly feeling the need to escape.

"Faith?" he called, but she disappeared into her room and locked the door behind her.

Fain, despite everything that he'd seen the past year, was surprised by her sudden reaction. He honestly believed that she was making rapid progress toward her single life and hoped that nothing had got in the way of that. Faith's actions spoke clearly about how she felt, and he wanted to respect her space, but she'd come much too far, and he couldn't allow her to slip back into herself. She was much stronger than this. Hours later, Faith still hadn't joined him. He had to discard her lunch and dinner and he was hoping that her breakfast didn't have to suffer the same fate. It was evident that something had changed. He knocked on her door on separate occasions, but he eventually gave up. He had spent the entire day to himself and despite what was happening, he realized that the time spent alone helped him a great deal. It helped him realize a few things. Maybe he too needed change. He was unsure of what it was, but, whatever it was, he had to find it.

After what seemed like an eternity, another beautiful day had cast its golden ray upon the lovely Island. Faith still hadn't joined him and he was beginning to care less about her stubbornness. He refused to spend the day preparing meals and waiting for Faith to come around. Maybe it's been a while since he'd a moment to himself, but he was going to have a blast. After a shower and a shave, Fain ran toward the wooden dock and got into a small dingy, cranked the engine and sped toward San Francisco bay. He thought that maybe he should have left Faith a note but this time he didn't give a care whether she was dead or alive. He wasn't sure how long he'd be gone, but that was beside the point. It was the weekend and he was going to have a good time. Fain docked the small boat near Pier 55 on Fisherman's Wharf. Despite the early hours of the day, he strolled into a slightly crowded bar and ordered a stiff one, straight up.

"Wow hold up there young man, show me some ID," called the bartender, a friendly looking guy who appears in his mid-fifties. While Fain reached his back pocket for his wallet, he noticed a gorgeous blonde staring at him from across the room but pretended not to notice. He slapped his ID down and said,

"Happy now!"

"Not quite," said the pretentiously grumpy bartender who realizes that Fain was a foreigner, who may not know the ropes.

"What now smart ass!"

"I see, we're getting real pretty, but you forgot your lipstick boy."

"I see you are of legal age, but then there's one more requirement...what do you do for a living?" Fain, not realizing that the bartender was kidding, responded...

"I'm a professional French Manny." The suddenly noisy bar turned silent and you can hear a pin drop. Then the silence was interrupted by combined hysterical laughter. Fain, for the second time today, ignored the response and downed the crown royal that the bartender poured him while laughing heartedly.

"Hat's off to you son."

A few hours later, feeling slightly lightheaded, Fain strolled out of the bar. For the first time in months, the twenty-nine-year-old, felt alone. He stared at his watch. Realizing he hadn't had anything to eat all day, he strolled into a diner and ordered a burger to go. As he was about to take a bite into his lunch, he was interrupted by a New York accent.

"Hi there! I swear, my homemade burgers are a lot more satisfying than Jacky's!" Fain looked at her and realized that she was the blonde that was at the bar.

"Ha, really?"

"Is this an invitation?" The woman rolled down her window and signaled Fain to enter her Ferrari. Without hesitation, Fain entered the gorgeous vehicle and was soon speeding toward the unknown. He glanced a few times at the strange woman. He didn't care about the outcome. Anyone promising to make him a real American burger was reason enough. A major plus, if he was the one being served for a change. The stranger drove for what seemed like an hour and parked on a hill in front of a two-story mansion with lots of glass windows.

"Please join me," she called, shutting the door behind her. Fain glanced after the woman, she appeared to be no older than her mid-forties. He tried opening the door to let himself out of the Ferrari, but it was apparently stuck. After trying for a few moments, realizing that he had no idea how to let himself out of the car, trying to not embarrass himself, he climbed out of the window. Relieved, Fain entered the woman's house and had no idea where she went. He made himself comfortable on a recliner in what appears to be a beautiful guest room. A few minutes later, he was greeted again by the strange woman who handed him a tray with the largest burger he'd ever seen and a mug of beer taller than the Statue of Liberty. After devouring the enticing meal, Fain burped loudly.

"How despicably, delightful" the woman said lighting up a cigarette. Fain's sleepy eyes widened at the sight of an immensely, muscular, tall black male taking his tray and handing him another beer.

"Oh, thank you!" he said relieved.

"You're welcome," the gentleman said in a deep but kind tone.

"To what do I owe this pleasure?" The woman smiled but didn't respond. Satisfied and overwhelmed, Fain fell into a deep sleep.

A few hours later, Fain awoke to a female voice in an emotional dispute. He listened to the argument and learned that the woman's name is Kate. Realizing the time, he tries to leave before she notices.

"Fain Collins," where are you going?"

"Wow, how do you know me?"

"Don't be ridiculous, have a seat kid!"

"No, not until you tell me who the hell you are!"

"Is this how you thank a kind stranger, by yelling at her in her own home?" By then Fain grabbed his leather jacket from the recliner and headed out the door. Kate realized that he may have had a bit too much to drink when he had got into her car earlier. She was hoping that he would have recognized her by now. He obviously didn't realize where he was or else he wouldn't have taken off on foot. Kate followed him in her Ferrari and when he'd walked about a mile, she pulled up in front of him.

"Fain, please get in the car."

"You're weird," he called.

"You know kid, you're lucky. I don't usually care about anyone, but I notice something different about you. Now get in this fine car before I change my mind!" she warned.

"So you think you know me, huh, what if I had my way with you. What if I had an unknown motive, you silly bitch!"

"Exactly what I had in mind. I'm Kate, you were a guest in my movie a few weeks ago," she said tearing off his shirt.

"Really?" he said doubting as he plunged toward her. As she reclined her seat and rolled up the windows, he reached for her gorgeous face, kissing her tensely. She was in excellent shape. Her prominent abs shaped as the former irritated, now calm French boy had his way with the unexpectant beauty.

Chapter 8

Hank was sure that despite Faith's stubbornness, that she would have joined him for dinner. Maybe she was profoundly disturbed by his boldness and needed time to think. He understood, but he's never felt that way about anyone ever and he wasn't sure how long he could wait for Faith to come around. As difficult as it is for him, he's going to leave her alone for now. Having been single the past three years, this was the best he could do for someone that he was quickly falling in love with. He glanced around his rustic bungalow and was thankful for the silence. He'd learned to make the best of the little and despite how small, he is going to embrace the silence until it returns a reward worthy of forgetting Faith. He could almost hear that very familiar, invisible, fictitious Hank making fun of his efforts but he didn't mind. However, he was becoming frustrated, very quickly with invisible Hank calling him names, and arguing with him about his ridiculous excuses for not giving his best effort at a second chance. But he was going to ignore that jerk. He'd listened to him many times before and had always regretted the outcome.

It was already after six in the evening, but it appeared much earlier. Hank wrapped up dinner and went for a stroll down the wooden docks. It was like a vision looking upon the gorgeous horizon as it attempted to bid the day farewell. Each day, he was slowly falling in love with this place and had no doubt that his fairly new home was a worthy investment. As he strolled further down the docks, a feeling of assurance came over him and he continued for miles until his Bungalow appeared like a dot in the distance. Twilight was now enforced, and an even more magical display of gold glistened across the evening sky in remembrance of the day's joy. Realizing the time and remembering that he had a conference call with his Editor and Literary Agent, he picked up a light pace. He needed to be in front of his manuscript in less than five minutes and his light pace turned into a full-blown sprint. The last time he'd ran this fast was his famous high school days of track and field. He chuckled as he thought of how terrified his opposing rivals were of his team. To him those days were all symbolic of the future. They reminded him that the race is never finished when the gold medal is awarded; it's really only the beginning of every race that he would ever run, this time with a more rewarding, less than tangible result.

As he sped off the dock, his mobile rang. Almost out of breath, he answered with an exhausting HELLO…

"Hank? Hey pal, is this a good time?" Adam asked.

"Hey Adam, yeah, no problem."

"You sure?"

"Yeah, yeah, I'm good. Just need to get behind the computer," said Hank reaching for the front door keys.

"You sounded like I interrupted a hot moment," Adam joked.

"Adam, I've never told you this, but you're a jerk; actually, an ass, a real one." Adam laughed.

"Whatever man, you're lucky I like your writing, butt face."

"You know what, I'm going to kick your ass the very next time I see you. Mark your calendar, that's exactly one week from today." "Done and done, big dudes never scare me, Scottish Kilt," said Adam laughing. Both laughed at their combined sense of humor. As Hank and Adam laughed, there was another call on the line…"

"Hang in there Adam, I think it's Jill." And sure, it was…

"Hey Jill, I have Adam on the other line."

"Oh, patch him through, let's connect," she said. There was a positive tone in her voice and Hank took it as a good sign. The three colleagues connected and as Hank had hoped, Jill informed him that there was an offer on the table…that his novel is selected for a feature film. He had ten days to consider the offer which was not negotiable. He gave Adam the ok to convert the Novel into a Screenplay but Adam was to contact him with every revision. This was going to slow the publication process of his fifth book, but it was a great offer and he promised Jill that he would deeply consider it. Both her and Adam had worked endlessly on his behalf and contributed a fair percentage to his bestselling author status. This indeed is excellent news and their feelings about the direction he should go were obvious, but he never envisioned his work on the screen; he hoped that the ten days were sufficient.

61

Faith's slowly blinked her eyes to an open. A feeling of refreshment came over her as she tossed about her silky bed linen. That dated overwhelmed feeling combined with that dreaded headache had fled the scene, and she hoped it was permanent. She refused to repeat the previous months; the days that she swore would claim her life into an eternal abyss of never return. After a long sigh of relief, she jumped out of bed with a spring in her steps. A refreshing shower added a plus to her feeling of spontaneity and she got into a gorgeous one piece floral pantsuit summer wear, with matching heels and flower necklace. She then threw her Jeanne York designer handbag over her shoulders. She had no idea where she was headed but her hot Lamborghini Convertible parked in her garage for months awaited. At the sight of her beautiful babe, she threw her legs over the side, slipped on her sunglasses and sped toward Sandy Island Blvd. As she sped away, she felt alive until an emergency sound caught to her attention. She looked in her rearview mirror and noticed Patrol George speeding after a small speedboat. "Patrol George, you are overrated, give those kids a break, it summer," she laughed, knowing if he'd heard her she too would have suffered the consequences.

As she turned corners, speeding toward the Golden Gate Bridge, something caught her eye which became clearer as she neared the Bridge. Her heart sank noticing that the tiny white object was a tent, possibly with someone fast asleep on a very unsafe corner of the bridge and freeway. Any wrong move, this person could plummet into the rough waters below. She also wondered why the highway patrol has not spotted this yet. It crossed her mind several times to simply ignore this and drive away, but she couldn't. She searched for somewhere to pull over. As soon as she pulled over in a no parking zone, she hurried toward the bridge. As she climbed the small foothill, she noticed that whoever it was were comfortable. Fully equipped with the essentials of a camper… At that point she had no idea how to proceed. "Hello, is anyone there?" There was no response and it was very windy, so she tried getting closer. "Hello, you must be crazy, what are you doing there? I mean of all the places you could pitch a tent, why would you pitch it there? This is nuts? If you wanted some attention; you could have simply flipped off the Senator, and it would have easily been justified, but you're obviously out of your mind!" As she turned to leave, she heard someone sneeze...

"It's the best view in the city, and it's free," a female voice called as a pair of eyes peeked out of a tent camp window. Faith removed her sunglasses.

"What are you doing here?"

"Are you okay?"

"How old are you?"

"Eighteen," the girl replied. An African American girl who appeared to be no older than fifteen was now standing in front of her Pink and White Craftsman's tent.

"Are you in some kind of trouble?"

"Lady, you should try minding your own business. I could be anyone."

"What's your name?" The girl sucked her teeth and went back into her tent.

"I don't believe you're eighteen!" Faith called.

"Now you're really beginning to piss me off lady." Faith was hardly bothered by her demeanor. For some reason, she wanted to help her. As she was about to ask her name a second time, she noticed highway Patrol pulled up next to her parked car. He was writing her a ticket and she took off running toward him with lightning speed. "Hey! Hey! Officer," she said waving her hands. The officer noticed her but he continued writing.

"Officer, hold up. I thought someone needed help. It was just for a minute," she called. The officer then responded to a call and left before Faith reached him. She pulled the piece of paper from her windshield. Realizing it was only a warning, she exhaled an exhausted sigh of relief. She looked at the tent on the hill one more time and smiled. Getting back into her convertible, she drove toward Fisherman's Wharf.

Chapter 9

Faith drove around the Bay, admiring the views that had always wowed her since her first arrival from Austria seventeen years before. The scenes took her back to when she was madly in love with Eric. The epic scenery and majestic tides revived her first love of the Bay. There was no better place to be on a surrendered Tuesday afternoon, filled with meaning. As she climbed hills and turned corners, admiring the beautiful North Bay Architecture, someone peeled through the intersection on their bike, cutting her off as she intended to run an Amber light.

"Hey, are you crazy?!" Faith shouted. The woman on the bike peeled to a stop and looked directly at Faith.

"Someone asked me that earlier?" Realizing that it was the woman with the tent on the bridge, Faith Laughed.

"You get around alright. I'm starting to think you're following me," the woman said with a disapproving look. Faith laughed a second time.

"Hey, is this funny to you? I swear if I see you again, I will report you!" the woman called. The lights were now green and incoming traffic beeped loudly at Faith and the strange woman. The woman looked at Faith, then flipped off the annoying traffic and peddled off toward the beach. As Faith traveled around the bay, she thought of the woman: seeing her for a second time that day, Faith thought that maybe it meant something. Her Mother-in-law had always told her that she was the superstitious type that tries to make sense of everything and that some things are simply coincidental. As she thought of this, she noticed a box of Cigarettes on the shelf above the glove compartment in her car. She had quit smoking after she discovered that she was pregnant with Katherine. It's a milestone she'd planned and had successfully accomplished. She thought that maybe the cigarettes belonged to Fain. As she thought of him, she remembered that she hadn't seen him in almost two days. Then she realized that Fain never smoked. At least, not that she knows of.

Whose pack of Cigarettes are these? She wonders. Faith thought of the last time she'd driven the convertible and it was over a year ago. She was now driving up Filbert Street and came to a stop at the plateau. She always swore that Filbert Street was the highest point of the bay and her fear of heights was calmed by the view of her Sandy Island Bungalow across the ocean. As she stepped out of her Lamborghini, the wind shuffled her scarf as she tried to gain her footing. The sound of the surf mixed with the sound of cars beeping awakened a brilliant idea. The view of her home across the Bay spoke for itself. The blue choppy ocean and the sound of the wind made everything seem almost futuristic in appearance.

"That's it, that's it!" she said her heart raced in excitement.

As the idea sunk further into her mind, she laughed. "Patrol George, I hope you drink enough beers this summer because this one will take a lot more than a fed-up San Franciscan turned Sandy Patrol Ticketmaster. As she digested that thought, the sound of a group of Sandy Bay University students grabbed her attention.

"Look at that view guys. This place is the Summer of dreams dude," said one of the students wearing a graduation gown.

"I know right, this view is the bomb. Wanna go for a drive?"

"Yeah, let's check it out" said the guy in the grad gown.

"Hey, hey guys wait," called an excited brunette holding onto her graduation hat, hurrying toward them. Faith smiled at the sight of the young group as they drove off in an obnoxious 2004 convertible, with a bad muffler exhausting thick white smoke as it peeled through a left turn, running a solid red. Faith laughed. How was it possible that no cars were interrupted during that illegal turn? She thought. The Bay can be boring, and not even running a solid red light could interrupt an open intersection with passage that could accommodate open traffic for miles. The inviting view across the bay spoke a million words.

Fain awoke to the sound of Kate's loud snores. It was after three in the evening and although it was a Sunday evening, he felt ridiculous. At Faith's house, he was always busy completing projects and chores: ones he was proud of and gave him that feeling of accomplishment. He got dressed quickly, and dialed UBER. Less than five minutes later he got into his ride.

"The Wharf, Pier fifty-five please," he said to the driver and exhaled a sign of relief. Unnoticed to Fain, the driver glanced over at him suspiciously. The driver knows Kate well and having never seen Fain before this, she wondered what his hurry was, but said nothing. The driver pulled up next to the Pier. Fain slipped on his black leather Jacket and ran toward the boat where he had docked the day before. As he was about to jump into the dingy, he noticed that the boat wasn't where he'd left it. He thought that maybe he had the wrong dock but after looking around, he realized that the small boat was really gone.

Still in disbelief, Fain checked the other piers. The Dinghy was nowhere to be found and after a few hours, Fain called the local police to report the incident. He was almost ecstatic as he provided the details, but he could hear a slight comical tone in the officer's voice.

"Ma'am, with all due respect, do you find this funny?" But the officer was reduced to laughter. This time Fain was beyond pissed.

He yelled "Stupid Bitch!" and hung up. A few seconds later his mobile rang.

"HELLO! HELLO, Sir, it's officer Kelly Richards, you called a few minutes ago?"

"Oh, you mean Cadette Richards cause there's no way you're a Cop, Bitch!"

"Sir, you are going to have to stop with the name calling if you want your property back." Realizing Fain exhaled loudly.

"You're kidding right?"

"Sir, you docked your boat on Pier Fifty-five. You are only allowed a total of five hours per day. If after five hours you have not moved the vessel, you are assigned a warning to move your boat. But you've ignored the first ticket and your boat was removed by the Patrol in charge. In order to regain your property, you'll have to pay a port fee of three thousand dollars."

"Say What!" Fain hung up the officer before getting the details on the vessel's location.

For the second time officer Richards dialed the stubborn French boy. Fain answered on the second ring but said nothing.

"Sir, are you interested in regaining possession of your vessel?"

"Ma'am, please provide the location of my property and I will follow up in an hour," he said annoyed.

Fain jotted the details down on the back of his skinny hands and thanked the officer.

"You got it and thanks for getting my name right this time, you callous jerk!" She replied and hung up. Fain was too annoyed to be bothered. He then thought of who he should call. The Dinghy was a rental from Hank, and he knew that the three-thousand-dollar fee was not the only smack to his pocketbook he had to deal with that day. As he thought of the two-thousand-dollar deposit that he could lose if there was anything wrong with the rental, he swore and kicked rocks. As he contemplated what he should do, his phone rang.

"Fain, I got a call from the Wharf, how did this happen?" Fain knew now that his deposit was toast, especially the fact that Hank knew that he had romantic feelings for Faith. Hank yelled at him like a schoolboy. He told him that he would apply his deposit towards the impound and that he would still owe him the balance.

"Hank, C'mon, just let me explain." But Hank had already hung him up. His only concern now was to get a ride home. As he thought of this, he now feared that Faith may also be upset with him. As he contemplated these things his mobile rang. It was Kate wanting to know where he'd disappeared to.

"Kate it's not a good time, I'll call you later." He said and hung up. Kate phoned him several times, but he didn't answer. For the second time, he called UBER.

"Where too?" the driver asked. "Sandy Island," he growled.

"My, my, are we grumpy today," said the driver: a tough talking woman who appeared in her late fifties.

"Frenchie, as much as I would like to help you out, we don't travel to Sandy Girl.

"Are you kidding, this is Bullshit, let me out, now!" he yelled.

"Geeze kid, I was just kidding with you," the woman laughed. Fain was hardly amused.

"What's with your attitude anyway, good looking kid like you?"

"Yes, good looks don't pay the bills if it's dead. Now if you don't mind, keep your eyes on the road please."

"By the way, I'm Emily. Yes, obviously, it's tattooed on your arm," Emily laughed. Fain felt around his pockets for his wallet and grew concerned as the driver pulled up in front of Faith's Bungalow.

"You have arrived, your Royal handsomeness," said Emily in her flattering New York accent.

"Ahh, finally," said Fain, discovering his wallet on the floor of the Vehicle.

"Was it that bad?" called Emily. Fain handed Emily a bill and said, "Keep the change!"

"Hey, hey come here I don't need your tip you silly kid, you probably need that to pay off your hundreds of parking tickets, jerk!" Fain flipped her off as he disappeared inside.

White smoke clouded the Sandy Island Blvd as the Five new grads peeled through the surprisingly open road in their convertible toward Sandy Island Bay. They followed the signs that pointed toward Hank's boat rental.

"I should call my mom. We had plans to have dinner with her after the event," Rob said.

"Dude, when are you going to stop worrying about your mom?"

"Shut up Steve. You have no idea what it's like being raised by a single mom who paid out of her pockets for my college tuition." Steve looked regretful and apologized to Rob.

"Okay, okay, we're here for a little fun, it'll only take a couple hours and we'll head back," called Tony, pulling off the freeway onto Hank's parking lot. Stephanie leaned forward and pulled on Steve's collar.

"I need you to stop being a total jerk to Rob, this isn't High School ok."

Whatever," Steve replied. Stephanie pulled his collar tighter.

"Ouch, okay, okay. Good," she said, releasing him. Rob and Tony laughed at Steve's fake sense of regret.

"Shut up," said Steve as Tony pulled the old convertible in front of Hank's place. He got out and pounded Hank's door several times, but he wasn't home.

"No one's here," he called.

"Let's wait for a few minutes, there's time," Said Stephanie.

"Okay, but I can only wait for a half hour, and then I got to split," said Rob, looking at his time piece.

"Pussy," said Steve. This time Stephanie playfully smacked Steve upside the head.

"What is your problem? leave him alone or else I'll throw you off the boat. Everyone knows you can't swim. Now who's the real Pussy," said Stephanie. Rob laughed loudly.

"Dude, for real? You're kidding right!" Steve glared at Rob as though Stephanie was the only reason that prevented him from kicking his ass. As the friends waited, Fain came to see what they needed.

"We'd like to rent a boat," called Tony, observing the hundreds of rentals displayed on Hank's dock.

"He's not here but hang on I'll phone him."

"Oh you know Hank?"

"Yes, just wait a minute and I'll phone him for you," Sounds good," said Steve rolling up his sleeves. Stephanie eyed Fain seductively.

"He looks hot, I wonder if he's...."

"I'm single," said Steve finishing Stephanie's sentence. Rob laughs at Steve's attempt. As Steve was about to respond to Rob, Hank pulled into his driveway.

"Steve, you better forget it. The last time you rented my boat, I told you it was the last time and I meant it."

"C'mon man, that was two years ago, and you know Patrol George is the biggest Jerk."

"Yes, but twenty-nine violations in a day is completely ridiculous Steve, I meant my word."

"Geeze, what's got you so pissed off today anyway?"

As Steve tries to reason with Hank, Stephanie approached Fain and said a few words to him. She then approached Hank and spoke to him for a few seconds and minutes later, she was given the keys to a small Party Boat named Jen.

"Are you guys coming?"

"Hank, are you kidding me?" Fain chuckled at Steve.

"Let's go boys," called Stephanie running toward the dock, removing her summer dress revealing a one-piece white swimwear. Steve parked the Convertible in the visitor parking and the three slightly drunk college grads joined Stephanie on the party boat. Tony pulled some beers from his pack and handed one to Steve and Rob, but Rob refused.

"Sorry man, I don't want to ruin it for Stephanie." Stephanie smiled at Rob for being the more responsible of the boys.

"Okay boys, let's go for a spin, said Steph cranking the engine.

"Mind if I take over for a minute?" Steve asked.

"Steve, you just don't get it do you?" said Rob.

"Alright boys, here we go," Steph said as the boat name Jen jumped into action, landing Steve on his butt. Steph sped through the open water toward the small hidden beach under the cliff of Sandy Bay University. As they neared the Cliff, she noticed a group of new grads high above the surf and whistled loudly, catching their attention.

"Wanna Join us?" she called.

"Hell ya," someone said and a few moments later, the Party boat was overly packed with Sandy Bay University grads. Steve fished out his fifth beer and was hardly behaving. Rob noticed Ken, a tall blonde Freshman approached Steph and began rubbing her thighs.

"Hey, hey, back of dude," Rob said approaching.

"What are you doing here anyway; this party is for new grads only. How old are you?" Steph asked.

"Old enough," he responded.

"Don't be a smart ass, answer the question," said Rob.

"Back off dude, what the heck is your problem?" said Ken approaching Rob with his fist clenched. Steph approached Ken from behind and touched him on the back. Ken, already on edge, turned around sharply smacking Steph in the face causing her to fall backwards.

"Ouch," she cried. With that, Rob punched Ken in the face and the two engulfed into a full blown, all out fight.

"Stop it!" Steph called. Steph had bruised her back and the loud music deafened her cry for help. Ken and Rob were smashing each other against the wall, causing damage to the boat.

"Stop it! She called.

"Rob, get off him!" Jake finally noticed the struggle aboard and hurried toward Rob who had Ken in a headlock.

"What the heck, Rob, I think he gets the message. Get off him," said Jake grabbing Rob from behind and finally pulling him off Ken.

"Ken, what are you doing here?"

"You know him?" Steph asked.

"Yeah, that's my little brother Ken, what the heck are you doing?"

Whatever man," Ken called. I'm eighteen, I don't need you looking out for me," said Ken wiping moisture and blood from a scratch on his forehead. Steph, hurried to the Captain's cabin and came back carrying a first aid kit. Rob noticed the bruise on her back and offered to look at it, but Jake took the kit from Steph and dressed the wound. As pissed off as he was at his little brother, he was disappointed in Rob. After dressing the bruise on Steph's back. He handed the kit to his brother.

"Here go take care of that scratch, you look terrible."

"Gee, thanks," said Ken, walking away embarrassed.

"Rob, I expected better of you. Can't you tell he's just a stupid kid? Steph defended Rob, by explaining what Ken did.

"Sorry Steph, if you don't mind, let's turn this boat around. I need to get Ken out of here. Steph was terribly upset as she took the steering wheel and turned the boat around. Everyone else aboard was drinking and partying and didn't notice what had just happened. As they neared the surf, Rob offered to fix the damage done to the deck. He told Steph that his uncle owns a similar boat and he taught him a few things about making repairs.

"Sounds great, but where are you going to find the time to do all this? I have to take the boat back in less than an hour." Rob reached for his mobile and called Hank. He explained to Hank that they would like to extend, and Hank allowed an additional two hours. Steph was impressed with Rob for taking responsibility.

"What's that?" she said, noticing a red stain on his collar.

"It's nothing," he said.

"Are we playing tough?" she said removing Rob's shirt and patching up a small bruise on his shoulder.

"There you go, tough guy. And promise me you will not be getting any more bruises today.

"I'll try," he said. Pulling her closely, kissing her.

"Now look what we have here," said Steve staggering toward them. "I knew it!" he laughed. Steve staggered toward Steph and attempts to kiss her. But Steph had moved out of the way to avoid Steve's kiss and he plummeted over the edge, splashing into water.

"Oh my gosh, are you okay?" Steph called tossing Steve the life preserver. Rob laughed hysterically.

"That's not fair Clark, because you know Lois can't swim!" Rob said mocking Steve. As Rob continued to pick on Steve, Stephanie pulled him close pretending to kiss him and then tossed Rob overboard.

"Now here's your chance to kiss and make up," she says walking away. Steve and Rob struggle to stay afloat using the single life preserver. Rob then tries to fight Steve for the preserver. As the two struggled, their friends on deck noticed them in the water.

71

"Hey boys, how can we help you?" They laughed.

"What's wrong, you can't swim?" and laughter follows. Jake opens a can of beer and began to pour it in the water.

"Here you go boys, drink up. That's the last one; I wouldn't want it to go to waste.

"Jerks, hammered shit!" The group called. Steve then punched Rob and got the life preserver away from him. As he tries to escape, their friends began to root for Steve as Rob peeled through the water like a speed boat trying to catch him. Steve noticed the iron bars against the stern of the boat and made his way on Deck. He then pulled the life preserver up before Rob could get a hold of it. Tired from chasing after Steve, Rob dog paddles his way to the stern of the boat and finally makes his way on deck. The friends laughed, and high five Rob for the last-minute show. Stephanie approached Rob and reminded him of the repairs that still needed to be made to the damages him and Ken made earlier.

"C'mon Steph, you almost drowned me."

"Hey, you, get over here, you're going to help with the repairs, now get up from your cat nap and get busy," said Rob tossing a hammer at him.

"I couldn't agree more," called Steph sipping on an iced lemonade, stretching out on a lounge chair on deck. Steve and Jake pitched in and a half an hour later, there was no signs of damage. Stephanie was beyond impressed and high fived her crew for a job well done.

"But, guys remember, prevention is better than cure, this cannot happen again. Okay boys," she said looking at Rob and Ken. Ken smiled and winked at her in response. She laughs.

"Very cute, but you are too young, and you are not my type," she said winking back at him. Jake shakes his head at his little brother's attempt.

"I don't think I could have a girlfriend with you around," he said placing his hands around his little brother's shoulders. Ken laughed. Rob sat next to Stephanie.

"Now where were we?" he asked kissing her as the sun disappeared beyond the horizon, leaving the sky in an orange display.

Chapter 10

Fain was surprised to see Faith as she pulled up in her convertible.

"Wow, you look great. What have you been up to?" He asked helping her out of the car.

"I can ask you the same. It feels like I haven't seen you in years," she joked. He was suddenly quiet, and Faith knows him only too well to ignore his sudden static silence.

"New girlfriend?" she joked. He glanced at her in response and when they were on the balcony, he removed her sunglasses and scarf and kissed her passionately. Realizing that Hank could see them, Faith tries to pull away from Fain, but he pulls her into his strong arms and empties the joy he felt to see her.

"I, I love you Faith. I've never felt so lonely waking up in someone else's bed. It ate at me for hours and I couldn't wait to see you." Faith looked at him confused.

"What are you talking about? Fain, you're very young. You have your entire life ahead of you. I wouldn't want you to throw all this away, just for me."

"Please don't say that," he said sharply. Faith tries to hide her slight feeling of betrayal and wonders who he had been with.

"It's Hank, Isn't it? I've seen you through the worst the past few months and this is how you repay me."

"Fain, I have no time for your tantrums. You're my Employee and I've allowed this to go much too long. I blame myself for this," she said regretfully.

"Tantrums, how dare you treat me as a child? Where is this coming from?"

"Fain, please stop it! I know you've seen lots of women during the very dark months of my life: the ones that you claimed to have seen me through. I also know that you've taken my convertible to drive your women. So, don't you dare try to play coy with me, Fain Collins."

Fain couldn't doubt Faith's accusations and he went to his room and slammed the door behind him. A few moments later Faith peeked through the window overlooking the driveway and saw him got into a rental and sped away. Her heart sunk at the thought of how long he would be gone, and she went to his bedroom and looked at his closet. She noticed that his closet was almost empty and there were several packed bags on the floor. She knew that it would take him more than a few minutes to pack this many clothes and she wonders how long he's been thinking of leaving. She reached for her mobile and thought of phoning him but didn't. She wasn't sure that he was really moving out and if he was, she wasn't certain that she was ready to be without him. Despite his dishonesty, he's been a great employee. As she thought of the previous months, tears welled up in her eyes and she stopped herself. Despite how the day ended, she had a wonderful time driving around the Bay. She was much stronger than she'd been and she was not going to allow herself to sink back into the epitome of depression that she swore would have kept her captive. She had freed herself and chose to look forward to the history of her life that has not yet occurred. As she thought of this, her mobile rang and it was her beloved Katherine.

"Hunny, I miss you so much, are you coming home today?"

"But mom, I thought you said that I can stay a week. I still have two more days with Grandma."

"Oh that's, that's right baby. Don't worry." But Katherine knew something was wrong. She could sense sadness in her mother's voice and wanted to know what was wrong. After a forty-five-minute conversation, Katherine was convinced that her mom was the happiest she's been in years. Faith was happy that her baby was coming home in two days, but she also hoped that Fain was back by then. She was not prepared to explain to Katherine what had happened to him. Other than Eric moving out, she knew that Katherine was not nearly ready for the adjustment of losing Fain.

Faith paced back and forth as she prepared for her daughter's arrival. She had not heard from Fain since the day before and the static silence of her beachside home was almost intolerable. As she thought of possible distractions or excuses for Kat, her lifetime movie was interrupted by an Entertainment headline.

"Kate Hayden has done it again. Prepare for this exciting new Romantic Summer adventure starring Fain Collins as the handsome

Kyle Morocco and the beautiful Kate Hayden as Madden Kenna." Hardly surprised, Faith realized that she hadn't renewed Fain's contract which left the door wide open for him to pursue new opportunities. As she thought of what she'd just learned, her phone rang. Seeing it was Fain, she answered quickly. They spoke for a few short minutes. He was only calling to inform her of his plans to get the rest of his things. Then she realized that he was coming the same day that Katherine was arriving and she phoned him back quickly.

"Fain, it's best you come by as soon as possible, Kat is coming home tomorrow and I don't want her to see you leave." A little surprised, Fain agreed and told her that he would be there in an hour. After a quick shower, Faith slipped into something comfortable and went for a walk down the pier. She left the spare keys where she knew he would find them and hurried toward the pier. It was almost afternoon and not a cloud could be seen, and the familiar, natural sound of the bay relaxed her. A few moments later she sat on the dock and let her feet touch the clear water. As she admired the small schools of fishes in the water, she was interrupted by a familiar voice…

"Hey there." She looked up to see Patrol George walking toward her with a beautiful horse.

"Wow, what do we have here," said Faith approaching the Sandy Bay Patrol TicketMaster. As she approached him, the animal appeared uncomfortable.

"Easy there girl," he said, patting her back.

"Where in the world did you find this beautiful creature?" Patrol George removing his cap and sunglasses.

"I want you to have her," he said a smile slowly forming on his stern face.

"Are you serious, no way, to what do I owe this lovely treasure. Besides, I'm not sure I know how to take care of her." Patrol George pointed to the fenced acres behind Faith Bungalow and chuckled.

"That's all you need my dear. Lots of open terrain where Becca can run freely." Still in disbelief, she reached out her hands and patted the gorgeous creature gently. She neighed softly.

"Wanna climb on?" He asked.

"You must be crazy. I've never rode on a horse before," she said hysterically. As his eyes met hers, she noticed that they were soft a grey. His stern face appeared much friendlier and he said almost in a whisper.

"*Trust me.*" To her surprise, the horse appeared to nudge her to climb on.

"Okay, but just for a little," she said climbing on. When she was seated comfortably, Patrol George said

"Okay girl," and Becca began walking away slowly.

"Might want to hold on tightly to those reins," he called.

"What!" But instead the Ticketmaster whistled loudly, and the horse picked up speed and took off down the bay. Faith screamed and held onto the reins tightly. She then heard another whistle and Becca turned around and headed back toward Patrol George, with Faith barely hanging on. As they neared, Patrol George's broad smile turned into a giggle.

"See, you're a natural," he joked. Faith was hardly amused, but slowly broke into laughter as the horse came to a stop.

"I can tell she likes you!" he said excitedly, or she wouldn't have let you climb on.

"She is beautiful," Faith admitted.

"Do I hear a… but…then she's all yours," he called and hurried toward his truck attached to a horse trailer parked in Faith's driveway.

"But Patrol George," she called. The tall dark, grey eyed gentleman ignored her and drove toward Sandy island Blvd. Faith turned and looked at Becca; a beautiful, almost white horse, except for the soft brown fur on her front and hind legs.

"Let's go girl, I can hardly believe it, but it looks like we're stuck together, at least for now." After letting the horse into the backyard, she noticed Fain pulled into the driveway. He didn't notice her, and she stayed with the horse to avoid him. As she looked around, she noticed a large crate with hay and apples sitting beside the fence.

"Hmm, looks like your pops left you a snack. But look at the size of it; how am I supposed to get it inside the fence?" The horse looked at her as though saying…

"You talk too much, go get me my snack!" She laughed and headed toward the large wooden crate, filled mostly with apples and separate compartments of fresh hay and water. As she attempted to pull the crate, and it began to roll.

76

"Oh wheels, that's great!" She pushed the crate inside the fence and locked the gate behind her. The animal excited to see his meal hurried toward the crate and began to munch. She then looked up at Faith as though to thank her.

"You're welcome," Faith called. As she headed back toward the beach, she saw Fain drove off. She was relieved that he hadn't seen her. She was warmed by the unexpected visit from Patrol George, which had bought her the most unlikely gift, one brave enough to ride through the tides of change and new beginnings.

Later, as she enjoyed a quiet dinner, her phone beeped. It was a text from Fain.

"Where did you go?"

"I was avoiding you," she responded. He replied with an angry Emoticon. She then texted him a humorous Emogi with its tongue sticking out.

"Who taught you that?" He replied.

"My new horse!" she replied.

"Ha, ha, ha. WOW! You replaced me with a horse? I'm offended, definitely offended."

"What are you going to do about it?"

"I'll break in and make out with you." She responded with a yellow rose.

"Wait a minute, a yellow rose means caution. Faith Elizabeth French, you are toast."

"Expect the unexpected; I'll have you for dinner."

"You wish. I saw your new schedule. Looks like I won't be seeing you for a while..."

"Says who?"

"Says your new movie, coming this summer..." He didn't think she saw the ad and wasn't sure how to respond.

"It's okay Fain, I understand. I'm really happy for you...I always knew that you were too cute to be a Manny."

"Really?"

"Silly kid, you made it to my bed, didn't you?" He responded with a laughing Emogi.

"I love you, Faith...see you around kid. I'll put in a good word for you with Katherine." As they chat, Faith strolled through the hallway and entered Fain's empty room. Everything he owned was cleared out except for a note and framed photo of him covered with birthday cake from Katherine's sixth birthday... she smiled, remembering that moment.

"Faith, are you there?" he called. But she didn't respond and after reading his note...she fell asleep in his empty room. Faith awoke the following morning to the sound of heavy rain. As her foggy thoughts of Fain disappeared, she looked at her phone and realized that she had three missed calls from Hank and five missed calls from Patrol George. Remembering Becca, she hurried out of bed and rushed toward the backyard. Still confused, she saw Patrol George and Hank hurriedly throwing up a tent covering to provide temporary shelter for the horse.

"What are you doing?" she called.

"Want to lend a hand?" he called sarcastically. Remembering Becca, Faith pulled on some water boots along with a yellow raincoat and hurried toward the men at work.

"Where is Becca?" she called in panic.

"Over there," Patrol George said pointing.

Becca was laying down and appeared to be shivering from being rained on.

"Oh my God, Becca, sweetheart." She cried hurrying toward her. Faith patted her wet fur and looked into her deep brown eyes.

"You'll be okay girl," she cried. Faith then hurried toward the storage in her garage and grabbed a handful of towels and blankets for the terrified animal. She spent over an hour, drying off the beautiful creature and then covered her with the blankets. By then, Hank and Patrol George were finished with the tent and was also wet and shivering. Becca looked up at her strange new home and appeared content. Faith looked at Hank and George and giggled.

"My gosh, I'm so sorry guys, looks like you're cold and starving...great guess," said George leading the way up Faith's stairs.

"I'll make coffee. Sounds great," said Hank following George to Faith's Kitchen.

Faith prepared a hearty breakfast for the men and enjoyed watching them scuffle down each bite with deep satisfaction.

"Haven't had breakfast like this in a long while," said Patrol George, wiping his mouth and hands the tenth time. Faith smiled broadly.

"Well, you're welcome anytime."

"Really? careful, I might just take you up on that," he warned. The look in his eyes told Faith that he meant it.

"How romantic," Hank jokes.

"Thanks for your help out there Hank."

"No problem at all. Saw you out there fighting with that thing and had to pitch in."

"So, where'd you get the horse?" Hank asked looking at Faith. George noticed something in Hank's eyes when he looked at Faith.

"It was a gift from George."

"Sweet."

"Sure, I thought she could use the company."

"Well, I thought it would be too much, after everything..." Hank said pausing. Faith noticed the tension building between the men.

"I should be heading back: I have a conference with Adam and Jill."

"Happy for you, Hank, you must be a fantastic writer." Faith complemented.

"So I've been told."

"You're a writer, good luck with everything," George called.

As Hank heads out, he thanks Faith for breakfast and flashed George a thumbs up. There was something different about him. Something in his eyes had changed and she wondered if it had anything to do with where they'd left things off. After George left, she prepared for her daughter's arrival.

Faith was excited and nervous as she waited for her Katherine. The weather hadn't led up and it was now pouring rain outdoors. Faith kept her eyes peeled at Sandy Island Blvd, hoping to get a peek of Elizabeth and Katherine's arrival. She then looked over at Becca who was now munching her fresh snack and appeared much happier. She's excited and couldn't wait for Katherine to meet her. As she gazed at the beautiful creature, she thought of Patrol George and how much he surprised her by his sudden visit. She's known him since they first moved to Sandy Island over fourteen years ago and have only waved at him on a few occasions; but he was never friends with the French Family. Maybe it's never too late to be a friend, she thought... Faith looked at the clock on her kitchen wall; it was almost noon. She reached for her mobile to phone Liz, but noticed the no service icon on the screen. Since Faith's Mother-in-Law was not into computers, her only option was to wait. The slightly sunny and grey sky she awoke to, was now completely grey. It was only noon, but it appeared a lot later outdoors. She then remembered that she could put in a call through her Gmail account, and she hurried to her computer. She dialed Liz's mobile which went directly to voicemail and there was no answer on her landline. She glanced at her mobile and the no service icon was gone. She attempted to call Eric, but the call had faded. She attempted Liz and Eric several times but to no avail. She grew more anxious by the second. She went into her parking garage, got into her corvette and sped out of the driveway. She was going to pick her daughter up herself. She loves her Mother-in-Law but she couldn't let her guard down when it came to her only child. After all, Eric and his new Fiancé' was also visiting Elizabeth this weekend and her level of trust plummeted to zero as she continued to speed away from Sandy Island, toward San Francisco's Marina District.

Faith slammed against the brake to avoid colliding with a black Cadillac that had barely pulled off the road. Recognizing Elizabeth's car, she pulled against the curb and ran toward the vehicle, nervously opening the passenger door. Noticing her Mother-in-law's forehead leaning against the steering wheel motionless and her daughter in tears… she grabbed her mobile, which by some miracle had a signal and she frantically dialed emergency. An emergency copter arrived within minutes and as though in slow motion, Elizabeth was air lifted from Sandy Island Blvd.

"Which Hospital?" she asked the medic.

"Hope Memorial!" the Paramedic replied. Faith lifted her daughter out of the crashed vehicle and hurried toward Hope Memorial Hospital. She could hardly believe what was happening. Katherine was still in tears and had not spoken a word until they arrived at the hospital.

"Mommy, is Grandma going to be okay? I tried calling 911 like you thought me, but I Grandma's phone was dead. I couldn't dial. It's all my fault," she sobbed.

"Oh, no, no sweetheart," she said lifting Katherine out of the car and hurrying toward the hospital reception.

"Elizabeth French, which room is she in please," Faith called hurriedly.

"Are you family?" Before Faith responded her mobile rang. It was Eric. He couldn't reach his mom and thought she might be at Faith's.

"Eric, please get here as soon as you can…your mom had a crash and we're at Hope Memorial." Less than ten minutes later, Eric arrived, and Faith was happy that he came alone.

"Where's mom, what happened?" he asked frantically?"

"I, I, but Faith couldn't find the words and Katherine continued to sob uncontrollably.

"I'm Doctor Zyll. Are you the family of Elizabeth French?" Said a tall blond spiky haired individual putting on a white robe.

"Is Grandma Okay. Where's my grandma?"

"Did you kill her you little jerk!" Katherine screamed. The almost packed waiting room almost filled with guests, busted into laugher.

"Please follow me!" the doctor called. Eric, Faith and Katherine followed Dr. Zyll to the fifth floor of the hospital and pointed to the room where Elizabeth laid.

"We have no idea where she went."

"What!"

"Sir, with all due respect, find my mom or I'll have my attorney flatten this place with a suit!"

"Son, that's no way to talk to the nice young doctor," said Elizabeth slipping on her rain jacket.

"Now, who's going to give me a ride home? I don't suppose it would be my granddaughter," she said leading the way.

"Sir, please speak with your mom, if she leaves this hospital against medical advice, I'm afraid we're going to have to permanently bar her from this life saving institution," the doctor warned. Eric wanted to tell Dr. Andrew off but he agreed with him. It's not the first time his mom had walked out of Hope Memorial and this time he had to do something.

"Grandma, you, you look great!" Katherine beamed.

"Thank you sweetheart, let go home!"

"Mom, please, can I have a word with you?"

"Son, you know you're just wasting your time. I'm perfectly fine and I don't need you or anyone for that matter."

You can simply help me find my car or tell your dad to get his butt over here. By the way, where is that TV bum?" Realizing what was happening: Eric spoke to the doctor and assured him that his mother is in good hands.

"We'll contact you if anything changes," Eric said hurrying toward Elizabeth.

"You can forget it!" the Doctor replied.

"Your mom is no longer welcome in this hospital, we've had it with Elizabeth French and we will no longer tolerate her ridiculous behavior."

"Well, you just violated Policy by blurting out my mother's name to a bunch of strangers!" Eric yelled. Frustrated with the French family, Dr. Zyll stomped out of the room and warned staff that Elizabeth was no longer welcomed. Despite his threats, Staff knew that there was nothing that they could do to prevent the inadvertent Elizabeth French from being driven, air lifted, or carried to Hope Memorial hospital, any day.

Chapter 11

Elizabeth fretted at the sight of her beloved SUV Cadillac being towed into her driveway on Bellevue Ave. This has been her favorite car as a wedding gift from Eric French Sr. on their 10th wedding anniversary, over thirty years ago. As much as she remembered, this was the second time her favorite Caddy was towed. Despite Eric's outburst that it's been the fiftieth time she's been towed since his father's passing four years ago. The entire family was gathered at Elizabeth's home in the Marina district, including Fain, Hank and Patrol George who's known Elizabeth for over twenty years. Elizabeth was hardly interested in their ridiculous intervention. She's made arrangements to meet with her best friend Laura for tea in an hour and has no intention of cancelling her plans.

"Son, if you have something to say, you'd better spit it out so I can get back to business."

"But mom, you must understand how important this is! We love you mom and we need to decide what's in your best interest."

"Mom, you almost hurt Katherine. You were in an almost fatal accident with your granddaughter and you're not the least bit concerned."

"Stop it Eric. Can't you see she doesn't remember any of this!" said Faith seating next to her beloved Mother-in-law.

"What's he talking about?" Elizabeth asked looking at Eric disapprovingly. Faith and Eric didn't realize, but there was a different argument being formed by Fain, Hank and George glaring at each other from across the room.

"You're the dude that almost gave me a ticket a few weeks ago for trying to save someone's life, jerk!" Fain said. George ignored him and Hank tried not to laugh. Hank realizing, called Eric aside and spoke to him privately.

"Eric, I apologize for the intrusion, but I was invited by Faith to show support. If you don't mind me saying, my mom also suffered from Alzheimer's disease and I can offer some advice based on experience. I also took care of my mother until her passing," he said firmly.

Eric wasn't interested in Hank's advice until he mentioned his mom.

"You said your mom had a similar experience?"

"It was a nightmare. I wasn't convinced how seriously ill my mom was until she almost burned down my condo trying to make me dinner."

Eric almost laughed but stopped himself seeing the deep concern in Hank's eyes.

"Are you saying that my mom might have Alzheimer's Disease?"

"Based on what I've heard so far, it's very possible."

"Well, she's much too stubborn for us to find out. I have absolutely no idea where to start."

"She's AMA'd every hospital the past few years since our dad passed."

Hank smiled but understood Eric's frustration.

"I know that we hardly know each other but, do you mind joining me, I need to speak with mom privately. My bother Calvin is better at convincing her, but he's not due back in San Francisco for another week."

"Absolutely," said Hank.

As Eric and Hank discussed the best way to approach Elizabeth, the sound of her garage opening caught their attention and a few seconds later, Elizabeth drove out of her driveway, speeding down Belvedere Ave. Hank giggled.

"Eric, I apologize, but you don't expect your mom to suddenly adjust her schedule and stop living."

"She needs time."

"If you're interested, my only recommendation at this time is to hire your mom a Personal Assistant to move in with her until your family figure out the best course of action."

"Great idea," said Fain. Eric shot him a dirty look.

"What's up man," Fain asked.

Eric responded by pushing Fain's chair out of frustration, causing him to fall backwards.

"What the heck, are you nuts?" Fain said touching the back of his head.

84

"Wow, wow, wow," said Patrol George, hurrying toward Fain with a first aid kit.

"What are you going to do about it, water boy," Eric said leaving.

"Eric, please wait!" Faith called following him.

"Faith, not now," he called getting into his Lamborghini.

"Eric, you owe me this much."

"Okay, what is it!" he said slightly calmer.

"Oh, never mind!" she said leaving. She's never seen him so upset and she thought that maybe there were other things on his mind.

"Faith!" he called but she ignored him and went to her daughter who was up from a nap. All she wanted was to take her home and forget that this day had happened. Having this much reality thrown at her in a single day reminded her that she still had so much to figure out about her own personal life and as much as she loved Elizabeth, she was in no position to help solve the new equations and maize of her new realities. Maybe they were on a similar journey and had much more in common than she realizes; but even in the midst of all that is possible, the roads of her life points in a direction that only she could pave. She had to take each step on her own to create a new journey; ones where the unknown characters of her future await her presence. Faith glanced at Patrol George handed Fain an ice pack. She wanted to assist the men, but instead she called to Katherine and slipped away unnoticed.

A few hours later, after putting her daughter to bed, Faith poured herself a glass of her favorite wine. It was a beautiful night and the almost full moon cascaded a golden reflection on the slightly rough waters below. She has often contemplated moving away from this hidden paradise, but her plans are often halted by the natural beauty that holds the contours of her heart, at bay. The wind is steady tonight and a soft breeze shifted the rose branches below. There was a mysterious stillness about this night, and she wished that she had company. As she continued to be enamored by the golden beauty of the night, she heard an excited neigh in the distance. Puzzled, she strained her eyes against the white sandy curves of Sandy Island and noticed a beautiful horse speeding toward the bungalow.

"Becca, Is that you? How did you get out?" Faith hurried down the stairs toward the beach.

"Becca, where are you?" she called panicked. Faith hurried toward the fencing and noticed the door was opened. Her fears were confirmed. Becca had gotten out. She reached for her cell phone and dialed Patrol George but there was no answer and of course he had a voicemail that was not yet set up. She looked over at Hank's Bungalow and noticed that he was already in bed. She was still getting familiar with Becca and wasn't sure if she could manage, but she was on her own to capture this stubborn girl.

"Becca! Come here girl!" she called. Then the sound of loud chews coming from inside the fence caught her attention.

"Becca?" The horse responded by thrusting her hind legs in the air and whined loudly.

"Great! You're already inside," she said hurrying toward the gate and securing the latch tightly.

"Ha, gotcha!" she laughed. Becca look at her as though saying...

"You really think that this could keep me in?" Faith laughed at the horse's intelligent nonverbal expression.

"Maybe we'll go for a ride tomorrow. There's someone I' want you to meet," she said heading back inside.

"Good night Becca!" The horse neighed in response. After checking in on her daughter, Faith poured herself another glass of Cabinet Sauvignon and flipped open her computer. The wind shifted the silky gold and white curtain covering her windows and she noticed that the lights in Hank's kitchen were now on. She felt like she was spying on him and stopped but looked again when she heard a woman's laughter. She quickly turned off the light and peeked through her curtain. This time, she noticed Hank pouring the woman a drink and then they toasted. Faith continued to observe Hank and the strange woman. She and Hank were not officially dating each other, but she was thrown when Hank kissed the woman. From the way they were conversing, it appears that Hank may have known this person for a while. Feeling slightly unsettled by her new discovery, Faith drew her curtain and after briefly looking at her dating profile, she turned into bed. Not even the two hundred plus possible romance on her dating profile were sufficient to pique her interest. The sound of the wind shifting the leaves outdoors and the soft golden moonlight kissed her, as she sank beneath the soft linen; sufficient to comfort the rough edges of the previous day's storms.

Faith awoke the next morning to the sounds of gleeful laughter and happy squeals coming from the beach. As the sounds settled in her ears and the soft morning breeze brushed her cheeks, she jumped out of bed, recognizing her daughter's joyful laughter.

"Come on girl, faster, faster," Katherine called as the gorgeous creature pranced slowly in circles on the soft green lawn. Faith looked on in disbelief: Katherine and Becca had formerly met as confirmed by her daughter seating in triumphant comfort on the horse's fetlock.

"Katherine, be careful!" Faith called panicked. Startled by the sound of Faith's voice, Becca took off down the beach with Katherine holding on tightly to her long brown mane. Faith almost fainted at the sight of Kat barely hanging on.

"Faith Elizabeth French, you're an idiot!" she called hurrying out the door, toward her daughter and the even more panicked horse. The horse and Kat were at least a half mile lead ahead and there was no possible way she can catch up on foot. She had to think on her feet and quickly.

"That's it!" she called opening the garage and a few seconds later, she was on her forerunner, speeding on the sand toward her daughter and Becca. As she neared the edge of the beach near the sand corrals, she exhaled a sigh of relief that her daughter was still holding onto the creature. She was now moving toward them at max speed gaining on the horse as it attempts to take a detour into a wooded area of Sandy Island. Faith lifted herself off the recreational vehicle and with one had holding onto the handle bars and with the other hand she reached for her daughter quickly transitioning her from the horse onto the forerunner, quickly navigating away from a large coral, making a sharp U-turn toward the beach. Katherine sobbed embracing her mom tightly, both still shaking with fear.

"Is everyone okay?" called a young couple who'd observed the entire event.

"Yes, we're okay! She's a bit shaken up, but she'll be okay," Faith called.

"Great job hanging in their young lady!"

"Thanks again!" Faith called and pulled into the front lot.

"I'm sorry mom," Kat cried.

"No sweetheart, it was all mommy's fault. I scared her."

"Oh mom, I was so scared. I was afraid I was going to fall off and I held on to her mane to tightly. I was hurting her, so this made her ran faster," Katherine cried.

"Oh hunny, I'm so happy you're safe, you could have been seriously hurt," Faith said hugging her daughter tightly.

After fixing them breakfast, Faith placed a call to Patrol George. She told him that she needed to see him urgently. He was at work and promised to swing by later. Faith noticed Katherine peek through the window several times. She knew that she was looking to see if Becca had returned but it's been over three hours and there was no sign of the creature. As she waited for George's arrival, she thought of Elizabeth. She felt badly about her hurried departure the day before and placed a call to her. After several rings, the voicemail answered. Leaving her mother-in-law, a voicemail message on her landline felt ancient, but she did. In her message, she encouraged Liz to listen to both her sons' advice not forgetting to mention how much she loves her and the fact that she meant so much to her and Katherine. Faith feared that Elizabeth's continued behavior and lack of responsibility for her health could cost her, her relationship with her granddaughter. Thinking of the many changes that had occurred the past year, Faith's sense of family felt shaken. Her heart raced as she thought of other uncertain possibilities. As she contemplated these things, Katherine entered the living room where she sat.

"Mom, where's Fain?" As her eyes slowly meet Katherine's, she opened her mouth to respond to her beautiful daughter but couldn't find the words.

"Mom, why didn't you tell me?" She didn't want this to cause her daughter more upset; the early events of the day were sufficient, and she searched for an answer. As she thought of ways to respond, her doorbell rang.

"Hold that thought honey," she said and went to get the door.

"Hi George, glad you could make it, please come in," she called. She was about to introduce him to Kat, but she'd went to her room.

"Have I ever mentioned what a beautiful home you have Faith, large enough that even if the horse moves in you would hardly notice," he jokes.

"Ah, yes, that is exactly the reason I requested your lovely presence. What would you like to drink?" she said leading the way to the kitchen.

"Scotch straight up!" he called following her curiously. When they were seated, Faith looked at George directly.

"George, exactly how long have you owned Becca and where in the world did you find her.

"Ah, I knew you would love her, she's extraordinary, isn't she?" After downing the last of his scotch, tired from a long day of Sandy Bay Patrol, enticed by the gentle ocean breeze, George places his Patrol hat over his face, stretched his legs out on the lounge chair and dozed right off to sleep. Faith chuckled as the rugged Patrol man engulfed in snores.

It was after six in the evening and there was still no sign of Becca. Patrol George was still fast asleep on her balcony as confirmed by the loud snores dancing their way in circles with an echoing effect that seem to bounce against the walls. As unprepared as she was for George's longer than expected visit, she started dinner in the hopes that he could join her and Katherine. It's the least she could do for a hardworking Sandy Bay employee. After placing dinner in the oven, she went to check on her daughter. She heard her laugh, and realized that she was on the phone, but with whom, she thought. Then she heard her mentioned Fain. She was relieved that Kat was in better spirits. As she walked back toward the Kitchen, she bumped into Patrol George, who catches her as she almost toppled over.

"Careful," he said.

"You startled me," she said laughing.

"I thought you were asleep."

"I was, until I was awakened by the delicious smell of Bake Ziti, my favorite, how did you know?" She almost blushed at his coy mannerism.

"Great, because I made plenty, and was hoping you could join us."

"Well thank you love." As they dined, George gazed at her intensely, but she tried to avoid looking into his piercing eyes. He was very tall, and his tanned complexion and trimmed beard complemented his rugged good looks.

"I've been thinking of retiring for several years now and today, I finally put in my application for retirement," he said on a more serious note while wiping his lips.

"Really?" He nods in response.

"I'm surprised. But I'm happy for you. Any plans on your next chapter…"

"Not sure yet, but I was hoping to do some traveling."

"George I almost forgot the reason I invited you over. I really meant to tell you that Katherine met Becca... and then the rest is history," he said finishing her sentence. Faith looked at him curiously.

"She came back this morning. I knew in part that's why you might have invited me over," he laughed.

"You're kidding. Becca is at your house? What an ungrateful brat, after all that she' put me through, she returned to her owner."

George giggled at Faith's cute anguish. After sipping the last of his wine, he stood up to leave.

"You and Katherine can come by anytime. I'm free this weekend." Then he paused. How about I teach that girl Becca some house manners before returning her to you and Kat?"

"I have to admit that it was unfair to bring her to you like this."

Like how?" Faith asked eyes narrowed. He smiled at her stoic curiosity.

"She's only a year old, with no training. Thanks for dinner, it was quite delicious," he called pulling his hat over his head as he hurried off.

"You're most welcome, but just you, not Becca," she called.

"Oh, you love her and you know it," he called. He honked loudly as he drove off. From the way he left; Faith sensed that he might be meeting with someone. But to her he seemed more like the private type; one cannot easily see past those mysterious grey eyes without reaching for a lifeboat.

Chapter 12

The summer months have long set her sails away from Sandy Island and Fall's gusty winds swept the tides into a choppy state of closure. The majestic ocean tides have always given her a sense of direction, but today as she glanced far beyond the grayish horizon, for the first time in forever, the endnotes of grayness seems to bid farewell, with no sense of continuance. Yet, despite these uncertain endnotes, the pages of her life will turn; in a direction that she was certain will take her on an unexpected journey; one where she would be certain to have the lead. It's been weeks since she visited with anyone and she was beginning to fear that the next chapter of her life may never start. It may even continue to be interrupted by short term romances or temporary attractions that seem to take away from her plans for change.

As though reading her mind, the grayish skies that she awoke to fled as though it had lost a battle against the savage winds now attempting to carry her to her next chapter.

"*Well, by all means, maybe just this once, I beckon thee,*" she whispered, as the wind attempts to remove her silken garments before carrying her away to her desired haven.

"Well, If it weren't Faith Elizabeth, I would swear the wind was one lucky bastard," said Hank, lighting a cigar.

"Hank, how long have you been standing there!" she said annoyed.

"Long enough," he grinned. She was in no mood to chat with him and turned to leave.

"Faith, please wait," he said putting out his cigar.

"I have great news."

"Oh yea? I doubt I would be impressed with your new girlfriend," she said and turns to leave again.

"Faith, please wait, please." But she'd left the balcony.

A few seconds later her doorbell rang. She was in no mood for Hank's company but opened the door to a creek, like when they first met.

"I'm sure your daughter's puppy is not missing this time Hank," she said and attempts to shut the door. But Hank stopped it from being shut, pushing gently against it; he enters Faith's mansion and takes her in his arms.

"I missed you," he said and kissed her passionately. "But, umm…," she says attempting to stop him. But he placed a finger over her full pink lips and kisses her. She was enamored by his strong embrace and sunk in his arms. The sound of the door shutting behind them made her thoughts skip, as she was lifted up far above the grey skies into a newness that she only hoped would cure the growing blossom of hope she swore would submerge into the deep. Hank had stopped kissing her and her eyes opened slowly.

"You're breathtakingly beautiful," he said. A tear rolled down his cheek.

"What's wrong?" she said brushing the tear from his princely face.

"I love you. Faith, I am head over heels in love with you. I knew from the very first time I saw you." Shocked, relieved, yet puzzled by his admission, she pulled away from him.

"But….umm." Unable to find the words, Faith ran to her room and shut the door behind her. She leaned against the shut door.

"But you were with someone last night, who was she? You looked like you were having a lot of fun."

"Faith, please let me in… I can explain."

"You must be hung over from all that fun last night," she laughed.

"Please go away Hank, I cannot afford to be hurt again." Her fragile heart was just beginning to recover from her long marriage to Eric. She wanted change but was not certain if she was ready to take another leap. And besides, they'd just met.

"Faith French, that was my agent and editor, she and Adam flew in from New York last night to celebrate. My first book got contracted for a feature…Faith, are you there?" But there was no response. He tried the door to her room, and it opened.

"Faith, I'm coming in okay. Where are you?" Her bedroom looked different than he remembered. Then he heard the shower. Then soft sobs.

"Faith, I'm coming, I promise I won't bite." She giggled at his humor.

"There you are." She was sitting in her large tub and appeared to be crying.

"Honey, what's wrong. Did you hear a thing I said?" Her pale skin looked like it hadn't seen summer, and she appeared frailer than he remembered.

"Are you going to take a shower or a bath, because your shower is on but you're sitting in the tub? Please talk to me," he said turning off the shower.

"You know you can tell me anything."

"Hank I'm at crossroads. I have no idea what to do with myself. It's been almost two years since..." He nods realizing she meant her split from Eric.

"Faith, I would be returning to New York for a week to wrap up some loose ends. Please come with me; both you and Katherine. And besides Syd would be thrilled to see her."

"Hank?"

"Yes Sweetie?"

"Are you asking me out?" He smiled and then leaned over the tub and whispered.

"How am I doing?" She smiled as she turned on the faucet tossing a handful of water at him.

"That's it, you're toast!" He laughed and got into the tub.

"You still didn't give me an answer," he said removing his shirt.

"Mom, mom are you in here? I just got off Facetime with Sydney and she really misses me. I want to see her. When would she be back?" Hank tried to hide himself, but his feet were too long for the bathtub and his hairy legs stuck out partially.

"Wow mom, you really need to shave your legs. When did you get so much hair on your feet?"

"Kat, hunny, could you please give mommy a minute?"

"Okay mom, but that's just weird," she said closing the door behind her. Hank finally came up for air, his face covered in soap suds. Faith giggled, reached for a hand towel and wiped the suds off his face. They both felt silly and laughed. As she wiped the suds off his lips, she couldn't resist them and she kisses him. He returned her affection, taking her into his arms, kissing her tenderly. Her small figure plunged against his muscular build and oceans of fire kindled beneath the subtle waves of her life waiting to be explored.

Faith had given Hank's proposal some serious thought and agreed to accompany him to New York. It's been two weeks since his invitation and they're leaving for New York this weekend. It was sudden, but she was excited. They had spent almost every day together the past few weeks and she could hardly wait to spend time with him in the Big Apple.

Hank whistled loudly as a stretched limo pulled into his driveway. He pointed for the driver to park in front of Faith house. Faith and Syd were elegantly dressed and despite still being in the tropical climate of Sandy Island, they were already dressed for New York's weather. Faith and Kat's face lit up at the sight of the shiny black limo. He winked at Faith as he took their bags and helped the driver load them into the trunk.

"Mom, can I be homeschooled like Sydney. That way we won't have to hurry back before school starts."

"But hun we'll only be in New York for a week."

"But school starts as soon as we get back."

"Hey Kat…lets chit chat about it when we get there. How does that sound?" Kat grinned broadly. By Hank's tone she knew that she had a good shot at convincing her mom.

"We're only two blocks from Sandy Island City Airport, please ensure that all passengers have all required travel documentation," said the sharply dressed limo driver.

"Thanks Sam," Hank called.

"You're fantastic, said Katherine.

"You're welcome kiddo," he called and winked at her through the rearview mirror.

"Hey Sam, by any chance are you single? My friend Syd have a boyfriend name Ben and I wanted to make sure that I have a boyfriend before I see her, that way we have lots more to talk about."

"Katherine?" her mom called looking at her daughter crossed.

"Shhh mom, can't you see I'm asking someone out?" Sam and Hank choked back laughter. Sam turned into the airport and came to a stop in front of Delta Airlines terminal.

"Well young lady, may I call you Katherine?"

"Yes, that's my name, isn't it pretty?"

"It's quite lovely. I heard your mommy called you several times. You see, Katherine, not only am I happily married, but I have a daughter your age."

"You have kids?" Katherine asked surprised.

"Katherine, darling that is enough, come let's go get checked in," her mom said, taking her hands.

"Hank remained behind, chatting with the driver and arranged for him to pick them upon their return.

"Oh and thanks for playing along, Kat has quite the imagination." Sam tapped the tip of his hat.

"Safe landing," he called and drove off.

An hour later, the three Sandy Islanders were en route to Hanks native home.

"Is Manhattan really as pretty as it looks on postcards?" Faith asked smiling childishly.

"Is this your first-time visiting New York?"

"Is it that obvious?" He leaned forward and whispered in her ears.

"*yes.*" Hank Glanced over at Katherine who had dozed off.

"Look," he said. She's the splitting image of her mother.

"It's the only time she doesn't appear to be a handful." Katherine engulfed in loud snores that sounded like a baby chainsaw cutting logs. Faith apologized to an elderly couple sitting across from them.

"Not at all, we have four grandchildren and two about your daughter's age." Faith exhaled a sigh of relief and placed a pillow she borrowed from the flight attendant under her daughter's head which subsided her snores. Hank took Faith's hand in his and patted them tenderly.

"I'm so happy you're here. Why do I get the feeling that Eric kept you hidden in his Sandy Island tower? You're so beautiful."

She blushed at his boyish charm.

It was after nine pm when they arrived at JFK. Katherine had stuffed her little tummy on the flight and was still asleep when they arrived. Faith was about to lift her up, but Hank tapped her shoulders gently…

"The honor is my mine," he said and lifted up the exhausted seven-year-old. After picking up their rental, Hank sped toward the hectic **I-678** and headed toward Manhattan.

"Wow, I can't wait to wrap things up and get out of this city."

"Hank this traffic is nuts."

"Welcome to the New York. Funny I'm welcoming you since I'm only here to leave."

"Well, maybe one week is all we need to help recreate some new memories."

"Ha, I like the sound of that," he replied keeping his eyes peeled against the highway that knows no speed limit. Faith looked over at Katherine still asleep.

"How far away is your place?"

"It's about a half an hour's drive from JFK, we should be there in another ten minutes."

"Gorgeous city Hank…"

"Thanks, born and raised. But I would love to put the last decade in the past." He continues to chat with her and didn't notice that she'd fallen asleep. Less than ten minutes later, he pulled up to his tiny parking garage at the Ambience Luxury Tower.

"Faith darling, we've arrived," Katherine and Faith awoke, but after a good stretch, Katherine looked around puzzled and went back to sleep. After throwing Katherine over his shoulders he typed in the pass code to lock his garage.

"I saw that, now I can break in anytime," said Katherine waking up. "

"You little rascal, you're up." Kat giggled. The two and a half-overwhelmed Sandy Islanders, jumped on the elevator to the fifty-seventh floor. Faith took Hank's hands in hers and Kat hugged him tightly as the elevator began to move.

"Ha, first time in an elevator too." Both ladies giggled for the fiftieth time.

It was a beautiful night and the city's skyline could be seen, as the elevator traveled at an accelerated speed then gently slowed to a stop. The gliding doors opened to reveal a very modern upper deck which led to a barely furnished apartment.

"My apologies, it looks like Candace might have left me another surprise." Faith looked   in shock as Hank went from room to room and returned to confirm that all three bedrooms were still fully furnished.

"Hank, this is fantastic, look at that spectacular view."

"Mommy, is this Sydney's home?"

"I'm sorry sweetheart, Sydney is with her mommy tonight, but you will see her tomorrow."

"*Okay*," Kat yawned. After showing Kat to her room, Hank gave Faith a tow of his Bachelor apartment, then invited her to join him on the balcony. She looked around in awe of the amazing views.

"This is amazing!" she called. There's a full moon out tonight over Manhattan's skyline.

"Look, it seems like I can reach out and touch the moon. It's not fair because I live on the ocean, and I don't think I've ever seen a more beautiful moon." Before she said another word, Hank gently turned her around to face him and kissed her tenderly. Captivated by his sudden move, Faith sank into his arms and let him have his way for a while. It was the kiss that sent lightening volts through her paralyzing her thoughts into nothingness, reigniting every forgotten desire that she'd never felt before. Each moment she thought he would withdraw; he continues kissing her. His rock hard body wrapping her as a blanket in midair. Both still fully dressed, their bodies tremble as he continues to kiss her with every bit of affection that rose, being even more enamored by the previous as she gasped in utter passion for that expected moment she hope would follow as he kisses her deeply, tenderly, fervently, agonizingly, possessively with unrelenting passion.

Faith's eyes opened slowly to the distant sound of emergency Cyrene's in the streets below. She sat up quickly realizing that she'd spent the entire night on Hanks Apartment lounge. As she stood up, she caught the attention of two young men sitting on the lounge next door smiling at her. She hurried inside and looked around for Hank and Katherine, but they were nowhere to be found. Then she noticed a note on the refrigerator.

"Took Katherine to my favorite bakery, be back shortly-Hank." She looked around and smiled at her sudden change in environment. Wow, she thought. After starting coffee, she looked for somewhere to have a seat, but Hank's unfurnished apartment was not ready to accommodate her, so she made herself comfortable on the kitchen counter, sniffing the steam as it rises from the coffee pot. After a cup of coffee, Hank and Katherine still hadn't return. After a quick shower, she slipped into something comfortable and as she was about to fix her hair, the doorbell rang. She wondered why he would ring the doorbell, but hurried to let them in. Without looking through the peephole, she opened the door and paused...

"Who're you?" the women asked simultaneously.

"It's Faith!!" said Sydney running into her arms and embracing her tightly.

"I'm so happy you're here, and you're still wearing my necklace!" she said excitedly. At that moment, Hank and Katherine returned from the bakery carrying several brown bags which filled the apartment with a delicious aroma.

"Candace, you're early. I didn't expect you guys till later."

"Katherine!! Sidney!!" The girls said hugging each other.

"I can't believe you're here."

"Same here," said Katherine excitedly. Candace looked on confused.

"Candace meet Faith, Faith, Candace," said Hank annoyed.

"Pleasure to meet you," said Faith stuffing her mouth with a Chinese pastry. Candace ignored Faith's greeting and looked at Hank.

"I didn't know you were seeing anyone."

"Seems fitting, I didn't know you were getting married until you invited our daughter to the wedding," Hank shot back.

"By the way, where's my furniture!?" Noticing where this was heading, Faith took the girls to the lounge and shut the door behind her. She peeked at Hank and Candace several times and by their body language, could tell that things got loud between them.

"I'm sorry Faith, I'm sorry I didn't tell mom about you and Kat, because I knew this would happen," she admitted ruefully.

"Aww, it's okay hunny, no apology necessary," she said kissing her forehead.

A few moments later, Hank joined them on the lounge. He appeared ruffled but calmed at the sight of Faith sitting with the girls.

"Warm delights anyone?"

"Daddy, thanks for bringing Faith and Katherine. But how did you manage to bring Faith? Did you have kick Fain's butt?"

"Hunny?" They all laughed and sat down to enjoy Hank's favorite pastries.

Chapter 13

Elizabeth strolled around her home thinking about the new set of rules that her son's had put into place for her. She felt like she was under house arrest in her own home.

"How dare they order me around," she fretted. It's been weeks since she's seen her granddaughter and was growing tired of the strict diet that Eric's fiancé had her on. She refused all doctor's appointments that Eric had scheduled for her. However, Calvin's friend who does concierge medicine in the bay area paid her a visit. After several tests, he diagnosed her with stage one Alzheimer's disease. Despite his outrageous diagnosis, she refused to let any of it keep her from her granddaughter. Rachael was watching her every move and at Eric's request, had hid her car keys and telephone from her access. As she flopped on the sofa, she noticed that Katherine had left her Skype opened on her Ipad.

"What do we have here," she said relieved.

"Liz? Liz, are you okay?" Rachael called.

"Yes sweetie, I'm in here relaxing by the fire," she called hiding the Ipad behind her and lifting her feet onto the ottoman.

"Great, let me know if I can help with anything, here for you mom," she called, her voice retreating.

"You're the best hun," Elizabeth mocked, her eyes rolling.

Elizabeth reached for the Ipad and dialed Katherine's phone. Faith noticed Kat's phone ringing in a unique ring tone and picked it up curiously. As she was about to answer the Skype call, Katherine came running into the Kitchen and almost bumped her mommy over.

"It's grandma, it's grandma," she said excitedly grabbing the phone from her mom and disappeared down the hallway.

"What was that about? Faith wondered. Katherine and Sydney locked themselves in the closet.

"Grandma are you okay? You called me on the special ring tone." You remember, the one that tells me that you're in danger."

Elizabeth went into detail about her current situation with Eric's fiancé and Kat was appalled.

"OMG, that's terrible. Grandmas listen to me. I'm in New York with Sydney. Yes Grandma, we got here last night and I'm horribly jetlagged."

"Hello, this is Sydney can I help too?"

"Sure sweetheart. The more the merrier."

"Great!"

"Shhhhh," said Kat placing her index finger over Sydney's chocolate covered lips.

"Syd, I have a great idea, I think Grandma should come be with us, we can make much better sandwiches that Rachael."

"Umm, should we talk to my dad first?" Katherine looked at her with the *are you kidding me* kind of look.

"Okay Grandma, here's what you should do…"

An hour later, Elizabeth had packed a small carryon suitcase and slipped out the back where a UBER was waiting.

"Sandy Island Airport please," she said to the driver who eyeballed her curiously.

"Why Sandy Island?" he asked.

"Well for one, my son works at San Francisco International and two, the views are much nicer when you fly out of Sandy Girl," she said annoyingly.

"Maam, are you sure you're alright?" Elizabeth handed him a rolled of cash.

"Yes maam, Sandy Island Airport it is," he said and sped out of Belleview Ave.

Elizabeth purchased her ticket at the counter just in time to catch the last flight out of Sandy Island to JFK. Less than an hour later, she found herself enjoying first class treatment on her way to meeting her girl buddies. She sipped on Champagne and high-fived herself for a job well done.

"Katherine! Syd! Where'd you go and what are you up to?" Faith called searching under the beds and closets to find them.

"Kat, I need an update on your conversation with Liz. Is everything alright with her?" But the girls had locked themselves in the elevator and could not hear a thing.

"I still can't believe that Grandma is coming to join us," Katherine grinned showing her missing teeth.

"This was a great idea Syd."

"Sure, not at all. And besides, why'd you leave your Grandma all by herself out there?"

"Well, I love her, but but…"

"But what!"

"Oh it's nothing," Kat said leaving. As Katherine ran off she almost bumped into her mom.

"Kath, where were you?"

"On the Elevator," Syd called, stepping away from the shutting steel doors.

"Are you girls okay?"

"Yes, why?" they answered simultaneously. Faith eyed them suspiciously.

"Kat, I know that look." Just then her mobile rang and the girls ran off.

"Eric? You sound upset, what's wrong?"

"No, we're in New York, just got here last night."

Faith hardly appreciated his attitude and she interrupted him…

"Eric, I'll tell you what? I do not need to inform you of anything, this is none of your business."

"We'll be back this Sunday. Is this why you called?"

"You're kidding!"

"Well, she couldn't have gotten very far."

"Have you tried her friend?"

"Tell Rachael not to worry."

"You tried to what?" She laughed when he mentioned that he'd placed his mom on house arrest.

"Eric, was this really necessary? You expect her to stay locked up inside all day. If I were you, I would start thinking outside of the box. Think about it, no access to her cars, no car keys, no phone access, how far could she have gotten?"

"You're welcome. Okay, keep me updated…and Eric, please don't be too hard on her."

"I'll try," he replied.

"Okay, bye now."

Katherine and Syd monitored Kat's Skype as promised, being careful to not miss her grandma's call. As they waited, a few moments later, feeling totally warm and cozy in the tight closet space, one after the other, they dozed off; Katherine for being jet lagged and Sydney for simply being caught up in the moment.

Hank was just returning with a few bags filled with shopping.

"Someone's been busy," Faith teased.

"I don't mean to pry, but I've been meaning to ask, was everything okay with Candace this morning?" He avoided her question planting a soft kiss on her lips.

"Pretty lips like yours should not utter such a name." Suddenly, Faith felt like she was caught up in a new story….*The Manhattan Luxury Tower of Secrets.* It was obvious that he didn't want to discuss Candace and she changed her mind for now.

"I just got off the phone with Eric and…" before she finished her sentence, Hank looked at her directly. Surprised, she chuckled at his response.

"Do I have your attention now?"

"No, it's not that, I was just thinking that I might have forgotten to get Onions."

"But yes, what did Eric want?"

"I knew it!" She laughed. Faith poured herself a glass of wine and retreated to the lounge to escape Hank's intense stare. He followed her. "

Seriously, what did he want?"

"Hank, stop it, you're scaring me."

"Not unless you tell me what you and Candace were arguing about…"

"I'll tell you later, I promise…suit yourself," she said walking toward the pool. As soon as she placed her glass down, Hank lifted her up and with lightning speed they plunged into the freezing pool. As they submerged, she looked around at the large bubbles, and as if in slow motion she was greeted by an electrifying kiss. A few romantically terrifying moments later, they surfaced. After catching her breath, she embraced Hank and dined to another moment of bliss.

"Jack, I feel like I'm on this romantic escape, except, you're not here." Liz said speaking to her deceased husband as she exits JFK.

"Let's call your granddaughter to see if she could get us out of this one," she said reaching for the Ipad from her purse. She looked at the screen and tried turning the device on the way Katherine had taught her, but nothing happened. She tried several times, but the result was the same. She then realized that it might have died and she searched for the charger. She then realized that she'd left the charger behind.

"Oh boy. Jack these things are useless, especially when you need them urgently."

"Over there," a soft male voice said. Elizabeth looked over her shoulders and saw her husband's apparition for a moment pointing to a device charging port in a less crowded area. When she looked over her shoulders again, he was gone.

"Oh Jack, thank you, we're going to have so much fun in the Big Apple," she said hurrying. Luckily, there was a cord that fitted her Ipad. A few moments later, the device automatically turned itself on and she dialed Katherine. The girls were still asleep but woke up to the sound of Kat's phone vibrating.

"It's grandma," she said answering hurriedly. "Grandma, I can't believe it, you made it! I'm going to hand you over to Syd, but first, I want you to locate the UBER icon on my dash and request a ride."

"Okay sweetheart, Google Maps says that my ride is only three minutes away."

"Okay great job grandma." She handed Syd her mobile.

"Gramma Liz, can you hear me?"

"Okay great, please tell the driver to take you to 5747 York Ave, Manhattan"

"Got it sweetheart. Girls, please tell Hank, that I'll be making dinner...."

Sydney called from her bedroom window overlooking the lounge at her dad making out with Faith.

"Daddy... Dad!!!!!" Just then, Kat also stuck her head out the window and screamed...

"Mommy, mom!!" Hank and Faith looked up at the girls.

"What's the matter kids?"

"Grandma said she'll make dinner."

"What's that?" Hank called.

"I think they said that Grandma was going to make dinner. But which Grandma?"

"Great question. Only that both Syd's grandparents are no longer in the picture." Just then Faith brought her hands slowly to her mouth.

"This can't be what I think it is. Hank, I think we're going to have a visitor, but who? I think we better go have toast with the girls," she said climbing out of the pool.

"Oh no, Katherine, I think we forgot that Grandma's visit was top secret and might have blown our cover.

"Oh, no! But wait, what if they think it's your Grandma?"

"Both my grandparents on my mom and dad side are gone."

"Quick, we must hurry," Syd called heading toward the stairs.

"The Stairs?"

"Yes because they'll look for us on the Elevator."

"But that's a lot of stairs Syd."

"Okay, you're right, hurry the Elevator..." The girls jumped on the elevator and quickly shut the door behind them.

"But wait, I forgot my phone, we have to go back."

"We can't, let's wait for Grandma at the gate." A three-minute ride to the lobby, and out the back toward Hank's Garage entry.

"Quick, this way..."

"Hey, what are you kids up too?!" the guard called. Startled, the girls ran in different directions.

"Kat? Syd? Where are you? Girls?" the panicked couple called searching frantically. A few moments later, the Guard came to the office where Hank and Faith was speaking to the office employees.

"Anyone lost two pretty packages?" At the sight of their daughters with the Guard, looking terrified, both parents felt that both girls have had enough. They thanked the staff and the guard and headed toward the Elevator.

Elizabeth flopped her bags down and typed in the code that Syd and Katherine had given her earlier. Exhausted she climbed onto the strange looking elevator and keyed in the 57th floor: a speedy ride that came to an abrupt end almost made her tumble.

"Looks like we made it Jack." As she was about to get off, the elevator started moving downward. She got off in time, but her bags were left on.

"Oh I hate these things!" she fretted. She pressed the call button several times and just as she was about to reach for her bags, the door shut, and her bags descended a second time.

"Katherine!" she called.

"I think I heard something," said Faith.

"Wait a minute, whose bags are these?"

"GRANDMA, GRANDMA LIZ, you made it!" Hank and Faith looked at each other.

"Sweetheart, I missed you. And you must be Sydney. You are just as I imagined. Thanks for inviting me." She then looked at Hank...

"What are you two doing standing there? Get over here."

"But, Liz..." before Faith said another word they were all submerged into an epic Grandma Hug with Hank's face smudged in the middle like a handsome giraffe.

"Where are your chairs?" Unsure of how to respond, Hank held back laughter.

"Elizabeth, what are you doing here?" they asked simultaneously.

"Well it's also great to have you," she replied hurrying to the Kitchen to start dinner.

Fain scrolled through his phone to locate Faith's number; after searching through every app, it was confirmed that he'd mistakenly forgot to save her number to his new phone. He'd forgotten his surfboard in her garage and needed her to mail it to him.

"Fain you idiot, you didn't even memorize her email," he fretted. He then remembered that she'd sent him an email over a year ago in France when he was preparing to move to Sandy Island to start his position as her assistant. He scrolled through his email and searched the email subject. Lucky for him Gmail indicated that the email was still in his Drafts folder from when he attempted to ask her a question but had phoned her instead. Just as he hoped, her home and mobile phone number was in her email signature from her first email to him.

"Jackpot!" It's been almost four months since they spoke and he felt weird about calling her, but finally did. Faith was in the shower when he called. Hank heard her phone ring and answered on the first ring.

"Yello!" Fain laughed lightly...

"Hey, who's this?"

"It's Fain, is Faith around?"

"Fain..? good to hear you man, haven't heard from you in a jiffy, what going on?"

"Hey Hank, is this you?"

"Yes kid, it's me."

"Listen, I'll have Faith give you a call in a little bit, she's temporarily occupied."

"Gotcha, okay, thanks! Great hearing from you man, we missed you around here."

"Thanks man."

"You got it! Chaw for now"

Fain sat on the balcony of his airy Santa Monica apartment and looked at the moonlight glistening upon the angry tides. About an hour later his phone rang.

"Fain, what going on, I thought you've fallen of the edge of the globe, where have you been friend?" They spoke for about a half hour and Fain learned about her new relationship with Hank. He couldn't wait for her to return from New York to get his surfboard, so he told her that he'd simply purchase a new one. He needed it for a scene in his new movie that was debuting in only a few weeks. He'd missed her and was surprised of how alive and happy she sounded. She'd move on and he had his new career to distract him for now.

Chapter 14

Elizabeth was happy that her daughter-in-law had taken the plunge into the world of dating. She woke up early and after taking her meds, she made breakfast and created a list of things that her and the girls could do for each day that she spent with them. It was still only eight am when she'd finish making breakfast and since everyone was still asleep, she poured herself a cup of coffee, picked up a copy of Hanks novel and sat on the lounge to relax. As she sipped on her coffee and flipped through the pages, a sudden buzzing sound got her attention. Looking over her lounge chair, she saw the name Candace and the face of a blond woman popped up on Hank's mobile. She was tempted to answer fearing for her daughter-in-law but didn't. When the phone had stopped ringing, she noticed sixteen missed calls from Candace and fourteen unread text messages. Tempted, she picks up the phone and read through the messages.

"Wow, what a *bitc*..." she said under her breath. Realizing that this was Hank's ex, and was insisting that Hank bring Sydney home or she was coming to pick her up in minutes...it was then that Liz realized that Candace might have already been on her way. She scrambled thinking of what she could do to make sure that Hank's ex doesn't get anywhere near his apartment.

As she ran through the kitchen, she heard the Elevator door make that pinging sound like when it's getting ready to open. As it opened, she noticed the face of the woman that popped up on Hank's phone when it rang.

"Oh no you don't," Elizabeth said and pressed the close elevator door and increased speed button that sent the Conveyor traveling back down toward the lobby at an accelerated speed.

"Yes," Liz said celebrating her temporary victory. A few moments later, Liz heard the vehicle heading up at an even faster rate. She prepared herself and as soon as the elevator stopped, she hit the same buttons again. This time, nothing happened. Then she realized that she was holding onto the wrong key, keeping the door open. She noticed that there was an option to lock the elevator. Elizabeth jumped and hit the lock above the panel. Confused about who this woman might be, Candace, started kicking against the door, causing a vibrating sound to travel through the apartment and down the conveyor.

"Oh, you've got to be kidding me," she fretted. Liz looked around and a villainous smile appeared on her face noticing a water release button on the far corner of the elevator. Quickly grabbing a step stool, she reached for the water release button that should only be punched in an emergency and sharp spraying sounds could be heard followed by loud screams. Finally, she was able to hit the increased speed which sent the horrible ex speeding toward the exit.

"Finally!" Elizabeth said exhausted, returning to her book. Liz slowly lifts her eyes from Hanks novel and noticed an emergency stair entry. As she neared the stair, she heard loud individual thumping and stomps. Someone was climbing the stair and they were not happy. Liz looked over the balcony and noticed that the determined little missy was already halfway up and screaming Hank's name over the top of her lungs. Just as Liz was about to hurry down the stairs to convince the monstrous little darling that Hank, Faith and the girls had stepped out, the overly soaked and pissed off ex was escorted from the building by security. Once more, Liz high fived herself and returned to her book. A few minutes later, Faith joined her.

"Morning darling, I made fresh coffee."

"Morning Liz, you know your coffee is the best," Faith called pouring herself a cup. She sat next to Liz, reached for her mobile and showed it to her. There were ten missed calls from Eric. What's it with phones this morning? Liz thought to herself.

"Eric, what does he want?"

"Here's what, the next time he calls, just answer and please tell him, there's nothing he can do to get me back on Bellevue Ave to eat Rachel's salad." Faith laughed so hard; her head started to hurt.

"I missed you. I'm so glad you're here," she said hugging and kissing the only mom she's ever known in the US.

"By the way, did you hear strange noises this morning?"

"Umm, no, why?" Liz asked looking at her with that familiar glare.

"What are you up to, Elizabeth French?" she asked eyeballing her mother-in-law suspiciously.

A few minutes later, Hank joined them on the lounge scratching his almost shaved head.

"Morning ladies, have anyone seen my phone?" Liz looked at Faith and that familiar look appeared in her eyes again.

"Umm, no, I've been up since six. I haven't seen or heard anything." Just then, Hanks phone buzzed, and Liz tried to suffocate it with her towel.

"Oh, I think I heard something," he said searching. Liz looked at the screen and as sure as her word, it was Blondie. She quickly turned it off.

"Oh, I think I hear something. It should be somewhere around here," Faith said. Just then Sydney came hurrying toward them.

"Daddy, it's mommy, she wants to speak with you, and she sounds really, really, mad!" Sydney said handing Hank her mobile.

"Candace, this is not a good time!"

"Do you think you and your crazed lover can stop me, I want my furniture, all of it!" she demanded.

"Candace, I have no time for your ridiculous *bullshit,*" Hank said under his breath stepping away, hoping Faith did not hear him. He stepped onto his apartment elevator and locked the door. After giving Candace a piece of his mind, he told her that he was suing her for full custody of Sydney.

"You can have all the furniture you want but stay the hell away from my daughter!" he yelled and hung her up. He remained in the elevator for a few minutes. After catching his breath, he rejoined the group who was slowly becoming his family. Hank sat beside Elizabeth and ruffled her hair playfully.

"Liz, I'm really glad you're here. To think of it, I should have asked you to join us."

"Well don't you worry about it, they don't call me Elizabeth Thunderbird for nothing, I always find a way to get my way," she laughed. Hank and Faith laughed at her entitled sense of humor.

"I see where Katherine got her stubbornness from."

"But, But, But...said Katherine peeking over the window overlooking the lounge. All laughed.

Later as they watched Elizabeth prepare dinner, Faith noticed a look of concern on Hank's face.

"What's new?" she asked, gently tapping the tip of his nose.

"It's the last thing I ever thought would cross my mind but, I'm going to have to try to get my daughter away from Candace."

"Oh no, I'm sorry, is this about this morning."

"It's about everything, and the most difficult part is that I'm going to have to spend more time in New York than originally planned," he said looking at her hoping that she would be okay with staying a bit longer.

"How long do you think you would need?"

"It depends on if I'm successful at the first hearing, but you never know, these things can drag on for months."

"I see," she said looking away from him, thinking of Sandy Island and wondering if she could spend more than a week away from home.

"I have an idea; why not talk to her about your plans to have Sydney full time. Who knows, maybe the both of you can come to an agreement." Faith had a huge point, but she has no idea the kind of person Candace is. He smiled and took her hands in his.

"That's a great idea. I will go see her tomorrow." Later Hank phoned Candace and she answered on the first ring.

"I knew you would call; you always do after an argument" she said assuming that he was calling to apologize for earlier. Hank giggled.

"Candace, can you meet for lunch tomorrow?"

"Ha, I love this, really?"

"Yes, your pick. How does Lucio's sound. 2pm?"

"Sounds great, thanks."

"You're welcome, I'll see you then," he replied and hung up.

Faith watched as Hank got dressed for his meeting with his Ex. A glimmer of jealousy came over her, and she thought of accompanying him.

"Are you certain you don't need company?" He nods and smiles at her.

"Trust me, if the convo calls for it, I'll have you on speed dial."

"Are you sure?"

"Positive," he says and kisses her on the lips.

"See you later daddy, and don't forget to ask mommy if I can stay here for another couple days, okay daddy?"

"Absolutely hun, daddy thinks that's a fantastic idea" he says slipping on his sunglasses and disappearing onto his now famous elevator.

"Wait, what does he mean by that? Syd asked looking at Faith with narrowed eyes. Faith winked at her in response.

As he drove to Lucio's Hank thought of how he might introduce his idea to his fiery Ex about his new custody arrangement but there was no ideal way to break the news to her without expecting an explosive response. He hopes that the almost three years that they have been apart is sufficient to assume otherwise. He pulled into Lucio's tiny lot and was surprised to have found a parking spot. He exhaled loudly as he shuts the door behind him. As he walked into the small restaurant, the scenery stirred up old memories of when he was first separated from Candace. The loneliness he felt all those years played games on his emotions. Maybe this was not such a good idea, he thought. But then he thought of his daughter and at that moment he looked into the same familiar face he wishes were Faith's.

"Candace? Wow, what happened you look...."

"Thanks, I knew you'd like my new look," she said completing his sentence as she led the way to the lounge upstairs.

"Guess who's playing in the lounge tonight?"

"Who?"

"Sax!"

"No way."

"Yes way!" Hank hardly recognized Candace. She'd lost a tremendous amount of weight in the four months since he'd seen her and was dressed rather seductively for her newly wedded status. Sax was playing what used to be him and Candace's favorite song and she started slowly shaking her head to the beat.

"For old time sakes...?

"Candace?" As he was about to respond she places her index finger over her lips.

"Shh...I'll be right back, got to go to the little girl's room..." she said and hurried off. As he tried to relax, he was interrupted by an overly sweet...

"What can I get you started with cutie?"

"Two Manhattans please while we're at it!" Candace twirled and twist, slowly dancing her way toward Hank.

111

"Ahh, gotcha, coming right up!" the waiter called and disappeared before Hank could change his mind.

"I have to say Hank, you look great!" she says gently patting his hands.

"Thanks!" He wanted to complement how great she looks but instead...

"You definitely look...different. But in a good way." He said holding back his true thoughts.

"Come on Hank, you can do better than that. You've always wanted me to get these done," she said cupping her chest."

"And you always wanted me to look this good. Come on admit it," she says taking his hands and forcing him onto the dance floor.

"Candace, I really need to speak with you... but she ignores him and threw her arms around his shoulders.

"How long have you been here?" He asked slowly removing her hands from around his neck and stepping rhythmically with her across the dance floor.

"Since lunch," she admitted. I forgot and showed up a couple hours too early. Really," he giggled.

"Candace, what's going on? Is everything okay at home?"

"Oh, ya it's fabulous, everything's fabs." But Hank wasn't convinced as Candace squeezed his buttocks and locks her eyes in his as they strolled around the floor.

"Candace?"

"Ya baby."

"How much have you had to drink today?" he asked as she almost tripped over his feet for the third time. As she was about to respond, she collapsed into his arms and spoke gibberish...

"Candace? Candace...but her only response was...

"Baby, Syd baby...." Hank lifted Candace up and carried her out of Lucio's.

"Oh boy, where's your car...Okay, I'll drive," he said laying her in the back of his convertible... he then searched her purse and located her keys. He pressed the panic alarm and realized that she was parked right next to him. As Hank was about to get into his car, a gentleman he recognized from the bar approached him.

"What do you think you're doing with the lady's purse, sir? Hank laughs realizing what he thought.

"You see, this lady here is a regular, she comes here often, and alone. I've never seen you." The intrusive guy then looked through the window and noticed Candace passed out on the back seat and quickly got the wrong idea.

"Wait a minute, what's really going on here?" I don't know what you think is going on, but why don't you just turn around and go back to minding your own business.

"Why don't I?" he pretended to be turning around to leave, then quickly caught Hank off guard with a punch to the face, knocking him to the ground.

"What the…Hank quickly jumps to his feet and responds with a revolting jab tossing the individual against Candace's parked vehicle.

"Back off!" Hank warned. But the stubborn muse who appears in his mid-fifties was hardly ready to back down. He came at Hank with lightning speed, but Hank got out of his way and watched as he plummets in the open gutter. Hank then got into his car, backed onto the highway and sped off. He laughs at his strange encounter and wondered what would have happened to Candace if he had not shown up. Still uncertain of Candace's odd behavior, he drove to her condo, the one she'd just purchased only a few short blocks from his apartment. He was surprised with her decision to be this close, the fact that they hardly get along. The last three years of their marriage was hardly a memory, ones he hopes that he would soon forget. He was now even more certain of his decision to have full custody of Sydney.

As he pulled into the parking lot and drove up to the fifth level, his mobile buzzed loudly. He'd forgotten Candace's apt number and drove around the lot for a while.

"Candace? I could use your help." But she continues to make meaningless sounds. He reached for his mobile to phone Syd and noticed that Faith had called. He called her back and she picked up on the first ring.

"Hank, babe is everything okay?"

"Yes, why."

"There were two police officers here asking for you…?"

"What?" Then he realized that it must have been about his run in with the individual in the restaurant parking lot.

113

"It's okay honey, I'll be home in a little bit, will explain then. In the meantime, could you ask Sydney for her mom's apartment number? She has had a bit too much to drink and I had to drive her home."

"Hmm, really?" Faith responded suspiciously. Candace made kissing sounds at Hank from the back seat which Faith overheard.

"Hank? Who is that?"

"Babe, I promise I will explain shortly. You certainly have a lot of explaining to do Hank… but I'm not the one with the Handcuffs."

"Syd darling, your daddy needs you."

"Okay," she replied and came running. "Daddy, what did mom say, can I spend the week?"

It's okay baby, dad didn't get a chance to ask her yet."

"Well, what are you waiting for daddy, and why was the cops at the door asking for you!"

"Syd, calm down honey, daddy just needs mommy's apartment number."

"Unit 4489," she said and hung up.

Hank giggles and shakes his head at the strange evening he was having.

"Candace, you must wake up, I'm not carrying you into your apartment. Last time I did, I got the living daylights knocked out of me. So, as of today, your Hank privileges have been suspended." Hank opened the door and Candace tries standing up, but almost collapses and he caught her and helped her to her unit which was only a few feet from where they were parked. Luckily, for her she punched in her password and the door buzzed opened. By then, she was slightly less intoxicated and laid on a sofa in her living room. After grabbing her a bottled water….

"Candace, I'll be right back, I have to go take care of something and get you your car."

"Okay Eddie, I love you babe," she called still confused. Hank laughs and hurries off. As he drove home, he phoned Faith and asked her to meet him in the Lobby. Faith left the girls with Liz and hurried to meet Hank who was already waiting for her in the Lobby.

"Hank, darling, is everything okay," she asked relieved to see him in good spirits.

"Better now that you're here," he says kissing her softly.

"Come on, I need your help to drive Candace's car back to her apartment." He says feeling more relaxed. As they drove, he started explaining the previous three hours. Faith laughed hysterically.

"Who do you think he was? And why on earth does Syd's mom visit this place, alone?"

"Beats me. She called me Eddie earlier and I'm starting to think that the guy she just got married to is the kid that used to live next door to her parents. Her parents used to babysit that kid after school. Eddy's parents hardly had time for him. They are the owners of Paxel Inc. on the Hudson. This one over there," he said pointing to a high rise near the Hudson River. Faith's eyes widened as Hank continues.

"Are you saying that you've never met the guy your ex married?"

"I mean, she mentioned Eddie, and kept mentioning the guy but it never crossed my mind that it might be the same kid until now...I mean I'm not concrete on this but I won't put it pass her." Faith giggles and stares at Hank unbelievably. Luckily, they had arrived just when a tow truck was about to tow Candace's vehicle which was parked in a one-hour lot for more than three hours. Hank pulled in quickly and hurried toward the men

. "Hey, hey wait...you don't have to do this."

"How much do you need to remove the clamps," he called reaching for his wallet.

"Sorry man, it's too late, we have our orders," the grumpy, overweight driver called.

"I hear you, one k?" Hank said counting a thousand bucks. The driver who had already started up his truck paused.

"Okay," he says. As Hank was about to hand him cash, the owner of Lucio's recognized him and came hurrying.

"Hey, wait, Hank is this your car?"

"Yes, I had a little emergency earlier and had to take a friend home."

"Okay, my apologies guys, but the tow is no longer needed.'

"Well you still got to pay up," the other guy called.

"Sure, how much?"

"Well, he offered me 1k, you'll have to beat that!" he barked.

"Geeze Hank," Lucio sulked.

"Sorry man."

"Okay, here you go he said handing cash to the still unhappy driver." He then gave his men orders to release the vehicle. The men removed the clamps while the tow driver count the cash that Lucio gave him.

"Hey, this here is five-hundred bucks!"

"Hey, it's what we agreed to, now beat it!" Lucio said making a fist. The upset driver got into his tow and drove of angry.

Faith watched as Hank and Lucio discussed his run in with the gentleman earlier. Lucio told him that he took care of everything after watching the surveillance tapes. She watched as they hugged. She was warmed by the nature of their friendship, realizing the love he shares by those who knows him well. She rolled down the window as he approached.

"Ready?"

"Hank, I'm from Sandy Island, lanes with no traffic and I'm the only driver for miles, forgot?" He kissed her through the window.

"Okay honey, I'll see you at my Ex's, he called and peeled out of Lucio's lot.

"Hank, wait!" She pleaded following closely behind. He was speeding on purpose. Weaving through traffic like a maniac then she lost him.

"Panicked, not knowing her way around, she peeled her eyes through the crazy maize but there was no sight of a Black Range Rover for miles. Keeping her eyes on the road, she reached inside her purse feeling around desperately to locate her mobile and her purse fell.

"Dang it! Frustrated, she then chuckled realizing that he was putting her to the test. He obviously thinks that I am this Sandy Island Barbie, she thought. Swerving sharply, she cuts off incoming traffic and took the first exit. Then she spots him…he appears to be searching for her; however, she wasn't ready for him to find her.

"I'll teach you…" She then remembered that she had no idea where Candace lived. She then pulled up next to him unnoticed. Finally, he glanced over and noticed her speeding and keeping up with traffic. He whistled loudly and winks at her. She blew him a kiss and he grabbed it and ate it. She laughs.

"Next exit," he said pointing and swerved of the nightmarish traffic, into Varsity Lux apartment complex. Faith followed close behind. Relieved, she followed him to the fourth level parking lot.

She spun the convertible around several times and lines it up perfectly next to him.

"Okay, be right back!" he said pretending to not notice that she was trying to impress him. She sat in the convertible hoping that he would say something about her terrific driving genes. But instead, he stood there staring at her for a while…

"Coming?" He asked. She shook her head no. He then tossed the keys through Candace's doggy door and agreed. "Yeah, let's not, we'll check on her later," he said walking back. She scoots into the passenger seat and observed him…

"Is everything okay?" He glanced at her from the steering wheel. His eyes swelled with tears. As she reached to brush a tear from his face, he leans over and kisses her gently. *"Oh my gosh,"* he says in a whisper. He shakes and trembles as his lips caresses her lips and face and he cried. Unsure of how to respond, Faith embraced him as he immersed in uncontrollable crying. Unable to find the words, she allowed him to submerge into any state of anguish, regardless of the reasons. It was allowed. Only one question… *"Why?"* she asked in silence. Hank finally pulled himself together and tire screeches could be heard as he pulled off the ramp into the evening traffic, speeding his way toward the Hudson. She had no words, no thoughts, no image…just the silence of the uncertainty that lingered, waiting to be relieved by his generous display of affection…

Chapter 15

The ten days they'd originally planned quickly evolved into weeks as the small tidbits and loose ends seemed more demanding despite a team effort. Faith and Katherine packed the last of their things and watched as Hank consoled Sydney. They had tried endlessly to have her accompany them back to Sandy Island, but other arrangements had to be made. Her mom had agreed to have her reside with her father, but it would be several weeks till she sees him.

"That's almost eight weeks away dad," she sobbed. Unable to resist, Faith and Katherine joined in and all four submitted to the tightest group hug in Manhattan on a cold, rainy day, in the hopes of bringing the deepest comfort to Sydney. Hank sobbed softly, and all four kissed each other's faces several times. Their warmth could be felt for miles, chasing away any fog, and cascade any gloomy day into flawless perfection. The sound of the elevator's ping followed by random keys being pressed brought feelings that they all dreaded.

"Dad, please," Sydney pleaded, but there was no better arrangement that could be made.

"It's okay sweetheart. It feels that way now, but daddy promise. The time will go by quickly and you will get to be with us in no time. Plus, you'll still be able to video chat with Kat." Candace watched as Sydney say goodbye to her friends. She appears less bubbly and a bit frailer than when Hank had seen her the week before. He worries that there was something much more serious than what she had told him. As Faith embraced Sydney one last time, her mobile buzzed. It was Elizabeth. Her flight had just landed in San Francisco and she wanted to see how things were going with their departure. After a short conversation with Faith, Liz wanted to speak with Syd. While Hank spoke with Candace on the lounge, Faith did one last sweep of Hank's condo to make sure that they had packed everything. She has enjoyed every moment of their time in New York. Especially their evening strolls along the Hudson. Each day brought its own special meaning and the three short weeks felt like its own unique lifetime, one she would never soon forget. Goodbyes could be heard, and Sydney sounded much happier after speaking with Liz.

"Bye honey, only it's not goodbye because? I'll be seeing you yesterday," Syd replied enthusiastically blowing Kisses at Faith and Katherine. But she shot a daring stare at her dad just before she disappears behind the door of Manhattan's most famous elevator.

It was already 8:00pm when they landed in Sandy Island and was surprised how warm it felt for October. Kat misses Syd and was already counting the days till Christmas. Sam pulled the limo into Faith's driveway and made a long sigh at the sight of Katherine fast asleep.

"Don't worry Sam, you'll get to pop the question the next time you take us to an airport." Sam's wife Jenny who accompanied him to the airport, laughed.

"Please tell my little doll, that she has my permission to bring Sam flowers anytime. But, however, Aunt Jenny's homemade cookies require a written permission slip from daddy that says, 'Good to go.' Along with a thumbs up drawn on the signature line." Faith giggled at the cute joke and kissed Jenny on the face.

"It was lovely to see you Jenny, you too Sam."

Hank was too exhausted and emotional to entertain Sam and Jenny.

"Thanks again guys, we'll be seeing you at the Christmas party," Hank called sitting on his luggage and watched as the limo disappears off Sandy Island Blvd. Faith invited Hank to join her for the evening and he accepted. After tucking her little darling into bed, feeling excited about being home and the gorgeous weather outside, Faith ran to her balcony. It felt like an eternity since she last stood there overlooking the tides. There was a gorgeous moonlight out and the waves basked about excitedly as though revealing their joy of her return. Overcome by the moment, she took to the stairs and ran toward the beach. Hardly thinking, she removed her clothing and plunged into the surprisingly inviting water. She laughed and plunged about excitedly. Hank hoping to join her on the balcony, carrying two glasses of her favorite wine did a double take when he noticed her in the water.

"Care to join?"

"No way, this is nuts, come up here."

"Nope, this water is heavenly, beats Hank, even if he's handsome and holding two glasses of the finest wine in Sandy Bay." Hardly able to resist her reflection in the moonlight, carrying two glasses on a wicker tray along with two bottles of Chardonnay, he headed to the beach, the wind blowing against his unbuttoned shirt. As the wind subsided the moonlight glistened against the now calmed waves and appeared golden. Yet he was surprised by her spontaneous lack of fear. Quickly removing his shirt, he dove into the water.

"Wow! This is great," he called. Looking around for Faith, who suddenly seem to have disappeared in thin air? He looked up in time to see her fleeing the water like the day she was born except she is a stallion. He bolts after her like lightening, but she was fast. Out of breath and enamored for her affection, he closed in on her as she flaunts tirelessly ahead, slowed to a stop by a gentle grasp, as they tossed about tirelessly in the sand. The tides basked against their entangled feet.

The following week, Faith prepared Katherine for her first day of second grade. She wished that she had taken the advice of seven-year-old Sydney who is currently homeschooled. But she saw the positive in having Katherine attend the next eight weeks of school at Sandy Island Elementary. She needed the distraction and it will help her adjust to not having Fain and Sydney around.

"But mom, I promised Syd that I would enroll at her home school so that way we can help each other with homework."

"I love you sweetheart. You are both in the same grade and can still help each other with homework."

"But mom...please mom...can you please call Fain to take me...?"

"Oh sweetheart. You know that's not possible."

"Okay, then let's phone him."

"Okay, but let's keep it short, school starts in less than thirty minutes," said Faith dialing Fain. He answered on the first ring.

"Faith?"

"No BFF it's me Kat."

"Wow, hey Kat, you sound all grown up!" he joked.

"Well that's cause I'm in second grade now."

"No way."

"I am too," she said proudly.

"Okay sweetheart, you can call Fain after school."

"Okay Uncle Fain, I have to go now, but I'll call you after school."

"Okay, bye." She was in better spirits as her mom drove her the short distance to the Elementary School on the corner of Sandy Blvd. Her teachers and Principal were expecting her and were waiting to welcome her to her first day of second grade. After a tight hug and two hundred smooches, Kat waved at her mom and joined her teachers and students out front.

As she drove home, she noticed her phone ringing on silence. It was Liz. She wanted to pick Katherine up from school.

"Sure Liz, I know she would be happy to see you. Yes, she did okay, we had to call Fain and that helped. Okay, love you too Liz, chat later." Suddenly, her world felt renewed. The trip to New York gave her a refreshed feeling and suddenly she wanted to do something different. She thought of the beach house. With four large bedrooms downstairs and three medium size rooms upstairs, she thought with this location, it would be ideal to list the rooms downstairs on SandybayBnB. She felt a sudden excitement about her new idea. She couldn't wait to see what Hank thought of her new venture.

Hank paced back and forth in his mind, still undecided about putting his Manhattan condo on the market. His new arrangements to have Sydney most of the time also meant that he would no longer need to be there as often. It was his first major purchase since his Divorce, and he had a strong, very special connection to it. He thought maybe his connection to the condo was mainly due to the verbal abuse of his previous marriage that made him feel inadequate as a husband and father. This purchase was the first most mature event that he has ever experienced. It also got his Ex to shut up about his failure as a husband and father. He was absolutely in love with his first purchase, but he knew that it made no sense having two mortgage payments, let alone sitting empty. He also thought that his heightened connection to his condo might be the short time he had spent there with Faith. It was a new chapter for him and the happiest time he'd spent in Manhattan. He thought that maybe he should discuss it with her before making his decision.

Hank peeked through the blinds of his kitchen window and saw Faith's Lamborghini parked outback. All the blinds in her downstairs

121

were drawn to let light in and he wondered what she was up too. After listening to the fifty plus messages that Sydney had left on his voicemail the day before, most of which are of what a bastard he was for leaving her in New York. His combined emotion of missing Syd and needing Faith, gave him a sense of closure.

"Hey cutie what are you up too?" He called surprising Faith with lunch. Startled, she sneezed as she looked up at him. Her hair tied up in a yellow San Francisco scarf. Her pink, low-cut V-neck knitted sweater covered most of her shorts.

"I found this great idea," she sneezed. "I, I, I, ahhhh Chooo!!!" Hank's eyes narrowed, as he waits for her to catch her breath.

"I have a great idea that can't wait. I'm really excited about it!"

"I see. And a very dusty idea it seems," he joked noticing dust on her pants bottom.

"Yes, dusty pending a marvelous makeover," she says and sneezes once more. Hank hands her a box of napkins.

"I haven't touched this room in over a year."

"Hmm, so what kind of assistant was Fain?"

"I see what you're getting at, but he was hired for the exact opposite."

"Ahh, how opposite? May I ask, in what direction?"

"Somebody's so cute when they're jealous," she teased. As they ate lunch over a dusty computer desk, Faith discussed her plans to list her available rooms on SandyBaynB.

"That's awesome. Actually, that's a fantastic idea."

"Really?"

"Yes, definitely. So, when do you think you'll be ready to launch," he asked looking around.

"Well, I'm listing all four rooms down here, so I'll probably be ready in a couple of weeks. I don't think that I'll have to register a business name or anything like that. I just need to have the rooms ready and order a few items that my guests would need, to make their stays one they would never forget," she declared, greening broadly. As she explained her plans for renovating each room, her eyes sparkled. He's never seen her more excited about anything. As though it's the first time she's been allowed to think for herself and there was no one to challenge her decision.

"Well, I think it's brilliant, but there's one thing…and…"

122

"And what's that?" She asked fearing what he might say. He smiled at her momentarily lack of confidence.

"That you're going to need some help."

"No, there's no need. I can manage," she says confidently, removing her scarf and shaking her hair loose.

"Umm, so are you going to limit your guests to couples only?" She laughs realizing his thoughts.

"Nope, so long as they're eighteen, tall, dark and handsome, they're in. The more the better." she giggles. Hank narrows his forehead and squint his eyes as Faith continues to highlight her specifics. As she concludes her most desirable guests, he stood up and cracks his neck muscles.

"Hey, I hate that look. Stop it!" she laughs and tries to run away from him. He pursues her. Faith tries to run to the stairs, but her pursuer came from the opposite direction cutting her off in time and kisses her lovingly.

"Having you around, I might get nothing done," Faith joked, looking at their half-eaten lunch and clothing spread out across the floor.

"You're bad for business Hank." He laughed at how adorable she appears lifting one eyebrow.

"Say that again."

"Nope."

"Come here."

"No."

"I said, come here right now. Faith Elizabeth French. I love you!" He looked over at her standing in one corner of the room, holding the sheets up to her chin.

"*I love you... but you cried when we dropped of your Ex's car*. You cried in the parking lot. Hank, you still have feelings for her." She says, staring at his boyish face. He didn't respond, only stares at her blindly.

"What are you thinking about…?"

"What?"

"You didn't hear a thing I said, did you? Where were you a minute ago?"

"In Manhattan, there's still something I have to take care of…"

"You mean like, explain why you still have unresolved feelings for her."

"No, what? Wait a minute." He was surprised by the sudden change in her tone..,

"Who's her and what make you think that?"

"You're so emotional when she's around...You cried in her parking lot. You still love her Hank."

"What? No, I was crying because I am in love with you, and you never responded when I told you. Remember when I asked you to accompany me to New York a few weeks back?"

"No, it's okay. I remember," she says becoming more distant.

"Faith, what's really going on?"

"Maybe it's because you're back home and all the old memories are flooding back..." His voice faded as he tries to connect with her on this unknown level. He wasn't sure how he was doing so he stops speaking and approached her. There were tears welling up in her eyes when she finally looked at him.

"I think you're right. All the old feelings and memories…"

"They can have that effect," he added finishing her sentence.

"It's the reason I moved here because as you noticed, in Manhattan, I was feeling exactly as you're feeling now. I think we are in the same place babe." She leaned against him and he embraces her.

"I have an idea. Maybe we should call this Days of Our Ideas," he joked. She smiled.

"You always find a way to make me smile Hank. "*I love you.*" Her eyes slowly met his. His heart races.

"I love you more my darling."

"So what was that idea you had earlier?"

"Actually, it's mostly your idea," he admitted.

"Really?"

"Faith?"

"Yah?"

"I think you should move in with me and list your entire house on SandyBaynB. It's a lot to think of in a single day so I'll let you think about it. Take as long as you need no pressure." She nods yes.

"Okay? They both nods yes together before enjoying another tender moment.

Later Hank went home to attend to some business with his agent and Faith busied herself opening the windows and curtain allowing the ocean air in. It's a gorgeous property and maybe it was too much space for her and Katherine. Of course, it's not just up to her; she would have to see how her little Kat feels about the business venture as well as a move as big as moving in with her boyfriend. It was strange thinking of him as her boyfriend, the fact that she feels so much closer to him. As she researched ideas for her venture, her phone rang. She answered and almost froze at a male voice what sounded like her Ex's.

"Omg, Calvin, is that you?"

"Hey, what are you up too? It's been forever," he laughed. "I swung by a few weeks ago but you weren't home. You were gone for a while."

"Oh, sorry yes, I was in Manhattan."

"Manhattan? I didn't know you knew anyone there? But don't worry, mom told me all about it.

"Yes, it almost drove your brother crazy when she came to join us unexpectedly in New York, but it was a great idea. She came in handy."

"I have no idea why my brother thinks that he could lock mom up all day with Rachael, eating vegan salads." She chuckles at his familiar humor.

"Hey, I was calling to invite you and your friend, Hank I think mom says his name is."

"Yes Hank, Hank Hutton."

"Ahh, hope he's as handsome as his name," Calvin teased.

"What does your schedule looks like this Saturday?"

"I would love to invite you and the lovely Mr. Hutton to a Black and White Fundraiser Gala at the Fairway Palace-Penthouse."

"Sounds lovely, absolutely, I would be delighted. Let me run it by Hank to see what his schedule looks like."

"Fantastic! Chaw for now."

"Chaw...and Calvin, thank you!"

"Absolutely, we'll see you two there," he replied.

"A Fundraiser Gala? Sounds uppity! Not sure if I have anything that fancy too wear. I mean, I'm just an old school Writer with a closet full of cargoes and tennis shoes.

"You mean fancy writer with a film that's about to launch. Let's see," said Faith going through Hank's crowded walk-in closet; hangers sitting empty and tons of unopened boxes.

"OMG," she laughed.

"Yes, probably just clothes in there."

"Right, someone's a packrat."

"Yes, it's been six months and I'm still living out of boxes."

"I'm not sure you really moved in," she joked. After opening and searching through about fifteen boxes, she was convinced that Hank Ben Hutton owned every cargo pants from here to Tahiti. She came out of the closet and was greeted by the sound of her boyfriend's loud snores and the soft ocean breeze that's the likely culprit for his untimely nap. There was still four hours before the Gala and she refused to go through the rest of Hank's unopened boxes to find him proper attire. While he slept, she grabbed the keys to his convertible and made a quick run to Sandy Bay Men's boutique. Their fine selection of men's clothing along with the help of a charming young lady, name Stephanie, made it a breeze.

"Are you Hank's girlfriend?" she asked surprised. Faith looked at her curiously.

"How do you know Hank?"

"My friends and I chartered one of his boats over the summer. It was a blast, the best summer I've ever had. Please say hello to him for me and hope to see him next time my friends and I need a spin around the Bay."

"I sure will, and thanks again for your help with the suit." As she turns to leave, impressed by Stephanie's friendly demeanor…

"Umm, Stephanie." She motions for her to come. Steph hurries toward her…

"I was wondering, what does your schedule looks like during the week?"

"Well, I work here three days out of the week, but I'm currently searching for something more fulltime."

"I think I have the perfect opportunity for you. You just graduated from Sandy Bay University this summer, right?"

'Sure did!" she grinned broadly.

"Here's my card, come by on your day off next week, let's talk. I'm the house opposite Hank's."

"I sure will," she said bubbly.

"Great, then it's a date!" She thanked Faith with a hug then hurried off to assist the line of waiting customers.

"Perfect fit," said Faith folding Hank's tie.

"I still can't believe you bought me a suit!"

"Well, cargos would have been the only event to interrupt what could be a successful fundraiser."

"So you think each time someone tries to bid on an expensive piece of art, they would have a look at my shorts and change their minds."

"Ahh, so you get it..." He giggles at her nonchalant sense of humor and composure as she applies eye shadow around her already gorgeously appealing eyes.

"Well I doubt that would be the case. Even in cargos, my unbelievable gorgeous date is all that's needed for off the hat bidding. I might as well be ready for a bidding war and hope to get you to come home with me tonight..." Their conversation was interrupted by Sam honking the horn of his shiny new white limo, waiting for them outside.

"Well, if Cinderella's name was Faith," Hank complements as the ocean breeze gently tosses Faith's hair and flowing white evening gown into a vision like twirl. Sam greets them warmly and jokingly criticized Hank for not giving him an invite.

"I promise Sam, it was Faith's idea to give you the stiffy. If it were the lovely Katherine, you know, every gentleman from here to the Golden Gate Bridge would be lined up, collecting their golden ticket."

"I quite agree," Sam nods. Sitting comfortably in the Limo, Faith glanced at her date as he pours them champagne.

"Oh Sam, you don't really believe him, do you? He didn't even want to wear a suit; you should see my boyfriend's closet. Nothing but boxes and boxes of chummy brown cargoes, he wasn't even worthy of the invite!" Sam laughed heartedly.

"You too are quite the pair...and possibly becoming one of my favorite couples."

"Ahh, we love you too Sammy," Faith says sipping on her Champagne. Sam pulled up to the crowded parking lot of the Fairway-Palace Penthouse. There were several parking lot attendants directing traffic who pointed them to available parking.

"Well this looks like it's going to be an incredible turnout," Sam said, getting the door for Faith. He took her hands and helps her up and she thanks him with a kiss on the cheek imprinting him with lipstick. Sam blushes.

"She's beautiful Hank. Promise you will take care of her."

"You have my word," he says shaking his hand.

"I'll be here after Midnight, before the Queen of Sandy Bay loses her glass slipper," Sam tips his hat and drove off.

The couple handed in their personalized invitation to the courteous doorman who showed them to the great hall that was already packed with people. And an open sitting area lined with chairs to accommodate thousands. Hank glanced at the fine architecture and exhaled a sigh of relief.

"Are you okay?" She asked noticing that he's adjusted his tie for the tenth time since their arrival. She could tell that it was possibly his first time attending one of these and she hid a small chuckle that almost surfaced.

"Faith, Hank, glad you can make it!" Calvin said greeting them excitedly.

"Come, there's someone I want you to meet." Taking Faith's hands guiding them through the crowded room.

"Faith, Hank, I want you to meet my friend Gerry. Gerry, please meet my sister, Faith and her handsome date, Hank Hutton," he said enthusiastically.

"Oh, it's an absolute pleasure to meet you, I've heard so much about you love," said Gerry, a medium built Italian. As Faith was about to ask Gerry how he knew Calvin, Calvin revealed excitedly that Gerry is his boyfriend and fellow co-pilot from Italy.

"Oh, my goodness, I had no idea," Faith said trying to hide how surprised she was discovering Calvin's sexuality.

"Calvin, I had no idea. I'm so happy for you."

"Shhh, I plan on telling mom at another time."

"Absolutely, I understand," she smiled still surprised. Calvin looked up at his mobile.

"Eric and Rachael's just arrived," he said, hurrying toward the door to meet them. Gerry chatted with Hank and Faith and revealed that he was one of the main sponsors of the event.

"I just learned that we're still short of a male model for the Entourge MedVouge clothing line. Gerry glanced at Hank and asked his size.

"No saying," Hank joked.

"I'm certain that you're a size fourteen, you should be perfect. Would you be interested in modeling my friends' new line?" Gerry asked.

"Who me?" Before Hank had a chance to respond, Gerry took him by the hand and led him toward the back of the room.

"Here's our replacement, get him dressed NOW we're about to begin."

"Wait, wait a minute." Before Hank could refuse, he was stripped and dressed in the finest piece of attire he has ever encountered.

"Hank?" Where did everyone disappear too? Faith wondered looking around. Faith stuffed a French hors'd'oeuvres in her mouth and reached for a glass of Champagne from the passing trey. A few moments later Gerry stood at edge of the stage and announced that they're about to begin. There were over five thousand guests attending what she could define as the finest Celebrity auction in San Francisco. As attendees took to their seats, Faith found herself seating unexpectedly alone. Unsure of where her very nervous handsome date might have disappeared too, she took her seat and hope that at some point he would turn up. A tall, very attractive auctioneer in her mid-thirties took to the podium and a young man in an Elvis costume appeared on stage. Loud whistles and bidding could be heard as the young stud strut his fine outfit in model like fashion.

"Hey, where's Elvis's Guitar?" someone shouted, and laughter followed. Hardly concerned by her sudden fate, she held her breath as Hank appeared on stage endowed in a bare chested Humphrey Bogart outfit. Hardly shy, he removed his hat and unbuttoned and unzipped his tight shiny bell bottomed pants. Hank gently removing his shirt and tossed it across the stage. Of the wall bidding could be heard and a hair edging question followed.

"How much to have the lovely Mr. Hutton to myself all evening?" asked a fantastically dressed maiden in French apparel.

"All gratitude Madam, however, the clothing is up for bidding, models are not included."

"Such a shame, he's such a handsome bloke," the Mademoiselle sighed.

"Just a minute, I'll allow it," Faith said standing up. All eyes were now focused on her and a sudden brush of moisture graced her forehead.

"Who's the lovely woman?" A gentleman called.

129

"That would be Madam, Faith Elizabeth French," the sister of our sponsor. The Madam endowed in French Apparel removed her hat and bowed lowly at Faith.

"Very well then. My bid to have the Handsome Mr. Hutton for the evening is Seventy seven thousand. I'm not interested in the outfit and you're welcome to have it," she said pointing to a shy young man who made the highest bid for the Humphrey Bogart outfit.

"Very well, your bid is accepted pending the approval of Ms. French."

"Approved!" Faith said enthusiastically gracefully returning a bow.

"Very well, Mr. Hutton, please join Madam Annabelle on the dance floor preceding this event. Later, after all bidding wars were settled, Gerry joined Faith on the dance floor.

"You're a fantastic dancer," she complimented him.

"It's an absolute pleasure, my love. After all, it is my fault that a fine woman like yourself finds herself alone on an evening like this.

"So Gerry, how long have you and Calvin known each other on a personal note?"

"As a matter of fact, today is our second anniversary. This event is our celebration."

"How wonderful." Faith said stepping gently to accommodate Gerry's twirl.

"You're a beautiful woman Faith. Here' my card. I have a friend that hires young models like yourself."

"Young model?" Faith blushed.

"Don't be shy…you'd be perfect," he assured. As they danced, Gerry received a gentle tap on his shoulder.

"May I please cut in?" asked a mysterious gent wearing a masquerade mask. Unsure, Gerry looked at Faith and she assured him that it was alright.

"By all means," Gerry said handing the lovely Faith to the mysterious stranger. Before leaving, Gerry whispered in the stranger's ear…

"I'd be very careful if I were you, this woman has some very private eyes on this floor, you creep."

The stranger ignored Gerry's warning and lifts up his hands snapping his fingers, and, in an instant, the music delved into a fast-rhythmic cha *cha*. Guests stare in amazement at the couple who stole the evening's spotlight. Faith appeared as a vision instilling her best moves, maneuvering through the ambivalence of a talented stranger. Her angelic appearance complimented by a flowing waterfall upheld the integrity of a proven talent. Hank glanced briefly at Faith, surprised by her unsound grace. Fully surrendered by an upheaval of daze, spiraling through thin air, warring through the conflict of elegance and enchantment.

Chapter 16

Hank gazed at Faith from his airy sea front balcony with her new Assistant Stephanie. Her home was now almost unrecognizable and her new venture SandyBaynB was about ready to be launched. His heart skipped each time he looks at her and some days it was almost unbearable to be without her. Someone of her elegance and grace can calm the winds of any storm. He couldn't wait to begin helping her make the short move into his life. One that will close the gap of the many miles of loneliness he felt the many years before she'd graced his life with her dignified presence.

"Hank Hutton, I'm ready," Faith called carrying a duffel bag in each hand.

"What are you doing?"

"Put that down babe, I got this," he called hurrying toward her. He took both bags from her hands.

"This might take a week, even if we live this close," she called.

"Yes, you have lots of pretty dresses in there," he joked. A few hours later, exhausted the couple flopped down on Hanks patio enjoying Fall's cool evening air.

"How do you think Kat girl will respond to the move?"

"I've thought of this several times and I've decided that I'm not going to have to tell her."

"Is that so? But how?"

"Well, she's staying with Liz until the end of the Fall school year and by that time Syd will be with us for the holidays…" Hank nods.

"You're right, she spends most of her time in that spare bedroom when Syd's around anyway."

"Exactly my thought."

"You're like a feather, what I perceive as difficult, you make them appear seamless…what can I do without you?"

"Want to find out?" she asked, eyes narrowed.

"I love you!" her eyes shifted.

"I love you my handsome Mr. Hutton."

"No I love you more…"

"I love you Faith Elizabeth, Hungry?"

"Strangely not."

"Same here, I don't have much of an appetite for anything home cooked."

"Want to order take out? I heard that new Chinese restaurant on Sandy Hilltop is raving, up for it?" She smiled without responding and he wondered what she was up too. Before he realized, Faith playfully covered his face with whip cream, laughing, she took off down the pier. Hank grabbed the can of whip cream and took off after her. As he closed in on her…

"Oh boy, look who's about to get it," he laughed out of breath. She was fast and as she looked over her shoulders to see if he was gaining on her, she tripped on a loose log barely missing a major plunge.

"Ouch," she laughed grabbing her bleeding right knee.

"Oh honey," Hank said hurrying to her. Despite a badly bruised knee, she laughed at how horrified he appeared, his blue eyes widened.

"Let's have a look at that," he said kissing her knee, getting a bit of blood on his bottom lips.

"Wait, you've got some of my blood on your lips, right there," she said reaching to remove it. But he reached his tongue and tasted it.

"Ahh, you taste like my favorite Vampress, now I'm going to have to finish the job," he said finally spraying her face with whip cream indulging in a kiss at sunset.

"A bruised bandaged knee, take out and whip cream make for an evening of indulgence. Let's just hang out. I'm not sure about you, but I'm wiped out from all this moving," Faith admitted.

"I agree, let's lay back and do absolutely, nothing! I love this, most couples deeply desire this time together. Let's enjoy it." He said making a silly face. His career of choice has given him the schedule that he had wished that his Ex would have appreciated, but Faith has led him down a path that is quickly unfolding. Paths that he never imagined that he would ever venture.

"Come here, you're too far away," he said to her. But she was only laying on the lounge chair next to him.

"Too far?"

"Yes babe, I want you to lay on my chair."

There was a sudden softness about him, and she knew that he meant it. After cuddling next to him, he spun noodles with chopsticks from his Chinese bowl and placed them in her mouth. Her eyes shut as her gorgeous full lips chewed slowly. Unable to resist he kisses her. With each mouthful, his heart raced as if her very presence spoke life into his heart. He could hardly do without her. Her eyes opened slowly meeting his...

"What are you thinking about...Mr. Hutton?" He took her in his arms and kisses her unfolding the storms within his oceanic heart, with more desire than the depths of the Bay. Her face shining from the ingredients of Chinese takeout as their hearts plunged forward awakening the tides as the waves of the sea basked joyfully below.

"Welcome to my bachelor pad hunny." He lifts her up and carries her to his gorgeous main room where the flavors of a variety of unplanned meals fell freely from the showers of passion.

Chapter 17

Patrol George's eyes slowly blinked to an open at the sound of his horses neighing and whining loudly. As he stirs to a tiresome wake, the smell of smoke fills his nostrils. Puzzled by the strange sentiment, he threw on a robe and peeked through the window overlooking the stables. He then searched hurriedly around his Cabin but there was no sign of fire. Then a fleeting moment he did not expect. At the corner of the eyes, the sun was beginning to dawn upon the Sandy Bay horizon but was darkened by a grey smoke blanketing against the sky. Horror struck as his mind raced almost freezing his momentum. As if kissed by an invisible force, he raced toward the stables as he tries frantically to free the horses. Loud receding gallops could be heard as he opens the stable doors as terrified horses run from the growing heat and blanketing smoke quickly approaching.

Suddenly alone, Patrol George reached in his back pockets to locate the keys to his vehicle but remembered that he was only wearing a robe over his boxers. As he attempts to make a dash up the stairwell to save a few treasured items, Becca came out of nowhere. She neighed, beckoning loudly for him to get on. "Becca get out of here girl," he scolded, But the horse as if insisting that he climbs on refuses to leave him behind. A sudden chilly feeling of assurance came over him like before and he jumps onto the horse and she peeled out of the now enflamed Cabin carrying her owner to safety.

Hank strolled lazily into his kitchen half asleep and poured himself a glass of water. As he lifts the glass to his lips, he noticed that it was almost six a.m. Curious of the foggy grayness outside his window, he walked toward the window for a closer look. It never fogs in Sandy Island, he thought. As that thought cleared…

"Is that smoke I smell," Faith strolled into the kitchen rubbing her eyes.

"Smoke? You smell smoke?" he asked looking around the kitchen. As if she'd seen a ghost, Faith pointed to the window.

"That's not fog, we don't get fog in Sandy Bay." She said hurrying to the window.

"Oh my God! Hank there's a fire!!!!" she screamed. Hank hurried out the door and looked in horror as thick grey smoke and fire ripped through the hundreds of water vessels docked a short distance from his home. He then turned in time to see Faith sprang into action, reaching for a hose to prevent the already domineering fire from spreading.

"Faith, no baby, it's too late!" he called hurrying toward her. But as he tries to decide between getting dressed, saving his home and stopping Faith, he was distracted by the loud noise of hundreds of fire engines en route to Sand Island. Suddenly pressed for time, he sprang into action as he tries to stop Faith as she ran toward her bungalow attempting to save a few prized processions. As if time stood still, Hank sprang after Faith to stop her as blanketing smoke and growing heat forced him to abandon his home. He looked around desperately and noticed a Jet Ski parked further away from the rest of the vessels. Without further thought, he dove off the now inflamed wooden docks and swam toward the small vehicle. He looked toward Faith's Bungalow but there was still no sign of her.

"Come on baby, we need to go," he pleaded. He circled the Jet Ski and parked it near the surf. He noticed hundreds of items from Faith's house being tossed out the back as Faith attempted to save her treasures. Then just as he was about to run toward her home to rescue her, Faith bolted out of her garage on a Quad 4Runner and almost ran him over.

"Faith, we have to go, now baby, forget all that crap!" he said panicked.

"Come here baby," he said, taking her hands and leading her away from the intense heat unto the Jet Ski. Faith wrapped her arms around Hanks waist tightly as the small watercraft sped into action as the two escaped into open waters. As they reached further out into Sandy Bay, they were now able to see clearly swerving in time to avoid colliding with hundreds of other Sandy Island residents attempting to escape. Hundreds of Coast Guards and other vessels were en route to the small Island. Hank swerved a second time to avoid a head on collision with a large incoming vessel.

"Please clear the open water!" said a rescue from a helicopter who threw a ladder over the side urging them to get off the Jet Ski to prevent larger vessels from crashing into them. Hank slowed to a stop and help Faith climbed onto the swinging ladder.

"Hank, it's too windy, I can't get a good grip," she cried.

"Come on babe, you have to do this, for us," he said. She looked terrified but held on tightly and slowly made her way up the ladder and safely into the chopper. Hank followed closely behind, shivering from the cold water and excessive wind created by the powerful whirring blades of the chopper. Now safely inside, the team of all female rescues handed Hank and Faith robes and sandals for their bare feet. A quick check of their vitals by the team of medics confirmed that they were both okay and only suffering from mild smoke inhalation.

Now able to catch her breath, Faith cried at their sudden fate, hugging tightly onto Hank as the chopper carries them away from Sandy Island.

"It's okay baby."

"No it's not, what about all our stuff!" she cried. The chopper landed on the roof of Hope Memorial Hospital. The team of medics gave them extra robes, and military rattan for their breakfast.

"You two are going to be okay," said a young red head and winked at Hank as the chopper took off to rescue more residents now crowding into the Sandy Island harbor.

Having a clear view of the entire Bay from the roof of Hope Memorial hospital, the couple looked on in horror as firemen and rescue teams fought relentlessly against the growing flames to no avail. Their homes, hidden by thick smoke erased any hope that their processions had survived the flames. Faith sobbed softly…

"You saved my life Hank."

No baby, you saved mines," they embraced each other, thankful that they are safely together.

Despite being cleared as safe from the team of rescue medics, the couple got lost in the midst of the growing numbers as hundreds of Sandy Island residents transported by Helicopters and Ambulances crowded the hospital. The nurses insisted that they waited to be properly examined. Patients filled the hallways waiting to be seen and cleared by staff.

"Nurse!" Faith called.

"Please wait Ma'am, we will be with you in just a minute," the Nurse replied sharply.

"No, I am fine, I need to reach my family to let them know that I'm okay," she fretted. But the Nurses ignored her for the hundredth time.

"Does anyone have a phone?" she asked desperately looking around the noisy hallway.

"*I have a phone*," called a tiny voice. A little girl called handing Faith her pink toy phone. Faith looked at her and smiled.

"Thank you, sweetie," and kissed her tiny hands.

"It's the only thing she managed to save," her mom smiled between tears. Faith hugged her. Tired and a little hungry, Faith continues to search for a phone.

"Please try admin," someone said to her from the crowd.

"Great idea!" she replied hurrying toward the elevator to get to the first floor. It took forever for her to get onto the elevator, but when she did, it was a very tight ride and she feared that there might be too many people on the ride down. It was a very loud squeaky ride ten floors to the lobby. She hurried to admin.

"Please, I need to use the phone!" she cried frantically. A guard showed her to the phone, but there was an awfully long line.

"You've got to be kidding me!" she fretted.

"Ma'am feel free to try the emergency room but the lines there are not that much shorter," the Guard assured. Looking at the crowd trying to get onto the elevator, Faith knew that there was no way to avoid the lines and her only option was to wait. Through weeping, and a mountain of different emotions, as residents confirmed their status to their loved ones, two daunting hours later, Faith finally got to call her mother-in-law. Tears of joy and anguish rushed down her cheeks as she explained their miraculous rescue.

"I'm so glad you're safe honey, I was so worried," Liz cried.

"Everyone's here and Calvin have offered to come to the hospital to get you and Hank home," Liz cried.

"But I need to find Hank first," she cried.

"Okay honey, we'll wait for you in the Emergency Room lot," Liz called before hanging up. Relieved that the worst of her troubles are behind her, she searched desperately for Hank.

"Nurse, can you help me locate a patient?"

"Yes are you family?"

"Are you kidding? Yes, I'm family, his name is Hank. Hank Hutton!"

"And you are?"

"Faith Hutton!" she lied.

"Well ma'am I still need to see your ID!" Frustrated Faith turned away and as she turns to leave, she bumped into Hank.

"Hank!" she cried excitedly.

"Where have you been? I love you." She cried hugging him tightly. The nurse smiled in appreciation of her luck amidst a growing crowd.

"Where have you been love, I've been searching for you everywhere!" Hank almost felt bad at the frustration on her Face.

"Well babe," he said holding up his wrist revealing a blue hospital band with the words cleared marked in bold white.

"I had a very stubborn nurse that insisted I get properly checked out before leaving. By the way aren't you supposed to be wearing a pink one darling?" he said winking at her. And for the first time today, she smiled.

"See, baby, I made you smile." They hugged each other tightly.

"Oh, I was able to reach Liz and they're going to be here shortly."

"That's great!" Hank said relieved as they pushed gently through the crowds, anxious and fearful of the unknown.

Calvin had already arrived when they finally exited the hospital. Faith ran to her favorite brother-in-law and hugged him. Then as in slow motion, Katherine came running to her…

"Mommy," the two embraced tightly.

"Mommy, there is a great big fire at the beach. I saw lots and lots of smoke."

"I love you sweetheart. Mommy promised to get you the whole world."

"It's okay mommy, I'm just really happy that you and uncle Hank are safe." Hank dried tears from his eyes at Katherine's bravery, overwhelmed by her statement. Most kids would have been fussing over their stuff, he thought. After a tight group hug, they drove off the crowded lot. Exhausted from a long day, they both fell asleep on the drive home. As Calvin approached Sandy Island Blvd, he thought of swinging by to see the extent of the damages, but all entries to Sandy Island were blocked off and the Sherriff was already directing traffic to alternate routes. He knew of another off-road route but as he was about to make a U-turn onto the bypass…

"Don't even think about it, Uncle Calvin," Katherine warned.

"We need to get my mommy home, she's very tired and smells like smoke so I'm sure she would appreciate a shower and to get out of those horrid jellies!" Kat yelled. Calvin laughs in agreement.

"Okay sweetheart, you got it, home it is," he said and avoided the bypass. He shook his head all the way to the Presidio Heights.

"You know your mommy is so blessed to have you sweetheart," Calvin admitted as he pulled into the driveway. Katherine smiled but that smile was quickly replaced with her stern protective instincts. As they pulled into the driveway, Liz came hurrying to meet them.

"Kat, your friend Sydney is waiting for you on Skype. She's worried as she hasn't heard from her dad." Katherine hurried inside to fill her friend in.

"Syd, don't worry, your dad and my mom made it out safe. My mom was like Spider Woman and flagged down a helicopter. She even climbed up the ladder while it shook!" she boasted.

"But Liz told me that it was my dad that got them away from the fire in his awesome Jet Ski."

"But, but, but it was my mom that got the helicopter to come get them of that tiny Jet Ski, what was your dad thinking? He could have got my mom killed on that stupid thing!" she yelled. "That's not fair! Well, I'm glad that they are both okay. That's all that matters! What's got into you anyway?" Sydney yelled and signed off. Katherine was livid that her dad had invited Rachael to a family emergency. How could he be so selfish, it's not like Rachael cares about anyone but herself, she fussed, pacing back and forth, shutting the door behind her. A few minutes later she remembers her mom and hurries to her.

"Where's my mom?"

"She's in the guest bedroom down the hall sweetie," her grandma called.

"Mom, please let me in, I'd like to draw you a bath."

"It's okay sweetie, uncle Hank already took care of it."

"But mom...as she was about to dispute...but changed her mind and walked away. "Is she okay? She seems a little upset," Hank admitted.

"She's feeling territorial and protective," Faith admitted.

"Your bond is amazing. Funny, I haven't heard from either Syd or Candace..."

"Want to put in a call to them? I'll be right back...let me go check on my daughter," she said tiredly.

"Please do not be long, you should try and get some rest."

"Love you, be right back," she called as she hurries to her daughter.

"Katherine? Where are you sweetie?"

"I'm in here, mom." She tried to dry the tears from her face as her mom approached.

"Sweetheart, you're crying..."

"Well mom, I almost lost you," she said now crying uncontrollably.

"Oh sweetheart, I'm okay," she tries to console her daughter, but she could tell by the way that she was crying, that there was something else the matter...When she pulled herself together...

"Mom, would you sleep in my room, I really missed you mommy."

"Oh sweetheart, absolutely. I'm all yours baby." Faith realized that she had hardly seen or spent much time with her daughter since she started school a few weeks before. She cuddled her like a teddy bear and before long they both fell fast asleep. After speaking with his daughter and Candace, Hank checked in on Faith and Katherine. He smiled seeing mother and daughter cuddled into a ball. He tippy towed back to the guest room and flopped onto the soft inviting bed he had hoped to share with Faith.

"She's all yours Kat," he yawned. And before long, he too fell into a tiresome sleep.

Faith awoke to the sound of Hank's frustrations on the small balcony outside her bedroom.

"Son-of-a-Bitch!" Faith got into one of Liz's robes and joined her very upset boyfriend. Hank pouring himself another shot of Brandy staggered as he looked at her.

"Honey, what are you doing, let 'talk about it darling?" He ignored her, leaned his head back and downed another drink, burping loudly.

"Hank?"

"It's okay sweetie, just go back to bed, you're up way to early Syd," he said softly.

"Hank, it's me, Faith. Come on baby let's get you inside, it's only 5am, you must be tired baby," she said reaching for his large, toned arms.

"Syd, I said you should go to bed honey, daddy will be with you in just a sec!" he repeated removing his arms from Faith.

"Hey Liz, you're up early, and who's your new hunk?" a neighbor called.

An embarrassed Faith hid herself. The neighbor seeing Hank standing on the balcony alone and shirtless was enflamed.

"Hey, want to join us tonight. My daughter's coming home from her studies in France and I'd love for her to meet you?"

"How old is she?"

"Twenty-one…so what do you say?"

"Okay, why not?"

"Great, I'll see you tonight."

"How does 7:00pm sound?"

"Splendid!" Hank called lifting his almost empty bottle of Brandy to a toast. Faith chuckled. And after he had finished the last of his cinnamon brandy, she approached him. This time he didn't resist, and she escorted him to bed. A few hours later Faith, unable to return to sleep borrowed a pair of tennis shoes and gym clothes from Calvin and went for an early morning walk around the Marinas. She walked briskly uphill for a little over a half an hour and stopped when a familiar image came into view. There beyond the thousands of rooftops, almost as a silhouette in the distance stood a lonely blue Sandy Island Bay and not a single house could be seen. She did not need to wait, it was confirmed. Slowly lifting her hands to her lips, tears ran down her beautiful face as she beholds her Utopia standing alone. Far beneath the lonely waves and joyful tides that greet her each morning. Now alone to greet the still charred lifeless forms that was once inhabited by love's eternal rose. Unable to leave, she cried…

"I'm here, my darling, I have not left you, I have not abandoned you, my love…though I'm far, I am near, for your love has complete me and I will never leave you. You are my Sandy!"

"Who are you talking to hunny?" an elderly woman taking a morning stroll asked…

Faith turned around and looked at her surprised.

"Sandy."

"Oh, you mean you're from the island…"

"Yes."

"You two must have quite a bond huh?" Faith smiled in agreement.

"Alright then, I better leave you two alone," she said moving along.

"By the way, I'm that one over there," the woman called, pointing to her house on the cul-de-sac.

"That is if you ever need to talk."

"Thank you."

"Bonnie, my name's Bonnie."

"Thank you so much Bonnie. Such a pleasure to meet you."

"Pleasure is all mine baby girl," the woman called. Surprised by her sudden encounter of Sandy Bay and overwhelmed by the kindness of this sweet stranger, Faith sat on a bench near the neighborhood park and stared at Sandy Island till the sun was well above the horizon. As she walked back to Liz's, she thought of Fain, surprised that she had not heard from him. None the less she was proud of him that he managed to keep himself busy in Hollywood. As she thought of Fain, she remembered that his production is due to be in theatres today and she hurried back.

"Mom, where were you?" her daughter said wrapping her hands around her mom's waist. Everyone including Eric and Rachael was sitting at the dining table enjoying Liz's breakfast.

"Great, I'm glad everyone's here.

"I have an announcement,"

"Eric, do you remember my assistant?"

"Who you mean the swishy Frenchman?" Everyone except Hank and Faith laughed.

"Well, he's made his first film and it's going to be in theatres today, I would really appreciate it if we can all go and show him our support…?"

"You mean, Fain, he's on television now?" Liz asked surprised.

"Well, I won't miss it for anything!" she said taking her meds.

"I'd love to support, but we have plans," Rachael said coldly. Katherine sneered at her remark.

"It's okay honey, we could be there," said Eric after whispering in Rachael's ear.

"Thanks' dad!" Katherine said excitedly.

"So everyone's in, great! Calvin feel free to invite Gerry."

"Absolutely."

143

"Who's Gerry?" Elizabeth asked, staring curiously.

"Mother this is not the time, but I promise 'I'll tell you later." Faith was surprised that Liz did not know about Gerry and felt terrible that she'd put her favorite brother-in-law on the spot. Calvin glanced at her and winked...she mouthed words, *"I'm sorry."* Elizabeth continues to implore. Calvin stood up, both hands placed in his pockets and his face as serious as when he is addressing his passengers.

"Mother, I love you with all my heart. I met someone a little over a year ago, his name is Gerry. He is also a Pilot. Gerry has asked me to move in with him and I said yes!"

Elizabeth sat quiet for a moment.

"Son, what are you saying, that you're gay?! You mean you've been seeing him an entire year and you didn't bother to tell your mother!"

"Well mom, I..." Elizabeth interrupted him, a smile slowly forming on her face.

"I always wanted another son. I've always dreamed of having three boys...you kept him from me an entire year. Son you rascal!"

"So you mean, you're not...dis...disappointed?" he stuttered.

"Are you kidding? Get me my son Calvin! And I'm sure you picked a handsome one to, you mamma's boy you."

Everyone was surprised and found themselves laughing at Liz's reaction. Hank, still slightly hung over from his early morning rendezvous, excused himself and went to find Faith. Laughter continues in the background as he walks away from the group he hardly feels connected too.

"Faith?"

"Hank? I'm in here babe," she called from Liz's office.

"Hey, what are you up to?"

"Just getting us tickets for later," she said removing the Regal Theatre receipt from the printer.

"I love you," he said solemnly. She looked in his eyes and could tell that there was something bothering him deeply.

"I love you too, baby. What's wrong?"

"Other than the obvious, is there something else...?"

"I know of another route into Sandy, mind going for a drive with me?"

"You mean, you're ready to see Sandy?"

"Don't worry we'll be back in time to see Fain's movie."

"Okay, should we take Kat with us…?" Hank pondered…

"Umm, maybe not just yet it can be traumatizing."

"You're right. Let me go talk to her and I'll be right back. And oh, you might want to ask Liz if we can borrow one of her cars…"

"That's right, I keep forgetting," she laughed.

As they exited the Marina District onto Sandy Island Blvd, Hank began to speed.

"Son-of-a-botch!" he yelled as the wind whipped his hat off his head onto the freeway.

"This baby is fast. God, for the first time in twenty-four hours, I feel alive.

"Hank, look. This road is closed."

"Darn it! When are they going to open the frigging road, oh forget it!" he yelled and drove through the yellow cones and wooden road-closed signs.

"I need to see if I still own at least the darn Jet Ski that saved my life," he yelled. Faith laughed at his sudden defiant boyish way. As they drove through the burnt rubble and ash, Faith suddenly became distracted by a familiar sound.

"Hank, wait, pull over babe."

"You heard something?"

"I think so," she said stepping out of the vehicle. Then she heard that sound again. It was clear, obvious to her now.

"BECCA! Where are you girl? Honey, please keep calling, so mommy can find you. Becca?"

"Baby, I don't think it's safe, and I don't hear anything," Hank called. But she ignored him and continued toward the thick brush.

"Hank! It's her, it's Becca, I know her sound, she was my horse for about eight hours, but I know her sound. Come on, we must find her."

"Faith, honey, please don't do this, it's not safe." But she did not respond, so he parked the convertible off road behind some tall brushes and followed after Faith.

"Honey, wait up, I'm coming." He ran toward her and she motioned for his silence.

"Look, it's Becca and she's with some of Patrol George's other horses."

"Wow, but how?" Faith looked closer and it looks like the horses are all sitting in a circle. "That's strange," Hank said taking the lead. Then he stopped in his tracks.

"What is it?" Faith implored. Without responding, Hank took off running toward the horses and scared them off.

"It's Patrol George," he called and when he couldn't locate a pulse, he began mouth to mouth resuscitations and chest compressions. Patrol George lay lifeless on the damp sandy forest ground. Faith screamed at the sight of him and wished that they had brought a phone with them.

"Please tell me he's alive honey?"

"I can't find a pulse," Hank called. After about two minutes of CPR, Hank stopped and asked for Faith's help to carry George to the car. They sped at a hundred miles an hour to Hope Memorial Hospital, in the hopes of saving their friends life.

They peeled into the Emergency parking lot and Faith ran inside for assistance. A few moments later they both waited patiently for a word. About a half an hour later, Hank looked up in time to see a team of five medical professionals heading in their direction.

"Are you the Family members of George Stone?"

"Well, we are the closest thing to family he has right now," Hank replied.

"Well, I'm sorry but I cannot release any information to you."

"Sir, with all due respect, you need to tell us how our friend is or I'm going to kick your ass!" The cocky doctor rolled his eyes.

"Please call security," he said and walked away.

"Oh doc?" Hank said approaching him. I though you should know... Assuming that Hank had additional information on George, the Doctor leaned in to listen and Hank smacked him upside the head. He then took Faith's hand and they ran into the laundry room and hid themselves as Security ran past their hiding place. Determined to learn the status of their friend, when the hallway was cleared, the couple hurried down the hallway and peeked into the room where George was last seen, but they had moved him. They sneaked around and hid themselves, listening for any information about their friend.

"Wait, what's that? Faith said reaching for a document that appears to have been left by accident in George's room. As they go

146

over the difficult to read doctor's hand writing, their eyes stopped on the same acronym and numbers…T.O.D: 11:47am. "Oh my God!"

"Shhh, come, we must go. "They both hurried out of the ER and drove out of the parking lot for a second time this week. Faith sobbed. Hank pulled off the side of the road and embraced her as she processes the sudden shock of the loss of her friend. The kind of person that everyone in Sandy Bay has grown so fond of, the love of all their lives. Her thoughts ran wild… He cannot be gone, she sobbed. Though he hardly knows the Patrolman, he knew that any person that Faith loves is well deserved. Be it a friend or a stranger, was worthy of her affections, so long as it was sealed by Faith's admiration of love and friendship.

Varying colors danced about in a dividing haze of nothingness. The light divided the colors and varying rainbow-like colors parted the darkness. Each individual color revealed a separate purpose and submerged the dark colors. The darkness circled the light and at times appeared to dominate the light. The brightness flickered to a single spark and became overshadowed by a single spark to suffice the nothingness, growing from a tiny flame into a glowing flower of light. Each light bonded with the darkness folding and forming yet transforming into an untold story of one…

"George Stone. George Stone. George Stone!" A plain voice called as though to scold a child.

"Behold the beauty of your untold, yet ever unfolding, ever unfinished work, George Stone, wake up!" At the sound of his name, George exhaled loudly and stared at the unexplainable whiteness that lay above him. Why is it so white out? It never fogs in Sandy Bay. What is this terrible fog? As his mind races, he heard someone whimpers fearfully as footsteps recede and a door slammed shut.

"Becca, Is this you? Where are you girl, are you going to get me away from this. Come here buddy!" At that moment, he sat up and exhaled loudly. The white linen covering his nakedness fell to his waist. As his vision cleared, Patrol George looked around the room. He looked directly at the digital clock on the wall which indicated: 12:05pm. He then gazed around the room. Why are there so many guys sleeping? What is this? It's the middle of the day. Why are all these people asleep? He thought.

"Hey you, hey there," he called to the woman lying next to him.

"Geeze, what is this? Is this your way of getting back at me for ticketing all these drunken summer vacationers? These guys look drunk. I mean look at those bastards. They look paler than the Vanilla Brandy they had last night. I wonder how long they have been drinking and boating. Get up you lousy bastards!"

A medical crew entered George's room single file, gazing curiously at him.

"Should I call a Priest?" the Nurse asked, refusing to come closer.

"Not necessary. At least not yet," the Physician replied. Everyone else giggled under their breaths.

"What is this? Can someone tell what's really going on here!"

"Sir, you're in a hospital morgue."

"Say what!"

"Well, sir, you were considered medically dead until someone heard you."

"Sir, do you remember your name and how old you are?"

"Ahh, come on, you got to be kidding me. I'm George, Patrol George. I'm fifty-seven and the last thing I remembered was trying to get away from a lot of smoke. Then it got warm and I don't remember much after this." The staff members looked at each other.

"Sir...."

"Patrol George is fine, no need to call me sir."

"Well, George, do you have any family that you'd like us to call?"

"Well why don't you try getting me out of this morgue first, do I look dead to you?" They all laughed. A few minutes later a nurse brought George a pair of matching blue sweat suit and he was carted out of the morgue where he underwent several hours of tests and observations.

Later Hank watched as Faith shared the news of the loss of their Friend to Eric. It was the only time he had seen them converse for over an hour or even touched. This is something they shared. A friendship that had brought them together for the first time since he'd met Faith and he almost felt jealous. He knew that Katherine appreciated the view of her parents sharing a tender moment together. As they continued sharing their fond memories of George, Faith's mobile rang.

"Hmm, that's strange, it's the hospital. Yes, this is Faith Elizabeth." Eric watched as Faith's facial appearance went from

148

stunned to utter shock as her eyes widens and moves about her forehead.

"But that's not possible. Yes, sure, no problem. Okay then, bye." As she hung up, Hank noticed that something might have changed. He hesitated to join them but did.

"What's new...?"

"I can't believe it. He's up, he's alive. Patrol George woke up in the morgue and they phoned me because he had me listed as his emergency contact," she laughed.

"What!" Both Hank and Eric said simultaneously.

"They said that he was calling all those stiffs' drunk sons of bitches!" Faith repeated covering her mouth as Liz joined them.

"Oh, and by the way he needs a ride from the hospital and personally requested that we bring him a stiff drink," she rolled.

Liz watched as George request another dish to be passed his way, as he devoured every last bite and she smiled. Her home has become a sanctuary for family and close friends. For the first time in years, she felt complete. It was also a time of great loss, yet the beauty of such an event brought tears of sadness and joy. She remembers that it was also the anniversary of the death of her beloved husband Jack. Unseen by her guests, she lit a lavender candle on the kitchen counter as tears rolled down her cheeks. The soft candlelight caused her tearful eyes to sparkle. She took that moment and retreated to her suite. The soft trickling of water from the tiny fountain nearby and her CD playing her favorite classic submerged her overwhelming emotion, to contentment and rest. As she dozed off, she dreamt that she was trying to catch a happy adorable baby girl who ran around in circles, then she ran through silky white curtains that shifted about by a soft ocean breeze. She followed her through the curtains and saw her run into Faith's arms, who picked her up and kissed her face lovingly. Her senses were awakened, and the dream felt as though it was real life. She wanted to reach out and take this beautiful child into her arms, yet an invisible force prevented such contact as an unseen curtain. Yet as they embraced, the child looked upon her with such admiration, that one's love cannot help but to be kindled by the joy that exists within.

Faith tossed and turned throughout the night. It was almost five am and she hardly slept a wink. Finally annoyed, she went into the kitchen and filled the tea kettle with water. As she waited, soft dragging footsteps approached, caught her attention.

"Are you feeling okay?" Hank asked rubbing his eyes. "It's okay darling, I need a minute…The kettle started to whistle loudly.

"What is that?" called the sleepy, half-dressed New Yorker.

"Want to join me for tea? There's enough for two," she said hoping he'll refuse.

"What kind of tea is it?"

"Cinnamon," she said, stirring her cup.

"Smells good, sure why not," he replied feeling a bit disconnected from her since their escape from Sandy Island.

"I still can't believe any of it. It feels like I am part of a dream and I'm waiting to get up. It seems that I'm visiting with Elizabeth and I'll be home in the morning," he said sipping on his tea.

"Cinnamon huh, pretty good," he admitted.

"The only cup that tastes better are your lips," he teased leaning forward and kissing her tenderly. Hardly able to resist, she placed her cup down and embraced the moment.

Chapter 18

"George, you're welcome to stay as long as you like dear," Liz called placing more bacon and harsh browns on his plate.

"Thank you, Elizabeth! You are quite the host," he admitted crunching on his meal and winking an eye at her. She smiled and turned to hide a blush that rushed to her face.

"George, I forgot to mention that we found Becca."

"Becca, you mean, you found Becca, my horse. You mean, wait a minute, you guys are the ones that saved my life?"

"Yes sir," Hank joked joining them this time fully dressed. Everyone laughed at his coy sense of humor.

"Hey, you guys up for a little adventure?" Eric asked.

"Hmm, what kind of adventure?"

"Well, if you're ready. I heard you arguing couple nights ago." Faith laughed at the strange conversation between Hank and Eric. It was odd seeing them get along so well. For some reason it seems like an invisible force had brought them all together.

"You all saved my life! I can't believe that you're just telling me this…"

Don't worry man, you were really heavy to lift…I promise, it's the last time I save you man, never again," Hank joked. George got up and embraced Hank so tightly, that he was almost out of breath when he released him.

"Where are you going dad?" Kat asked.

"Take a look at this sweetheart," Eric said pointing at the news as everyone turned to face the television.

"That's great! The roads to Sandy Island are open!" Elizabeth said excitedly. The memory of what they had lost, refreshed in their memories and they all slowly walked away from the kitchen.

"Wait a minute; you guys aren't up for that little adventure anymore? I'm in," Calvin, said joining the group.

"Come on guys, I insist!"

"We must face it at some point!"

"You're right Eric, but we're not going to do this today. We need time."

"I agree with Hank. Eric, this is their loss, not yours. Last time I checked, you were out of the picture," Calvin scolded.

"Shut up! Shut up Calvin, I already told you to stay out of my family's business!" Eric said leaving.

"Stop it Calvin, this isn't the time for this," Faith said hurrying after Eric.

"Eric, wait please don't leave, Katherine needs you," she pleaded. Eric paused.

"How are you?"

"How are you holding up…?" he asked in a hesitant voice. Faith noticed a look of sadness in his eyes and she almost wanted to embrace him.

"I'm not sure I've really faced it.," she said tears rushing to her eyes. Eric looked around, then embraced Faith.

"Faith I'm so sorry, I'm sorry for what I've put you through. I love you." Faith looked at him surprised and he released her.

"Okay, thank you," she said and hurried back inside.

"Mom, are you okay?" Katherine asked, noticing that familiar look on her face.

"Sure *baby, mommy's great,"* she said trying to avoid eye contact with her smart defying daughter as she retreated into the hallway bathroom, locking the door behind her.

"Mom, I know that look. Ah ha, spit it out mom, who kissed my beautiful mom? Who kissed her?" She shouted. Hank walked into the room and overheard.

"Well, last time I checked, I'm the one that kissed your beautiful mom.

"Hmm, well it's not the first time, so why does mommy look so surprised?"

"Great question," Hank thought.

"Honey, is everything okay?"

"Sure, I'll be right out," Faith called in a muffled voice, blowing her nose loudly. Hank waited by the bathroom door arms folded, tapping his feet and humming a little tune.

"Honey, can I come in? Please baby…" he pleaded. She didn't respond. She was feeling confused and had no idea where her life was headed. She tossed another tear drenched tissue into the trash and looked in the mirror. Her face pink from being over wiped and her large green eyes looked terrified and confused. When she finally opened the door, Hank was still standing there.

"Hi there!" he said cheerfully. But she was in no mood.

"Baby, I love you, please tell me what's going on." unable to find the words, she submerged to tears.

"Oh baby," he said kissing her face. He lifted her up and carried her to their room.

"Here, here, you don't have to say a word…I'm right here baby, right here madly in love with you. Take all the time you need hunny." He got into bed and wrapped his arms around her. She opened her pretty large eyes and looked at him. He kisses her forehead. She began to gently remove his shirt. He smiled and a look of doubt appeared in his eyes.

"What?" she asked.

"This feels different. I mean, I miss our bed," he admitted. She smiled broadly. She brushed her hands over his toned abs.

"You're so hot, Hank Hutton. You look like something straight from Soap television."

"Soaps, you mean the shows my mom used to watch. No way," he laughed. As he catches his breath he was met by Faith's soft lips. He pulled her close to him. Tears stream down her face as the bittersweet thoughts of uncertainty and pleasure; rearrange the unspoken words of lost perception.

The sound of George's voice caught Faith's attention as the sunrise peeking through the partially opened window, causes her eyes to squint. She crept out of bed and went to the window overlooking the grassy backyard. George was patting the horse's face lovingly and hugging her in appreciation. She looks as he stared downhill at the sloping landscape preceding Liz's hillside mansion. The hills continued for miles, beneath thousands of Marina style homes that appears to dominate the tireless twisting route that led to Sandy Bay.

"You see that girl, see that. This hill takes us to the bay. Let's go find your siblings," he said and climbed onto the horse. Faith was amazed by how much Becca had grown in the three months since her visit. She watched as they continued downhill until they disappeared beneath the Victorian homes and the sun rose gracefully over the distant horizon.

"Good morning beautiful," Hank said yarning loudly.

"Good Morning darling, guess what? There's a trail back there that can take us all the way to Sandy Island," she said opening the curtain. Hank squinted his eyes from the brightness of the sun coming through their window.

"Look at you, come, let's get out of bed, we are going for a little walk," she said throwing him a pair of Eric's pants and shirt.

"What, no baby, I can't. This is nuts, and it's way too far," he said with a yarn.

"Honey, I think it's time we sit down and go over our options. I mean, this is a huge deal, we can't avoid it forever."

"And you're right honey, but not today."

"Yes, today baby, we must."

"And besides, you can rebuild your house any day, you just made a movie deal, Hank Hutton, so what's the sweat about."

"Well, to be honest, I was unprepared for the fire. I did not have sufficient insurance." he admitted, his voice fading. Faith ran her fingers through her hair. Then she looks at him defiantly.

"What!"

"Well, I just barely moved there less than a year ago and I thought I had time…" Faith still couldn't believe it. She almost laughed but didn't at the boyish look on his face as though he was being scolded by his Ex.

"Well luckily, you have options and you still have your Manhattan condo. Thank goodness you didn't sell it," she said trying to cheer him up.

"That's good right?"

"Yes, it is, but my movie won't be release for another few months and in the meantime, the condo is my only option for now. It's wonderful of your mother in law to have me, but I know that I cannot stay here forever. If I want my own place right now, I will have to move back to Manhattan."

"Is this necessary. Hank, I love you, and my family is all here. I'm not ready for this move," she said laughing nervously.

"See that's why I didn't want to discuss it," she said turning to leave.

154

"I mean what about you. You don't have another place right now, unless you plan on staying here...what other plans can you think of now? I mean you can come with me to New York, at least we'll have our own place and privacy...and the girls can make up...and...." His voice faded and Faith just stared at him with no words. He didn't seem to get it. Her life was just slowly coming back together after the divorce and now this...she feels that all the progress she has made had disappeared without a trace.

"Still up for that walk honey?"

"I think it's a great idea," he said getting dressed. Faith peeked through Liz's bedroom door and her and Katherine was still fast asleep. Before leaving, Hank left a note for Liz on the refrigerator.

The sound of her handset caused Liz to stir. She reached to answer it and almost rolled over tiny Katherine almost buried under her soft pink blankets and linen. She reached for the handset a second time and answered with a sleepy...

"Yes hello, this is Liz. Who? The Senator's office? Really? Pardon my manners, but what can I do you for darling?" It was the Senator's assistant and she spoke urgently...

"The Senator would love the opportunity to speak with Faith?" Said a young female voice on the other line.

"Oh, absolutely, yes just a minute." Liz hurried down the hall calling Faith at the top of her lungs. Then after several knocks she opens Faith's bedroom door to a creek. Noticing they were gone she lifted the handset nervously to her ear.

"I do apologize but Faith is not home at the moment, would you please give me one hour to find her and I'll be certain that she's available if you try her again in exactly one hour."

"Are you certain that she would be available because this is quite urgent? And I need clearance and confirmation for each outbound call made from this office."

Absolutely, you have my word," Liz replied.

Liz got dressed and tickled her granddaughter to wake her.

"Come honey, we must to hurry."

"Hurry, where to Grandma Liz?" Both still in their PJ's hurrying toward the garage. Moments later Liz joined the sparse traffic headed to Sandy Island.

"I hope that's where they are, and I know she went on foot because there were no cars missing from the garage. Elizabeth drove

155

pass hundreds of apparently displaced residents who were taking photos of what was left of their once beautiful lives.

"Grandma who are all these people and why does everything look brown and charred?"

"It's alright sweetheart, grandma Liz will explain later, we have to find your mommy and I hope that's where she went."

"But Grandma, I heard that nice doctor said that you aren't supposed to be driving," the cute sandy blond said looking at Liz with narrowed eyes.

This time she ignored her.

"Grandmother, I would not be ignored," she demanded.

"It's okay darling, I know it's time for your breakfast."

"No Grandma, you're avoiding my question. I know what you mean. You are saying that I am being grumpy because I've not eaten my breakfast yet." As Liz drives through the deserted Island, she heard horses neighing playfully near the surf. Then playful giggles followed.

"This sounds like mommy," said Kat.

"Sure does," she said, pulling up near the surf.

"Wow, oh my goodness," she said looking around astonished. Then remembering why, she was there…she looked and saw Faith, Hank and Patrol George trying to round up the horses.

"Looks like George found his missing horses," Said Kat following her Grandma.

"FAITH, FAITH darling…"

"MOMMY, Mr. Senator wants to speak with you mommy," Katherine's tiny voice cut through the roaring sound of the ocean and horses combined, reaching her mother's ear. Faith looked around startled and came hurrying toward them.

"Oh my God, sweetheart, Liz, what are you guys doing here?"

"Thank goodness," Liz said looking at the time on her watch.

"A very urgent call came for you from the Senator's office."

"The Senator? You mean…yes apparently."

"You poor guys," Faith said looking at both of them in their PJ's. Hank came hurrying after Faith.

"What's going on?"

"It's okay babe, you can stay and help George with the horses. I have an important call, from the Senator's office…"

"Really?"

"Yes, I'll be right back."

"Okay, I love babe," he said kissing her on the lips.

"Here you go honey, you drive," Said Liz, tossing the keys to Faith.

"Wow, I mean, this is unexpected. I wonder what it is about." She said, pulling into the garage. Five minutes after they arrive, the phone rang, and Faith answered.

"Yes, this is Faith French, what can I do for you?"

Hank and George harnessed all seven horses and took the wooded trail that led to Liz's place in the Marina. Exhausted, Hank looked at George and laughed.

"George, you didn't even break a sweat...You're really strong for a dead guy!" he joked. George laughed uncontrollably at Hank's candid sense of humor.

"Kid, you're a trip. I like you. How long have you been seeing Faith?" Little over six months."

"And you didn't pop the question yet. I'm telling you, she's a catch. Probably the most beautiful woman you've seen around here. I wouldn't waste time."

"Is that a warning?"

"Better believe it, I'll take her for myself," George joked. Hank laughed almost believing the stern mysterious Patrolman. As they led the horses through the trails, a distant look came over George's face. It was obvious that there were other things troubling him and Hank wondered. It could be a million things including the obvious, yet he respected his silence. He wanted to ask George about possible relatives but didn't.

"So, what are your plans for Sandy Girl...?"

"Well, I was thinking of rebuilding the ranch, exactly the way it was. I'm very fortunate that all the horses made it. It's definitely a sign. I think you are right..."

"What are your plans?"

"Not sure, I might have to wait a while before making any plans."

"All of my assets are tied up. I heard you have a nice little apartment in Manhattan, you can get a pretty penny for that, probably take care of most of your rebuilding cost."

"Yes, Faith had mentioned the same thing but I'm still not sure if Sandy Island has the magic that first brought me here...I'm feeling a bit unsure about a few things," He admitted... glancing at the

157

bareness and charred remains of what he thought would be a new beginning for him and Sydney.

"Well, you can't give up now, you're much too young," George said staunchly. He wondered if Hank's uncertainty also included Faith and he grew concerned for her and Katherine.

Liz dove headfirst into her closet and pulled out another outfit, holding it up without looking and Faith refused for the twentieth time. She laughed at her mother-in-law's attempt to have her properly dressed for her appointment with the Senator later today.

"You were a total little hottie, Liz. Look how skinny these pants are and these all look like they used to belong to a supermodel. They will never fit," she laughed. Then something caught her eye. A gorgeous white Jacket with black and gold trim along with matching black pants. Both swinging on a hanger as Liz continued to shuffle through her large untidy wardrobe.

"What's this?" she said pointing.

"Oh that old thing...yes, it has a certain class about it," Faith said stepping stylishly in her pink bathrobe and hair still wrapped in a towel.

"Wow, this old thing is a Liz Claiborne suit," she said peeking at the collar.

"I think I found the one," she called hurrying into the bathroom to try it on as Liz stared at her surprised but curious.

"Is there a wide brim hat that goes with this darling outfit," she asked from the bathroom.

"Yes, but I never wore it with a hat!" Liz replied.

"But is there one?" Faith insists. Liz searched the shelves and noticed a shiny, circular gold brim hat peeking out amongst hundreds of other hats. Faith stepped out from the bathroom and exhaled a sigh of relief...she looked in the mirror and whistled loudly.

"Wow, Liz, this is it, our search is over. This is the suit that could win me the presidency," she joked. Liz reached for the hat on the crowded upper shelf and found herself tumbling and was instantly buried as hundreds of hats and purses fell on top of her.

"Ouch!" she screamed.

"Oh it's about time I clean out that stupid closet," she fretted. Faith peeked at Liz and noticing her feet sticking out from under the pile, she wasn't sure if to help her or laugh.

"Liz darling, are you okay?" she asked, holding back a chuckle. Liz sat up quickly and sneezed, still clutching onto the hat to Faith's outfit.

"Ahh you found it," she said, taking the hat from Liz's outstretched arm.

"Knock yourself out kid, you look great. I had my doubts, but you look fantastic."

"Thanks mom, I love you," she said hugging her tightly.

"Okay baby, I don't want to get dirt on your outfit," Liz said, releasing her.

"Liz, I still can't believe that these used to fit you."

"Well, when you get back from your appointment, I'll take you down memory lane…. I have lots of stories and tons of photos too."

Faith smiled as she placed the gorgeous hat on her head and leaned it to one side. Liz smiled pleasingly at the sight of her daughter-in-law.

"That's it Hun. I never wore the hat, but you are a fine woman, Faith…and today, you are my masterpiece, ready to take on the world," she smiled pleasingly.

An hour later, Hank kissed the finest woman he'd ever seen as she stepped gracefully into a stretch Limo en route to the Senator's Estate for a private meeting with Senator Floyd Henley. She felt a bit uneasy and unprepared as they neared the Senator's home. The Chauffeur lowered his divider and reminded her of the chocolate and champagne he had brought her.

"Thank you, I really do appreciate it," she said. As his divider began to close, she hesitated, but quickly asked the chauffeur if he knew what the meeting was about. But he only winked at her and smiled. Nervous Faith popped open the champagne and poured herself a full glass. She downed the flute in one shot and poured another. After her fifth glass, Faith placed the cover back onto the almost empty bottle.

"Madam French, you have arrived," the chauffeur called as the doors glided to an open.

"Oh boy," she said nervously as a small burp traveled slowly up her throat. She was feeling sociable at best. She stepped out onto soft grass.

"Are you the Queen of Sandy Island," asked a young boy no older than twelve looking down at Faith from the upper balcony.

"Hi there," Faith waved at him, still tickled by his question.

"Hello Tommy," the Chauffeur called.

"Madam French, please follow me," he said leading the way to the entrance.

"Well this certainly is a lovely Estate," she exhaled nervously. Then chatting and conversations could be heard as the door opened and Senator Henley hurried toward Faith, excited to greet her.

"It's an absolute pleasure to meet you, Senator."

"The pleasure is all mine Mrs. French."

"It's now Ms. Winter, as I'm recently divorced from Eric French."

"I see, certainly Ms. Winter," he smiled looking at her from head to toe.

"I'm certainly pleased that you could come on such short notice."

"Absolutely, I understand that the matter is quite urgent."

"Very much indeed," he agreed, leading the way to a private office overlooking a gorgeous landscaped garden in full bloom. Faith felt embarrassed as she was feeling drowsy.

"I'm sure your question remains constant; why did I request your presence, and of all the people in Sandy Island, why you, of course?"

"Certainly, it's like you read my mind completely," she smiled warmly.

"I promise to keep it short and to the point. Ms. Winter," he smiled. Before the recent devastating fires that tore through Sandy Island: Sandy Bay, as we have called her for years was an extension of San Francisco. Recent legislation was passed to consider the small Island a separate entity. As the first and longest standing resident of Sandy Island, you were selected to fill the position of Senator of Sandy Island. Due to the current state of the Island, the people of San Francisco agreed that an upstanding citizen should be handpicked to represent the Island and govern the affairs thereof with the full support from the city of San Francisco," he said pausing to take a sip of water from a glass nearby.

Did he say Senator of Sandy Island? Maybe I'm not hearing correctly...Are you there with me," he asked resuming.

"Did you say Senator of Sandy Island?"

"Yes, certainly."

Faith removed her hat and began to fan herself as a sudden shot of warmth caused moisture to appear on her face. As she processed the Senator's words, there was a soft knock on the door.

"Yes it's open."

"Dad, it's me Tommy."

"Yes Tommy, what can I do for you?"

"I was wondering if Ms. Faith would join us for dinner. I also brought her a glass of lemonade," he said carrying the glass carefully on a tray.

"How wonderful, you are an amazing little host Tommy," she said proudly reaching for the glass and glancing disapprovingly at the Senator. He smiled at her charm.

"Thank you, Tommy, daddy will be with you shortly."

"But, but, dad," he fretted as he shut the door behind him.

"Okay where were we...Are you saying that I don't even get to think about this?"

"Certainly and that's what I was about to discuss. Due to the current state of Sandy, you have thirty calendar days to decide if this is for you."

"But have you thought about my qualifications in terms of whether I could manage a position like this."

"You are the daughter of a well-known Senator in Germany. Isn't Senator Rickford Winter your father?"

"How did you know that?"

"Well, my staff has done our homework."

"You certainly have. Well, it's the very reason I left Germany, because the spotlight has never been of interest to me. I really thought that I had left all that politics behind."

"Why do I get the feeling that you're upset with me...?" he said and spun around in his office chair.

"Well, the last time I tried doing anything for myself, I was in the process of opening a humble little Air-Bay-and-B," she said walking around the room, her hands tucked into her pockets. Not trying to take over the world." He laughs at her unexpected sense of humor. As he continued to encourage her, he couldn't help but notice her striking appearance.

"Well, I think you're perfect for the position and I hope that you'll consider it," he said in a formal tone.

"The twenty thousand displaced residents of Sandy Island await your time sensitive decision, for such a time as this. Is this the reason Tommy referred to me as the Queen of Sandy Island?"

161

"He's quite the optimist and must have secretly attended one of my meetings. Since his mother passed, he accompanies me often."

"You're a wonderful father and you might very well be grooming a future candidate," she replied. Henley smiled and raised his eyebrows in agreement.

Chapter 19

"Thirty days? That's it! You have to call him back and tell him, no way. Sounds like a lazy son-of-a-bitch trying to pawn his work off on you in a not so subtle classy kind of way! Tell me you're not considering this?" Faith didn't respond. She sat quietly watching Hank huff and puff back and forth and finally attempts to toss an empty soda can out the window, landing only a few feet away.

"So thirty days huh?"

"Yes babe, thirty days."

"You know, a lot can be done in thirty days," he said on a more positive note.

"I think you need somewhere, quiet, where you can think. Somewhere, you can forget about everyone and everything else. I'm sure you need time to make a fair decision. What do you say?"

"So what do you have in mind?"

"It's a little bit of a drive and I prefer it over Lake Tahoe…Ever heard of Big Bear Lake?"

"I might have heard it somewhere or may have come across it when I was doing research for the Air-Bay-and B. So, not really."

"babe, I feel like picking on you. You've sheltered yourself from the world. I am going to have to steal you away and take you to the Wild." He was now much calmer and imitates a Bear when he said 'wild.

"So what do you say?" She thought he was kidding, but that familiar look tells her that he really wanted her to leave town with him…She laughs…

"Okay, I'll let you know in the morning." She says and as she turns to leave, she bumped into Liz, smiling ear to ear and in a very celebratory mood, carrying a bottle of Champagne and a microphone.

"I had no doubt sweetheart. You made Senator. I knew it!" She poured her and Hank a round of champagne then attempting to reach the entire neighborhood. She stood on a lounge chair and lifted the microphone to her mouth.

"My daughter is now Senator. Therefore, Elizabeth French is now your second in command! This also means no tickets for me, regardless of my exquisite wine collection! You donut stuffing rascals! Oh my goodness, darling, I knew at some point that someone would see this beautiful young lady for what she's worth. Sweetheart, you made me so proud," she beamed, embracing Faith with the strength of a boxing champion.

Now responsible for the direction of every legal event on the small Island, Faith realizes that Hank may have a valid point. Her only escape for the rest of the evening was her very wise seven-year-old daughter.

"Katherine, mommy need you darling."

"Yes mommy," the tiny angel came running and jumps right into her mother's arms as they embraced tightly.

"What is it mommy. Is it about your big job? Mommy, did the President get fired, is that why you got his job?"

"Well sweetheart, that would be great, but not quite."

"Well mommy, what about what Uncle Hank said? He said we should go up to Big Bear. I heard you guys talking about it earlier."

"You sneaky little cutie."

"Well mommy, I couldn't help it, you guys were standing under my window," she chuckles. Her mom kisses her face. A few hours later, mother and daughter, exhausted from a long day, fell fast asleep, snoring small and large Z's as night clouds and stars danced around the ceiling.

Chapter 20

Fain yawned and stirred to a wake, digging his hands under his pillow to grab his favorite Roku remote control. It's been weeks since he's spoken to his friends in Sandy Island since the fire and he turned on the news in the hopes of an update. He knew it was the reason they hadn't shown up to his movie premiere but didn't think it was sufficient. He's been a fantastic friend and employee, and none the less, two weeks after the horrible fire was sufficient time to think of him. It's been almost three months since he last saw Faith and Katherine and he couldn't shake that feeling. He was doing surprisingly well for someone that had just entered the Entertainment Industry. Yet, the attention of millions of new fans and one-night relations could not satisfy his longing for the only thing he's always wanted. As he stared at two strange women laying in his bed, he was distracted by Sandy Island breaking news update.

Tons of reporters were on the scene at Elizabeth's Marina home in the hopes of obtaining an update from Faith.

"Ma'am it's been twenty-four hours since your election, have you made a decision?"

"Any plans on the displaced families and children. Are any arrangements being made to employ and relocate the displaced Teachers and students from Sandy Island?"

"Please be respectful, it's only been a day since her election, you are terrifying her," Hank Said and escort Elizabeth and Faith inside shutting the door behind them.

"Wow, Faith was made Sandy Bay Senator?" He says getting out of bed.

"Hey, wake up! I'll make you ladies some breakfast, and then I'll call you a cab!"

"No thanks you Jerk!" One of the women called and hurried to the bathroom. The other got dressed in front of him.

"Hey Vik, you coming?" she called. A few moments later, both women flipped him off and left his Beverly Hills Apartment. He was now used to the Hollywood night life and nothing hardly surprises him anymore. Both his Twitter and Instagram pages had over two million followers since his movie debut and he had to hire professionals to manage his growing popularity. Having moved five times in the last three months due to crazed fans and ticked off girlfriends, he missed his quiet life in the Bay and wished he could find a way back. But this was no longer an option. It was a faded dream engulfed by fire and tainted feelings of the past from what he now considers norm. Kate had written another script and had already cast actors for her newest production, this time excluding him all together. She made him a celebrity and she was hardly pleased with his growing popularity. He was disappointed in her the fact that she was hardly appreciative of the role he played that influenced the film's positive ratings. Having lost a second employer in less than two years, he was not prepared to start a different career. He loved acting and he was going to stick to it. He's positive that his performance in his last role would pave the way to his Hollywood career as proven by the hundreds of messages from producers on his voicemail.

He's never been a big fan of the news, but Fain was glued to the television since the news of Faith's random election as Sand Bay's prospective Senator. He knows better than anyone that she needed to be around someone who would support her. She's brilliant, yet without positive support, she would easily fade into a world that he was only too familiar with. He packed a bag and began a seven-hour trip to San Francisco. He plans to call her when he gets within an hour of the city. As he drove, he thought of ways in which he would provide support in the event she rehires him as her assistant. With only a French high school diploma, he felt very underprepared, even ridiculous, thinking that he would be a prime candidate in comparison to the hundreds of others that would be vying to be her assistant. Placing all doubts aside, he drove nonstop for what seemed like hours and pulled off the freeway to nap.

What seemed like a moment later, Fain awoke to a blinding light. Panicked, he sat up quickly.

"Is everything alright sir?" a highway patrol asked, shining a bright light around his vehicle.

"Yes sir, everything's fine. I've been driving from Los Angeles the past few hours-just stopped for a quick nap." Noticing Fain's

166

accent, the officer asked Fain for his immigration documents. Fain didn't like where this was headed, and he told the officer that he was here on an employment visa and that it was still current.

"Do you have this document with you?"

"Well, sir, I didn't think that it was important to bring it along with me."

"Well, young man, I will have to ask you to follow me back to the station to verify your legal presence in the US."

"Sir this is completely unnecessary. I'm just heading to San Francisco to see a friend."

"Sir, I will have to ask you to step out of the vehicle. If you corporate, I will not put cuffs on you," the officer said staunchly.

"I can't believe this," Fain fretted and followed the officer to his parked vehicle and before he could collect his thoughts, he was seating comfortably in the back of a squad car being transported to God knows where. He knew that his employment visa was expired over six months ago and had asked Kate his employer to help him renew it. She said that she would, but she never followed up with him about it so he had no idea what would happen to him. He was now wishing that he had drove off and avoided the officer altogether. He doubted that his brand-new Jaguar F Convertible, left on the side of the road would be there when he returns.

The officer pulled up in front of Santa Cruz police department. Still unsure what to expect, the officer let him out of the vehicle and led him into the building. Please have a seat and this young lady, will have a few questions for you in a few minutes," he said referring to an attractive female officer shuffling papers at her desk.

"Bob, what's he in for?" she asked staring at fain suspiciously.

"He's possibly undocumented. Do a quick search to verify his visa. He's supposedly here on an employment visa," he responded.

"So where are you from?" She asked appearing a bit softer. He was pissed off and wanted to tell her off but responded under his breath.

"France."

"France huh? So what's your name and how long have you been in the US?" she asked taking notes.

"The name Fain Collins, been here eighteen months." He was growing fed up of the questions, some of which he swore was completely irrelevant. A little over an hour later the officer took his answers and entered them into the system. Fain had no idea what the officer would find, so he thought of making a run for it but noticed the highway patrol officer was staring at him from across the room. The Officer running a check on him started glancing at him repeatedly and he knew it was not good. He was nervous and assumed the worst. After what seemed like hours, she printed out some documents and took it to the Officer who he now realizes is her lead. They were both speaking under their breaths and he could not hear what they were saying. Both officers approached him, and as he attempts to stand.

"Please remain seated sir," the highway patrol growled.

"Sir, do you have a more recent work visa-because what I have here is an employment visa that's been expired over six months ago?"

"What! That's not possible. I mean I just got finished with a major production and my manager said that she would take care of extending my visa."

"Well, unfortunately, it does not appear that she did. There's no new application in the system so we're going to have to keep you here overnight. Just until we verify with immigration on your legal status."

"What! This is crazy. You can't do this!"

"Yes we can," the officer said placing Fain's hand behind his back and placing him in a cell next to a large tattooed male.

"C'mon, this is ridiculous. What's your problem?" he yelled. You know, if anything happens to my car, I will personally sue this department."

"Sir, your car has been placed in impound to ensure its safety. You will be able to regain procession as soon as you are cleared."

"Cleared? What's that supposed to mean? Do you even know who I am?" The officers as well as his cellmates laughed at him.

"Buddy, I arrest Celebrities every single day. You guys are my favorite. By the way, you will have to pay fees to collect your vehicle, if you get out of here soon enough, by the way, you're being billed by the hour."

"This is nuts. You hear me!! This is crazy!" he yelled.

"Hey kid, come here. He hesitated but approached a woman dressed like a lady of the night. She whispered…

"Did you get your phone call?"

"My phone call?"

"Yes, you're entitled to one phone call to a friend or family member who could help you get outta here."

"Really?"

"Yes kid," she replied softly.

"Hey, hey no touching," the officer who brought him in called.

"Hey? No hey you, you forgot something."

"What's that?" he replied sharply.

"You forgot my phone call, dipshit," said a more pissed off Fain. I would watch my mouth if I were you. And free phone calls are only for Citizens of the United States," he sneered.

"That's a crack of shit," the woman called.

"Give the kid his call," the cellmates said together. The Santa Cruz PD was interrupted by arguing and noises until the officers gave Fain his one phone call.

"I need my phone, the number I need is on that phone. I don't have it memorized," Fain said feeling embarrassed.

"Buddy, you have one shot to make your call, take it or leave it!" the Patrol man called.

"Here you go, make it quick," the officer who took his questions said handing him his cell phone. Fain scrolled through his phone and found Elizabeth's phone number. He dialed the number and handed the cell phone back to the officer. It was already after one am in the morning and the line rang for a while. Just as the officer was about to interrupt him, Katherine answered.

"Hello, this is Elizabeth French's home, how may I help you," she said sleepily.

"Kat, this is your BFF Fain, I need a huge favor," he pleaded.

"You're not my BFF anymore, you moved, remember?"

"Okay sweetheart, yes I did, but can you go get your mommy for me?"

"She's asleep," Katherine said yawning. Just as Katherine was about to hang up, Faith overheard her and came into the kitchen where she stood holding the phone up to her ear.

"Who is it sweetie? Mommy its Fain and he wants to be my BFF and I can't because Sydney is now my Bff. Good bye Fain," she said and hung up.

"Fain? Was that Fain?"

"Yes!" she said and stormed off. Confused why Fain was calling so late, Faith looked at the handset and noticed that the call came in from the Santa Cruz Police department near Seaside.

"That's it buddy, one call that's all you're allowed," the officer said removing the phone from his hand and placing it back on the handset.

"This doesn't count. Isn't there a rule about the age of the person who answers?" he asked looking at the woman in the cell next to his. The woman nods no.

"Sir, that's it, please return to your cell," the officer said sternly. The only other chance is if someone calls you back," the woman called. Just as she said that the phone rang. The officer answered. Surprised, she handed the phone to Fain.

"You must be the luckiest kid alive," the woman called and everyone was now smiling at Fain's struck of luck.

"Fain, why are you calling me from the Santa Cruz PD?"

"Long story," he responded, relieved to have gotten her on the phone.

"It's something to do with immigration," he fretted. Faith knew immediately what was happening and she knew that she would have to do the two-hour commute to Santa Cruz in order for Fain to be released from Police custody.

"Fain, it'll take me a couple of hours, I'll be right there," she said hanging up.

"Faith, are you coming?" but the line beeped loudly.

Faith woke Liz and told her what had happened.

"Here, please take the keys to the Lamborghini and go get him out of there. We both know he would be on a flight back to France by morning if we don't get him out of there tonight," Liz said. A few moments later, Faith was on the freeway speeding toward Santa Cruz, fearing that they might transfer him out before she arrives. She felt partially responsible for what had happened to Fain. She thought that if she had renewed his work visa, he would not have been in this situation. Coming from Germany, she is all too familiar with US immigration laws. She was prepared to expedite a visa renewal for him; her only hoped is that it was not too late.

It was already three am when she arrived in Santa Cruz. Her mobile GPS directions was on the dot. She parked in front of the PD and hurried inside.

"How may I help you?"

"I received a call from my employee. What do I need to do to get him out of here? It's really my fault. I completely forgot to renew his employment visa," she said brushing her hair with her fingers, trying to appear calm.

"Well, Ma'am, you'll have to fill out some paperwork. If you intend to renew his work visa, you will have to do so before we can release him from custody."

"But it's after three a.m., I don't think it's necessary for him to remain here overnight."

"Ma'am, as you're aware, USCIS is not open until 8:00am. He will have to wait here."

"This is ridiculous; you mean my presence here serves no purpose?"

"I'm afraid so Ma'am."

"Can I speak with him?" Faith asked.

"Sure, please follow me," she said leading the way toward the back of the station. Fain was lying on the cold leather seat and at the sight of Faith, he stood up quickly.

"Faith, what are you doing here?" he said feeling embarrassed. He reached through the bars and embraced her.

"Please no touching," the Patrol Man who had fallen asleep said waking.

"I'll renew your visa. There's an office not too far from here," she said. Fain continues to apologize to Faith.

"No, it's alright Fain. I'll get a hotel room, and, in the morning, I'll go take care of the paperwork, okay," she said smiling at him encouragingly. After thanking Faith and apologizing for the fiftieth time, Faith drove to the Hilton. She set her alarm for 7:30 am and flopped exhausted onto the bed and fell asleep.

Faith was at the USCIS office right at 7:45am and there were only a handful of cars in the parking lot. A feeling of fear shivered through her. She hoped that everything goes well for Fain to be released from custody. It was terrible seeing him behind those awful bars, over a simple immigration flaw. The doors opened right at 8:00am and she hurried to the lobby and approached a friendly Security Officer.

"Good morning, which department processes Visas?"

171

"Sure, all Visas are processed on the 3rd floor." he said politely and showed her to the elevator.

"Thank you!" she said feeling less nervous by the friendly encounter. She was first to arrive in the waiting area and took a seat. Less than a few minutes later the room was almost filled, and two bright red zeros appeared on the computer. Immigration officers took their places behind individual window stalls respectively and the numbers 01 appeared on the computer. Slightly confused, she looked around and realized that she needed to print a number from the kiosk when she first arrived. She now realized that she was at the very end of the line and it would take several hours to complete Fain's Visa request. As she walked to the kiosk...

"Ma'am, ma'am," she heard on the intercom. She turned around startled that the entire room was staring at her.

"Me?" she signaled with her hands.

"Yes, please come to window four," a friendly voice called. Soft murmuring could be heard as she walked pass the center Isle.

"Isn't this Faith French, Sandy Island Senator?" she heard someone whispered. She approached the open window and took a sit.

"Madam, Senator, French, how may I assist you today?"

"I noticed that you were here before everyone else and was surprised when the first number was called and someone else answered." Faith laughed nervously.

"Yes I'm not very familiar with the process and missed my chance to grab a number when I first arrived."

"Well, you're in luck because I noticed," the woman smiled warmly.

"How can I help you today?" Faith explained the situation regarding her employee and as she spoke the immigration officer's eyes widened and she placed several forms in front of Faith.

"My apologies," she said empathically. You will have to sign this form for Fain's immediate release, because he will have to be present in order to sign the documents to process his Visa extension. Faith was overjoyed that the process was quite simple.

"I have to admit, it was absolutely unnecessary for them to keep him at the station overnight since you, his employer showed up and explained the situation," the officer admitted.

"That's exactly what I thought. They're just a set of bullies," she fretted. A few minutes later, she shook the officer's hand.

"Once he's released, have Fain fill out this form and return it to this office before the end of the week. I have made an appointment for you both."

"Is it possible to come back in today? I'm not exactly from the area."

"Absolutely, I'll keep an eye out for you, so you don't have to take a number from the kiosk."

"You'll just have a seat and I'll call you once my desk is free."

"Thank you, Amy, you're a lifesaver," Faith said, shaking her hand enthusiastically.

Relieved by her struck of luck at USCIS, Faith headed over to the Santa Cruz PD. Feeling a bit more empowered with her release form, she stormed into the station and demanded Fain's release.

"Ma'am, you'll have to wait your turn," said a younger, very polite female officer. Noticing that the night shift had already left for the day, Faith handed her the form.

"Oh' I see. She has an immigration release for the gentleman," called the younger officer named Kim.

"Let's see," said another officer almost grabbing and reviewing the form.

"I'll be very careful with that if I were you. Remember, no one's above the law, not even you," Faith warned.

"Alright," the officer said handing the form back to Kim. She then stamped it and the grumpy officer released Fain.

"Oh, so you think that's all, where's my car?" he yelled.

"Fain, please try to stay calm," Faith reminded him.

"Your car is out back. Your immigration release covers everything in custody so there's no charge," Kim said, smiling at Fain.

"See, you lucky Jack," Faith said and chuckled at his pissed of demeanor.

When they finally left the station, Faith told him about his appointment with USCIS. He was less than thrilled.

"Well, you can be thankful for the little things," she reminded him.

"By the way, where were you headed? Aren't you a long way from Los Angeles?"

"Yes, I was coming to see you," he said leaning up against his car and folding his arms.

"Me, but why, shouldn't you be with your girlfriend? Or better your millions of fans?" There was that familiar look in his eyes and Faith didn't want to pry him for answers.

"Alright then, let's go take care of your Visa and we'll catch up later, okay," she said leading the way. Less than an hour later, as they leave USCIS, Fain embraced Faith tightly.

"I would kiss you, except..." She chuckled realizing what he was thinking. He kissed her on the cheek instead.

"Thank you," he finally said.

A few hours later they arrived in Marina Heights. Noticing them from the balcony, Liz came out to greet them.

"Wow, young man, I heard you were in a bit of trouble. Is everything okay now?"

"Yes, thank you ma'am," Fain said respectfully.

"Would it be okay if I be your guest for a few days?" he asked politely. A bit flattered by his mannerism Liz stared at him.

"You look starved, why don't we get you started on breakfast. Sounds great," Fain admitted.

"Great, I'll see you in the kitchen. Faith will show you to the guest quarters," she called.

"Wow, how hospitable of you? You're most welcome," she said leading the way toward the back of the building to a private guest room with a separate entry.

"The keys are under the flowerpot. I'll see you in a little while." As she turns to leave...

"Faith?"

"Yes? He wanted to tell her that he loves her and how much he's missed her but instead...

"Thank you." She could feel his stare as she walks away.

"Where's everyone?" asked an exhausted Faith, taking a seat at the table.

"Faith is he in any other trouble that you know off? Remember, your image is important."

"Fain was on his way up to see me and Katherine and pulled off the side of the road to rest. An officer approached him and before he knew what was happening, he was being asked questions he could not answer and got hauled off as an undocumented immigrant."

"Oh," Liz said hardly satisfied with Faith's answer.

"Do you think he still cares for you? How would Hank feel, having him around?" Liz questions made Faith realize that maybe Hank was right about leaving town for a few days.

"Lizzy, I'm not sure I have the answers."

"I see the way he looks at you..."

"Now's not the time Lizzy..."

"Alright, I'll leave you adults to figure out your own prerogatives."

"What smells great?" Fain asked joining them in the kitchen. Liz poured him coffee and placed a delicious breakfast in front of him.

"Wow, thank you," he said taking a seat at the table. Liz and Faith smiled as they watched him devour his breakfast as though he hadn't eaten a home cooked meal in forever. At long last, Fain burped loudly and kindly asked for seconds. Faith and Liz engulfed in laughter.

"Uncle Fain, ah ha, I knew you're planning on asking me to be in your next movie," Katherine said jumping into his arms.

"So, where's the script?" she asked letting herself down.

"Sweetheart, wow, look how much you've grown!" Fain said taking a step back.

"Well I don't have a boyfriend yet if that's what you're thinking. But I know you got dumped again, this time by that actress me and Syd really likes. Yes you got dumped by Brit. How'd you let that happen?" she asked scowling at him curiously.

"Wait a minute, how'd you know this?"

"On Celebrity Wats app...Me and Syd have an account on there?"

"You what?" asked an appalled Faith.

"Well they don't stay little," said Hank joining in.

"So tell us Kat, what else have you seen on Celebrity Wats app," Hank asked sitting down. Liz held back laughter, trying not appear to be entertained by her tiny gossip princess.

Chapter 21

Surrounded by all those who mattered on a rainy Saturday evening, in a room warmed by a fire, Faith announced her decision to accept her position as Senator of Sandy Island.

"My experience this weekend assisting Fain with a minor immigration issue. My love for Sandy Island and the eternal passion I feel for the home that I missed each day at Sunrise. The majestic tides that repaired my torn soul during the many months I felt lost. The sounds of summer laughter that echoed deep beneath the waves. The fresh air that greeted me each morning as I graced my balcony overlooking my faithful love. The new faces that added new meaning. The sound of Seagulls beaconing each morning, and the vision of sunrise cascading the horizon has prepared me for this moment. I did not choose this path, it chose me," she stated boldly.

"Hank, I'm sorry, I wanted to go away with you this weekend but I couldn't keep the people of Sandy Island waiting, they need me now," she said and hurries to Liz's study to phone Senator Henley with her decision.

"Faith, wait!" Hank said hurrying after her. "Are you sure that you don't need more time to think?"

"I'm sure Hank, the Island is a disaster. The residents cannot afford to wait. Besides, I really missed my home. I want it all back, in the exact location with the same view over the balcony, as though nothing had changed!" she said reduced to tears. Hank embraced her and Fain told Liz that he was going for a walk.

"Fain, can I come?" Katherine called.

"Sure sweetie," after putting on her tennis shoes, they were off.

News of Faith's decision to rise to the occasion for the people of Sandy Island made Nationwide headlines. The quiet little life that she once knew had long set sail beyond the seas as she prepared for a journey that only time will prove. She knows that there is no better time than the present to make a difference for the people who need her now more than ever.

Faith Scrambled through the hundreds of boxes in Liz's garage. Liz looked on at the mess that Faith had made and chuckled.

"Honey is there something I can help you find?" Faith lifted her hands holding up a pair of flippers and snorkel.

"Honey, I think you should confirm with the Senator first." Liz said taking a photo of Faith in the clutter.

"Says who?" Faith responded pulling herself up. I just sent him your photo holding onto the fins and snorkel and guess what? He's headed over. He should be here any minute," Liz laughed taking more photos of Faith standing in the rubble.

"Wait a minute, you mean, you don't mean what I think...."

"Liz, NO! You must call him off, no, no, no!"

"Yes, yes, yes way!" Liz replied. The doorbell rang and Liz hurried off to answer it.

"LIZ!" she called almost panicked. She tried to escape from the garage before the Senator arrives. Faith scrambled and made it to her room as the sound of San Francisco's most familiar voice echoed throughout the house.

"Oh no," she panicked at a soft knock on her door. Faith hesitated as she opens the door to a tiny crack. Her eyes were met by a disciplining stare that seems to imply, what are you up to?

"Senator, what are you doing here?"

"I heard you were going to pay Sandy Bay a visit...mind if I join you?" he asked. She remembers his suit and tie and the stern professional look he wore. She didn't expect him to be wearing it for a swim. She held back a giggle.

"Sure...why not...let me grab my accessories and we'll be off," She called feeling nervous and excited at the same time.

"Wow, nice ride," Faith said tossing her bag in the back. "Wait let me get that for you," Floyd called hurrying to get the door for her.

"Mom, can I go to New York with Hank? He's leaving tonight."

"He's what? Henley, this will take just a minute," Faith called hurrying toward her daughter.

"Hank, what is Kat talking about? Are you going to New York?" She swung the door open to see Hank packing a small suitcase.

"Yes, I'm going to Manhattan to get Syd, her mom just checked into rehab again and I got a call from Lucio. Remember, my friend who owns the restaurant and Pub. Lucio...?"

"Yes, you won't believe it. Candace left Sydney at the Bar and asked Lucio to call me to come get her."

"You're kidding me...Wish I was," he said grabbing his small carry on suitcase. Katherine can tag along if that's okay with you?"

"Yes mom, please say yes, please, please, please mom," Kat pleaded. Are you sure?"

"Yes, I'm sure Sydney would love the surprise."

"Alright then, that's fine, please have her back ASAP."

"Great!" Katherine said excitedly disappearing down the hallway. Faith embraced him tightly.

"Sorry about Candace, I can't imagine. And thanks for having Katherine tag along." She kissed him on the face and left as she remembers the Senator waiting.

"Ready?" he asked as she approached.

"I hope you are?" She replied and sat in the comfortable leather seat beside him. As they drove, he glanced at her. She appeared so much stronger, maybe even wiser since their visit two weeks before. The expressions on her face changed from soft to stern as they approached Sandy Island Blvd. It was as if she'd left a sunny vacation and was about to enter the eye of a storm.

"So, is this the interview before the Senate seat is decided?" she joked. Floyd laughed at her unexpected sense of humor.

"Relax Faith, I just want to see if you know how to swim...after all, the Sandy Island Senator, should at least be able to rescue an unprepared swimmer," he laughed.

"You're not kidding, are you?" she laughed. There was something about him that made her nervous, the way he dresses, even the way he spoke. She wondered why he was dressed in a suit and tie to the beach. His sunglasses hid his eyes and his boyish bangs were even more of a mystery. As he wondered what was behind her long silence...

"Nice shoes," she said slipping on her sunglasses. He smiled suspecting her thoughts. As they neared the beach, an unexpected image graced the scene... a white double-decker Yacht sat enthroned upon the calmed surf.

"Wow, is this....?"

"Yep, that's our ride," he smiled removing his tie as they approached the lonely Bay.

Faith grabbed her bag from the back of Senator Henley's Jeep. She watched as he tore off his well pressed office attire revealing his tight-fitting swim trunks. As his gaze met hers, she quickly looked away to avoid meeting his eyes.

"See you there," he called and jogged toward the tides and dove beneath the waves. He disappeared and when he surfaced again, he was climbing aboard Vixen. The name spelled in wild Italics, yet boldly in gold and black across the stern. So, you want to know if I can swim…I see, she said thinking out loud. He watched as Faith twist her chin left then right. She removed her expired ponytail, then her sundress and shades and stared at him with the look of death. "How dare you test me on my Bay, I'll show you, she thought in silence.

"Henley look what's that?!" she called pointing. As he turns to look, she dove headfirst into the surf and surfaced a half a mile away from Vixen. She laughed as he drove the boat in circles searching for her in the water. When he'd searched for a while she whistled and almost deafened him.

"Wait a minute, how'd you get over there?" He steered the boat toward her, but as he neared her, she swam further away to prove her point. What is she doing? he thought. He followed as she swam all the way to the coral reef and she climbed onto the snow white rocks.

"Point well made, you are now crowned, Senator of Sandy Bay, now please, if you would climb aboard the Vixen for your celebration…?" he called over the microphone. She laughs at his obvious lacking in knowledge of Sandy Island. A short while later, she dove into the water and continues to swim away from him.

"At least you must be exhausted by now," he calls over his fading microphone. She responded but he was too far away to hear her. He must have looked away, but when he looked again, Faith was nowhere in sight. By now he knew her only too well to be concerned. Vixen arrived at the snow white barriers and he releases the Anchor in time to avoid a collision with the seemingly innocent yet daring reefs.

Faith climbed the steel stairwell and swung her legs over Vixen's iron beams, landing with a soft thump on deck. She lay there for a while and glanced at the familiar gold horizons. A sudden sense of entitlement came over her. A million thoughts of how to restore this once miraculous island ran through her mind. If she were going to be

Sandy Island Senator, she would promote and argue the 'status quo,' Maybe with minor changes. This Island is an original and cannot be substituted with its motherland, San Francisco. As she pondered these thoughts Senator Henley stumbled upon her, almost crushing her perfectly painted toes.

"So, what's your big plan for this thirty mile Island?"

"You pay for it," was her response.

"What excuse do you have for San Francisco's million-dollar real estate market and the thousands of people that landlords are putting on the streets daily? Senator, I think you already know the solution."

Wait a minute, I think I remember Katherine, my daughter had mentioned that the Bay Area belongs to St Francis. There's no way he'd dispute my plan for Sandy Island."

"Wait a minute, you're quoting St Francis. I mean I don't see the relevance... San Francisco is named after St. Francis... not Sandy Island. You guys are a separate entity."

"How dare you Senator." she scolded. Faith and Senator Henley argued into the wee hours of the morning and just as the Sun was dawning upon the Bay, they had both reached a conclusion.

It's been several weeks since Faith awoke to sunrise on Sandy Island. The clear blue waters and warm sun on her face birth new hope for her plans to restore what appears to be irreparable damage to paradise. The refreshing smell of coffee brewing and the sight of Senator Henley approaching instilled possibilities.

"I must say, I slept better than I did in months since our time-wasting arguments."

"Kid, where have you been our whole lives? Every Senator including the President would be on vacation with you in charge. You're something else Faith French..." he chuckled as he handed her a cup of coffee. She shied away from his conversation. After all it was morning on Sandy Island and despite her prospective Senator Status, she refused to discuss politics. Maybe no one including Senator Henley was prepared for her unique stance as Senator-but Politics would never be part of her office.

Vixen is a gorgeous boat with two decks and lots of privacy from her presumably neglectful acquaintance, Senator Henley. It's been several hours since the eve of sunset and he's been on his mobile almost the entire day. Only sixteen hours with him and she can tell that his responsibility to the people of San Francisco is of pivotal

180

importance. There's no doubt that his hands were filled and his heart was in the right place. So far, her day spent with the Senator gave her a peek into her new life. As she pondered her new responsibilities, she realizes that Henley's responsibility to the people of San Francisco is one that bore a much greater responsibility than that of Sandy Island. At the thought of this, her heart sunk. Unbeknownst to her, she was in training: The test that almost ended before she'd even begun.

A golden twilight kissed the evening skies when Henley approached Faith in a blue bathrobe and smoking a Cigar.

"Faith, the people of San Francisco has agreed to fully fund the cost of rebuilding Sandy Island. There was a bit of hesitation with your stance on insurance however there was a large turnout on the public debate. The people agreed that Sandy Island belongs to the people of San Francisco and since it's an Island that is well under thirty thousand in population, the Island should be rebuilt by the people of San Francisco."

"I knew it, you're not even in office yet but you're already scoring goals. This call for celebration... Bernard, please bring our finest champagne," he said speaking into his tiny earpiece.

"Who's Bernard?" Faith asked looking puzzled.

"He's my Retriever," he smiled as the lab approached placing a bottle of Napa Valley's finest at his feet. The pup then approached Faith and sniffed her hands and feet. After wagging his tail followed by a playful bark he returned to his quarters. Faith laughed.

"I had no idea we had company. Yes however, he watches over you at my request."

"Really?"

"Indeed," he replied exhaling a puff of smoke.

"What a good girl."

"Actually, he's a boy," Henley teased. As they chat, Faith's mobile buzzed.

"Hi Fain? No, that's not possible. No way. Katherine cannot remain in New York for a week, this was not our agreement."

"Hank said he tried to reach you a few times but there was no answer." She checked her phone and noticed that she had several missed calls from Hank. As she stared at her phone, she felt a sudden wetness gush down her legs and a bright red fluid formed a small puddle in her feet.

"Oh my gosh," she panicked. Fain still on the line....

"Faith, is everything okay, I mean it's only Hank. I think Katherine would be okay for a week, but I understand, it's up to you so I'll pass the message onto Hank. Fain heard her scream and then silence followed.

"Faith?"

Puzzled by Faith's reaction, Fain rubbed the top of his head. Still unsure of what to tell Hank, he flopped on Elizabeth's recliner and returned to enjoying his weekend. A lot has happened the past few months since he left Sandy Island and he felt slightly distanced from Faith. He was unsure of his reasons for being in San Francisco, yet, somehow, he wasn't in a hurry to drive back to Beverly Hills. Patrol George and Liz had left for a horseback ride down the beach and with everyone else away, it was an unexpectedly quiet weekend for him. He felt like he'd lost the only family he's known and with all the new development that's on the horizon for Faith, he knew it was only a matter of time before he became a distant memory. As he poured himself another shot of whiskey, he remembers that his thirtieth birthday was only two weeks away. He thought of the many friends that he'd made in Los Angeles most of whom were women who would care less about his birthday. Even with a major production in theatres, and all that he has accomplished since his previous position as Faith's assistant, a bit of hopelessness crept over him. It's been almost two years since he'd left France with no intensions of returning. A renewed feeling came over him and he contemplated seriously about his previous decision and saw how childish they were. He knew that it was time for him to pay his parents a visit. After all, up until his engagement to Camille, he was close to his mom. His father's sternness had put a wedge between them, yet it wasn't sufficient to keep him away from them. He'd missed his large extended family and as he sat in solitude, he'd made up his mind that it was time for a visit. He was going to keep his plans to himself. He intended to leave within the coming week to be home in time for his birthday.

Senator Henley carried Faith to the very top deck of Vixen where a small chopper awaited. Still unsure of why she'd passed out, he placed her securely into the chopper and air lifted her to the roof of Hope memorial. He picked up the emergency phone and dialed the hospital's private nurses unit urging them to come quickly. Less than a minute later the unit arrived on the roof. Still unsure what was happening, the nurses, approached, and realized that it was Senator Henley, they hurried toward him.

"Sir, are you, all right?"

"Yes I'm fine, it's not me, it's Faith, the Senator Elect for Sandy Island," he said pointing to the chopper. The Nurses hurried to the vehicle and lifted Faith, placing her onto a gurney. Within minutes, she was in the care of the most skilled nurses at Hope Memorial. Senator Henley knew that this was the only way that news of Faith's emergency would not leak to the press. He did not want the people of San Francisco and Sandy island to be further alarmed by this new development and he was careful in securing the most private option for Faith's care.

Faith was now fully conscious and was unsure why she was at the hospital. She pressed the buzzer and two nurses arrived both smiling at her and addressed as her Senator French. They both appeared in their late twenties and was looking at her as someone from their favorite soap television. Faith narrowed her eyes…

"So, can you ladies tell me what's going on?"

"Congratulations Senator, you're having a baby, you're about eight weeks pregnant," they said smiling at her proudly. Senator Henley arrived in time to overhear the conversation.

"Is that so?" he smiled. His eyes narrowed, I know we've only spent the evening on Vixen, but any chance it could be mines," he joked. Faith laughed. The nurses congratulated her again and excused themselves.

"Pregnant, my God, this can't be, and surely, this is not the time," she fretted. The smile that was slowly forming on her face slowly faded as she wondered who the father of her child might be. The nurses wants to keep you overnight for observation, is there anyone you need me to call for you?" he asked growing concerned of how this would affect Faith's new responsibility to the people of Sandy Island.

"My daughter is in New York with a good friend and Liz is on a date with Patrol George, the only person left to call would be Fain or Calvin. Let's not tell anyone just yet. Let's keep this as a surprise until everything is settled with Sandy. I don't want the Residents to become distracted or concerned by this."

"Absolutely, I agree," he said happily.

"By the way you look lovely, did they say eight weeks pregnant?" You don't look a bit of it," he smiled. Faith smiled at his coy sense of humor.

"Well, if there's no one that I can call, I would hate to leave you here alone. I would love to stay here with you…"

"I'd be delighted. How sweet of you, but I couldn't do that to poor Tommy."

"Oh, no worries at all. Tommy is spending the weekend with my parents in Pacific Heights. He loves it because it's his old neighborhood and he has more friends up there."

"Are you certain?"

"Absolutely, my pleasure." Despite his strict professional approach to his work, outside of his profession, Henley has this laidback, overly sweet personality. He took Faith's hands in his and brushed it slightly and smiled. There was a sparkle in his eyes.

"You look tired, come here," she said patting a space next to her on the narrow bed. He giggled.

"Okay, if you insist." He snuggled next to her and placed his hands on her tummy.

"You don't deserve to be alone tonight, I'm really glad that I'm here with you," he said kissing her on the forehead. Faith smiled at his caring nature as she slowly drifts off to sleep.

The next morning, Hank woke Faith very early around six am and suggested that they sneak out of the Hospital Secret Unit.

"Are you sure, but why?"

"Trust me, it's the reason they named this ward the Secret Unit, it's for very private events like this one, that's to do with San Francisco Royalty." She chuckled and then agreed to his secret plot. A few moments later, they flew off the roof of Hope Memorial and headed for a Vixen landing. As they neared Sandy Island, Henley made another proposal.

"I would love to show you around the bay, are you up for it?"

"Absolutely, she said excitedly. Faith gazed in awe of the breathtaking views of San Francisco Bay. She's heard of this gorgeous sky view before, but no words could accurately capture the city's majestic sky line which seats like an ancient, yet futuristic City on the sea.

"Senator, this is so unexpected and lovely, I had no idea that my weekend would be this fun."

184

"The pleasure is all mines," he said with a wink.

"And I had no idea you're such a skilled Pilot," she said proudly.

"Is that so?" he said and pretended to release the controls. She screamed and they both laughed. As they headed back to the Vixen he remembers breakfast...

"Hungry yet?"

"I'm starved," she said remembering the precious life growing so tenderly inside her.

Henley took lovely care of her ensuring that she ate a healthy breakfast. He refused to let her help and has been spoiling her since he learned of her pregnancy. She almost felt guilty as she thought of Hank. They'd grown slightly apart since Sandy Island and she was still unsure of their relationship. A lot had happened and even Hank has a few new developments that beckoned him in a direction that she could not follow. She thought that this may be the reason she agreed for Katherine to accompany him...Maybe it would appear that a part of her was with him and that he wouldn't feel that she was slowly slipping away. Then she thought of her baby...maybe it was the beginning of the end to a new beginning, for her and the men in her life.

She didn't notice but Henley was gazing at her for about fifteen minutes wondering what could have occupied her thoughts in such an emotional way. There was something almost mysterious about this beautiful woman he'd heard so much about. Still the mystery of her life and the unknown created a feeling of hope within him. It was apparent that her romantic life was one that was at best complicated. Yet, it was a conflict that he wanted to be a part of, whether personally or professionally, it was a paradox he is willing to solve.

Her eyes met his admiring stare which almost startled her. She blushed and placed her hands on her tummy.

"Sorry, I didn't mean to scare you, you're so beautiful, I couldn't help it."

"What were you thinking about?" Then he realized...

"It's alright, sweetie it's none of my business," he admitted.

"Not at all, I was contemplating my new life...and what I'm going to do with myself..." she laughed. He approached her and took a seat next to her at the small dining table for two. He took her hands once more.

"I'm here for you, you don't have to be alone, if you would allow me," he said. There was a plea in his eyes and his caring nature was quickly winning her heart. A tear rolled down her gorgeous face. Unable to withstand her emotion, he took her in his arms and kissed her softly.

"Say yes, say you'd let me take care of you and help you through this," he pleaded between kisses.

"Yes," she whispered as he kisses and caresses her gently high above the surf aboard the Vixen on an unexpected turn of the tides.

Chapter 22

The following morning, Faith awoke cuddled up in soft sheets as she glanced around the room for her host. The smell of coffee brewing assured her that he was in his new favorite department making them breakfast. As she stretched her arms tiredly, she became distracted by her mobile buzzing. She searched around the room for her phone and realized that it had fallen under the bed. She lay flat on the soft carpeting and peeked under the bed. She spotted the device and as she reached, Henley came into the room carrying a tray with her breakfast surprised to see a pair of legs sticking out from under the bed.

"Wow, if I was sure I would admit that you're not that great at playing hide and go seek," he laughed. She giggled and made a muffled statement about her phone.

"I think it would work better if you had both legs under the bed," he laughed.

"Oh, you're silly," she laughs finally pulling herself up. Her hair was a messy ordeal and he poked fun at her.

"Don't worry Senator, you will figure it out," he said placing the tray on her bed.

"Let me grab my breakfast and I'll join you," he said. Faith glanced at her phone and noticed that she had sixteen missed calls from Hank and ten missed calls from Liz. She listened to Elizabeth's messages first and her final message stated that she and Patrol George had flown to New York to bring Katherine home. Faith realizes that things with Candace may have been much more serious than Hank had realized, and that he might have decided to remain in Manhattan. She was saddened, yet thankful to not be alone at that moment. She phoned Katherine immediately and regretted her decision allowing her to tag along with Hank. It was unwise and careless on her part. Katherine was in tears and wanted Sydney to come to San Francisco with her and she wanted her mom to be okay with it. She did not want to leave her friend, it was difficult. Hank

187

had promised that she would be spending Christmas with them and she didn't believe his story that they would come once things had calmed down with Sydney's mom. She admitted to her mom that she'd told Hank that she hated him and Faith was now in tears.

"Darling, I love you, I'm so sorry. Mommy wishes that Syd could come back with you, but it's not my decision, there's nothing mommy could do." Mommy, you're his girlfriend, you can talk to him, please mommy!"

"I love you baby, Grandma Liz and George is on their way to you. You will be home soon baby. Mommy love you more than life... I promise everything is going to be okay," Faith sobbed.

Henley returned with his tray to join Faith for breakfast only to find her hugging tightly onto a pillow in tears.

"No, tell me the eggs couldn't be this bad. I swore scrambled was your favorite," he joked. Faith chuckled between tears. As they ate, she revealed some personal notes to him about the nature of her life and its complications. Henley is a great listener and never once took his eyes off her as she poured her heart out to him. Even as deeply saddened as she is now, his only desire is to comfort her to the point where she would forget the loose ends of her life. Even in tears, she is an undeniably beautiful, wise woman who would inspire and bring life to the distressed people of Sandy Island: Displaced residents awaiting a beautiful heroine in tears to heal the hearts of her people.

Eric was furious as he sped into the driveway and rang the doorbell repeatedly. Katherine had phoned him from New York when she couldn't reach her mom. He was livid that Faith would allow Katherine to accompany her boyfriend to New York without his permission. When there was no answer, he swiped his hands on the ledge above the stained-glass door for the spare key.

"Eric please calm down, you cannot be sure unless you know the whole story," said Rachael.

"How is she supposed to manage an entire island and she can't even manage her own daughter?" Eric was hardly listening to Rachael as he pushed the door open.

"Mom, are you here?"

"Faith, Calvin? Is anyone here?" He'd dialed Liz's phone several times and it went directly to voicemail. Liz was avoiding Eric's call because she realized that Kat might have phoned him. He only phones this often when he's upset, and she was not about to hear how wrong Faith was about sending Katherine to New York with someone she hardly knows. She still blames him for everything that has happened with Faith and she refuse to give him a chance to be right. She knew that he would only use this opportunity to right his many wrongs. Patrol George glanced at Liz's mobile as she declined another call.

"Secret admirer," he joked. Liz smiled at him.

"Thanks for accompanying me George. I'm so happy you're here."

"Not at all, I was overjoyed when you invited me. I needed this," he replied taking her hands. They had landed at JFK an hour ago and was in a UBER Taxi heading toward Hank's apartment in Manhattan.

Fain sped up Lombard drive toward Amber Heights. He'd received a text from Kate earlier inviting him to join her and some friends for drinks. He almost declined, but he didn't feel like spending the weekend alone. He would be leaving for France in a few days and drinks with a few friends sounded like the perfect conclusion. His heart ached for the days spent in Sandy Island with the family he loves. There was nothing he wouldn't give to have it all back, but it was too late and too much had happened. As he thought of Faith and Katherine, he turned up the volume on his favorite song, "Both Sides Now" by Joanie Mitchell. Tears streamed down his handsome face as he pulled to a stop in Kate's driveway. He sat in his convertible until Joanie subsided. As he exhaled in satisfaction, he was interrupted by loud music as Kate swung her front door open.

"Coming?" she asked. He glanced at her doing his best to hide his boyish emotions.

Faith opened her laptop and logged into her email. She was shocked at the several thousand emails from fans, romantic interest, and one that was too difficult to ignore. It was an email from Hank sitting above the pile. Vixen was on the move and the most appealing subject line in the midst of her many emails were a public invitation from the people of Sandy Island to meet their new Senator Elect. As she rolled her cursor over Hank's email, Henley leaned his head into her doorway in a playful way…

"You have to see this," he said.

"There's nothing else that could amaze me about this place. I promise you; I've seen it all." As she stepped onto Vixens uppermost balcony, her sentence was interrupted by dozens of excited swimmers.

"I can't believe it, dolphins...! I've never seen them this close before," she beamed.

"They are attempting to attack Vixen, it's her color. They think she's a giant Killer Whale," Henley joked.

"You're kidding," she grinned.

"Hey guys, over here," she called.

"They're just beautiful," Faith said leaning over the iron beams.

"Careful," I've haven't hired you a lifeguard yet," Henley said.

"Oh, don't kid yourself, I can swim this entire island," she boasted placing her hands on her hips.

"I should tweet this. Sandy Island Senator just sassed me," he said winking at her.

"Twitter, you do Twitter...Where do you find the time?"

"Do you mean you don't have Social Media?"

"Not that I know of...do I?" He chuckled at how naïve she appeared.

"Trust me hun, you're going to need SM...or your email will blow up and your computer will grow legs. You're famous now kiddo...you have to get with it," he smiled eyebrows raised. Faith made a face at him, rolled her eyes and headed back to her emails.

"Hey wait. What's so important? Where're you going? I brought you here to get away from the crowd. Trust me; you'll have all the crowds you need in a short while." She walked to the door and stopped. She stared at him as he steered the boat.

"You might be right about that, but I'm steering," she said approaching.

"Feeling fearless I see. Okay here you go, take the rudder and I'll stand behind you until you feel comfortable, okay?"

"Okay," she replied. Henley noticed an immediate confidence about Faith. It was almost metaphorical how she eased her way in front of him and took the lead. Instantly, he knew it was an immediate sign of her preparedness to take the lead on Sandy.

Henley docked Vixen in front of his Ocean front estate. He watched Faith gracefully descend the three-story stairwell and finally stepped onto the small private dock. He swore that there's a peace about her that could calm any storm.

"Got everything?" he asked trying to change his thoughts.

"Yep," she replied throwing her beach bag over her shoulders.

"But you forgot something," she played.

"And what's that," he asked.

"Your car, you forgot it on the beach, the one you picked me up with on Friday," she grinned.

"Oh, that one; you would have been right, but Lenny, my Chauffeur grabbed her the same evening we got there."

"Oh, I see. Seems you have these secret Agents that follow you around unnoticed. So, tell me, who else is on that boat that I don't know about?" she said adjusting her sunglasses. He continued to observe her ladylike demeanor.

"Henley, I know that the minute you get inside, it all turns into politics. You might as well take me home."

"Hmm, some Senator you are Frenchie. You think you can be Senator and avoid Politics?"

"Absolutely," she said turning to leave.

"Some guest you are, where're you going?"

"I think that's the second time you asked me that today Henley. I've called a UBER, I'm going home," she smiled.

"You're kidding?"

"Watch me she said hurrying toward a vehicle that had just arrived.

"You know this is a no UBER zone, private property, you're lucky that I just called of my shooter, or that Uber would have been toast." She laughs at his defensive humor. She knew he was only trying to get her to stay with him the rest of the evening.

"Can you meet me tomorrow to discuss rebuilding plans? I've also hired a Communication Specialist to prepare a public speech for you. We must do a public address ASAP." She turns to face him.

"Sure, sounds like a plan. How does 2:00pm tomorrow sound?"

"That's ideal. Would be even better if you can show up a half an hour early to go over your speech."

"You got it," she replied. "Henley.... I had a lovely time. Thank you!" She flashed him another smile before getting into the Uber. Henley shook his head and smiled. He still couldn't believe that she took off like that. She is the perfect fit and he couldn't wait to see her tomorrow to get things started.

Faith was surprised to see Eric's car drive out of Liz's driveway. She was glad that he was leaving just as she had arrived because she could not handle hearing any comments about her mistakes; especially not from him. As soon as she stepped inside, her phone rang. It was Liz. They were at JFK on their way back and would be arriving around 6:00 p.m. this evening. The second she thought of her daughter, a sudden feeling of guilt came over her. Then she remembered her baby: a precious unexpected life growing within her. In one single weekend, her life was completely changed. As she thought of her baby, she remembered Fain.

"Fain? Are you here?" She searched everywhere but there was no sign of him. There was a white envelope with her name sitting on the dresser in the guestroom where he slept. Then she remembered Hank's email. The silence of her unread email and a sealed envelope was much louder than any unspoken words. She took the envelope and slipped it into the dresser. Suddenly, she couldn't wait to see her daughter; the ripple effects of her tiny voice can calm the many storms of her life. Faith arose surprised to find herself asleep on Liz's recliner. She couldn't remember whether Liz and Katherine had arrived and looking at the time on the wall, her thoughts raced. It was after 5 a.m. and after a quick look around, her fears were confirmed. Where's everyone she thought. She looked at her mobile and there were several text messages from Liz. The most recent text message read

"Hunny, we'll be at the Fairway Palace-Penthouse downtown. I know that you must prepare for your public debut tomorrow, so I'm going to keep the girls for the rest of the weekend. We'll be home tomorrow evening." She wondered what Liz meant by girls. Maybe it was a typo, she thought. She wanted to place a call to Liz but realized it was too early. She tried going back to sleep but an hour later she was still awake. There was no doubt that she was nervous about her public debut later today. Henley was wrong. She needed to write her own speech. There was no way that she could read a professional speech to the public that was written by someone else. On that thought, Faith sat in Liz's office and wrote a twenty-five-page speech to her people of Sandy Island.

A few hours later, Faith peeked through the window; a warm golden haze could be seen over the horizon. She knew the signs that depicted a gorgeous day from the many years she'd adored the sun kissed skies of Sandy Bay. It was only seven am when she packed a bag and drove Liz's convertible out of the driveway and headed to Senator Henley to present him with her speech. As she pulled into the driveway of the Senator's private residence, she was almost blinded by sharp piercing security lights.

"Hold your position," a female robotic voice called.

"You've got to be kidding me," she said hardly intimidated. Henley looked over the balcony. Faith could see a white robe and a cloud of smoke being blown into the air. Seeing her large, terrified eyes peering through the windshields, Henley blew another puff of smoke and said...

"Alexa, it's alright," he said pointing a remote control attempting to deactivate the security sensors. Faith stepped out of her vehicle.

"Why so early?" He called opening the gates.

"I heard you make the finest coffee, I couldn't afford to miss out," she replied shading her eyes from the blinding light.

"Henley, do you mind?"

"Actually, I do." He jokes. "Yesterday, you took off like a bullet, and now you showed up at seven a.m. As far as my guns and security cameras are concerned, you're an intruder." She reached into her purse to remove her speech.

"Faith no, please wait till the lights go out," Henley called in a panic.

"Or what?" she ignored. Hanks security lights flash about and the alarm beeped loudly.

"Faith, please no," he called in a panic. The lights went dim and just as she entered the gates, buzzing sounds could be heard and the smell of smoke and sulfur clouded the air.

"Yikes!" she screamed. Henley pressed against the remote repeatedly and successfully disarm his security.

"Looks like I need a new battery for this thing," he said looking at the remote and a frazzled Faith as she entered his residence.

"That's not very funny Henley," she said between giggles.

Several hours later, Faith sat in an air lifted Caterpillar Crane near the surf of the ruins of Sandy Island and addressed the twenty plus thousand residents of Sandy Bay. Senator Henley was beyond impressed with Faith's preparedness and speech preparation since the untimely illness of their Communication Specialist prevented him from preparing the original speech. The crowd applauded and cheered as Faith addressed them with the enthusiasm of a true leader.

"Grandma Liz, this thing looks pretty scary; is my mommy safe all the way up there?" Kat asked nervously.

"Looks fun," Syd said grinning. Patrol George smiled proudly as Faith concluded her speech with plans that are in place for her beloved Island. News of building plans as well as San Francisco's Insurance full coverage for each resident lifted the emotions of once distressed families. A wave of satisfaction swept the Island, restoring joys, filling the void of loss.

Chapter 23

Faith removed her sandals and stepped onto the soft green grass that sprouted along the green lawns where the abodes of Sandy Island residents once stood. She watched as hundreds of residents observed from a distance as their homes are rebuilt by the finest Architects and Engineers who's been contracted by the Senator to rebuild Sandy Island. It was a joyful event yet much more than a daunting task sitting in a tiny office awaiting the instructions of Senator Henley. It seems that she was simply a Senator in training who needed direct instruction from a superior source. After only three hours of her first day on the job, Faith fired her mentor: Senator Henley and began making Executive decisions for Sandy Island. Ben: Faith's Communication Specialist's drove her from point A to point B almost continuously all day as she cautioned onlookers and answered hundreds of questions to the excited new owners, eager to recreate the image of a lost memory.

As the day concluded, at the request of Senator Henley, Ben drove Faith to the Senator's residence to settle an argument. Faith had fallen asleep on the way. Her eyes opened slowly as Ben pulled to a stop at the Senator's residence.

"Why are we here?"

"Hi sweetie, mind joining me for dinner?" Henley called.

"Henley, I haven't seen my daughter in a week, I'd much rather spend this time with family."

"Hi mom!" Katherine called standing on the Senator's balcony. Puzzled, Faith stepped out of Ben's truck.

"Honey what are you doing here and where's your grandma?"

"Grandma's in the Senator's kitchen making dinner for everyone."

"Hi Faith!" Syd called excitedly.

"Syd?" As Faith wondered what was happening, Grandma Liz and Patrol George joined the girls.

"Darling, where's your shoes?" George giggled at the sight of Faith after her first day on the job.

"Hey!" George shouted at a crew of camera men from Sandy Bay News hurrying toward Faith.

"Hey back of dude," Ben called, taking Faith by the hand and shutting the gate behind them. The insistent reporters collectively shouted random questions at Faith, while some placed their cameras over the gate in the hopes of capturing a word or maybe a glimpse of the beautiful woman named Senator of Sandy Island.

Fain sat at San Francisco International Airport; awaiting his flight to Paris. He'd arrived almost two hours earlier and had learned that his flight was delayed another four hours due to an unexpected hailstorm. He lowered his visor to hide his face as a handful of teenagers took photos of him.

"That's Fain Collins, the guy from that movie. Hey, can we get your autograph? Your awesome dude," they said speaking simultaneously. He tried to avoid them pretending to not notice, but all three boys approached him with questions of his role as a Stuntman. He shared some of his secrets of how he'd pulled of several daring stunts. He then autographed the back of their shirts. The boys then high fived him and took off. He smiled at their responses, glad that they were the only ones that had recognized him. Fain stared curiously at hail the size of a fist on the runway, and for a moment it felt like he was in a different city. According to the news forecast, the excessive hail was caused by a sudden drop in temperature and low laying fog that had clouded surrounding areas. He smiled at the possibility that this was a significant sign that he should remain in San Francisco, but his mind was made. His thoughts were interrupted by a flight update on the monitors. The fog had cleared a little sooner than expected and a team of Airport field workers had successfully cleared the excessive hail. His flight was now leaving in thirty minutes. He was tempted to call Faith and Katherine, but he assumed that by now she'd read his letter and had possibly ignored him or needed time. Moments later, he boarded Air France. As he took his seat comfortably in first-class, a feeling of assurance came over him and for the first time in years, he felt like he was close to home.

Faith woke up to the smell of coffee and scratching sounds from her window. It was raining heavily outside and the palm trees near the bay bent and swayed by heavy winds.

"Faith, come quickly, I should have done this earlier. Follow me," Senator Henley called, showing Faith to an office whose structure was pure marble.

"Henley, this is gorgeous."

"Glad you like it because that's your office," he said smiling broadly. She smiled, "It's lovely, however, I need different pictures on the wall. These are too political looking. I need more colors."

"This reminds me, you need an assistant."

"What about Ben?"

"Oh Ben only handles communication; emails, phone calls, press conferences, and of course your public speeches," Henley said, staring at her with narrowed eyes in her soft pink PJ's.

"You look ready," he called walking away. Faith called after him...

"Senator?"

As she thought of an immediate solution for an assistant, Kat entered her office.

"Mommy, I know who would make the perfect assistant..." she grinned, revealing her missing teeth. Her mom laughed...

"And just who might that be?"

"I know you know what I'm thinking mom...and you know it's Mr. Collins, our very own fearless Stuntman with a movie an all," Kat said placing her hands on her hips tiptoeing stylishly across the marble floor.

Her mom giggled...

"Well sweetheart, mommy promise to think about it, okay," she said approaching her and embracing her. As Kat wrapped her tiny hands around her mom, she felt a softness on her tummy. She slowly released her mom took a few steps back.

"Mom, what was that?"

"What love," Faith asked feeling her face becoming flushed as she realized that Kat might have felt her tiny bump.

"Mom, are you okay?" Kat asked realizing that her mom was embarrassed. Faith tried to think of a quick excuse but there was no way around her daughter's curious eyes.

"Sweetie...there's something mommy needs to tell you." Just then Syd called out to Katherine.

"Kat, where are you, there's something I want to show you."

"Please hold that thought mom," Kat called and hurried off.

197

"Kat...?" Faith called but both girls disappeared down the long hallway. Faith placed her hands on her tiny bump; feelings of anxiety and excitement raced through her emotions.

Retching sounds could be heard as Kate lifted her head from her porcelain toilet for the hundredth time. She wonders why Fain hadn't returned her call. Weakened from dehydration she knew that it was time to pay a visit to the ER. A feeling of loneliness crept over her as she struggles to get dressed and finally drove out of her driveway on the isolated cul-de-sac. As she pulled into the parking structure of the ER, she rolled her window down and motioned to the guard to bring her a trolley.

"Sure, no problem," he replied hurrying toward her. He places the chair as close to the driver side as possible and held Kate's hand as she sat carefully into the chair.

"I'm Paul, is there anything else I can do for you," he asked placing her purse in her hands and wheeling her to the entrance of the ER.

"Thanks Paul, you're a life saver," she called as two nurses hurry towards her. As she explains her symptoms to the Nurse taking her vitals, she retched loudly. The Nurse reached for an emesis basin and held it up to Kate's mouth. Her vitals indicated an extremely high fever and by the looks of her pale skin, the nurse knew that the popular movie producer needed immediate attention.

Several hours later, feeling rested and flushed with fluid, she was discharged. She hurried to her parked car and drove away from the Grace Memorial. Her heart raced as she reflects on the day's events. How could this be? She thought.

"It can't be, Dr. Rosenberg is quite mistaken, I'm not, absolutely not pregnant," she said laughing out loud. For years, her and her husband Gabe had exhausted every option to no avail, which ultimately led to their divorce.

"This can't be," she beamed with excitement.

"I'm not the dried-up old prune he thought when he shut the door on our marriage," she beamed rubbing her tummy. She turned up the volume and began to sing out loud occupying both lanes leading up to her estate when the sound of a siren and a robotic voice interrupted her excitement.

"Pull over to your right," the officer called flashing all the colors of the rainbow. As the officer approached, she rolled down her window, still basking in joy.

"Officer, what can I do for you today?" she asked shaking her head rhythmically.

"Ma'am I'm going to have to ask you to step out of the vehicle," the grumpy officer called.

"Is this really necessary?" Kate said stepping slowly out of the vehicle.

"Ma'am do you realize that you've been driving on both sides of the road for the previous five miles?" She removed her sunglasses and stared at the officer who appears in his early thirties.

"Five miles?"

"Yes, I've been following you the last half hour since you pulled out of the ER. I'm assuming that by the way you're driving that you might have gotten some unexpected news…?"

"Well, not that it's any of your business, but yes, I did," she responded.

"Not that I need any specifics, but I'm still going to have to perform a sobriety test."

"Kid, I have no time for this," Kate said getting back into her vehicle.

"Kate!" The officer called her out. She paused…

"Do I know you from somewhere?"

"You can say that," he responded. "We met a little over a week ago, I was one of your guests the weekend before last…" he said approaching her, removing his sunglasses.

"So what are you so excited about, mind sharing?" He asked now smiling.

"Sorry, I don't remember you."

"C'mon, remember, we made out for like an hour, but you refused to give up the goods," he joked.

"No way, I always remember who's been in my house, even when I'm having too much of a good time to remember," she smiled.

"Okay, I was sort of undercover; wore a ball cap the entire time and your friend Fain was making fun of me…cool dude. Is he going to be around this weekend?" Realizing, Faith's eyes narrowed.

"I'm not sure?" she responded.

"He's a nice guy." Kate watched as the officer reached into his pocket and jotted down a note.

"Here, give this to Frenchie, tell him to give me a call sometime, okay." Technically, you own this road, so I can't give you a ticket. But you owe me one. Have Frenchie call me sometime okay," he said and left to respond to a call. She watched curiously as the officer got into his vehicle and sped off.

"Who was that? I always remember a face," she said pulling into her driveway. Remembering her news, Kate's joy resumed. She was going to make some changes, a lot of changes to embrace the precious joy that has entered her fleeting life. As she thought of Fain, there was no doubt that she was carrying his baby. As she contemplates the events of her unexpected day, she knew that she would never disclose her joyful news to the Father of her baby.

Kat and Sydney wrapped Chance in a blanket. He licked their faces to thank them for his bath.

"Aww, you're most welcome Chance, look how big you got," Kat said drying him off.

"He's been with my mom the past few months. She had to come with us when mom went to the rehab.

"We better keep her away from Senator Henley's Doberman Pinchers, they'd have her for lunch," Kat joked.

"Oh no, not my puppy, you're such a good boy," Syd said petting his wet floppy ears. Kat stared at Syd as she hugs Chance. She knew that all the ups and downs with her parents must be difficult for her.

"Hey, want to take Chance for a walk?" she asked.

"Umm, sure but we can't go far…this place is filled with security cameras."

"I know, I really miss Sandy Bay, things were so much simpler."

"How do you feel about your mom's new Job?"

"Funny, you're the only one who's asked me…I miss her Syd, I'm afraid that I might not see much of her in the coming months and Fain has disappeared again. I'm really glad you're here Syd. Not to mention school. It's only been three weeks, but it already feels like a lifetime," she admitted. They hugged each other and Chance wined and sat next to them.

"Do you think your mom would let me stay? I don't think I want to move back to New York."

"Don't worry, I'll talk to her," Kat assured.

"Is everything alright ladies?" Senator Henley interrupted. Chance grumbled.

"Well, well, who do we have here?" he said patting Chance's ear.

"Umm," Syd responded nervously.

"He's mines, mom couldn't watch her. She had to go away to…

"But…" Kat interrupted Syd.

"Where's mom? There's something I need to ask her," Kat said taking Syd's hand and hurrying off, Chance following closely behind.

"Girls?" Liz called.

"Here Grandma," Kat responded from the kitchen.

"We're making sandwiches, would you like a Sandwich Grandma?" Liz chuckled at the sight of Syd in Senator Henley's oversized apron.

"If it's no trouble," she said in a friendly tone.

"Not at all, Grandma Liz," Syd responded with a wink.

"I thought you too might be bored, and George and I wanted to see if you want to go for a horseback ride on the beach."

"Sure, that sounds fun," Kat beamed.

"Actually, I don't know how to ride a horse," Syd cried.

"I can show you how," Kat called excitedly.

"Okay ladies, I'll go borrow some saddles from Henley. George and I will meet you two out front," Liz called excitedly. Kat knew that Grandma Liz enjoys being around Patrol George because there was an excitement in her eyes each time she mentioned his name.

Henley had spent a generous portion of his day attempting to locate an interior designer that specializes in political décor for Faith's office. He was about to give in when his phone rang.

"Yellow," he called trying to sound casual.

"Oh, yes, yes, can you come in the morning, say around 9:00am? Fantastic! I'll see you then." He said excitedly and hung up. As he searched the premises for Faith, he looked at the CCTV and saw her exit the back entrance. Realizing that she was alone, he slipped on his tennis shoes and followed her.

"Faith wait up. You shouldn't be alone…you have to be more careful, you're a State Senator now," he called almost out of breath trying to catch up to her. Realizing that he was exhausted, Faith picked up a light pace. She soon disappeared on the narrow trail.

"Faith, where'd you go Hun? C'mon, that's not fair, you know I can't fly," he joked. As he turned a corner, Faith jumped out behind a large tree trunk and called "Boo," startling him.

"You flinched," she joked. He stared at her. She seemed a lot happier than he remembered. She didn't realize but she was standing in a path of flowering plants which complement her soft appearance.

"You're glowing," he smiled. She followed his gaze to the wildflowers at her feet. When she looked up again, he was standing an inch away from her.

"Senator?"

"Shh," he whispered, and kisses her covering her soft lips. Overcome by Henley's sudden gesture, she leans forward and sunk into his strong embrace.

Chapter 24

As she concluded Hank's email, Faith stared at her computer monitor in horror. She wished that she had read his email sooner. It was sent almost three days ago from his iPhone. She learned that Hank's Ex-wife marriage to Eddie was annulled only three months after they wedded. He'd also chosen to remain in New York to offer Candace his support. While driving her to rehab, there was an accident of highway I-78…she could tell that there was more he wanted to say but might have been interrupted by something or someone. Trying her best to remain calm, she reached for her mobile and attempted to phone every hospital near the I-78 expressway. Her palms became sweaty and her hands shook as she dialed the numbers. After her fifth attempt failed, a thought came to her and she Googled the accident. There were several published articles about the accident, however, they did not disclose the names of the parties involved. As she searched the web frantically, another article was published by the Manhattan Chronicle. The short article was an update on the accident and revealed the names of the parties, and the Hospital that they were taken to be treated for severe injuries. In her state of shock, fear and uncertainty, tears streamed down her face as she dialed the number to Bellevue Memorial Hospital in Manhattan.

"Memorial Emergency," a soft voice answered. Shaking and in tears…

"Yes, I'm trying to locate my fiancé Hank Hutton, I'm calling from California. There was an accident there several days ago…"

"Ma'am, I'm sorry but I cannot provide specific information over the phone. I can only tell you that Mr. Hutton is here, however as I mentioned, I cannot provide specifics unless you're his family and is physically present here."

"How about Candace Hutton? Is she also at this location…?" Yes, she's currently being treated here, but that's all I can say."

"Okay, okay then, thank you so much," Faith cried and hung up.

Faith's heart raced as she reeled in uncertainty of Sydney's parents' condition. She had to get to New York but couldn't. She is now a Senator and her schedule belonged to the people of Sandy Island. As she thought of what to do, there was a soft knock on her door.

"It's me Henley, is everything okay? Can I come in?" he called

"Just a sec," she responded trying to dry her eyes.

"Okay, please come in Henley, what can I do you for?"

"Sorry, I thought I heard sniffles. Realizing, she remembers that this place is covered in security features and that she could hardly keep anything from Henley. For the tenth time since she'd read Hank's email, she was reduced to tears.

"There's been an accident, Sydney's parents, they've been in a horrible accident and I'm not sure if they're okay."

"An accident?" he asked confused....

"When did you learn of this?"

"Just now, Hank tried reaching me a few days ago, but I didn't have the time and I just got the chance to read the email he'd sent."

"I'm assuming that Sydney is the child I saw with your daughter and Elizabeth earlier?"

"Yes," she nodded.

"It's been quite busy around here and I haven't had the chance to properly meet Syd. My goodness, this is a nightmare. It's best we keep this to ourselves until we get more information."

"I've tried phoning Bellevue Memorial where they were taken but they refuse to give me specifics over the phone."

"Faith, I have an idea. This must be as private as possible, but you must get to Manhattan. I'll take you in my chopper, we should get there in about 4 hours."

"Henley, I should tell Liz... are you certain?"

"Yes, I have to at least tell her what I know..."

"Okay, but we must hurry."

"Okay, I'll meet you out front in ten minutes. Faith put in a call to Liz but it went straight to voicemail. It was almost too difficult to leave such a devastating message on Liz's voicemail, but she had no choice. Henley wrote a quick note for his son's nanny. He has plans to take Tommy fishing this weekend and assured him that they would go later that day.

Faith could hear the whirring sound of the helicopter's blades and hurried out front to join Henley. As she enters the vehicle, Henley reached out his hands and help lift Faith on board. Moments later they were en route to New York. As they neared Manhattan, Henley signaled ATC: local Air Traffic Controllers to receive clearance to land his chopper on the roof of the Hospital. Almost four hours later and a short while after receiving the greenlight from ATC, he landed safely.

"Looks like we made it, I'll have to fuel her up before we head back," he said taking Faith's hands as she steps carefully out of the chopper onto the roof. Faith braced herself for the unexpected.

"Here, put this on," Henley said cautiously, handing Faith a pair of scarf and sunglasses that she'd left in the chopper a few days before.

"Glad you forgot them, they'll come in handy now," he said winking at her. His cheerful spirit reassured her, and a feeling of calm came over her as they walked through the hallways and entered the doors to the Emergency room. As in slow motion Faith converse with the ER's admitting Clerk. She didn't mention to Henley that Hank was her fiancé before this, and her conversation with the Clerk revealed this to him. As she stared at him expecting a response, he was unmoved and smiled. He'd promised to be there for her no matter what, nothing he learns in the process would change his promise to take her by the hand and lead her through the maze of her life.

"Mr. Hutton is on the second floor in room 222. The elevator is around the corner to your left," the clerk whispered. As they walked toward the elevator, Henley took her hands…

"Together?" he asked.

"Together," she agreed. Faith cried as she approached the curtain and slowly drew it back. Henley stood a short distance away to allow them privacy. By the conversations, Henley knew that it was safe to assume that Hank was alive and just as he thought of approaching, Faith called him enthusiastically, a broad smile on her face.

"Senator, what are you doing here and to what do I owe this pleasure?" Hank was now sitting up in bed. There were bandages on his forehead and a white cast around his right hand. He'd suffered a broken arm and minor bruises on his face and shoulders. As he discusses the events from three days before…Hank was reduced to tears.

"Faith, she's gone, Candace, she… didn't make it," he cried. Faith slowly brought her hands to her mouth in utter shock. She sat next to him and wrapped her arms around him. As she thought of Sydney, tears sprang into her eyes and for the hundredth time today, she wept.

"Mr. Hutton, I'm deeply sorry for your loss," Henley said placing a hand on Hank's shoulder. Henley then remembered Faith's pregnancy and that she hadn't eaten…

"Oh, Faith, the baby, you need to eat. I'll be back with refreshments," he called and excused himself. Faith and Hank slowly releases each other from their tight embrace. He looks at her, unsure of what Senator Henley meant.

"A baby, you brought a baby?" he asked puzzled. For the first time today, Faith smiled.

"Hank, there's something I must tell you," she said placing her hands on her tummy.

"I'm pregnant," she said smiling while removing a tear from her eyes.

"You're having a baby?" she shook her head in response. A glimmer of joy sprang into his eyes.

"In the midst of death, I found life," he said now moved with tears, this time in complete joy.

"Oh Faith, I'm so happy you're here. When I didn't hear from you, I thought…she interrupted his sentence with another tight embrace and whispered…

"Shh." She didn't want him to learn of her pregnancy this way….still unsure whose baby it was…yet the joy her precious gift has brought to Hank…it was certain that there was no better time than the present.

Hank is being released from the hospital today and he was thankful for his unexpected company. He wondered how they'd managed to go unnoticed by the crowded ER and staff members.

"How's my daughter, does she know about the accident?" Hank ask, hesitating at Faith's potential response.

"We've had a busy week and unfortunately, I just got the chance to read your email this morning. I came as soon as I learned of the accident. We came here with Henley's chopper. Syd wasn't home.

She's on the beach with Liz and George. I tried reaching them but got Liz's voicemail," she said. "I'm hoping that she doesn't get my message, that way you can speak with your daughter." Remembering Candace, Hank and Faith was reduced to tears once more as the nurse helped wheeled him to the roof where the Helicopter waited. Henley removed his mobile and phoned AAA....

"Hey guys, it's me, I'm at Bellevue Memorial and I need fuel. Yes, in Manhattan. How long? Okay perfect," he responded and hung up. As they waited for emergency fuel, the three discusses next steps. Hank agreed to return to California and reside at Liz's place surrounded by his friends until he recovers.

"What about Candace?" Henley asked.

"I made arrangements to have her funeral in California. She will be transported in a week," he said tearfully.

A few hours later, Henley's chopper lifted off Manhattan's Bellevue for a short trip to Hanks apartment on the Hudson. A few minutes later, they landed on the roof of the Astoria. Faith took the memorable elevator to the unit and followed Hanks specific instructions. Moments later she returned with a few things he'd packed for his trip and once more, they lifted off and en route to California. During the trip, Hank discusses some of the plans that him and Candace had made during their marriage in such an event. We'd both agreed to cremation," he said tearing up once more. "

"It's okay darling, we can discuss it later," Faith assured him, wiping away his tears and kissing his face. As she fed him a snack, remembering... "Please have some," he smiled glancing at her tummy. Sharing a bittersweet moment, they are comforted by the joy of renewed hope. Henley hardly spoke on their trip back and a little over four hours later, the party of three landed safely at Henley's private Estate. Tommy ran toward his father. "Daddy, I'm glad you're back," he said as his father hugged him tightly. Elizabeth, George and the girls came out to greet their arriving guests. She appeared puzzled by Hank's condition. By Liz's reaction, Faith realized that she did not receive the voicemail that she'd left on her phone earlier and she was relieved.

"Daddy, what happened?" Syd called running toward her Father.

"What happened? Daddy are you okay?"

"I love you sweetheart," he cried embracing her with his one available arm. Katherine looked at her mom for answers...

"There's been an accident," Faith cried. As they all encircled Hank, Silence followed, and a soft wind ruffled and stirred the hundreds of flowering blossoms on the estate releasing a sweet fragrance into the air.

As Sydney sat on Faith's bosom, her Father, revealed to her that her mom was gone. He explained that the Doctors had done everything that they possibly could to bring her back. As her father unfold the events of that fateful day, Sydney's eyes widened in shock.

"No daddy, what do you mean? Why are you saying this to me…. please where's my mommy?" Faith held her lovingly and kissed her darling face. Unable to process what her father was saying, Syd slipped away from Faith and ran off. Hank was again reduced to tears as the cries of his beautiful daughter could be heard. Liz phoned her boys Calvin and Eric…she wanted Syd to be surrounded by her family.

"Calvin agreed to come with his fiancé. Eric sent his love but refused. "It's none of my business mom. It's not my family. Besides, I wedded Rachael last night in a private ceremony and we're currently preparing for our honeymoon." Stunned by her son's admission…Liz simply hung up without a word.

Sydney refused to be comforted. She's hardly spoken to anyone and has eaten very little since the news of the untimely death of her mother. She'd spent the last week in the private guestroom that Liz had put together for her. Despite the amazing support from the family that she's grown so found of, she felt alone. Climbing out of bed for the first time today, she drew the curtains and sat in a sofa near the window. It was raining heavily out and the sounds of the heavy rains as they splash against the windowpane helped calm her growing sense of loss. It was as though the pouring rains were nature's way of sharing in her sorrows. As she sat gazing at the sprinkles on the window, her silence was interrupted by a soft knock on her door.

"Syd, it's me, can I come in?" Katherine called. But Syd remained focused and undisturbed. Kat lifted her eyes to the pink handwritten note on the door…,

"Please, do not disturb," It read with a pair of tear drops drawn in pink.

"I miss you Syd, please say something, talk to me," Kat pleaded.

"Come darling, she just needs more time. We have to give her space and time..." Liz said embracing her granddaughter.

At Hank's request, Faith and Calvin went above and beyond to arrange a memorial service for Candace Hutton. Later, Hank handed Faith a little black book with a list of all of him and Candace's devoted friends. She dialed their respective numbers and each time, she handed the phone to Hank. After several hours they'd contacted over a hundred people to inform them of Candace's passing and to invite them to pay their respects at her memorial this Saturday. It was a very daunting, emotional task listening on the responses and conversations between Hank and his friends, but she was thankful that this part of it was now over. She giggled as he tosses his mobile across the floor.

"Sorry, but you have to admit, your arms are in exceptional shape to have held your phone to your ears this long." She joked. He flexes his right arm in response. He appeared to be in better spirits, but she knew it was only for a moment.

Calvin and Gerry had reserved the first hundred seats at the St Vincent De Antonio Catholic church for friends and family. It was already 9:00am Saturday morning; Calvin had already arrived at the beautiful parish to place the reservation labels on the seating that was set aside for friends and family. After the finishing touches, the men glanced at the gorgeous setting that they had created.

"This is truly a work of art," Gerry smiled pleasingly at Calvin.

"The flowers are an exquisite touch," Calvin admitted.

"This setting seems more appropriate for the beginning of a new journey." Calvin said and smiled broadly realizing Gerry's thoughts.

As Faith helped Hank with his tie, the doorbell to the main entry rang.

"Expecting someone?"

"No," he nods. She opens the door to see a large floral box completed by Gold and White Bows. It was addressed to Hank Hutton. Surprised, she picked up the strange looking present and carries it, extending it away from herself.

"It's for you," she said, placing the box above the fireplace.

"Looks lovely, what do you think it is?"

"Oh, it's Candace's Urn."

"Goodness, thank God I was careful," she said feeling weirdly awkward.

"Perfect, mind carrying it to the car?"

"Don't you want to have a look...?"

"No." Hank smiled.

"'Okay," she says and carries the Urn and places it in the back of Liz's convertible. As she thought of her odd encounter, she phoned Calvin to confirm that everything was arranged. As she thought of him, her phone buzzed.

"Calvin, I was just about to phone you."

"Yes, it's here. Her Urn has arrived. Yes, that would be lovely. I can't thank you gentlemen enough... wonderful" she beamed. A few moments later, Calvin arrived and carried Candace's Urn to the church.

Near the pulpit stood a gorgeous photo of Candace in a flowing white Spring dress. She was sitting on a swing in her mother's flower garden in Maine. The photo was placed between two large vases of fresh flowers atop a large black Organ. The gorgeous white Urn were placed on top the Organ surrounded by even more gorgeous arrangements of flowers. For the first time in over a week, Katherine waited to greet her friend to accompany her to her mother's memorial. It was like an image from a fairytale when Syd finally stood in the hallway dressed in a breathtaking black flowing girl's lace. It would have been a moment of epic splendor to run into her arms, but as much as she was happy to see her friend, her large green eyes were met by Syd's sad steady brown eyes. She simply lifted her hands out to hers and hand in hand, they walked out front where Liz, Faith, Calvin, and Gerry were waiting. At the sight of his daughter and her friend, Hank was once again overcome with emotion.

"Daddy," Syd cried running to him, embracing him. As they drove to St Vincent De Antonio Catholic church, Syd knew it was the longest journey she'd ever make.

It was an astounding vision as close friends and family filled the seats to pay their final respects to the Hutton Family. Many of which shared fond childhood memories of Hank and Candace filling the Parish with temporary laughter. As joys faded, Hank turned to face his daughter; she'd requested to play her mother's favorite song. Surrounded by friends on a sorrowful rainy day, Sydney played her mother's favorite song. "A Mother's Prayer," by Celine Dion on the large Organ where her memories were displayed so beautifully. She played magnificently, with all of her heart, and tears streaming down her beautiful face, she made her final tribute to her Mother, one that would never soon be forgotten.

It's been a week since Candace's Memorial. Syd continues to occupy her comfortable quarters at Liz's. She was grateful to be in San Francisco and despite her choice for solitude, she was comforted knowing that she and her dad were surrounded by those who loved them the most. Chance whined and scratched on the door to Syd's bedroom. It was almost as though she was attempting to speak perfect English when she made a sad melancholy sound that got Faith's attention. Unable to get Syd to let him in, Chance laid down in front of her bedroom door and yawned loudly.

"Hi sweetie," Faith said patting Chance's ears. "You're a good girl. You take such good care of her. Hang in there, she'll come around soon." Faith continued patting her ear and tickling her tummy, as Chance's tail tapped loudly against the carpeted floor.

Liz waltz into her kitchen dancing to Nat King Cole's "Unforgettable." Her promise is to keep things as positive and cheerful around her home as possible to lift the welcomed sadness that has swept away common joys. Patrol George smiled at the sight of Liz as she twirls and spin, entering the kitchen.

"Wow, I wished I was better attired," he said, slipping on a bathrobe over his PJs joining Elizabeth in a Waltz. The two spun around Liz's large kitchen smiling and giggling.

"George, I have butterflies," she blushed. Unsure if it was love or lust in George's eyes, she leaned forward to meet his lips.

Chapter 25

Faith stood at the entrance of her office, admiring the gorgeous marble architecture and sunny decor of Sandy Island sunsets in different variations. She also appreciated images of the picturesque Island refreshing her memory of the images that once were. Her new office is now an excellent representation of the vision she hoped to successfully reinstate into the perfect image it once was.

"I have to admit, this is a far cry from what it was a week ago," Senator Henley said, approaching with a cup in both hands.

"Thank you," Faith said, taking a cup of coffee from Henley's extended hand.

"So how're you and the little one this morning?" he asked, staring at her tummy. There was a sudden look of concern in her eyes.

"You know Henley, I have not been to see my OB, not yet."

"And why's that?" he asked.

"Hmm, well, the last time I went to see my OB. I was married and knew who my baby's father was." Realizing her fear…

"Come here," he said, taking her in his arms.

"I would love to accompany you to see him. I would love to be with you for every appointment" Henley offered.

"Okay, yes," she said, snuggling into his arms.

"You're letting Henley take you to see your OB, Faith this is so not cool. That's my place, it's my baby," Hank scolded. She wanted to share the uncertainty of her baby's paternity with Hank, but she didn't believe that he was ready for the truth. Despite being divorced from the mother of his child, she knows that it would take him some time to get over his deep sense of loss. She knew that he needed the joy that a new baby would bring into his life. She was not willing to devastate the possibility of this fact by sharing with him the result of an untested hypothesis.

"Hank, please I need you to trust me on this one. I wasn't sure where our relationship stood when you left for New York. Henley's been there for me and I can't turn him away. At minimum, you should be grateful that he's been so generous to us both." Hank turned away from her.

"You can't exclude Syd and myself. At this pivotal moment, this baby is exactly what we need."

"You'd have to trust me on that one Hank, she needs you more right now. Syd needs you. You both need each other to get through this, and it will get better Hank, I've been there. I promise," she said, remembering the death of her parents. He turns to face her, revealing the tears streaming down his face. It's now that she realizes how much he loves the mother of his child.

"Darling, I'm so sorry," she said, embracing him.

"If you prefer, I can have a private OB come to my residence, here to see you."

"Really?"

"Oh Sure, I have a few that I can recommend."

"Are they men or women?" Henley laughed at her question.

"Am I seriously hearing this from my newly elected State Senator?" He smiled, eyes narrowed.

"Well, sorry but the ones I know are all men." As she contemplated Henley's proposition....

"Um, you know Senator, I have to admit, I already have too many men in my life."

"Wait a minute, am I included?" he joked.

"I've thought about it, and I like having you around."

"Sounds charming," he said looking into her eyes.

"You can kiss me if you like," she invited, seeing the longing in his eyes. Placing his coffee cup on Faith's dark wooden desk. He kissed her forehead.

"I'll always be here for you," he said in a whisper and took her in his arms.

The following morning, Faith awoke feeling an icy cold draft coming through the window. Strange, why is it so cold, she thought, not remembering whether she'd turned on the air conditioning before going to bed. She then heard playful noises coming from outside. She looked out the window facing Liz's oversized backyard.... her eyes widened and her mouth stood agape at everything from grass, to miles of roofs and trees, blanketed by several inches of Snow. The playful noises were the sound of two beautiful young ladies sitting in red wooden toboggans, speeding down hill.

"Wow," Hank called, folding his hands and shivering, it's freezing out here. I love it," he joked.

"I wondered whose idea this was?" he asked looking up at the heavens as though speaking to someone.

"I think God is trying to tell me something," Faith called from the window, catching Hank's attention.

"I see that, can you ask him to make it quick." Faith laughed at the sight of him.

"What are you wearing?" She laughed, staring at his short cargo pants and flip flops.

"You can blame the girls. They were in a hurry to get out here, didn't care if I froze," he laughed. He appeared much happier than she remembered and as he glanced up at the window at her in silence, she could almost read his thoughts.

"I have to go get ready, to head to the office. We have a public conference this morning to discuss the progress on our girl Sandy," she called. She'd missed him and the days that they shared on Sandy Bay. It almost seemed that fate had brought him back into her life. She wondered if she and Senator Henley hadn't flown to Manhattan to see him...what his decision would have been. She was mystified by the uncertainty of the days ahead...Would fate also decide the direction of the days to come and the birth of her unborn child?

Senator Henley docked Vixen in the cove of Sandy Island.

"Dad, that's a terrible spot, you know we never catch anything here." I really hope that this isn't one of your lousy lessons, because I'm in no mood for them right now," Tommy said annoyed. Henley understood his frustration but there was a point to this. Since Tommy was old enough to go fishing, he'd used several real-life examples to teach him valuable lessons. He was only eleven but was already wiser than most people his age. As Senator, despite a demanding schedule, he'd promised a schedule that would allow him time with his son. Tommy was about to shout another question when he felt a hard grab on his fishing line. He looked over his shoulders for his dad.

"Hey dad, dad, where are you? But Henley had decided to hide from Tommy and watched him from around the corner. He could tell that by the way that Tommy's fishing line was bending that it was a small to medium catch, one that he could easily pull onboard.

"Dad, dad, where are you?" he screamed and threw a tantrum.

"Dad, I hate this" he yelled while actively reeling the aggressive fish onboard. Henley held back laughter as he observed his son's tiny stomach formed a six pack as he reeled the determined catch aboard.

"Dad, what should I do with this deplorable fish?"

"It's your dinner," said Henley approaching.

"I'm not eating that. Then you'd miss the point."

"Dad you know I hate these stupid games, I'm not eating that and I don't want a sibling," he yelled and stormed off.

"Tommy, what are you talking about?" Henley asked puzzled by Tommy's statement. As he contemplates Tommy's statement, he realizes that he must have overheard him and Faith's conversation and assumes that he was having a baby with Faith.

"Wow, hey Tommy, wait up kiddo," he said, following his son. Tommy had locked himself in his cabin and didn't come out till he heard Vixen's anchor splashed in the waves below. As soon as the boat had docked, Tommy ran past his father, scrambled uphill, and disappeared in the tall grass near the Estate. Henley knew that he was headed to the guest house where he would remain to his heart's content. Henley realized that he needed to spend some time with his son. It's been a hectic few weeks and Tommy was obviously having a difficult time adjusting to all the changes that were taking place. What was I thinking? He thought. He then realizes that his son must have a million questions that no fishing trip could solve.

After a long day at conferences, Faith relaxed at the office and stretched her legs out placing them on a stack of books sitting in the corner. She glanced around the room and noticed the mess that she'd made. She'd accidentally overprint a conference document that needed her signature, and there were tons of paper sitting on the floor. She'd removed her shoes which were sitting near her desk and a pile of boxes that had just been delivered was sitting near the entrance of her office. Several of her coats, some of which she'd forgotten after too many exhausted afternoons were hanging on a fire chair near the fireplace. As she sat at her desk, her white leather recliner felt overly comfortable. A short while later, loud snores could be heard, as Syd and Katherine joked that small Zzzzz's were floating down Senator Henley's stairwell. Liz and Patrol George had dropped the girls off at Henley's based on a text message that Faith hand sent earlier. Liz texted Faith…

"Hi hun, I just dropped off the girls, they're inside the gate and are on their way up. Hank will be swinging by to take you and the girl's home in an hour." But Faith was fast asleep, as the effects of her early pregnancy claimed her last ounce of strength.

"Shhh," Syd whispered as they tippy toed passed Faith's office.

"Where are you going?" Kat whispered.

"To find Tommy, he's so cute," Syd said smiling suspiciously.

"Follow me, this way."

"But Syd, he has a guard and those horrible looking pit bulls that sit outside his bedroom. You mean the ones that eat and farts all day?"

"Shhh, come on, let's go kiddo," Syd called and both girls disappeared through the back entrance and took the trail of Lily's that led to Henley's guest house. Syd crouched down and walked up to a partially open window. She looked over her shoulder for Katherine and saw her hiding in plain view behind a cherry blossom tree.

"You call this hiding," Syd laughed. Tommy glanced at the computer monitor. He noticed that the security camera had picked up some movement behind the window.

"He was still upset with his father and didn't care. He trusted that Greg and Sammy were sitting near the entrance. As he glanced back at the monitor, he couldn't ignore the blond hair that the camera had picked up sitting in the grass behind the guesthouse. A smile began to form on his face. He thought maybe the girls were just picking flowers. He then opened the gate and instructed Greg and Sammy to come in. He knew that his pets were only friendly during lunch.

"Come here boys," he called. Greg's ears popped up when he saw Syd's hands reach and knock on the window. He grumbled and Sammy joined in.

"Hey, quiet down boys, that's no way to treat the ladies." Tommy realized that they were not just picking flowers, they were trying to scare him. He was in no mood to hang out with little girls, so he had to think of something quick. He then remembered his very realistic Werewolf costume. He pulled it out of the hallway closet and slipped it on at lightning speed. He appeared so frightening, that both pets barked and hid themselves under the dining table.

As Syd and Kat circled the yard, trying the door handles, a pair of large hairy paws generously opened the door and beckoned them to enter. As the girl's eyes adjusted to the sight of a grotesque figure now fully apparent with large gaping teeth, bloody screams could be heard as they fled the flowery scene in utter horror awakening Faith from her nap. A little confused, she stared at the time on the wall. Just as she was about to investigate the screams, both Syd and Katherine fled past her and vanished.

"Girls?" Faith called. "Is everything okay?" Puzzled, she looked at the back entrance sitting wide open and an arrangement of broken flowers sitting scattered on the floor. Faith almost gasped as Tommy removed the mask.

"Geeze, Tommy, what are you doing?" Faith laughed picking up a yellow rose and tossing it at him.

"You almost had me there for a minute, where in the world did you find that thing?" she laughed.

"Oh, it's my old Halloween Costume. I put it on to scare the living daylights of your girls and the little one," he said pointing at her stomach. Realizing what he meant she called after him as he walked away.

"Tommy, Tommy...." she called. She knew it was time to speak with the girls about the baby before they learned it from someone else.

"What is it mom, what do you have to tell us," Katherine asked, holding Sydney's hands and wiggling her toes excitedly.

"Darlings, I've been keeping a secret."

"You have? But, but, mom you're not that good at keeping secrets," Kat replied, looking at her mom suspiciously.

"She's a Senator now Kat, and they're allowed."

Sydney replied, winking an eye at Faith.

"Really? Do Senators have secrets? What about Senator Henley?"

"Well, he's been a Senator for a very, very long time, so I'm sure he has lots and lots of secrets," Sydney assured.

"OMG, mom, what's your secret, what are you keeping from me mommy? Is it dangerous?" Katherine asked standing, placing her hands on her hips. Faith's eyes shifted to her tiny bulge, placing her hands on her tummy and circled it gently.

"Girls, we're having a baby," she smiled broadly. The girls looked at each other.

"A baby," they said simultaneously.

"Who's having a baby?" Syd asked, looking at Katherine.

"Not me," Katherine laughed. As Syd and Katherine argued about who's having a baby, Faith giggled, wondering if she could once more win their attention.

"Girls, Syd, Kat...I'm having a baby," Faith said now smiling radiantly. She now had both their attention.

"Mom, are you really having a baby?" Katherine asked optimistically. Faith shook her head.

"Yes baby." You're going to have a baby brother or sister," Faith said excitedly. A look of both concern and of astonishment formed on Syd's face. As she thought of Faith's baby, the words, the message, and moment has claimed her silence...yet a smile began to form as she thought of her dad, Faith, Katherine and the baby...

"You're having a baby?" She said approaching Faith and placing her hands around her and Katherine as all three embraced in the most loving way. Sydney's heart raced as a flowering secret glistened her innocent thoughts, restoring joy of the slightest chance that Faith's baby could be her sibling.

Chapter 26

As Faith thought of someone who would fill the position as her Legislative Assistant, she scrolled through her phone contacts to locate Stephanie. As she stumbled upon her, her thumb dialed the number on accident. The line rang for several minutes then an automated voice response answered.

"The number you've reached is no longer in service."

"Ugg," she said frustratingly and hung up. She wondered what had happened to her since the fire destroyed Sandy. Before the fire, they were both working on Faith's idea to convert her Sandy Island Bungalow into a Sandy Bay-n-B. She hoped at minimum that Steph was safe.

"Faith, honey, where are you sweetie?" Elizabeth called.

"Here Liz," she replied.

"Honey, I overheard you in the bathroom this morning, is everything okay? Look at you, you're glowing. How could I have missed this...as her thoughts cleared, the girls came running through the door.

"Grandma Liz, you won't believe it, mom is having a baby!!" Katherine said ecstatically.

"It's true Liz, we're both going to be big sisters," Syd said excitedly.

"I still can't believe it," Kat said, jumping around like a bunny rabbit.

"As sure as my thoughts. How far along are you darling?" Faith took Liz's hands and placed them on her tummy.

"Oh, sweetie, you already have a little bump. Secrets are for senator's love," Liz joked embracing Faith, once more the girls joined in as they all submerged in a tight embrace.

It's been almost three months since project Rebuild Sandy began. The view from Senator Henley's balcony showed incredible progress as almost ninety percent of the residential community appears complete.

"Sandy looks better than I remembered," said Henley joining Faith.

"Yes, she's a beauty, and you have the best view."

"An amazing unobstructed view. Or should I say, a specific view." she smiled, staring at him suspiciously. He approached her smiling and rubbed her back gently.

"Wait a minute, are you saying that's your house over there?"

"So how long have you been spying on me Henley?" she kidded. Since I first spotted you in a gorgeous summer dress. Standing right there," he said pointing.

"The wind had the tip of your dress and it stirred your hair. Each morning, faithfully, you would grace this view. Then for several months you never showed. It was then I asked my assistant to perform some research to find out who lives there.

"Henley, I'm sure you're aware that I'm entitled to my right to privacy."

"Indeed, but for six months?"

"Where were you? I was concerned. I felt like I got to know you. Then suddenly, you disappeared. I swear, you made my day, each morning, there was a grace about you, so refreshing, I had to find out..."

"Oh, Henley, I almost forgot. I might have a slight conflict with my schedule today."

"How so? Our meeting with the Sandy Developers is in an hour and I also have an appointment with my Obstetrician in an hour."

"Any progress with your search for an assistant?"

"I have someone in mind but didn't have any luck reaching her. You mentioned research earlier, if your Assistant isn't too busy, would you mind if she does some research to locate a Stephanie Bradley for me please? She's one of the dislocated residents of Sandy Island. Very bright young lady and recent grad from the University."

"Sure, jot down Stephanie's info on a sticky note and I'll ask Kim to give it priority."

"Thanks Henley."

"You got it. Anything else I can do for you, my lady? Oh, I have it, that doctor's appointment needs to be pushed back..." he said, hurrying off, his robe tossing behind him.

"You're the best," she calls after him.

Tommy got on his bike and began a two-mile ride to Liz's house on Belvedere Ave. He pulled into the driveway and set his bike against the garage. As he was about to ring the doorbell, the door swung open.

"Tommy? It's Tommy right?" Liz asked.

"Yes it's me, Ma'am sorry to bother so early in the day, I'm here to see Hank, is he in?" he asked, his eyes drifting to his feet.

"Yes, is he expecting you?"

"No, but it's important that I see him. I haven't been sleeping...and..."

"Please come on in Tommy, how did you get over here?"

"I rode my bike."

"Your bike?"

"Hank, you have a visitor. It's the Senator's son, Tommy."

"Who?" Hank asked peeking from around the corner.

"Oh, sure, give me one sec, I'll be right there."

"Can I get you something to drink Tommy?"

"Yes Ma'am some lemonade will do, please thank you."

"Coming right up," Liz called.

"Tommy, Henley's son right?"

"Yes."

"What can I do for you buddy?"

"Mind if we talk somewhere private?"

"Sure, I know just the place," Hank said leading the way.

"Here you go darling," Liz said, handing him a tall glass filled with Lemonade and a napkin. "Thank you, Ma'am, again sorry for the intrusion."

"Not at all Tommy, you're welcome anytime," she called.

Hank led the way down a long corridor that led to Liz's private balcony overlooking the rest of the neighborhood.

"So how can I help you buddy?" Tommy remained silent and sipped on his lemonade. Hank smiled and shook his head.

"This must be really good lemonade." Tommy shook his head.

"Yes Liz has a way of making everything edible, absolutely delicious. I think it's the reason I still live here. It's quiet and the meals are to die for," Hank admitted. Hank continued to wait for Tommy to say something, but he only listened as Hank led the conversation. As Hank continues to chat with Tommy about his life and the things he did when he was Tommy's age, he began to

221

suspect that the reason for the boy's unexpected visit was simply casual. He realized that he was possibly feeling isolated due to his Father's schedule and not having kids his age around.

"Tommy, you're homeschooled right?"

"How'd you know?"

"I suspected so, my daughter Sydney is also Homeschooled."

"It's a great option but can be boring for an only child," Tommy admitted.

"Yes definitely," Hank agreed. But that was all he said, and his silence resumed. Hank continued to share details about his childhood with his unexpectedly silent visitor. About an hour later, after enjoying a couple slices of Liz's famous cheesecake and another glass of lemonade, Tommy thanked Hank for his time.

"I can give you a lift back to the estate," Liz offered but he declined. Tommy got back on his bike and rode home. Both Hank and Liz were left mystified.

"So, he said nothing at all."

"Nothing," Hank replied.

"Strange...I think he might just be bored.

"His dad's schedule hardly makes time for him."

"I used to be his age at one time and as an only child, I can relate. Are you sure we shouldn't tell his dad...?"

"No, I'm sure he'll come by again. Maybe he's trying to establish trust and in time he will open up, when he's ready.

"You're right Hank. When I was growing up, my mother always used to say that children have a good sense for people. Maybe he knows he can trust you."

Strong winds from the X-19-SX helicopter's powerful blade stirred the trees and plants nearby. Faith and Henley boarded the aircraft for their meeting with the Contractors.

"We only have room for one more," the pilot called.

"What!"

"Well you'll have to come back because I need to see Sandy's progress. I have a public conference in the morning, and I need to be prepared to address the people of San Francisco."

"Paul, listen, this aircraft is not to be used for entertainment reasons. It is Government property and should only be used for official purposes. You know what, please come back in the morning," Henley said frustratedly.

"Henley is this necessary?" Faith said looking at him questionably.

"There's room, at least, I should go."

"Sorry Faith, I have to accompany you on this one. A large percentage of the residents of Sandy Island are currently residing in San Francisco, this makes it my prerogative as well as yours. In the morning, we must both be present to address the public."

It's been almost five months since the fire devastated Sandy Island and the displaced residents are growing more concerned.

"I must warn you; this conference is going to be emotionally demanding, are you sure you're up for it?" Faith smiled as his concern was obvious.

"Henley, when you recommended me for this job, I would like to believe that it was for the right reasons and not just the wind in my hair."

"Of course not. But you can't blame me for being concerned about your current situation. Faith you're having a baby and in all my years as a Senator, I can tell you that these public meetings can be daunting. It's no place for someone who's emotionally fragile."

"Henley, you're being ridiculous, at some point, the people of Sandy Island will have to learn that their Senator is pregnant, and that she has no idea who the father of her baby is. Is that what you're so ashamed of Henley?" He didn't respond and he could tell that by the look in her eyes that she was beyond frustrated with him.

"Henley, an office in your house is no longer appropriate, if I'm going to be successful as a Senator, you'll have to give me some space," she said firmly and walked away.

"Faith, please," he called.

The next morning, Faith arrived earlier than usual to meet Henley for their meeting with the Architects. Their meeting couldn't last more than an hour as shortly thereafter they had to be downtown at the Congressional District on Golden Gate Ave. Paul arrived on schedule.

"Hi Paul, thanks for being here," Faith said in a cheerful spirit.

"Morning," Henley called icily.

"Morning, Sir, Madam," Paul responded respectfully. After apologizing for yesterday, the trio headed southbound for Sandy Bay. It was an incredibly beautiful day out as the early sunrise radiated its transparent light on the glistening horizon.

A few hours later, after several missed phone calls and text messaging from the Congressional Office, the two Senators were finally on their way.

"I really like that idea that Sam proposed," Henley said, finally breaking the ice since the meeting with the contractors concluded.

"You mean the idea of broadening Sandy Island Blvd?"

"Umhm," he nodded.

"I'm not sure I like the idea of too much traffic coming to our little Sandy."

"Well, we must learn from experience. The two lanes were not sufficient to allow most residents to escape by car. I was thankful to learn that most residents were expert swimmers and own private boats."

"I don't see much difference in escaping by boat or car."

"Actually, a car starts up much faster than an engine boat which can take several cranks to get warmed up," Henley smiled. She wanted to argue with him, but it was not the time. She had to save her energy for the large crowd that according to Jeremy, their Communications Specialist, had already assembled in the Senatorial Hall. The X-19-SX helicopter landed on the heliport where they were met by four secret service agents who drove them to the Congressional Office on Golden Gate Ave.

At the sight of their Senator approaching, Jeremy hurried toward Faith to greet her. He reached for a napkin in his shirt pocket and gently wiped the drops of sweat that were forming on her forehead.

"Senator is everything alright?"

"Certainly, just a bit annoyed," she replied.

"As he continues to gently remove the moisture from Faith's face and forehead…

"What's your position?" she asked.

"Oh, I'm Jeremy, one of your Media and Communication Specialist."

"Oh, pleasure to finally meet you Jeremy, why weren't you at the meeting this morning?"

"You mean the Contractor's meeting?"

"Right… I wasn't aware that I had to be present Ma'am."

"You might want to access the transcript from the meeting to prepare my speech."

"I already did, Ma'am."

"Excellent," she replied.

"Senator?" Jeremy called hurrying after her.

"Yes....?"

"Ma'am Senator Henley wants to stand with you for the first address. He wants you to meet him in the conference room to go over your speech. Faith exhaled frustratedly.

"Faith, it's time," Henley called. As they entered the Senatorial Hall, Faith was surprised at the large crowd that had assembled. It seemed that everyone was shouting questions. Jeremy took to the podium and addressed the crowd.

"One question at a time please!" he shouted. He then whispered to Faith

"Ma'am, you're all set." Faith glanced at Henley and smiled as she took to the podium to address the public; most of whom are residents of Sandy Island as well as concerned San Franciscans. He'd change his mind; he would watch from a distance as she faced the crowd, for the first time, this time in a different way. As she addressed each question, she appeared wise and confident. Henley and Jeremy continued to observe from a distance...they smiled proudly at how well she addressed each individual question. Several hundred hands were lifted, and Faith selected an individual toward the back of the Conference room.

"Sir, you, yes, you in the white beret."

"When would Sandy Island Blvd be open to the public?"

"As of 12pm today, all access to Sandy Island, including waterways would be fully accessible to the public."

"Excellent," the gentleman replied. As her eyes scanned the crowd to select her next question, she noticed a familiar face. As she searched her memory, she realized that it was the young woman she'd seen camped out near the Golden Gate bridge, earlier in the Spring. Realizing that Faith had recognized her, she smiled broadly and waved enthusiastically. She was dressed quite sharply in a pink lace Jacket, Jeans and knee-high boots. Faith returned the smile and waved enthusiastically. The crowd turned to face the woman.

"How are you my friend? I don't believe that I'd get your name that day...remembered?" She smiled remembering her conversation with Faith several months ago.

"It's Margaret, but my friends call me Maggie," she replied.

"I see, now that wasn't so difficult now, was it?" Faith jokes.

"Everyone, please meet my newest friend Maggie, I've had the pleasure of meeting her back in the Spring, she was a bit reluctant to give me her name. But I assure you, she's a very bright young lady and quite the conversationalist." The crowd applauded, while bystanders shook Maggie's hand. Maggie remembered her conversation with Faith and knew that the Sandy Island Senator was simply being kind.

"Maggie, do you have any questions for me today?"

"Just one," she replied confidently.

"My mom and I did not lose our home to the fire, but it was foreclosed on, and sold at auction. We are residents of Sandy Island and have been displaced since we lost our home…" she paused for a moment, as though to remove a tear from her eye. Faith realized where her questions were heading, and she met her halfway.

"You would like to know what provisions are being made for Sandy Island residents that have been in transition, prior to the fire?"

"Yes ma'am," she said, lifting her eyes to meet Faith's. The press was eager to hear Faith's position on the issue of homelessness in San Francisco and on the Island as they shuffled among themselves to capture the best view of her from the growing crowd.

"The City of Sandy Island recognizes the economic divisions and societal norms that form our different ways of life. During my discussions with the contractors earlier this morning, I was informed that a surplus of two hundred fifty homes were built to address the issue of homelessness in the Sandy Island District. During our initial meeting with the Developers, I've advised our contractors to not only communicate with businesses and homeowners, but to also rely on Census Data, to accurately accommodate the residents of Sandy Island. In doing so, we're now able to reinforce our promise to the dedicated residents of Sandy." Loud whistles and applauses could be heard as Faith delivered the news that they all awaited.

"It is official: The construction of Sandy is now complete. As of today, displaced families can begin to return to their respective homes. Businesses can resume normal operations as soon as shipments and supplies are restocked. As of today, employers can rehire laid-off employees to prepare their businesses to open their doors to the public. It is presumed that all businesses and residents would be completely settled within one month from this address. The City of Sandy Island, thanks San Francisco and surrounding counties for their patience, generous contributions and accommodations to their temporarily distressed neighbors of Sandy Island." As her speech concludes, a soft wind shuffled the nearby trees. The early morning fog gracefully lifted as the sun cast its golden rays across the Bay, warming the hearts of the people from the city on a hill. Loud applause resumed as the press photographed their new Senator leaving the podium to mingle with the public. Tears streamed down her face as she shook hands and embraced children and adults alike.

"She's lovely," some complemented while others expressed their appreciation for her beautiful appearance and genuinely kind nature. Maggie approached her and extended her hands, but Faith instead leaned forward and embraced her.

"Maggie, what does your schedule look like this weekend...?" As Maggie was about to respond, Jeremy tapped her on the shoulder.

"Please Senator, we must hurry, the Secret Service is waiting to escort you and Henley back to the helicopter," he urged.

"Maggie, I have a better idea. Jeremy, come here please, I need your help. Please communicate with Maggie, I need her contact information. I also need you to arrange a meeting between Maggie and myself for this weekend.

"Absolutely, I'm on it."

"Thank you, Maggie, if it's appropriate, please provide Jeremy with your contact details and I'll see you this weekend..."

"Thank you, Senator," Maggie called. Faith looked over her shoulders one more time and waved as she was guided away from the crowd.

Chapter 27

As Faith scrolled through her hundreds of unread emails, she noticed one from her Communications Specialist. Titled "Maggie's info." There was no physical address, just a P.O. Box and her mobile number…As she contemplated the issue of homelessness and families, Faith realizes that it was a topic that was almost foreign to her, yet, one that cannot be ignored. As she prepared for her meeting with Maggie, she read several short essays and publications about the issues of homelessness in San Francisco and surrounding areas; with the issue much more prevalent in the downtown areas and southern districts of San Francisco Bay.

"How is it that Henley never once mentioned these things to me?" After a long sigh, she phoned Maggie.

"Hello, this is Maggie, how can I help you?"

"Hello Maggie, it's Faith."

"Mom, it's, it's…Miss Senator, hi Senator," she said excitedly.

"You can call me Faith, we're friends now, remember?"

"Yes, I, I remember Senator, I mean Faith."

"Maggie, how're you and your mom doing today?"

"We're doing great. Mom's happy, I told her about the possibility of having a home and she's really excited."

"Maggie, I'm going to ask you some personal questions, if you don't mind."

"Sure, sure Senator ask me anything. Faith, do you mind if I put you on speaker phone, that way mom can hear you and ask questions if needed."

"Absolutely," Faith responded.

"Maggie, quick question, are you and your mom alone…do you have company?"

"No, not at all Senator, we're by ourselves. We're sitting here at Dolores Park having breakfast."

"Good, very good," Faith replied. As they chatted, Faith learned that Maggie's mom resided in a temporary shelter on Bovard street, while she camps out in random locations around the city. She told Faith that she checks in on her mom daily.

"I'm really worried about my little Maggie, Ms. Senator," her mom said.

"She doesn't like staying in the shelter. She doesn't trust anyone here, or anyone for that matter. I'm surprised that she was able to make a friend, and with a Senator," her mom said proudly. Faith could almost hear a smile as she listened to Maggie's mom.

"Maggie's mom?"

"Yes Ms. Senator."

"What's your name darling?"

"Joyce."

"That's such a beautiful name."

"Thank you," she replied and chuckled softly. As Faith spoke with the daughter and mom duo, she told them that she would meet with them at the Park to make arrangements for their transition into permanent housing.

"Ms. Senator, I'm so proud of my little Maggie."

"Absolutely, and you should be. My mother-in-law once told me that some things are simply coincidental but when I met Maggie, on that beautiful spring day, in the most unusual way, I knew it was for an important reason."

After Faith's meeting concluded with Maggie and her mom, she phoned her brother-in-law Calvin.

"Faith, darling, I've missed you. How've you been? I've seen your public address and it was quite exquisite. The people love you," he beamed.

"Calvin? May I have your attention please," she laughs.

"Sure, what do you need, my friend?"

"That's the perfect question...because I need a huge favor."

"I'm listening?" he said in a deeply caring way.

"I have a little friend; her name is Maggie."

"Oh yes, Maggie from the Conference Hall?"

"Exactly, Maggie and her mom are having breakfast at Dolores Park. I need you to speak with your boyfriend and arrange a temporary stay in the guest suite at the Fairway Palace-Penthouse for two. Please inform Gerry. Additionally, would you mind running a quick shopping errand. The ladies would need clothing. How long do you think it would take to have this arranged?"

"Since the guest suite is already prepared to be occupied, it shouldn't take me more than a couple hours to shop."

"Fantastic, I always know that I could count on you," Faith replied.

"Who was that?" Gerry asked.

"Ooh, someone's jealous," Calvin Joked.

"I'm not going to answer this question. I'm only going to ask, are you up for a little shopping spree...?"

"And who are we shopping for, you or me?"

"Neither..." Calvin replied. He was enjoying Gerry's suspicion and wasn't about to relieve him of his jealousy.

"Well, I know just the place...I have a friend on Fillmore, she owns the cutest little boutique and carries the finest," Calving said excitedly. Gerry became even more suspicious of his boyfriend by the second. He's had a long day dealing with stubborn guests and their snobbish attitudes. He was in no mood for some spur of the moment shopping spree and flopped onto the sofa. Soft snores followed.

"C'mon, I can't do this without you. You have lovely taste in clothing. I need your help with this one."

But he didn't budge. Calvin looked in the mirror, threw on his favorite scarf and beret and said...

"You've got this, Calvin."

"Where to?" the door man asked.

"To Fillmore St. The sister-in-law has requested my services."

"Excellent," he replied and whistled loudly for the chauffeur. As Calvin was about to enter the limo, Gerry peeked out of the window overlooking Fenmore Palace Courtyard...

"Sneaking off without me?"

"I couldn't get you up. And I'm kind of in a hurry," Calvin laughed, getting into the vehicle.

"To Fillmore St. please." The Chauffeur pulled out of the courtyard.

"You and Gerry alright?" the Chauffeur called.

"Yep, he came home in one of his moods. He thinks I'm running off with someone else."

"Well, you're quite handsome. I don't blame him for being a bit jealous."

"Oh Hannibal, I'm not having this conversation with you, not now, not ever."

"Oh my, are we feeling sassy today?" Hannibal said rolling his eyes and pulled the limo into Fillmore St parking lot in front of Candace St John's Lilacs and Laces.

"Do you need me to wait?

"That would be great, thanks Hannibal. It shouldn't take me more than an hour," he replied, hurrying inside.

"I could have gotten the door for you," Hannibal called after him.

"Sorry, I'm in a hurry," he replied and slipped through the gliding doors at Candace St. John's.

"Faith, I'm here at Candace St John's and realized that I need a photo of the ladies as well as their sizes, so I can have an idea what to buy," he chuckles.

"That's right, but you see it's kind of a surprise, and I don't want them to figure it out. So you'll have to do your absolute best. Maggie is only eighteen, tall and slim. I'm assuming that she looks like her mom. Go one size above a medium and no more than an extra-large for her mom. Sorry I can't be of more help darling, I have to go now," she said and hung up.

"Candace, are you here?" Said Calvin, lost in the shuffle.

"I'm sorry, she's out of town this weekend and I'm here filling in for her," a young brunette replied.

"What's your name sweetie? You're the splitting image of Candace."

"Thank you, I'm her daughter, Stephanie...Stephanie Bradley..."

"Hmm, why does that name sound familiar," Calvin said, removing a hair from his face. About an hour later, with Stephanie's help, Calvin hobbled exhaustedly out of Candace's carrying what seemed like hundreds of bags of clothing.

"Need some help?" Hannibal asked, opening the trunk. Seems you bought the entire store...."

"Mom, mom wake up, it's Ms. Senator," Maggie said, trying to wake her mom. Faith threw a scarf over her head and slipped on some sunglasses to disguise her familiar appearance. Dolores Park was crowded and her white scarf and sunglasses were the perfect disguise as she approached Maggie and her mom who appeared to be asleep.

"Maggie, come, come with me, this way. I'm parked over here," she said pointing to her Lamborghini parked on the corner of 18th and Dolores Street.

"So good to see you Ms. Senator," Maggie said, hugging Faith so tightly that she couldn't breathe.

"You're welcome sweetie," I have a surprise for you," Faith said.

"Joyce rubbed her eyes and stretched to a wake.

"Ms. Senator, is that you? I can't believe it. Ms. Senator, what are you doing here? You should be more careful, you could get mugged on this side of town," Joyce said embracing the nicely dressed Senator, whose fragrance was beginning to mesmerize the crowd at Dolores Park.

"Where are we going Ms. Senator?" Maggie and her mom got in the back of Faith's Lamborghini.

"Wow, this is very nice, so comfortable," Joyce said, fastening her seatbelt. Shortly after entering the car, someone shouted...

"OMG, it's Faith, Sandy Senator!" said a crowd hurrying to get a photograph of the Senator and her friends. Faith fastened her belt and screeching sounds could be heard as she sped off 18th street towards Fenway Palace on Montgomery Blvd.

"Ms. Senator, do you have a CD player on your Lamborghini?" Maggie laughed at her mother's naive question.

"Mom, it's a Lamborghini...really?"

"You mean, a real-life Lamborghini?"

"Yes mom. Mom, this is Faith Winters French, she was married to Eric French, the District Attorney of San Francisco. And now, she's the Senator of the entire City of Sandy Island. Of course, it's a Lamborghini and of course, it has a CD player," Maggie chuckles at her mom's lack of awareness of the situation. Faith smiled and giggled at her friend's conversation.

"So if you're right, please tell me, what year is your Lamborghini?"

"It's a 2020, Lamborghini Urus. Hope this helps," Faith replied.

"No way, you mean, they make those now?" Maggie and Faith's chuckle turned into a full-blown laughter.

"C'mon mom, you're sitting in the Senator's ride...this is as good as it gets."

As Fatih pulled into the courtyard of the Fenway Palace, she glanced at her friends and realized that they were not properly attired to meet Fenway Palace dress code.

"Ladies, have you ever got changed in a vehicle?" Joyce laughed...

"Absolutely Ms. Senator, back in the day, when I climbed out my window to go to my girlfriend's high school party," she laughed.

"Well I did the same thing except I would dress all innocent in front of my mom, but when I got in my friend's car, I always had a change of clothes to look smokin for my boyfriend," Maggie admitted. Her mom stared at her in disbelief.

"Perfect." Faith replied and high fived Joyce. As she was about to phone Calvin, he was already hurrying toward her.

"Calvin, perfect, please meet my friends Maggie and her mom Joyce.

"*Hello*," The ladies said simultaneously.

"Hi there, pleasure to meet you both. By the way I saw you on TV at the Conference Hall and you look a lot prettier in person," Calvin said winking at her. Both ladies blushed.

"Calvin, come closer please, closer, closer..." As he leaned against the window Faith whispered something in his ear.

"Absolutely, be right back," he said. A few moments later, he returned carrying two pink handbags from Candace St. Johns.

"This one's for you, and this one's for you," he said, handing the bags to Maggie and Joyce.

"For me? well that's very nice of you sir."

"I'll park on the crowded lot so the ladies can have some privacy. Would you mind asking Gerry to meet us here to escort the ladies inside?"

"Sure, we'll meet you here in a few minutes," Calvin said and phoned Gerry on his mobile.

Faith parked in a crowded section of the parking lot to avoid the cameras.

"Wow, I look fantastic," Joyce said, slipping on her dress.

"Perfect fit, I'm in style," Maggie said, stepping out. Faith had placed her hands over her eyes. "Is it safe to look now," Faith giggles.

"Oh, sure, we're all ladies here," Maggie jokes.

"Absolutely, wow, I hardly recognize you two, you both look lovely, wow." As the ladies' excitement subsided, Joyce began to wonder what this was all about.

"Ms. Senator, why are we here? Are we going to be on TV, because you know, I'm not as brave as Maggie, I'm really shy," Joyce said her eyes widened with fear.

"Good question, why're we here?" Ms. Faith," Maggie said looking around. Faith removed her sunglasses and looked at both women.

"I have a surprise for you ladies, please follow me," she said smiling as she led the way to the entrance of the most luxurious Hotel in San Francisco where Gerry and Calvin stood chatting with the doorman, waiting to escort the ladies to a new life of great expectations. Calvin whistled at the sight of both women.

"You can both be models for our weekend Galas," Gerry said offering his arms to Maggie.

"May I," Calvin said, offering his arms to Joyce as they led them to the elevator to the seventh floor of the Fenway Palace....

"Okay ladies, we're almost there. On the count of three, I want you to close your eyes," Faith said excitedly.

"...3..2..1. you can open your beautiful eyes now darlings...."

"OMG, OMG Maggie and Joyce's eyes widened in disbelief. At the mountain of shopping bags and exquisitely furnished guest room...

"Exactly ladies, this is your guest suite for as long as you need," Faith said, embracing Joyce who had been reduced to tears.

"This is only the beginning of many wonderful things to come for you sweetheart. These are gifts from me to you. I want you to know that Senator Faith is your new friend and that I'll always be here for you," she said, reaching for a napkin from Gerry's hands.

"We'll leave you now to enjoy your gifts and get comfortable. "So how long can we stay?" Joyce asked.

"For as long as you like sweetie. Mr. Gerry is the owner and manager of this building and Calvin is his Fiancé, they will take good care of you both. You can have breakfast, Lunch and dinner in the Crown Lounge or if you desire, your breakfast can be served to you in your room. If you have any questions regarding dress codes, Gerry and Calvin are only a phone call away," Faith said cupping Maggie's adorable face.

"I don't know where to begin to tell you how thankful I am for all you've done for us Ms. Faith."

"Shh, you're most welcome Hun. You're such a strong young lady for taking such good care of you and your mom," Faith said, tears rushing to her eyes.

"Okay ladies, we'll leave you two now. Make yourself at home. Don't be afraid to let me know if there's anything else that I can do for you. Your Sandy Island Senator has an open office, which means you call or arrange to see me at any available day of the week." She looked at them one more time and blew kisses as the mom and daughter duo blew kisses in return looking around in disbelief.

"Bye for now girls, we'll see you in a bit to grab you for lunch," Calvin said, hurrying out after Faith.

"As Faith said, anything you need," Gerry said and flashes the ladies a wink before shutting the door behind him.

Calvin hurried to the elevator to catch Faith but he looked in time to see her drive out of the parking lot onto Montgomery Blvd. He reached in his pocket for his mobile and dialed her number, but obviously, she was driving and would not answer, and his call went into voicemail.

"Faith Hun, I forgot to mention that I might have ran into the young lady that you've been looking for. She's the daughter of my friend Candace who owns the little boutique on Fillmore where I shopped earlier. I'm not absolutely sure, but I'm sure that she mentioned that her name was Stephanie Bradley," He says and hung up.

As Faith drove home, she thought of Henley's conversation about the reconstruction of Sandy Island Blvd. It's been several months since she'd taken that route and there was an opportunity ahead to exit and take a short overpass that avoids the traffic to Sandy Blvd. A sudden excitement came over her as she made a sharp U-Turn onto Sandy Blvd. The loud hissing sounds of moving trucks and the natural joys of children's laughter resurrected the memories of the lively coast that was temporarily swept by silence. As she sped along her favorite route, she noticed Liz's black Range Rover pulled off of Belvedere Ave, onto Sandy Blvd. Whomever was driving didn't notice her and she followed when the Rover took a right turn on an unmaintained road that led to the beach. She continued to follow from a distance and finally took a right turn keeping a safe distance.

The Rover pulled off the road and parked on a narrow turnout, overlooking a sloping hill near a narrow grassy trail that led to the beach. There was barely enough room on the turnout for two cars, but she managed to park with just a small portion of her bumper sticking out on the unpaved road. As she got out of the vehicle to investigate...she was interrupted by a familiar voice...

"Faith? What are you doing here?" Hank asked, rolling down his window.

"I was heading to the Bungalow, my new place and I thought...what are you doing here?"

"I come here a lot," he laughs. "It's my little hiding place to think." He looked at her and it seemed like months since their last conversation.

"Want to join me...how've you been?"

"I must be heading back. I have some loose ends at the office."

"Can it wait,' he asked, opening the door to the passenger side.

"Okay, maybe for a minute," she said.

"Wow, this view is..."

"Beautiful right.... *I've missed you.*"

"It feels like it's been forever." Before she said another word, he leans forward and kisses her longingly. Faith found herself completely enamored by Hank and fell completely into his arms.

"Spend the day with me," he said, removing a strand of hair from her face...her full lips were red from his kiss.

"You've been taking care of everyone, let me take care of you today." She exhaled loudly and smiled as he placed his hands on her tummy.

"Hank, I think you still love her..."

"You mean?"

"Yes, Syd's mom, and it takes time. I think you need time." His eyes drifted.

"Faith?"

"Yes."

"Do you love me?"

"Hank...so much has happened...I'm not sure things could be the same."

"But the way you kissed me just now. You haven't answered my question."

"I do, but..."

236

"Yes, I lost the mother of my child, and yes a few months ago, I thought that I wanted to stay in Manhattan to see her through a difficult patch, but somehow, it seems the universe disagreed with my decision and I'm here, with you. And you're having our baby. Faith, I love you." As she was about to respond, her mobile rang. "Hold that thought, she said and stepped out of the Rover.

"This is Faith…."

"Senator, the new proposals are on your desk, would you be back to the office today... I need approval by morning."

"Henley, you did not discuss this with me. We need to discuss this. I'll be there in a few minutes.

"Hank, I'm sorry, something came up, I have to go," she said hurrying off.

"Faith, would you please wait," Hank pleaded.

"I'll call you later. I promise," she said and drove off.

Hank packed the last of him and Syd's belongings from Elizabeth's guest house, the tiny residence they called home the past five months. As he loaded up the Rover, his phone rang. He thought it was Faith, but it was only his Real Estate Agent, calling with an update on his Condo.

"Hank, you have an offer."

"That's great. How much…?" His eyes widened.

"Wow, let's do it...yes, yes take it. Can't beat that," he said and jumped in excitement.

"YES!" best news he's had all day. He had great news earlier this week when he learned that his Sandy Island Bungalow was completely rebuilt...but he was still concerned that he would not be able to manage the financial upkeep of both properties. He's now in an excellent position to keep his promise of being a stay-at-home parent to his daughter. As he thought of Faith, he hopes that she would see things in a new light when he moves back to Sandy Island. Maybe she would remember what they had and would eventually come around. As he drove out of Belvedere Ave, a feeling of renewed hope swept him like a fresh morning air, remembering the joy that had first brought him to this side of the world.

Chapter 28

"**H**enley, this is not up for discussion, it's too soon. The residents have just begun to settle into their homes. To begin construction on Sandy Blvd is not only annoying, it would create upset and I would never hear the end of it," she stressed. As she argued with Henley, she felt a sudden pain in her lower abs.

"Ahhh Ouch!!" she cried.

"Faith, here take my hands, have a seat. What can I get you!"

"Please call my Obstetrician…. OUCH," she cried. It was after hours and it took several attempts to reach Vivienne.

"Hi Vivienne, this is Senator Henley, we need you to come right away, Faith is experiencing some discomfort. Okay, thank you."

"Faith, she's on her way, but she said we should call Paramedics just in case."

"No, I don't want to spend the night at the hospital. This will make news and cause unnecessary worry from the public." A few minutes later, Vivienne pulled into the driveway, almost knocking over Henley's Lion figurine statue.

"She's laying in the lounge."

"Thanks Henley, please tell me paramedics are on their way."

"Sorry Viv, she asked me not too." Vivienne shook her head and followed Henley to the lounge where Faith lay curled up in the fetal position.

"Hi darling, how're you feeling?" she asked, taking Faith's vitals.

"What were you doing before this?"

"I was arguing with Henley."

"That's right, your office is here. Henley, please bring me a sixteen-ounce glass of water. Faith darling, your vitals are a bit high. I'm going to have to run some tests," Vivienne said, placing a tourniquet onto Faith's upper right arm.

"Oh sweetie, I can't even find your veins. Here Hun, I'm going to have you drink this entire glass of water. Then I'll wait ten minutes and try again," she said, removing the tourniquet. Hank paced the hallway, blaming himself for Faith's disposition. After drinking the glass of water, Vivienne took the baby's heart rate.

"Beautiful," she said smiling. "The baby is healthy; his vitals are on point. I believe this was brought on by anxiety."

"What a relief," Faith said, sitting up.

"I'm feeling a bit better. Can I sit up now?"

"No sweetie, I'm sorry, you'll have to lay on your left side for a bit. Henley, would you be a doll and grab a pillow. I need Faith to be elevated.

"Perfect," Vivienne said, patting her veins. After replacing the tourniquet, Vivienne quickly obtained Faith's blood sample.

"How are we feeling now Hun?"

"A lot better," Faith said and smiled weakly.

"You are almost three months pregnant and have only barely passed your first trimester. I'm going to have to put you on thirty days of bed rest."

"Sorry Viv, I love you, but I can't. My Sandy Island family needs me."

"Henley, I need your help with this one. I'm glad you're here. Faith, your baby needs you to be healthy. Thirty days of rest. And no arguments. I'll run these to the Lab and follow up with you in the morning," Vivienne kissed her Senator's forehead.

"Thanks Viv, love you, thanks for coming on short notice."

"Be a good girl for me now. Love you...kisses," she said and headed out.

"Thanks Viv, I can see why Faith's so fond of you," Henley said walking Viv to the door.

"Faith, where'd you go? I'm sorry, sweetie, I didn't mean to upset you. We can forget about this project for now," he said wondering where she'd disappeared too.

"Faith?" He checked her office and then the guest bedroom. "Faith?" then he heard flushing sounds coming from the hallway bathroom. "
Faith, is that you?"

"No it's me Tommy. Is everything okay dad?"

"Yes Son, don't worry. I'm trying to find Faith. Have you seen her?"

"She's sitting near the fireplace in her office," Tommy replied and shuts his bedroom door.

"Faith, I'm so sorry. What can I do for you darling?"

"Henley, please don't worry."

"Please stay the night, you can have my bed, it's very comfortable."

"Oh Henley, you've been wonderful, but I'll take the guest bedroom. I can't put you out. I didn't want to be alone tonight anyways. Liz and the girls called me from Lake Tahoe this morning. They won't be back till Monday evening."

"Can I grab you a change of clothing? Is there anything you need?" She pointed to a small carry on suitcase next to her desk.

"I'm always prepared for the unexpected," she smiled. She appeared exhausted and as he continues to gaze at her, he knew that he was falling in love with her. Henley approached Faith as she was beginning to doze off. He lifted her off the recliner and carried her to his Master Suite across the hall. She hugged the silk pillows tightly as she snuggled between the sheets. He made himself comfortable on his sofa near the fireplace. There he has a clear view of her. If she awakes during the night, he wanted to be right there. As he dozed off, he heard a soft sound of discomfort. Faith was shuffling as though she was having a dream.

"Faith, can you hear me? Her eyes barely opened.

"Henley…?"

He brushed her face gently. "Get some sleep darling," he said. Unable to resist how lonely she seemed, he climbed into the oversized bed and snuggled her. They both exhaled a sigh of relief.

The following morning was the weekend and Henley wanted Faith to sleep in. After making breakfast, he prepared everything that she needed and placed it in the Master Suite on an attractive gold-plated rollaway tray. The delicious smell filled the room as Faith began to slowly stir to a wake. What's the lovely smell, she thought. Sitting up, her stomach began to feel upset as she hurried out of bed to the bathroom. Unable to control her urges, she embraced the porcelain bowl and buried her head for an unbelievable relief. After what seemed like hours, she finally lifted her head out of the bowl and sighed…

"Oh God!" Realizing that she was sitting on the floor of Henley's bathroom, she pulled herself up quickly and got into the shower.

"Faith, honey," Henley called searching the room. Then he heard the shower.

"I'm here Henley, I'll be right out. Thanks for the breakfast, it smells lovely," she said, fighting back a huge gag.

"I want to feed you breakfast sweetie. Come let's eat before everything gets cold."

A few minutes later, Faith stood wrapped in a cotton robe and her hair stuffed in a towel wrapped neatly around her head.

"You look lovely," he said patting a seat next to him. Come, come sit with me doll.

"Henley, I'm so sorry, I didn't mean to put you out. And you went through all the trouble to make me breakfast."

"It's no trouble at all...Your Doctor, Viv, she asked me to take care of you," he said, interrupting his original thoughts. She could tell that he wanted to say something else but didn't.

"Okay, I'll try. But I haven't been holding anything down. I've just..." Before she could finish her sentence, he placed a few delicious red grapes in her mouth.

"Mmmm, yum," she said chewing slowly. He wiped her mouth slowly with a napkin. She looked in his eyes as he wiped the fruit juices from her lips and saw something familiar. She's never seen that look in his eyes before and as she was about to warn him about her morning sickness, he stuck a variety of fruit with a fork and placed them between her lips. She chewed with her eyes closed.

"Thank you, Henley, I think that's all I can stomach, for now," she said leaning her face into his hands as he patted her soft skin.

"Faith?"

"Yes...Henley."

"Can I kiss you?" She shook her head...

"Yes," she said shyly. He leaned forward and kissed the sweet savory fruit juices from her lips, kissing her affectionately. He cuddled her and embraced her tenderly. She looked in his eyes as he drew her to himself. As she submerged into his strong masculine embrace, she remembered her gentle physical state.

"Henley," she whispered.

"Yes," he whispered.

"I must rest."

"Okay love," he says with a gentle smile. He lifted her up and placed her on the silk sheets where she slept the night before.

"I care for you...Faith Winters." She smiled and almost appeared as an innocent child. He had discovered her nature.

"Come, lay with me, but promise me you'd be a good boy," she giggled. They snuggled under the sheets and Henley placed his hands on her soft tiny bump.

"Looks like we have company," he says kissing her forehead. Her ocean green eyes sparkled as he pulled the linen over their heads.

"Want to play, peek a boo, hmm?" he asked playfully kissing her fruit-stained lips. They had spent most of the day indoors and Henley's staff accommodated the Senators every requests.

"I never expected to enjoy such a romantic day while pregnant...I think it's my best date yet, or is it a date?" Henley could hardly contain himself and kisses her in response.

"Faith I'm in love with you, and I love your family." Surprised by his unexpected admission, she stared at him blankly...

"I, I, I'll be right back," she said and went to the guest room and shut the door behind her. She spent the rest of Saturday contemplating Henley's words.

The following morning, she awoke to a soft knock...

"It's me, can I come in?"

"Don't be silly Henley, come on in," she said sitting up in bed.

"Someone's in better spirits," he teased.

"It's Sunday Henley, don't you attend church?"

"Church?"

"Yes Church, you're the Senator of the second most expensive City in the U.S. are you not? Some example you are..."

"What's your excuse Faith?"

"Well, my church has been under construction for several months," she said, blinking her eyes repeatedly. Henley laughed.

"You're funny...That's no excuse Faith...are you kidding me. There's hundreds of other churches in the City of San Francisco...under construction huh..."

"How dare you judge me Henley?" she looked upset, and he was enjoying himself.

"I like it here, under this fine linen," she said.

"Two Senator's under a silk white linen. Must be a sign."

"Henley, are you making a pass at me...can't you see that I'm pregnant? And with someone else's child...?"

"All the more lovely, my dear," he replied.

"Now I feel like Little Red Riding Hood."

"All the better to love you my dear."

"Henley, didn't you hear me hurling in the bathroom yesterday?"

"All the better to care for you my dear..."

"Henley, can't you see that I'm barely dressed...?"

"All the better to make love with you my dear. Faith, do you love me?" She looked away from him as he waited for an answer. Then she turns to face him.

"Yes darling, I love you. But Henley, my life is complicated."

"Then we shall rhyme forever," he says taking her into his arms once more.

"Henley, I'm exhausted. How long is this trail?" Said Faith tagging along behind Henley who's standing on a little hill up ahead.

"I can't do hills today," she laughed.

"It's the perfect view. You can see Alcatraz Island from here. I promise, it's a gorgeous day."

"I know it's a gorgeous day Henley, but don't you have better things to do?"

"In time you'll learn how to take it easy. Haven't you read up on our Presidents? Especially Teddy Roosevelt? Teddy was the Leader of the Free World who used to disappear from the White House, thirty days at a time to go duck hunting. He would literally take off unannounced. No one knew where he was."

"You've got to be kidding me?"

"Not at all. I guess his point was, you just have to take it easy and learn to live a little."

"How am I supposed to climb this hill now that I'm weak from laughing," she said sitting on a nearby bench.

"C'mon, don't be a party pooper," he said, throwing a handful of flowers at her.

"You are such a meanie, I'm not climbing that hill, ever. Maybe this is some horrible test that you're trying to get me to pass to see if I'm fit to be Senator," Faith scolded. Henley laughed.

"Do you always have to over analyze everything?"

"Honey, I just wanted you to see a gorgeous view."

"You're awfully reckless, it was just last night my OB placed me on bedrest." Henley ignores her excuses and continues to taunt her.

"Faith, Faith, Faith, Faith, Faith, Faith..."

"Henley, truly, I can't believe you, how dare you...I'm in no position for this," she said angrily approaching the tiny hill. Just as she attempted to place her feet on the hilltop, she was suddenly taken upward at lightning speed.

"Ahhh! What in God's world! Henley, what are you doing?"

"It's a little game I set up for me and Tommy. It's perfectly safe but he hates it. I thought you might like it," he said grinning in a sinister way.

"What is this thing anyway...?"

"It's a catch-net. You step on the trigger right there and it releases an umbrella-like blanket that sweeps down, catches you and swoops you up in a canopy." he laughs.

"Henley, would you get me down from this tree now? And I mean, now."

"Dad?... Dad, did you set Faith up to get caught in that trap from Cutthroat Island," Tommy said approaching them.

"I heard someone scream. Faith are you okay? Dad, I told you this isn't for everyone. Sorry Faith, it's something he learned in the Army back in the day. Tommy said reaching in the hollow in the tree trunk removing a rope that he held with both hands.

"Okay, Ms. Faith, I got you. Dad, are you going to help, don't just stand there, are you drunk? She's having a baby dad, what the heck were you thinking about?" Tommy said now even more annoyed.

"Thank you so much Tommy, you're a lifesaver. I had the feeling, if you didn't show up, I would have spent the night in that tree." Henley looks at Faith between the netting. Her eyes were all he needed to know that he'd better not be around when she finally frees herself from that thing.

"Thrilled you showed up when you did, son. To think of it, I don't think I remembered how to release the darn Bazuka," Henley said, scratching his head.

"Dad you're such a jerk."

"Son, be careful, I'm still your dad," Henley said tossing a stick at him.

"Forget you dad, I'm going to go spend the day with Hank. I'm sick of this boring place and your stupid games," Tommy said leaving.

"Tommy, son get over here, let's talk this over. Tommy! Did he say Hank, when did him and Hank become friends?"

"Sounds like a smart kid," Faith said approaching Henley with a fist. He laughs and tries to run away from her, but she looked so adorable he couldn't help himself.

"What are you going to do with those?" Her messy hair and missing shoes spoke for itself.

"I'm going to rip your head off, that's what."

"No honey, you don't mean that," he said, backing away from her. He didn't realize what he was backing into and he tripped and fell over an old tree stump. Faith laughs releasing her clenched fist.

"Henley, are you okay? Why are we out here? Are you trying to say something to me... Something you're too scared that I might not be prepared for?" He sat up and placed his chin in his cupped hands.

"I...um, I just wanted to take you for a walk. I heard it's really good for you at this stage of your pregnancy. And I really enjoy spending time with you."

"Really...?"

"Yes, you're wonderful." She offered her hands to help him up.

"Come here. Let's get you home and make you dinner."

"What about my shoes? Oh, we'll find it later," he said, picking her a rose.

"Henley..?"

"Hmm, yes? Just wanted to say that this was kind of fun."

"Come here."

She giggles as Henley lifts her up.

"You're as light as a twig, sure you're preggers?"

"Henley?"

"Yes?

"There's something you're not telling me."

"Come...Let's get back, I have a surprise for you."

"Hank!..Hank are you here?" Tommy called, knocking and ringing the doorbell to Liz's front door repeatedly. After a few minutes he opened the side gate that led to the guest house.

"Hank! Where's everyone. Liz, Sydney, Kat...is anyone here?" Peeking through the open curtains, Tommy noticed that the small guest house was neatly put away and there was no sign of anyone. Looks like Hank moved out...he thought. As he searched the premises, he heard the sound of horses' neighing.

"Horses, hmm, hey where are you guys," Tommy said turning the corner, stumbling upon stables.

"You guys must be Patrol George's horses…" A younger horse approached him and sniffed his hands.

"Hey boy, you're a boy right?" Tommy leaned forward to see the horse's gender and he fell into the stall.

"Ouch! Hey boy don't be scared; I won't hurt you. Are you broken? I need a ride. I need to find Hank; I think he moved back to the beach. Do you know the trail that led to the beach?" Tommy asked reaching for the saddles hanging on the gate. "You don't look more than two, but just a bit too old to be a Foul." Tommy said, attempting to climb onto his back.

"Good boy, atta boy. Come let's go," he said leading the horse out of the stable.

"That's great, woohoo, yay. Come on boy."

The horse led the way to the grassy trail toward the beach and picked up the pace as Tommy held the reins firmly.

"Awesome!"

"Almost there boy." As the horse neared the beach, she must have recognized something familiar. She neighed happily and pick up a faster pace with Tommy barely hanging on.

"Where are you headed boy?"

"Slow down," Tommy yelled.

"Slow down boy," he cried.

"Where are you going?" The horse began to slow down as he approached Faith's Bungalow, completely rebuilt, and nestled in the exact same area before the fire.

"You know this place boy. Where are we?" As Tommy got off, the horse took off running and rolled playfully in the sand.

"Hey, wait come here!" Tommy called, running after him.

"She's a girl, her name's Becca," Hank said looking at Tommy curiously.

"Hank! It's you, I can't believe it's you. I was looking for you. Is this your place? How do you know her, I mean the horse?"

"She belongs to Faith. She's a gift from Patrol George."

"That's Faith's house," he said pointing to the beach house.

"Oh, okay, she must have recognized this place. Smart girl."

"Tommy does your dad know where you are?"

"By the looks of it, I'm assuming not. What are you doing here?"

"I was looking for you."

"Yes, you mentioned that, but why?"

"I just wanted to talk. I enjoy talking to you. You're a good listener."

"But what about your dad?"

"He's always busy. He never talks about her..."

"Who, who's her."

"Mom, my mom." Realizing, Hank's eyes drifted to the sand.

"I see."

"You just lost your wife, right? I thought maybe you would understand and that you would be a good person to talk too," he said tearing up. Hank felt awkward, as Tommy embraced him.

"Tommy, I'm sorry you're going through this, but I have to get you home."

"No, I'll take the horse back."

"Tommy no, it's not safe." As he tries to get Tommy's attention, his phone rang.

"This is Hank. Oh, hi Henley, please call me back in an hour. Okay, thanks," he said and hung up.

"Tommy, It's a nice day out, let's take a walk. May I ask, how old you are?"

"Almost twelve. I'll be twelve next month. On the day that my...On the day that I lost my mom."

Hank paused for a minute.

"Have you ever discussed this with your dad?"

"Yes, but he gets interrupted often, especially during our conversations. We've hardly ever finished a conversation," he continued.

Hank understood, especially as Tommy is an only child. As they walked along the shorelines, Tommy removed his shoes, wetting his feet in the surf. He looked over his shoulder and smiled noticing that the horse was following close behind. As they walked along the coast, Tommy told Hank about his life as a Senator's son and what it's been like growing up without a mom.

"I look at our family albums with photos of when I was a baby, but I don't remember...I don't remember what she sounded like, or if she sang to me or pushed me on a swing." About an hour later, when they'd reached the coral reefs...

"Tommy, that was your dad that called earlier. He's on his way to give you a ride back. You can call me anytime you need to talk. When the girls get back, maybe we can all go on a fishing trip. I just sold my Condo in Manhattan and I'm looking to repair my boat; Sandy Girl. She sustained some minor burns near the stern, but nothing to major. How does that sound?"

"Sounds great," Tommy smiled.

"Okay buddy, let's head back."

"Wanna race?" Tommy asked running ahead.

"Sure...On your mark, get set, go!" Hank said lifting his arm in the air and using his fingers to imitate a gun. And the two were off, with the horse leading the pack and Hank pretending that he couldn't keep up with Tommy.

"Wow, man you're fast," he pretends as the gap between him, Tommy and Becca widens.

Henley pulled off Sandy Island Blvd onto Bay View drive into Hank's driveway. He watched as Tommy and the horse concluded the race. Tommy laughed as Becca purposely tossed in the sand and rolled over a short embankment. When Tommy stood up, he noticed his dad's car parked in Hank's driveway. Henley got out of the car and approached his son. Seeing his dad approaching, Tommy lowers his head.

"Hi dad."

"Hi son, what are you up too? I see you made a friend."

"Her name is Becca. I think she used to belong to Faith. She's great."

"Really?"

Tommy could tell that despite his dad's formal approach, that he was upset.

"Tommy, please wait in the car. This will only take a minute." Tommy watched as his dad and Hank's conversation went from conversational to formal to argumentative.

"I'm glad that my son confided in someone, at least someone within our circle of trust. But you should have informed me. Someone should have said something to me. Tommy is my responsibility, he's my business, not yours."

"Aren't you being a bit hypocritical? You've been spending quality time with my fiancé who's pregnant with my child. Don't tell me that all this time you two spend together is strictly business. An office in your private estate is even more convenient. So tell me, what is that all about?" Henley removed his sunglasses and glanced at the time on his wrist.

"Let me guess, too busy right."

"Hank, whatever is going on between you and Faith, that's for the two of you to figure out. I offered Faith an office space in my home to direct her when necessary for the position. Being a State Senator is a huge responsibility and I couldn't simply throw her out there to sink or swim."

"You're smooth at talking your way out of things. I'll give you that. No wonder you don't have time for your own son."

"Hank, I don't think that my relationship with my son is any of your business. Thanks for being there, but you are spending time with my son and it is no longer appropriate," Henley says and turn to leave.

"Whatever man just be a father to him and don't blame me for your problems. Mind yours and I'll mind my own. Deal?" As Hank continues to argue, Henley took a call. Hank shook his head and left.

"Hank just give me a minute," Henley called.

"Whatever man," Hank replied. As he heads home, he remembers Becca and whistles for the horse. Becca was walking along the surf with her tail and ears lifted high.

"Hey Becca come here girl." She fluttered her ears straight up and began walking toward Hank.

"You look upset, what's with the attitude," Hank mimicked, assuming what Becca might be saying in her own horsey way.

"I hate arguments, I don't like em." He laughed at the thought.

"Come on girl, you can wait here," he said, opening the gate to his backyard and watches as Becca walks in and rolls playfully on the soft lawn.

Chapter 29

Faith's laughter could be heard through the window overlooking a gorgeous flower garden. It was a warm spring day and the sound of birds chirping could be heard as they leaped from branch to branch, bringing a long winter to an end and the heart of sleeping blooms to life.

"Mommy, is Sydney and Hank mad at us?"

"What makes you think that honey?"

"It's been six weeks since we've moved back to Sandy Island and Syd and I have only had one sleep over."

"Everything's going to be okay darling. Uncle Hank and Syd are trying to get settled in."

"What about Henley? He hasn't been around in like fourteen days?"

"He's getting ready for a conference in D.C, he leaves tomorrow. Your mommy is on Medical leave, so he's attending on both our behalf's. This means you and mommy can spend some quality time together. So, tell me sweetheart, how would you like to spend our day?"

Kat bounced around excitedly.

"I would like to help decorate the baby's nursery," she said excitedly.

Faith reached for her personal mobile and noticed a missed call with an international sort code. As she searched through her missed calls, her thumb accidentally dialed to voicemail.

"Faith it's Fain. I really missed you. I heard the construction on Sandy Island is complete and I've been thinking of coming back. I want to be there for you and Kat. If you'd have me." As Fain's message concluded, another message from six weeks earlier began to play.

"Faith, I forgot to mention that I might have ran into the young lady that you've been looking for. She's the daughter of my friend Candace who owns a little boutique on Fillmore where I shopped earlier. I'm not absolutely certain if it's her, but I'm sure that she mentioned that her name was Stephanie Bradley." As she thought of Fain's message, she looked at her image in the mirror. At five months pregnant, her tummy was now clearly visible. She looked around the empty unfurnished rooms. Windows without curtains and walls without paintings. So much have changed in a year, she thought, yet here I am standing in the same place. I've saved and rebuilt lives standing in one single place. Faith Winters French, it's time to fly, She thought as her memories raced.

Elizabeth and George were out of town attending a horse show in Sacramento. Hank has been distant since they'd moved back to Sandy Island and him and Sydney had taken his remodeled boat Sandy Girl for a fishing trip around the Bay. After pleading with Henley, Tommy got approval from his father to accompany Hank on his fishing trip. Tommy had taken a real liking to Hank and understandably so. She understood Hank's attitude toward her and at minimum, he deserved the truth. Yet, she needed time; maybe space to think of what she wanted for a change.

A silver moon graced the skylines beyond the coral reefs casting a stony reflection on the choppy night seas. The soft wind shifted the coconut palms, causing the waves to roll gently with the tides. Katherine had fallen asleep on the white Faux Fur futon with her pink apple ipad tucked beneath her pillow. It was the only piece of furniture she'd manage to unpack from the hundreds of boxes still seating in the garage. It was almost a dream being back in Sandy Island standing on her balcony enjoying her favorite view. As she sipped on Sparkling water the wind played in her hair as she remembers the new life that grace her womb. A feeling of adventure stirred within her. At 1 a.m. Faith was hardly thinking of sleep as she flopped into her office chair to research the next flight to Paris. It was past 4 a.m. when she finally curled up on the furry Futon next to her daughter. She was greeted by Kat's gentle snores that warmed her forehead inviting a long-awaited sleep.

"Mom? Mommy, please wake up, you never used to snore. I haven't slept all night, because you've been snoring and I was worried that my legs will get the baby," Kat said, sitting up with her hands folded.

"Sorry baby, but mommy is so tired," Faith yawned loudly and went back to sleep. Katherine looked at her mom curled almost into a ball. Regardless of whose baby is in there she was going to be a big sister and it's now her job to take care of her mommy. At least that's how she felt. Kat thought of all the people that have entered their lives. They all had their own lives and at the end of the day, there was her and her mom. She was going to take good care of her mommy, and no one dared think of coming over. She fretted in silence. Maybe she would allow Senator Henley, but even though he was a Senator like her mommy, he was the tall, gaunt, boring type that constantly talked about politics. Kat remembered that her mom hated politics. It's the reason she'd left Germany because she remembered that her mommy had mentioned that her Grandparents Emma and Uwe Winters were German Senators. It was the very reason why her mommy ran away to sunny California with her dad to get away from all that garbage. Her job is now to protect her mom from too much Politics, especially the Press.

It was already 9a.m. and Faith was still fast asleep. As she contemplated her new responsibilities, Kat strolled into the Kitchen and searched through the cupboards looking for ingredients to make her mom's favorite Armenian Pastry. Her search was concluded by empty cupboards and a magazine with local restaurants and companies that deliver the finest breakfast in the Bay. Kat folded the page which revealed a humble little restaurant named Nerfunteri's Egyptian Breakfast. She couldn't make out some of the words but read enough to understand the bold red letters that said, "We speak your language." About an hour later, there was a loud knock on the front porch followed by the obnoxiously loud doorbell.

"I'm coming!" the eight year old yelled.

"Please don't ring that bell, you're going to wake my mommy," she said annoyed swinging the door open.

"Hi sweetie, is your mom home?" A short Hispanic woman asked, smiling warmly.

"Come on in, my mommy is asleep. Follow me, I'll show you where to put everything."

"What's your name sweetie?"

"My name's Kat."

"Well Kat, you have a beautiful home," the woman said placing the items on the middle aisle.

"Well thank you. We haven't had the time to put everything away, that's why we have no furniture and the walls are still bare."

"Understandably so," the woman said heading back to her vehicle.

"Wait, I have one more bag," the woman called.

"What smells so lovely?" Faith said, waking up.

"Katherine Honey, what are you up too sweetheart?"

"I'm out front mommy," her tiny voice echoed through the bare hallways.

"Hello, I'm Maria, I work at the Egyptian Diner down the Blvd. Your daughter is very bright, and ordered breakfast," Maria said, hurrying to the kitchen.

"Really? Honey, you ordered in? Well that is very thoughtful, but you should have woke me up hunny. Thank you so much Maria," Faith said, handing her a tip.

Maria's eyes widened in appreciation as she stared at the generous tip.

"Thank you, Senator."

"No thank you Maria, so nice of you to bring us breakfast."

As Maria headed back to her vehicle, she looked over her shoulder smiling happily at the sight of her Senator.

As they ate, Katherine stared at her mom curiously.

"Mom, you look like you have a fever."

"I do?" Katherine leaned over the table and brushed her mom's forehead with the back of her hands.

"You're definitely extra warm," Kat said in a responsible adult like tone.

"I'll be right back," she called and left. Kat returned with her mom's Multivitamins.

"Mom, you should take your baby vitamins and drink extra water." Realizing what her daughter was up too, a tear rolled down her face. Why was Kat suddenly so concerned for her wellbeing? A feeling of guilt came over Faith as she watched her daughter poured her more sparkling water and piled more eggs and fava beans on her plate.

"Oh Honey, this is absolutely delicious, but mommy's okay now. I swear if I take another bite, I will pop." Katherine laughed at the comical expression on her mom's face.

"I missed you mommy," she said, climbing onto the table placing kisses on her mom's forehead and cheeks.

"Look honey there's cranberry sauce and beans in your hair," her mom teased.

"This means you're edible," Faith giggles and lift her daughter off the table.

"Want to take a bath in your brand-new tub?"

"Sure mom, but you won't be able to lift me up anymore because I don't want to hurt my baby brother."

"Baby brother? Hmm, we'll see."

"I know for sure mommy. He has big Sandy Bay eyes and auburn hair." Faith laughed and placed her thoughtful daughter in the tub.

"Here's my chance to take care of you for a change," Faith said shuffling the water to make bubbles. Katherine splashed around as the faucet gushed water into the sparkling whirlpool tub.

Later, Faith sorted through her and her daughter's things and selected their finest apparel to prepare for an unexpected trip. It would be Katherine's final few months as an only child and she wanted it to be a memorable one. Their flight to Paris would depart at 2a.m. and she had less than seventeen hours to prepare. A few hours later, she had two suitcases packed and all her credit cards were converted for foreign transactions. The thought of traveling to Europe alone with her daughter gave her an uneasy feeling, but those feelings was soon dissolved by the excitement of her unplanned adventure. Truly, why was she going to France, she asked herself.

"Mommy, I'm finished with my bath!" her daughter called interrupting her thoughts.

"Your bathrobe and slippers are hanging on the wall next to the tub," Faith replied.

"Mommy, I change my mind, can I have another bath? I love my bathtub."

"Sure darling, I'll be right there."

"Mommy I change my mind again mommy."

"Well, well, well, my indecisive daughter. WOW, honey, how much bubble bath did you put in there?" she laughed looking at the almost empty container and her daughter's face barely visible under a mountain of sudds, floating around everywhere. Kat laughed at the petrified look on her mom's face.

"I'm so happy to be back home mommy."

Sound asleep, Faith lifted her daughter out of bed and carried her to the airport taxi waiting outside. A drizzle started as the driver turned carefully off the Blvd.

"Ma'am, is everyone all buckled in?" he asked with a southern accent.

"Absolutely, we're all set, thanks Len," she replied.

"You're welcome Ma'am. You're my favorite Senator Ma'am. Because of you, my family now have a home." She only smiled in response.

"Madam Senator, we're almost here."

"Thanks Len. My apologies for the early departure."

"No worries at all," he replied as they pulled into the terminal of Air France.

Katherine woke up momentarily but then drifted back to sleep. The taxi driver helped Faith checked her bags into first class. She was greeted with smiles, whispers and pleasing stares, as the residents of Sandy Island and surrounding areas recognize their heroine. Some residents approached her and shook her hand, and others waved from a distance. After her and Katherine's luggage were checked in, the hostess directed them to the First-Class waiting lounge. They were greeted by well-lit Palace like settings with an open cafeteria. There were lots of sitting and an open game room to entertain children. There are also showers for last minute travelers running late and the option to dine, sit at an open Bar, or simply watch television. The last time she'd travel internationally was over four years ago to attend her mother's funeral and six years before that to attend her father public memorial in Germany. Her most recent trips were all domestic on private flights including Henley's Helicopter. Of course, the Bar looked inviting, but she could picture her baby's tiny head shaking saying… "No way mommy, wait till I come out." Faith approached the cafeteria and reached for a small plate and placed a variety of Olives and chopped fruit to satisfy her growing appetite. Katherine had taken off to the game room and must have forgotten where she was...

"Mom, where are we?"

"We're at the airport darling, in the lounge for specific travelers, we're going on vacation."

"Oh, okay. But where?"

"It's a surprise darling." She arrived an hour early for her flight and as she was about to glance at the time, she was distracted by the attendant's voice.

"We're now boarding first class travelers for flight 549 to Paris France at gate seven."

"Katherine darling, that's our flight."

"Ah ha, we're going to Paris. Mom isn't that where Uncle Fain's from."

"There's no keeping secrets from you Katherine French," her mom smiled in disbelief. They were the first to board the flight and Kat was fully awake and excited as her little feet stepped quickly to keep up with her mom's long strides.

"Yay, we're going on vacation. That's great! But mom, shouldn't we have invited Grandma?"

"Grandma is in Sacramento helping Patrol George with the horse show, but we'll check on her as soon as we land in Paris."

"Ok mommy."

Kat snuggled up in the spacious booth alongside her mom.

"Look mommy my chair reclines. And I have a television and a remote control. Wow, this is so cool," Kat said climbing off her reclined chair to explore. She disappeared into the next room and a minute later she returned.

"Mom, this is great, there's a shower back there, and another room, where two people are kissing!"

"Shhh," Faith laughed and panicked.

"Come here darling. Your iPad's in this bag. We'll be taking off soon."

"Ok mommy, I just wished that Syd was here."

"I know hun. We'll be back home before you know it."

Kat snuggled into her converted bed and covered herself with a blanket that was stuffed neatly on a shelf beneath the arm rest. After she played a few games, several minutes later, soft snores could be heard. It will be eight hours nonstop to Paris. That nervous feeling, she felt earlier had return and she wanted to open the champagne that she saw in the small refrigerator.

When Faith's eyes drifted open; it seemed the sun had vanished from the open sky and was already bidding the day farewell.

"What time is it darling?" she asked the Hostess who'd spoiled her rotten the entire night.

"It's 10:30a.m. your time in California, Madam Senator. But currently, it's 6:30p.m. local time in France respectively Madam. We'll be landing in less than thirty minutes. Can I get you another

Oui Yogurt? I enjoy watching you eat them," she said, smiling warmly.

"Sure, they're quite good," Faith smiled appreciatively. Her daughter's bed was already made, and her blankets were folded neatly next to her pillow. There were several empty snack wrappings and soda cans in her trash container.

"Katherine Elizabeth?"

"Oh she's made a friend over in the economy aisle and has been with her all morning while you slept." The Hostess said enthusiastically.

"Really?"

"Yes, she's a lovely girl and quite a joy to have onboard."

"Thank you dear, you've been a lovely host."

"It's been an absolute pleasure," the stewardess admitted. Faith peeked out of her cabin window. They were flying over the city of Paris. Its gorgeous architecture was clearly visible, and a clouded view of the Eiffel Tower could be seen in the far distance.

The pilot's voice came into the intercom.

"We'll be landing in Paris, France in exactly fifteen minutes. Ladies and gentlemen, please return to your seats and fasten your seatbelts." At that moment the seatbelt lights came on and Katherine came running down the aisle and flopped onto her bed.

"Hello stranger, I heard you made a friend. There's a button next to you that converts your bed back into a chair. Okay darling."

"Oh, let me help you with that sweetie," the Hostess said hurrying toward Katherine.

"I have it, but thank you," Kat said smiling proudly. Faith and the Hostess laughed at the confident young lady sitting properly with her seatbelt fastened and her legs folded.

"Wow, mom look we're back in San Francisco."

"No darling, we're in Paris. Its architecture is much like the ones in San Francisco but there's a distinct difference. Have another look."

"Oh mommy, there aren't very many tall buildings."

"You little genius," her mom laughs and tickles her.

"I love you too mommy. This was a really good idea. Are we going to go see the Eiffel Tower today?"

It's already seven p.m. Let's start fresh tomorrow and make it a date. High five?"

"High-five mom," she said touching her mom's warm hands.

Chapter 30

Faith and Katherine's first morning in Paris was cold and rainy, cancelling all plans for sightseeing. Faith was quite taken by the perfect view of the Eiffel tower from her hotel balcony. *"Fascinating,"* she whispered. She wanted to spend some time driving through Paris with Katherine, but she soon realized that it would be more meaningful to be in the company of Fain. She listened to the voicemail he sent a few days before and wondered what his reasons were to return to France. Maybe I should have read his letter, she thought. She was still unsure of her reasons to reconnect with Fain, yet there was no one more qualified to show her and Katherine an excellent time in Paris.

Katherine was terribly Jetlagged and while she slept, Faith performed several searches to find Fain's address. Each search result produced thousands of Fain Collins, and a few of which included a certain Fain Collin of Aragon with the same street address in Paris. She thought of phoning him but wanted to keep her visit a surprise. In comparison to every possible form of contact, showing up at Fain's door seemed to be the only possible option. She jotted down the strange address: House of Aragon: 79 Rue Des Floures 75006, Paris France. She recognized Rue Des Floures from her previous communications with him before his first arrival to Sandy Island, but she was unsure of the house address.

"Mom are you still trying to find Fain's address?" little Katherine said with a yawn.

"Why is it any of your business darling?" her mom teased.

"Mom you have that look that anyone can read. I just know these things mommy," she said running off to the bathroom. Faith listened as Kat sang Fain's address out loud in the bathroom ~~ 79 Rue Des Floures 7500 ~~ 79 Rue Des Floures 75006~.

"Of course she knows. Kat are you sure? It says House of Aragon, not house of Collins."

"Mom Fain and I are still Bff's and we never give away our secrets. But I'll tell you a little secret because you might be having his baby."

"Katherine love. I've never discussed this with you or anyone for that matter. Who told you this?" Katherine batted her eyes and replied.

"My buddy, last time I checked her name's Syd. She said her dad thinks that you're unsure whether you're having his baby."

"Katherine?"

"Syd overheard Uncle Hank chatting with his friend, the one that calls him about his books."

"Do you mean his agent?"

"I don't know mommy."

Suddenly Kat was reduced to innocence and her mom was left to figure out the details. What in the world does Bff mean? she asked herself, feeling irritated.

"Katherine, there's a Uber waiting for us by the lobby. They'll only wait 20 minutes," Faith called. Katherine presented herself in a sweeping summer dress, wearing a broad rim hat and an umbrella in her hand.

"I told Fain, I'll marry him someday and I want to look my best for him. What do you think of this dress mommy?" Faith held back a chuckle as she delivered the best compliment she could to her daughter.

"To Aragon House Madam sir," Katherine said to the driver after buckling her seatbelt. Faith wondered what had gotten into her daughter.

"Copy that," the driver said, reminding Katherine that he's an appropriately dressed Paris Chauffeur not to be mistaken for a woman.

"Thank you for the reminder sir but I really like your colorful scarf and blouse."

"Well thank you little madam, that's the best compliment I've received all day."

Katherine crossed her legs and practiced French on her Ipad as they drove toward Fain's Residence.

"Mommy, did I mention that Fain Collins is French Royalty?"

"Madam you've arrived," the driver interrupted pulling into the quaint driveway where a master gate with high-tech technology presented a TV like feature with a female voice response system that greeted them loudly.

"Bienvenue à Aragon House, êtes-vous un invité spécial de l'hôte?" The driver looked over at Faith and interpreted what the intel was saying.

"The security system wants to know if you're a special guest?" Faith thought about it for a minute and responded with uncertainty...

"I would think so?"

"Fain, it's me and mom!!!" Katherine said shouting out of her window. The Uber driver spoke in French and asked the system to communicate in English.

"Absolutely," the female voice intel responded.

"Are you a special guest and of whom?"

"Special Guests of Fain Collin, the Duke of Aragon."

"Very well, please select your name among the list of guests that the Duke is expecting today," the Voice responded displaying three names on a computer screen.

"The Duke? This has to be the wrong address," Faith said annoyed.

"I assure you, it's not," the driver responded.

"He's the only Fain Collins in the Republic of France. I know him very well. Believe it or not, I used to help him run away from his dad. I came to this address often," the driver said with a wink. Faith wondered why Fain never mentioned any of this to her. Other than the fact that he had this very rugged princely appearance; his resume was sufficient to have her disregard a pre-employment background check.

"Madam is your name on the list?"

"As you can imagine... Is there another way in?" Faith asked appearing somewhat sneaky.

"I'm afraid not Madam," he replied. The driver looked in time to see Katherine make her way over a flowering fence and slipped beneath a wrought iron beam.

"Madam, your daughter, she's made it inside the parameters. It's quite dangerous, the premises are protected by French Bull-dogs."

"Katherine!" The security system had gone nuts and sounded an intruder alarm. Followed by Katherine's blood curdling scream.

"Aaaah! Help! Somebody please help!" Katherine screamed.

"Madam, I suggest we wait for security."

"Security? Sir with all due respect, are you nuts? My daughter could be hurt. Please do what you can. I'll try to reach Fain," she said, reaching for her phone, dialing frantically.

261

"Katherine, where are you? Please tell mommy you're okay." Faith peeked through the wrought iron fence and saw a large Bulldog standing over Katherine licking her face. A few women dressed like chefs came hurrying toward Katherine. The driver who'd somehow made his way inside, tried to shoo the dog away as he ran in circles around the yard. The large animal who appears to be fond of Katherine obviously had a different opinion of the taxi driver and continue to pursue him.

The women hurried to Katherine and helped her up.

"Young lady, are you alright? How in the world did you get in here?"

"Through there," Katherine said pointing at the fence.

"Would you please let my mommy in, she must be really worried." One of the women nodded at Pauline; a young woman dressed in a different color uniform. The girl reached in her pocket and removed a remote control. After shutting off the security system, she entered a code that opened the gate.

"Wait a minute, why do you look familiar?" The older woman asked.

"Katherine!" her mother screamed hurrying through the gate.

"That's right, you're little Katherine. Duke Collins friend."

"Wait a minute, is that what you call him?" Kat laughed.

"What's all the racket about?" Fain asked looking out of a window in the tower room overlooking the front entrance. Everyone looked up at the Tower.

"Fain, is it really you?" Faith asked hiding a chuckle.

"Round here I'm known as the Duke of Aragon. Didn't you read my letter?"

He laughed and took a swig from a bottle in his hand.

"Well ladies of the house. Please don't keep my friends waiting, invite them in. You might also want to see who Nobleman is having for lunch in the back," he said and disappeared from the window.

"Oh no, the driver!" Faith said remembering. Everyone laughed at the sight of the dog hanging onto the driver's bum. The head housekeeper whistled loudly, and Nobleman finally released the driver and came running toward them.

"Fain I can't stay long. This trip's for Katherine. It's her last few months as an only child. And as you know, we hardly spent much time together the past year. I was hoping you could accompany us," Faith said, trying to be formal. As Faith stared at the Cathedral ceiling, Fain observed her closely and his eyes settled on her abdomen. Having noticed his continuous silence, Faith glanced at him.

"What?" she asked with a chuckle.

"Is it mine?" he asked without humor.

"What's yours?"

He sat on the large, royally made master bed and placed his hands on her midsection. At that moment the baby moved, and Fain became excited.

"Is this why you came? To tell me that we're having a baby. You mentioned that it's Katherine's last few months as an only child and I'm such a bloody idiot, I couldn't put two and two together." Faith watched as Fain's hands circled her tummy. Then suddenly he became distant. He slowly withdrew his hands and his eyes met hers.

"You're not sure, are you?" She looked away from him and he recognized that familiar look.

"You're afraid? Faith, what are you doing here?"

"I'm on Medical leave. I wanted to spend some time with Katherine, just the two of us, but I feel so exhausted. I couldn't have planned this trip at a more awful time," she laughed.

"No I'm glad, I'm happy you came. I could be a father. Do you know what this means?"

"What?"

"My parents had an arranged marriage in place for me to marry the Prime Minister's daughter, Camille. Rumor has it that the Prime Minister is a hidden Royal and could have potentially inherited my father's estate. I don't want to get into too much detail, it's kind of old school stuff," he said turning away from Faith and running his hand through his hair.

"Long story short, the arrangement is that I was to marry the Prime Minister's daughter Camille, who's my second cousin. Since that never happened, there was a lot of upset. Therefore, I left France. It's the reason I took the job you offered. After I returned to France, I reconciled with my parents. They told me that if I had a son, that it would mend our relationship with the other side of our family and could potentially save our family's estate. You see, the Prime Minister may be the real Duke of Aragon, but he only has two kids. Camille and Lucas. It is customary that the Duke with the most male relatives be the successor of the title Duke and the heir of the family's Estate."

"I see," Faith said sitting up.

"Fain darling, I don't think it is wise to share this information with your relatives.

We must be certain that we know what we both want. I know it's not fair to you and Hank, but I need time," she said exhausted.

Fain invited them to dinner and as they dined...Katherine giggled.

"What is it Kat?" Fain asked.

"You have a tummy now."

"Yes Fain, I must admit, you look happy," Faith chuckled.

"You mean I'm a bit of a chub."

Everyone including the housekeepers and chef engulfed into laughter.

"Well, when I got home, the ladies wasted no time in fattening me up," he laughed, pouring more wine.

"After dinner, I would love to show you two around," he said, burping loudly.

"Yeah, you were a bit on the skinny side," the head chef teased.

"Well, after Faith kicked me out, I lived alone for a while and depression kicked in. I hardly had the time," he joked.

"Aww, my poor Bff," said Kat, leaving her seat to embrace him.

"Well you're not that fat, so don't listen to them. Come let's get out of here," she said, taking his hand. Faith watches as Katherine escorted Fain from the dinner lounge. At that moment, she realized how much she'd missed her quiet life with Fain in Sandy Island. The simplicity of it all has been immersed by politics and the press. Was simplicity sufficient? As she reflects, she remembers that she's on vacation.

"Fain, I'd like a French cruise down the Saone and Rhone river. Are there any fleets that connects to Germany?"

"Funny you'd ask, the Saone and Rhone Cruises are the only ones that go to Germany. But why Germany?"

"I would love to show Katherine my hometown. The last time I visited was for my parent's funeral and I was pregnant with Katherine. She's never been. I was never close to my parents after I got married to Eric. They were both very much against my marriage to Eric."

"Are you sure that it's a good time to visit? There's a political upheaval there now and your parents were a hot topic. I'm not sure this is such a good idea," Fain warned.

"Anyway, it's early in the day and I'd like to show you two around. How does that sound?"

"Sounds great," said Katherine grabbing an umbrella.

"Why the umbrella?" her mom asked.

"Well mom this isn't Sandy Island where it never rains. It's Europe and besides, I got the weather forecast on my Ipad this morning." Faith laughed.

"Darling, where and when did you learn these things?"

"Mom, I'm the daughter of a State Senator, I'm supposed to keep informed of current events. You're also responsible for informing the Senate of your whereabouts. Mom did you know that you were supposed to register with the City when you travel internationally? You are no longer a civilian. You're supposed to keep your city officials informed. But don't worry mom, I took care of that for you. If you plan to visit Germany, you're supposed to enter that information in the State of California's Portal, as required of all Senators. If Senator Henley can't find you, he could declare a State of Emergency and you could be declared missing." As they continued to listen with their jaws being lowered by the second, her mom finally broke her prolonged silence.

"Katherine French, I'm on Medical leave darling, I don't need to register anything." Fain laughed at his Bff.

"Well we can never be too careful now can we. How about a good time in Paris first?" Fain said leading the way to his Hummer.

As Fain Sped off the A7 Autoroute...

"Where to homies?" he says trying to impress their American sense of humor.

"What do you recommend?" Faith asked, drifting off to a sleep. Fain drove around Paris for almost an hour. Both ladies were fast asleep the entire time. Stuffed silly by his generous staff, and a dose of jetlag on a rainy evening is the perfect killjoy for an exquisite afternoon of sightseeing in Paris. They were both still fast asleep when Fain headed back to the Aragon mansion. As ecstatic as he was to see them, he knew it wasn't the best time for a Paris German expenditure. He was glad that Faith made him aware of her presence in France, however, in the morning, he would try to convince her to make different arrangements. He parked his large Hummer in front of the Guest House. There were fresh new blooms and he knew that his friends would appreciate the privacy in the presence of gorgeous French blooms.

"Hunny, we're home," he joked propping his chin as he turned to face the sleeping beauties.

The following morning, Faith awoke to the sound of Fain arguing.

"Dad, I'm not willing to discuss this with you, at least not yet. I'm not even sure it's mine," Fain shouted.

"It's?" Faith wondered what Fain was referring too. As her feet landed on the floor, she was greeted by warm French sunshine and acres of roses. Unaware of Faith's presence, Fain continues to argue with his father.

"Dad, I love you and mom, but maybe it's time we let this go. Maybe we can sell Aragon Estate to the Prime Minister. If we sell, you and mom can still live relatively well. Dad, how could you say that? I thought we were passed this nonsense. No, I will not marry Camille, she's moved on and so did I. Last time I checked, she's an actress in California. Dad, everyone's moved on, it's time you did too," Fain said and hung up.

"You're awful, that's no way to talk to your father," she said coming out of her hiding place.

"Hey, how long have you been standing there?" he laughed.

"Does it matter?" she replied.

"You have no idea how stubborn my parents are. They're stuck on this old fashion Monarchical ideology while everyone's racing for the future. I had to give them a wakeup call." Faith just stared at him curiously. He had missed her wisdom and the taste of her Sandy Island lips that tasted of sea salt from the ocean breeze that graced her oceanfront balcony. He was still unsure of her visit at such a delicate time, but it was welcomed. As he stared into her fierce greenish/blue eyes, he felt at home. The memories of their sunny days on the Island came rushing back to him like the ripple effects of rain on calm water. As they stared at each other, Faith gave in to his new manly appearance as he took her in his arms and kissed her.

"Let's go home," he whispered.

Chapter 31

"C'mon sweetheart, almost there," Fain called leading the way up a plateau from a winding dirt trail beyond Aragon Manor.

"How much further?" Faith called exhausted.

"Mommy, I can see everything," Katherine shouted. She was sitting on Fain's shoulders and had no idea how difficult it was to climb up the narrow winding hill.

"What can you see, baby?"

"Come quickly mommy, I don't want to ruin the surprise, she called excitedly. As Faith caught up with the crew, her eyes widened in amazement. A perfect view of the city of Paris stood magnificently. It was almost sundown, and the final reflection of the sun shone beautifully across the city, creating an almost celestial ambience. Faith stood in complete awe, lost for words as she embraced an unexpected moment in Paris.

To relieve his parents of disappointment and an uncertain future, Fain wrote a letter to his Father, informing him that Faith was pregnant with his son. Their flight to Sandy Island is leaving later tonight and he didn't want to leave any stones unturn. After slipping the letter to his father in the mail, he phoned his mom to inform her of his plans to return to Sandy Island. Antoinette was overjoyed by the news. She loved her son's relationship with the entertainment industry and since he'd return to France, she was extremely concerned with his future.

"Darling, this is wonderful news. I will try to convince your father to visit you in California. I love you son."

"I love you mom," he replied.

Fain was much closer to his mom Antoinette than with his father Arthur. Faith's sudden visit to France brought a whirlwind of hope into his life. He looked in the mirror and pulled at his scruffy beard. He couldn't wait to bask in the sunshine and jog on the five-mile beach in front of Faith's bungalow. The days he's longed for, basking in the sea and sun.

The original trio landed at San Francisco International Airport at 7a.m. on a sparkling Sunday morning. After rescuing everyone's baggage at the crowded baggage claim, Fain threw his two duffel bags over his shoulders and held on tightly to Faith and Katherine's heavy three-piece luggage in both hands. Faith giggled at the sight of him.

"I thought I only had two Disney suitcases," Katherine said.

"Oh, I packed the extra one with gifts for you and your mom. No one visits Fain of Aragon and leave without bearing gifts," he said and flashes Kat a smile.

"Hey there, mind if I help with those," said an Airport employee hurrying toward him with a baggage trolly. Before Fain could refuse, the assistant reached for the suitcases in his hands, and placed them on the trolley.

"Hey buddy, I got this," he said as the employee reached for the bags on his shoulders.

"I know, that's what you say, then you sue us for not doing our jobs," the employee said in broken English. Faith was exhausted but couldn't help but laugh at the commotion between Fain and the employee who was much shorter than Fain and was growing very upset by the minute.

"Mom I think I should intervene."

Before her mom responded, Katherine got between the two men and broke up the argument.

"Fain cut it out and let the short little man do his job," she yelled. The argument stopped but Katherine's statement regarding the employee's height left him even more upset and pink in the face. As another confrontation was about to begin between Fain and the employee, Faith's rental arrived, and the three exhausted travelers entered the vehicle. After stuffing their belongings into the tight trunk quarters, Fain drove off San Francisco airport Blvd. He couldn't wait to plunge into the sparkling blue water.

Chance barked fiercely as Fain approached.

"Sorry boy I know I need to lose the beard and the gut," he said patting Chance on the head. Hank almost laughed at the sight of Fain.

"Hey, is that you Fain? Darn I almost mistook you for a burglar," Hank joked.

"When did you guys get back?"

"This morning."

"Hey man I need to rent or borrow a jet ski, got those back yet?"

268

"Oh, um yes I got most of my toys back yesterday but they're not insured yet."

"No worries, mind if I take this one for a spin?" He asks, climbing onto the craft. He cranked the engine and took off before Hank responded.

"Hey Fain!!"

"Just like old times," Fain calls and sped off on the crystal-clear water.

Faith and Katherine slept the entire day, while Fain splashed around in the evening sunshine. Later that day as Faith tried to pull herself together, she noticed a spot of blood on her nightwear. Katherine was sleeping next to her and she wondered if her daughter might have sustained a bruise that she didn't mention. As she observed her daughter closely, she felt a gush of warm fluid rush down her legs. Afraid to look she reached down her thighs and touched, slowly lifting her fingers to her face.

"Blood, it's blood," she panicked. As she reached for the phone to call her OB, it rang.

"Hello, who's this? Sorry, I cannot speak now I have an emergency," she said.

"Faith, it's Henley, are you okay?"

"I'm afraid not. Please phone Viv and ask her to meet me at the new hospital on Sandy Blvd."

"I'm on my way," he replied. As soon as Henley phoned Viv, he got into his car and drove as fast as he could to Sandy Island. As he pulled into Faith's driveway, an ambulance was seen speeding away from Faith's residence. He made a sharp U-turn and followed closely behind the fleeting emergency vehicle. Henley had made a good call following Faith to the Hospital because the nurses escorting Faith to the ER told her...

"I'm sorry Madam, but your daughter cannot accompany you."

"I have her," Henley said approaching.

"Uncle Henley," Katherine said, running into his arms.

"Is my mommy and the baby going to be okay?"

"Come, let's have a seat over here and wait. Your mommy is in the best hands, she will be okay." Henley assured.

As they waited Henley tried to keep Katherine entertained to keep her mind off things. About an hour later Faith's OB Vivienne joined them in the lobby.

"Senator Henley, so good to see you. It's been a few weeks," she said smiling warmly. I'm here to take Katherine to see her mom," she said embracing Kat.

"Mind if I join?" he asked.

"I don't see why not..." she said.

"How's she?"

Viv looked at him nervously.

"The baby arrived."

"But isn't it a bit soon?"

"Yes, she was only five and a half months along," she said.

"Mom had the baby?!" Katherine said excitedly and took off running.

"Katherine sweetheart, wait up, we have to take the elevator to the fourth floor," Viv called. Henley and Viv caught up with her at the elevator and told her that her mommy was in recovery in room 412.

"Hurry, hurry, hurry," Kat said pounding the elevator button impatiently. I want to see my baby brother!"

As soon as they got off the elevator, Katherine took off running. As she entered the room, she was surprised to see her mom in tears.

"Mommy, what's wrong?" Faith smiled between tears.

"Well, the good news is, you have a beautiful baby brother. But, sweetheart, he came just a little bit too soon and he must remain in Intensive Care for a little while. It would be a long time before he would be able to come home. Still not understanding what her mom was saying, she pulled her iPad from her backpack and dialed Grandma Liz.

"Grandma Liz, Grandma Liz, you won't believe it, mommy had the baby, we are at Faith Hope Memorial on Sandy Blvd," she said excitedly.

"Katherine, sweetheart, calm down. I thought you were in Paris."

"Yes Grandma, we got back early this morning. Grandma isn't that great!"

"Yes darling. But how's your mommy...?"

"Um, she's okay but she's crying, and I don't understand. She doesn't seem happy about the baby."

"Don't worry darling, Elizabeth Thunderbird is on her way."

"Liz, I thought I would feel like the city of lights, as they would say when you've just returned from Paris, but I feel like a peeled banana." Faith cries as Liz console her.

"Oh sweetheart..." Liz sigh as they embrace.

As Liz wiped tears from her face with a napkin, Faith remembered Fain.

"Liz?"

"Yes love."

"Please get word to Fain, he's at the beach and is probably going nuts wondering where everyone went. I didn't have the time to leave him a note," she said in between tears and laughter.

"Fain's here?"

Faith nodded…

"Oh, you shouldn't have, this kid is the last thing you need around. How does Hank feel about all this?"

"I'm not sure Liz, I haven't seen Hank in weeks." As Liz consoled her, Henley and Viv entered the room.

"Hello Vivienne. Hi Henley, I'm glad you're here, so wonderful to see you," Liz said excitedly.

"Hello Elizabeth, how have you been? It's wonderful to see you as well," he replied. His eyes drifting to Faith.

"How are you feeling sweetheart?" he asked, taking her hands.

"A bit exhausted and eager to see my son," she admitted.

"Are you ready to see him?" Viv asked.

"Alright, I'll leave you for a minute to go get word to Fain. Where's Katherine? I'll take her along and grab her a bite to eat," Liz said.

Before leaving, Liz kissed Faith on the forehead.

"Katherine darling? I'm right here Grandma Liz," she said hurrying toward her.

"Where were you. I was video chatting with Sydney," she said excitedly.

"You didn't tell her about the baby yet, did you?"

"Of course, I did Grandma Liz, that's the best news ever. Why is everyone acting so weird. I have a brand-new baby brother," she said skipping down the hallway.

Vivienne held Faith's hands and smiled warmly.

"Faith, your son has the strongest heartbeat I've ever heard. He weighed in at three and a half pounds and show incredible promise that he will make it through this. You were only five and a half months along. Most babies born at five months usually weigh around two and a half to three pounds. Faith, the good news is, your baby boy has made it through this. The not-so-great news is that he will have to remain here at Faith Memorial ICU for the next four months before he will be ready to go home. I'm so sorry sweetie," she said remorsefully.

271

"Are you ready to go see him?" she asked.

Faith wiped a tear from her face and nodded yes.

"Okay Hun, I'll grab a wheeler."

"Here, I got you," Henley said, lifting Faith out of bed and placing her in the chair. He then followed Viv toward the ICU. Faith was emotionally overwhelmed as she was greeted by the precious sound of newborn cries. She was almost distracted until her eyes rested upon her infant. It was like the entire world had disappeared as her eyes met her tiny human.

"My sweet darling. Hi baby it's your mommy," she said softly. At the sound of Faith's voice, it was as if his eyelids opened to a squint.

"He recognized your voice. It's the very first sound that babies become familiar with," Vivienne said smiling at mother and son's first encounter.

"He's beautiful," Faith cried. "I just want to take him home. Can I hold him?"

"Yes but it would have to be after twenty four hours, okay love?" Viv replied.

"Okay," Faith said wishing that she could place her index finger in his tiny palm.

Elizabeth was less than excited to greet Fain with news of the baby. As soon as she pulled into the driveway, Katherine took off running up the stairs.

"Fain, Fain where are you, the baby came. I have a baby brother. I knew it all along," she said ecstatically.

"Katherine, where have you guys been? I've tried your mom's phone like fifty times."

"Fain didn't you hear anything I said? Mommy's at the hospital, the baby came!" Fain looked at her slightly confused.

"What do you mean? But it's too soon...is the baby okay?"

"Fain please get a shirt on; Grandma Liz is out front waiting."

Fain looked over the balcony and met Liz's disapproving stare.

"Oh, right, okay, I'll be right there," he said.

He disappeared and returned wearing a shirt sunglasses and flip flops.

"C'mon let's go," Katherine said leading the way.

"Hi Liz, good to see you."

"Hello Fain...so I see that you've decided to return to Sandy Island?" Fain could tell by her tone that she was not happy to see him, so he quickly changed the conversation.

"I know Faith said that she's only five months along, so how's the baby?"

272

"It's not for me to say, you're headed to the hospital so you can discuss this with Faith," she said, slipping on her sunglasses.

"Did someone tell Hank, because I think he should know," Fain said.

"I did. I phoned him on my iPad app. Him and Sydney are already on their way," Kat said proudly.

"Katherine sweetheart, are you sure that this was a good idea? Your mom might not want it that way. You should have asked her first."

"Sorry Liz, I'm just really excited."

"It's fine, you boys will have to figure it out soon because I don't want my daughter-in-law feeling overwhelmed," Elizabeth warned.

"I... I... Captain," Fain said. Liz was less than amused.

"Mommy, wake up, Fain and Hank are here."

"Sorry hun visiting hours are over. The Senator needs to rest," the attending Nurse said.

"Oh okay, Syd and I just wanted to tell my mommy something. Our grandma is in the cafeteria grabbing us a snack."

"Okay sweetie. I'll give you guys five minutes," she said.

"Mommy, Fain and Hank are outside chatting, they were smiling at first but now they don't sound so happy."

"Oh no, they're both here. Who told Hank?"

"It was me mommy."

"Katherine?"

"Sorry mommy."

"How are you feeling, Ms. French?" Sydney said happily, revealing her new teeth.

"I'm feeling okay Syd, just slightly ripped off, because I can't feel my baby tossing around in my tummy anymore," Faith said smiling weakly. Faith's mood changed in an instant.

"Please tell those boys to get in here instantly!" she said annoyed. As soon as Hank and Fain entered the room...

"I need both of you to go home, now!"

"But what about the baby, I'd like to see him," Fain said.

"Is he going to be okay?" Hank asked. Faith exhaled loudly...

"Oh boy, okay, I guess I owe you both this much."

After calming herself, she explained everything that her OB had told her. A few minutes later, the attending nurse returned and attempted to kick the men out of the room.

"But I'm the Father," Fain said

273

"And I'm the uncle," Hank replied. He wanted to say that he could also be the father, but he wanted to protect Faith's integrity. A few moments later Henley and Elizabeth returned. Faith looked around the room at everyone and smiled.

"C'mon guys, you should go home."

"No, you shouldn't be alone, not now. You don't really expect us to leave you now," Fain said sitting next to her.

"Well, you're still my fiancé and I have good reason to be here," Hank said possessively.

"Well, if you're staying, I'm staying," Henley said folding his arms. Liz chuckled at the men.

"Well so long as you don't kill each other. It looks like there's room for everyone. We have a pull-out sofa, a rollaway bed and a recliner," Faith said. The recliner was close to Faith so Fain scrambled and took it.

"I'll take the roll away," Henley said.

"Well, I guess that leaves me with the cold hard sofa," Hank grumbled.

"Come on Uncle Hank you are tougher than that," Katherine teased.

"Better believe it," Hank replied flexing his arm. Fain burped loudly and rubbed his tummy in response. Everyone laughed.

"Well sweetheart, you've created quite the Sitcom," Liz said tucking her in.

"I can't complain. For now, you're in the company of Sandy Island's most eligible bachelors competing for your affection," Liz joked.

"At least until morning when I find my energy and bump their heads together," she giggled.

"Hank I'm taking Sydney to my place if that's alright."

"Thanks Liz, you're a lifesaver," he smiled.

"Syd hunny, please be good for Liz okay and daddy will see you in the morning."

After hugs, embrace and kisses...Liz took the girl's home.

The attending Nurse opened the door to Faith's suite and peeked at her company. She smiled and shook her head. If only I was a Journalist, this would make the front page, she thought. While everyone slept, the Nurse towed an electric breast pump next to Faith's bed and sat next to her. After removing the blankets, she noticed that her Pajama blouse was wet in front.

"Ah perfect," she whispered. The Nurse then slipped on some gloves and after lifting Faith's blouse, she places her hands on her breast. She almost chuckled as they felt like full size cantaloupes.

"What are you doing?" Faith asked.

"Hello Senator, your Son is ready for his first feeding. I've brought you a pump to help you express."

"Express? Well, thank you, Hun, but I'll manage," Faith said annoyed.

The nurse smiled at her.

"Okay Ma'am, but I meant no disrespect. I'm supposed to cleanse the nipples then attach the pump."

"Oh I see, okay, carry on."

"How's he doing, I need to see him."

"Absolutely, once he's fed, we'll take you too him."

"How do you feed him? Would it painful for him?" Faith asked, appearing more worried by the minute.

"Not at all Miss Senator, we feed him intravenously."

"I see."

"Alright then. We'll have to try to fill at least four of these bottles and refrigerate them. He will need at least eight bottles to get through the day," she said confidently. As the Nurse prepared the pump, she glanced at Faith.

"What is it?" Faith asked.

"Oh, it's nothing."

"C'mon, you have beautiful revealing eyes, I can tell you have something on your pretty mind."

She smiled at Faith's response.

"Um, we were wondering if you've decided on a name for your son?"

Faith propped her chin and squinted her eyes.

"I haven't really thought about it. I was still deciding on a name, then he surprised me," she smiled. Faith went silent for a few moments then she met the nurse's eyes.

"Lucas, his name is Lucas."

"Perfect, it suits him perfectly," the Nurse said excitedly placing the final bottle onto the pump.

Faith paced the hospital suite tugging against a lock of hair. Hank and Henley had left her a note. They had to go home to take care of appointments. Fain was still fast asleep. He appears as a child grabbing onto his pillow except for the dark hairs that grew all over his legs. Her smile faded as she came to a new realization. Would I have to remain here for the next four months? The thought of going home and leaving Lucas in the ICU was almost unbearable. She drew the curtains to let the sun in. She had a perfect view overlooking a coastal side of Sandy Island that she'd never seen before. How exquisite, she thought. She looked around the room at the paintings on the wall. They were rather vague, leaving her trail of thought in a paradox. Suddenly she wanted music… She wanted to dance, maybe for her son, maybe for the uncertainty as she began to move rhythmically across the room in circles.

Chapter 32

"**L**ook at your chubby little legs Lucas. I think you're ready to be interviewed for your first job. Let's get you dressed. What would you like to wear?"

Lucas kicks his legs excitedly at the sight of his sister.

"That's right, a diaper, a necktie and your resume in hand," Katherine says tickling the bottom of his feet. Lucas's temporary excitement turned into a fuss as Faith entered the hospital suite where they've stayed off and on for the past four months. The nurses are preparing Lucas's final paperwork and Faith's Obstetrician Viv is in her lab awaiting Lucas's paternity results. Faith had requested the test after a fist fight between Fain and Hank landed them in stitches.

"My, my have you grown my sweet darling," Faith said, picking up and kissing her baby boy's chubby face.

Katherine loved the excitement in her mother's eyes. Each time she played with Lucas she saw a spark that wasn't there before. As Katherine admires her mom and Lucas, there was a message chime from Fain on her iPad.

"Please text me when your mom exit's Sandy Blvd, okay."

"Sure, but why?"

"I can't say, but you're sworn to secrecy, okay young lady."

"Okay Agent Fain, over and out," Kat replied.

As Kat cuddled up next to her mom and Lucas, there was a soft knock on the door.

"It's open," Faith replied. She was surprised to see Henley walk in.

"Hi Henley, I thought you had a meeting."

"Yes, I got out earlier than planned."

"What a sight for sore eyes. I can see he's ready for the Senate. You're a handsome little guy," Henley said, removing Lucas's hat. You know I wouldn't miss this little guy's transition for the world. Yep I'm going home today," Henley said pretending to speak for Lucas. Katherine giggled at how great Henley is with the baby.

"You look ready," he said, winking at Faith.

Fain scrambled to make sure that everything was exactly perfect. He'd spent several weeks preparing Lucas's nursery and had employ the help of Faith's Assistant, Stephanie Bradley. So far, she's doing a fantastic job with the interior design of Faith's newly built, beachside elegance. The exquisite colors, decor, and lighting instilled the essence one would find in the modern ambience of a classic San Francisco estate. As Fain made the rounds double checking that everything was perfect and in order, he received a message.

"We've just exited Sandy Island Blvd, we'll be there in a little bit," Kathrine texted. He responded with a quick thumbs up and hurried to the balcony and whistled loudly.

"Everyone please take your places," he called excitedly. Hank, Sydney, Stephanie, Elizabeth, Patrol George, Calvin, and Calvin's friend Gerry as well as Faith's friends Maggie and Joyce stood together on the stairwell, leading up to a nicely decorated balcony, arrayed in blue and white balloons and a Princely touch. A large sign that read Welcome home baby Lucas hung just above the stairwell. As Faith exited Henley's car, she was greeted by familiar voices shouting… "Surprise!!!" The almost blinding decor lights took baby Lucas by storm as he screamed from the top of his lungs. Everyone responded with a heart breaking…. "aww." Unable to resist, the happy crowd approached Faith, hoping to get a closer look at the charming baby boy.

"Fain, it was a lovely Party, you've out done yourself," Faith said, collapsing on her sofa.

"I promise, this is the last party for a while. I don't think the little guy is very fond of classy, well-lit festivities," Fain said picking up the healthy newborn.

"I think he has my ears. Oh yah, you have my ears. But you are still the splitting image of your mommy. Look at those cute dimples. You are the definition of adorable," Fain said playfully.

As Fain entertains Lucas, Hank and Sydney walked in.

"What a nice surprise, come on in guys."

Sydney and Katherine embraced each other.

"Wow, it feels like it's been forever. I've missed you so much. We should ask my dad if he can homeschool the both of us together in the Fall."

"That's a great idea because my mom will be really busy with the baby."

"That's perfect," Katherine said happily.

"Come, I want to show you something."

"What is it?" Sydney asked following Katherine down the hall.

"I want to show you Lucas's nursery. Uncle Fain did a great job."

"Oh okay. Wow, it's amazing, gosh he's so adorable, I really hope he's my baby brother," Sydney said sniffing on Lucas's blanket.

"Yummy, boy do I love the smell of babies." As the girls try to tidy Lucas's messy bedroom, Sydney notices an envelope sticking out of the baby's diaper bag. As Katherine arranged Lucas's crib, she looked up at the sound of paper tearing.

"What's that," Kat asked, approaching.

"Not sure," Syd said, opening the envelope.

"Per...per...paternal results for Lucas Tommy Hutton."

"Hutton? Lucas's has the same last name as me," Syd said staring at the document excitedly.

"This could only mean one thing," said Kat.

"Oh my gosh, I think we're sisters. We're sisters," Sydney said hugging Katherine excitedly.

"Are you sure?" Kat said looking closely at the document.

"It's con...confirmed, that Henley Hutton is 99.99...um what's that symbol?

"It's a percent symbol."

"Thanks...percent the father of Lucas T Hutton."

The girls screamed in excitement.

"Oh, boy, umm, I'm not sure we were supposed to see that. I think that this is my mom's very private business. We should put it back," said Kat.

"But we already opened it," said Syd.

"No, you opened it, you shouldn't have," Kat scolded.

"Well, that's not so bad, because we found out that Lucas is our brother."

"Gotcha! What are you two whispering about?" Fain asked, entering the room with Lucas who'd fallen asleep in his arms.

"Oh, oh." The girls said simultaneously as they dropped the letter and ran out of the room.

Fain tucked Lucas into his crib and drew the curtain to allow fresh ocean air to come in. He looked curiously at the torn envelope on the floor and reached for it.

What are they up too? he wondered as he reached for the document in the envelope. He read the three sentences. He read them again a second and third time. He was hardly surprised by the results and always knew that there was a strong possibility, but he wasn't ready to face it. He wished the last few minutes had never happened. Fain set the envelope on the dresser and after switching on the baby's video monitor, he placed the receiver in his pocket and went for a walk to clear his head.

"What are you two whispering about?" Hank asked, staring at that familiar look in his daughter's eyes.

"Umm, nothing," Kat said.

Faith smiled upon her sleeping baby and gazed at his artfully arranged room.

"The girls are up to something," Hank said walking into Lucas's nursery.

"Shh," Faith whispered to him.

"Look what we have here," Hank whispered, smiling proudly at the sleeping infant. As they dote upon Lucas, Faith noticed the torn, familiar looking envelope on the dresser.

"I think I know what the girls are up to," she said, removing the document from the envelope and handing it to Hank.

"What's this?" he asked, staring at the three sentences.

"This says that Lucas is my son," he said excitedly, a smile forming on his face.

"I was so afraid he wouldn't be mine. Is this for real, or did the girls create a cute little document prank?"

Faith laughed at his boyish reaction.

"He's yours."

"Wow, I have a son, this is almost surreal. I mean, wow I can't believe it. Do you need me to sign anything because I've been thinking that if he's mines, I would want him to have my last name? Should we discuss it later?"

"He already does," she said, presenting him with another document for his signature.

"This one is for the Registrar for our son's birth certificate," she said smiling at how tickled Hank seemed by the news. As they discuss Lucas, Fain returned from his walk and noticed the apparent joy on Hank's face, and he knew that he'd gotten the news that he is Lucas's Father.

Over the next few days Fain slowly distanced himself from Faith. It was almost unreal how increasingly close Hank was becoming to the family that he loves. As his mind began to race with thoughts of what life would be like for his parents and the future of his family's estate, it was even more unbearable what life would be like without Faith. Soon, news of the birth of Faith's son will make headlines, and he had to think of something quickly. As he paced back and forth, an idea came to him. He needed a boat. Senator Henley's son Tommy had mentioned that his Father had placed Vixen up for sale. Perfect, he thought and put in a call to Henley.

"Henley, it's Fain. No, I'm not calling for Tommy, I'm calling about the boat, is it still up for sale...?"

"My apologies, I didn't realize it wasn't for sale yet. Faith told me that Tommy had mentioned this to Hank on that fishing trip they took a few months back."

"Yes, I would love to come and have a look at it. Perfect, I'll see you in a little bit," Fain said excitedly and hung up.

The short drive to Senator Henley's estate felt like a master heist in the works. Yet, his love for Faith and the purpose of his potential venture would set the path in motion for the woman he loves. As he pulled up to the security gate, Tommy stood on the balcony and said...

"Alexa, open the gate, it's a friend."

"Awesome feature, thanks Tommy. I have something similar at Aragon Manor in France."

"Hi, you must be Fain. Dad said Hank was coming over. Dad it's Fain, not Hank." Tommy said and left.

"Fain, my apologies, sometimes I get the names mixed up. Come on in, I'll take you to Vixen."

"Can I get you anything, Vodka, Brandy, can a beer?"

"How hospitable. Brandy sounds great if you can accommodate?"

"Absolutely. Go ahead and have a look at Vixen, she's right out back through this door, right there," Henley said pointing.

Fain was floored by the sight of Vixen.

"Wow, you're gorgeous," he said stepping on board.

"Three decks, you can probably entertain a party of at least two hundred."

"Here you go champ," Henley said, handing Fain a glass with ice and a bottle of Brandy.

"She's a beauty," Fain said excitedly.

Come don't fall in love with her yet, let's give you the grand tour," Henley said leading the way.

"Rumor has it, you're some kind of French Royalty?"

"Henley, with all due respect, if you ever call me Prince, sir I will kick your butt."

Henley laughed at Fain's unexpected sense of humor.

"Not looking to get my butt kicked, so I better stick to business," he chuckled.

Fain hesitated but thought at minimum, the Senator of San Francisco should know a bit of his background.

"Well, actually, the Prime Minister of France is my uncle, my dad's brother."

"Really?"

"Yep, him and my parents have been at odds over Aragon Estate since I was a kid."

"You mean they're fighting over inheritance?"

"Yes sir."

"I can see why you prefer to be away from home," Henley said as the tour came to an end.

"Sir you are quite the impressionist," Fain said.

Henley laughed.

"Senator, I would be delighted to be Vixen's second owner, she's a beauty."

"Perfect. It will take my assistant a few hours to put the paperwork together. I'll swing by later today and drop it off. In the meantime, you'll have to put some paperwork together to get a Sandy Island pier Permit."

Fain looked surprised.

"A Permit?"

"Yes, it's a new requirement that was signed into law since the reconstruction of Sandy. The good thing is that the permit is issued the same day."

"Oh, that's perfect. Thanks for your time today sir."

"Not at all. You're welcome, anytime."

Henley watched as Fain drove off. He wondered why he didn't mentioned Lucas. Faith has informed him that paternity revealed that Hank is Lucas's father and he's been growing concerned about the situation over at Faith's. He wanted to give her time to adjust to her new family, but he couldn't help but worry about her.

Henley glanced at the time on the wall. It was almost 5:00 a.m. and he'd hardly slept a wink. He had hoped to see Faith when he dropped off the signed documents to Fain earlier, but she wasn't home. Her life is headed in a new direction, moving faster than a freight train and the thought of intervening made him feel vulnerable. Maybe she didn't see it, but it always seemed that she needed to be freed. The first time he laid eyes on her standing on her balcony in a flowing summer dress, the wind in her hair as she glanced at the restless tides below, he knew she was searching for something...something that not even saving an entire Island could fill. Henley lay awake for hours, thinking of Faith. When the early morning sunrise finally casts its radiance, he fell into a deep sleep and had a dream of Lucas. He was about five and was throwing a red Frisbee to a golden retriever who jumps and catches it in its mouth. Then out of nowhere Hank and Fain came running toward him and Lucas did not appear to be happy by their presence. He dropped the Frisbee and ran toward his mom.

Henley's dream was interrupted by loud thumping on his door.

"Just a minute, I'll be right there," he said scrambling out of bed.

"What can I do for you son?"

Tommy hands him his mobile...

"It's Faith, she sounds upset."

"Hi sweetie, what's going on?"

"I can't find Lucas and Fain is also gone."

"Are you sure, maybe he took him for a morning stroll. Have you tried his mobile?"

"Yes, it's going straight to voicemail."

"Faith, I have an odd feeling about this. I sold Vixen to Fain yesterday. I thought he was acting strange but it's summer, so I assumed he was looking for a good time with his Hollywood buddies."

"He purchased Vixen?"

"Yes, he swung by after obtaining the permit and drove Vixen to the new Pier near the cove."

"Faith go ahead and phone the authorities. I'm sending two secret agents to your house to get you and the kids to my place as soon as possible."

It's been seven hours and there was still no sign of Fain or Lucas. There was also no sign of the yacht and Faith was now convinced that Fain had taken Lucas. Senator Henley had requested that the investigation remain private for 48 hours to keep reporters from swarming his residence. He also did not want the press to get a hold of this because in the event that Fain had kidnapped Lucas, he does not want him being informed that they're onto him.

Fain docked Vixen deep beneath several large coven reefs that he'd discovered about ten miles beneath Sandy Island. Despite Vixen's height, the tall coven rocks were a perfect hide. He looked over at Lucas who was still fast asleep on the captain's bed beneath two pillows. Fain had stolen the breast milk that Faith had pumped and placed in the refrigerator. He'd taken care to keep them refrigerated, then he would warm them in the microwave for each feeding. He kept his eyes on the news for when the kidnapping of the son of Sandy Island Senator makes headlines. He was pressed for time and could hardly wait to get a hold of the French Prime Minister, his uncle to inform him of the birth of his son. With success, his uncle will sign Aragon Estate over to his parents. It would be another three hours before his uncle came into the office. But he'd already inform his parents of Lucas's birth, and they'd gotten word to his uncle about Lucas. French Prime Minister Louie Lennox, jaded over the eternal dispute between him and the Aragon's said that upon video confirmation of the child, alive and well, that he would immediately sign all rights of his claim to Aragon Estate over to Fain's parents.

Fain hopes that he would successfully complete his mission before his actions are deemed an official kidnapping. He was terrified, moisture ran down his forehead as he glanced back and forth between the time and ABC9 news. He almost fell off his chair as Lucas awoke with a startling scream.

"Coming buddy," he said, hurrying to prepare Lucas's bottle.

"Shh, here you go," he said lifting the infant, gently placing the bottle in his mouth. As he concluded Lucas's feeding, Skype opened on his computer screen.

"That's our call buddy, come let's go chat with your Uncle Lennox, he needs to see you.

"Hey Uncle Len!"

"Fain, you are still a boy, what are you doing with a baby," he joked.

"Look what we have here, he's Aragon blood for sure. Look Fain, I don't have much time, but it's nice seeing you finally settled down, taking some responsibility for yourself."

"Thanks Uncle Len, so what do you think?"

"I must say, he's a cutie, and has your eyes and ears."

"That's exactly what I thought when I first saw him," Fain laughed.

"Is he healthy?" Lennox asked in a slightly scheming way.

"Nice try Uncle Len, yes he's as healthy as a storm and he's here to stay."

"Alright, alright, I signed the documents last night. I didn't want an innocent child to be the reason, after all, I'm nearing retirement."

"Very good, that's excellent news Uncle Len. You know this means the world to us. I cannot thank you enough."

"You are most welcome my boy. I must run along now, go ahead, and take care of my little nephew okay. Bye Lucas."

As Lennox exited the screen Lucas yawned loudly.

"Good boy," Fain said, returning him to the Captain's bed. As soon as he turned on his mobile, he received several text messages, most of which were from Faith. The most recent text message was from Kate. He opened Kate's message and there was a photo of her cuddling a baby boy. Wow, Kate had a baby. When did all this happen? he thought.

"I left you a voice message," the note said. After listening and reading through the mound of messages that Faith and Hank had left, he sat staring at his unshaven face in the mirror. He then listened to Kate's voice message. As soon as he heard Kate's message, he phoned Faith and gave her his location.

"I can't believe it. Lucas, can you believe it... I have a son, he's three months old and his name is Felix."

Lucas sneezed in Fain's face in response.

"Yes, I deserve that," Fain said, kissing Lucas on the forehead. There was two helicopters circling the area and Fain was concerned that Faith might have alerted the authorities. But she didn't mention this when they spoke.

"Alright Lucas, let's get you home, buddy."

As he drove Vixen out of the cove, he thought of what he would say to Faith and if anything, he's likely to get into a fist fight with Hank again.

"Oh well. You know, if I didn't hear from Kate, I would have likely taken you to France. That was the plan," Fain said as he changed Lucas's wet nappy.

As he pulled the boat into Sandy Island's new Pier, there was no sign of the helicopters and for a minute there, he felt like he was in the middle of a hostage situation with invisible guns pointed at him. As he walked down the wooden dock with the baby in his arms, Lucas smiled at him.

"Aww, Lucas, my buddy, I don't deserve your kindness. I really thought you were mine."

As he neared home, everyone including the Police and two Secret Service officials were standing on the beach waiting for Fain to safely surrender Lucas over to his parents.

"I tried talking them into leaving but they weren't convinced," Faith said, taking her baby joyfully.

"This isn't what it looks like," Fain said looking around at everyone. As the officers tried to get a statement from Fain, Hank shoved through the crowd and punched him, knocking him to the ground.

"What the heck were you thinking, you jerk. You had everyone worried sick."

"Dam it, what the heck, he's my son, I took him for a spin around the bay."

"No one was able to locate you and you weren't answering your phone!" Hank yelled.

"Stop it!" Faith said looking at Hank crossed.

"Fain did you have knowledge of this document," the officer asked, handing him the paternity results he saw a few days before.

"What's this?" he pretended.

"This says that Lucas is my son. I'm sure you saw the paternity result, that's why you took him!" Hank yelled.

"Officer, I swear, I've never seen this document before now. I am terribly sorry, but I thought Lucas was my son," he said hoping to appear convincing.

"Officers, thank you for coming, but I don't believe that he was attempting to kidnap Lucas. We all assumed that he was the father. Please return to your districts," Henley said.

"Yes, Senator," the men said.

Elizabeth was keeping an eye on the girls and wondered what was happening. Katherine sneaked out and got away from Liz. She saw when Hank punched Fain and she wanted to know if he was okay.

"Fain are you okay," she asked running towards him.

"Sure sweetie, don't worry, Uncle Fain didn't feel a thing. It's kind of a guy's thing," he assured Katherine.

"Faith, can I speak with you privately."

"Hank please, not now. I need some time alone to process. I need time to think about all of this," she said embracing Lucas snugly, walking away. Hank was furious and took Sydney home. How could she be so naive, he thought. It was obvious that Fain was up to something. When they were inside, Faith slapped Fain.

"What were you thinking. Have you gone bonkers? If you wanted to spend time with Lucas, you sould have informed me," she scolded.

"Faith, you have to see this," he said showing her the photo that Kate had texted him earlier.

"Who's this?"

"Do you remember Kate, the movie producer I met a year ago? It's her son."

"And…what does this have to do with anything?"

"He's my son, she told me in a message this morning. His name is Felix."

"Wow, really?" she said calming down.

"He's adorable, and looks a great deal like you."

"How old is he?"

"He's three months old."

"Oh, my goodness, that's incredible. So, what are your plans?"

"Not sure yet," he said looking in her eyes for any sign that she might need him, but she seemed relieved by the news.

"I think it's time you meet your son," she said smiling.

"Yes, I plan to take off for a few days, are you going to be okay?"

"Yes, absolutely." As he turns to leave...

"Fain?"

"Yes?"

"Congratulations," she said smiling proudly at him.

"Thank you!" After chatting with Katherine and kissing Lucas on the tummy, Fain tossed a duffel bag with clothes in his new Rover and drove like there were no roads up to the heights to meet his son.

Chapter 33

"Hank did you even read the contract before you signed?"

"Well, yes, somewhat," he said feeling unsure.

"you agreed to be on set for the entire production. You said that you wanted to be present for the shoot and we made provisions in the contract which you signed. And I must say, it's too late to make changes to the agreement."

"Adam, there's no way I could get away for an entire year. I have kids and I'm sure you've heard that I just had a baby."

"This is nuts, Hank, please don't screw this up for us. We've all invested a lot of time to get you this deal, please tell me you're in."

"But you said that production starts in two days and I have to leave for Hollywood tomorrow night. That doesn't give me much time," Hank said frustratingly.

"Hank, this is your only shot, you have twelve hours to figure this out. I'll check in with you in the morning," Adam said firmly and hung up before Hank could say another word.

As he thought of the sudden arrangements he needed to make, his phone rang.

"Daddy, I'm having dinner at Faith's, I won't be home for another couple hours, okay daddy."

"Sweetheart, are you asking for permission or are you telling me."

"I'm telling you dad, what's the big deal, and besides, we're all family now." Sydney says and hangs up abruptly. Why is everyone so impatient with me lately? My own daughter thinks that I'm optional, he thought. He knows that she's undoubtedly excited about her new brother.

"Ah forget it," he says, ruffling his hair and pouring himself a scotch before heading over to Faith's for dinner.

During dinner, Hank and Faith enjoyed the view as the girls competed to feed Lucas strawberries. Lucas was growing like a little vine and his chubby face was covered in red juices as he chews and makes yummy sounds with his mouth.

"Lucas loves his sisters; I can tell they're inseparable. Can you imagine seeing them apart?"

"Can we chat privately after dinner, it 'll only take a minute," Hank said, feeling anxious.

"Um, sure." Faith was puzzled by the suddenness of his approach, but she had a good feeling she knew what he wanted to talk about. After dinner, Hank helped with Lucas's bath. He then watched as Faith rocked him into a deep sleep.

"He's a beautiful baby."

"Yes, and he's starting to look more like Sydney."

"Nice of you to say, but he still has your gorgeous eyes and wavy hair," Hank said as they stroll onto the balcony.

"Ahh, it's a beautiful evening out, I'd hate to be the one to ruin it," he said.

"Why, what is it you needed to discuss," Faith asked, her eyes narrowed with concern.

"Something came up and I…" He looked away from her then.

"What's wrong? Are you having second thoughts about our engagement?"

"No, not at all. It's just that I didn't get a chance to read the entire contract and now I have to leave town. I have to be away for an entire year. I can still get away on weekends but…"

"An entire year? What's this contract about?"

"Do you remember the book I completed a few months back?"

"Sure, what about it. It was optioned for a film and I signed the contract without reading it in its entirety, and now I must be in Los Angeles in less than two days to begin filming.

"Wow, that's incredible, but in two days? Will you be taking Sydney along?"

"Actually, I can't, that's why I wanted to talk. I know it's a lot for you to process, especially with our baby but, there's no way to modify the contract. I wished I'd read the darn thing before I signed. At the time, all I cared about was the deal, so what's to think about, right?" Faith laughed at his childish humor.

"If you're asking if Sydney could stay with us, you know that's a no brainer, right?"

"I feel like I'm taking advantage. You gave me a Son, mourned my ex and now you're taking in my daughter. Dear Faith…have I ever told you, you're a Saint, and I love you, so very much."

"Never," she jokes.

He took her in his arms and kissed her on the forehead.

"Hank look, over there. The dolphins are back."

"Splendid, you know what this means. It's officially summer again on Sandy Island," he says kissing her tenderly.

A few days later, as Faith and the kids drove Hank to the Airport, an idea came to her. "Hank, it saddens me that your house would be unoccupied for so long. Of course, we'll visit when Sydney needs too but most of the time, it will be sitting pretty."

"What did you have in mind?" he asks.

"Before the fire I was working on a little project called SandyBaynB."

"You mean like to list it as a vacation rental?"

"Exactly my thought. It's summer and we'll have visitors coming from all over."

"Hmmm, not such a bad idea...Can I take a couple days to think about?" he smiled.

"Of course. Absolutely, all the time you need."

"You're still on maternity leave Senator. Do you have someone in mind who would be up to the task? You know I adore your brilliance but there's no way you could do this alone."

She smiled in agreement.

"Daddy I'm going to miss you so much daddy, but not so much because I get to stay with Faith and Katherine and my chubby baby brother who I love very, very much. So please don't worry about us because you know I am very, very helpful," his daughter assured. Hank hid his chuckle.

"Not one-bit darling. You know daddy couldn't be prouder." Sydney blushed in response.

"You have a way with the ladies Hank. To get your daughter to accept your sudden departure on such short notice is impeccable."

"I love you," he whispered. "I'll try to come home on the weekends, or as often as I can."

"I know you will," she says placing her hands on his as they pulled into Sandy Island Airport. After many tight embraces and kisses, Hank's flight soared against the fiery sky as the faces he loves became tiny dots in the distance.

For the first time in weeks Faith found herself standing in her favorite place staring at the stillness of the bay, lit by a full moon. After dinner and a splash in the pool, her babies fell fast asleep. She was hardly surprised when Sydney had suddenly requested that Lucas sleeps in her room. She had even prepared a neat little arrangement for him by placing one of his playpens next to her bed. Syd had an impossible year and with neither of her biological parents in the picture, Faith couldn't imagine the bond she must share with Lucas. It almost broke her heart the thought of what it would have done to her if Lucas were Fain's. There was a superior plan at work, surrounding the unplanned events of their lives.

"Are you absolutely certain that you don't need an Assistant? What about security? Faith for God sakes, you are a State Senator. You are adorable, but there are people out there, sneaky little haters you would never suspect who wants the impossible."

"Henley we've been on the phone for hours discussing my status and security. I assure you; I do not need these things. I've had the most exquisite of Assistants and I've never met anyone on Sandy Island who doesn't approve of me. I'm approachable, kind and I mingle with my residents; they are my neighbors. Would you like to know what I'm working on right now?"

"And what's that?" Henley asked in a disapproving tone.

"I'm in the process of learning everyone's names. Yes, after I get their names, I'll learn who they are, and I will make sure that they lack nothing. If my residents need to come to my door for a cup of sugar, they will have free access. No security, no secret service, and no guns. These are my people Henley and my prerogative," she said and hung up.

Henley was impressed with Faith's confidence but he was hardly listening. He phoned her Mother-in-law Elizabeth to get her approval.

"Oh Henley, I'd never forget the day when you called my home asking for my stubborn daughter's assistance, to step in as Senator. Have I mentioned what she did to my closet trying to find an appropriate outfit to meet with you?"

Henley chuckled by Liz's relentless humor that always get him in better spirits.

"She's refusing to have any assistance with the kids, and I think it's a bit too much for her. Did I mention that she also hung me up before I finished speaking? I think she's a bit stressed. She's got her hands full and she's taking her position a bit too lightly."

They chatted for a while and Liz mentioned that she would like to throw a summer party to celebrate her Grandson and all their accomplishments.

"Senator, is it possible to accommodate a family of over fifty on your Vixen?"

"Oh Vixen; you won't believe it, but I sold her to Fain."

"Oh no you didn't."

"Don't worry, I'll get a hold of him and see if we can arrange something."

"That would be lovely."

"When do you need Vixen?"

"Think you can have her in front of the Bay in a couple of days?"

"Absolutely, even if I have to repurchase, I'll have her ready. And just to confirm, do I have your permission to set up security for your daughter...?"

"Henley, please do whatever it takes to ensure her security and I'll handle the ripple effects," Liz replied.

Later Henley chatted with Fain and made him an offer for Vixen.

"I have to admit, I missed her like crazy, I wasn't quite prepared to sell her."

"Would you consider selling her back to me? You seem like you're in good spirits. What's new Fain Collins? A surprise, I see. Well, we'll see you at the party in a couple of days. Alright, I'll see you then," Henley replied.

After getting off the phone, Henley contacted the secret service to occupy a residential home, neighboring the Sandy Island Senator to set up security.

It's been almost six weeks since Hank left for Los Angeles and so far, he's been unable to visit for a single weekend. Fain was only a twenty-minute drive away and have only phoned on a couple of occasions, but Faith didn't mind. Poor Katherine woke up early trying to fill Fain's shoes. The look on her face when she thought she had failed was far more priceless than burnt cinnamon rolls on a rainy day. Sydney at such a tender age already demonstrates keen maternal instincts and loves helping with her brother. Faith keeps a close eye on the girls, since Sydney attempted to give Lucas a bath in water that was much too cold. Despite her efforts to comfort her, Syd still feels terrible about it. She assumes that Lucas is furious with her because of the way he screamed in the cold bath. Faith was simply thankful that it was cold water and not the other way around. Yet with each passing day, the love she feels for her little darlings are far more fulfilling than the restless waves against the cove on stormy days.

"Mom is Fain coming to the party? He's only come by twice and he takes forever to respond to my texts," Katherine said looking up from her iPad computer.

Faith and Lucas were fast asleep, and she responded to Katherine's question with gibberish and loud snores. It was a hectic few weeks and Faith wished that she had taken Henley's advice. Everything was a complete disaster. There were spills on the kitchen floor. Recipes and ingredients, pots and pans on the center aisle. There were at least five loads of laundry waiting to be done.

"Kat, should we take Chance for a walk, she looks awfully bored?" Syd asked.

"We should ask mom, but she's asleep. I'm really worried about her; she seems so tired."

As the girls chatted, there was a knock on the door; the entrance that led to the beach.

"Senator Henley, it's Senator Mr. Henley," Kat said hurry to let him in.

"Mr. Senator are you here to help us with all these chores, the place is a total disaster," Kat said placing her hands on her hips.

Henley chuckled.

"Hello, I remember you," Syd called looking up from her iPad.

"Hi there, I remember you as well kiddo," Henley replied.

Syd smiles and returns to her game.

Henley looked at Faith fast asleep with the baby in her arms. He wondered how she managed to hold Lucas so firmly while asleep. Yet he couldn't help but notice her undeniable beauty. As he looked around he understood where Kat was coming from. It's a huge place and being a new mom to three kids is a lot of work. He's now certain that she would agree to have him send an Assistant.

Vixen was docked out front as Elizabeth had requested. She'd invited family, friends, neighbors and acquaintances to celebrate her Grandson and all of their accomplishments.

"Okay girls, I'm here to help you get ready for the party," Henley called.

"Oh, that's right, today is Grandma Liz's party. Yay, let's go get ready, I know just what I'd like to wear," Syd said excitedly.

"Me too," Kat says as they ran off excitedly.

Lucas sneezed and Faith opened her eyes.

"Hi there," Henley called.

"Henley? When did you get here?"

"About an hour ago. I didn't want to wake you."

She blushed realizing that he's been looking at her while she slept.

"Please excuse the mess, I've had quite a week," she said appearing slightly embarrassed.

"I know what you're thinking."

"What am I thinking about Faith Elizabeth?"

A smile formed on her face.

"Actually, I haven't said a word," he toyed.

"Wow, why's Vixen out there?"

"Your mother-in-law's party is today, remember?"

"That's right, totally forgot," she said placing Lucas in his bouncy.

"Mind if I hold him for a sec?" he asked, approaching.

"Sure, not at all," she said placing Lucas in his arms. He stared at her seductively as he takes Lucas.

"Go ahead, I'll watch him while you get ready."

"Thanks," she called and hurried to the shower.

"Hey there little guy, what are you going to wear? Need some help?"

Lucas smiled in response, revealing dimples and toothless gum.

"You are a heartbreaker, what are you trying to do to me little guy," Henley teased, kissing him on the forehead.

"Let's get you dressed for your party. You're going to have the time of your life buddy and Uncle Henley will teach you the best dance moves ever."

Later, as they boarded Vixen, Faith felt relieve to be surrounded by all their friends including uninvited guests from Sandy Island.

"Faith, over here," Maggie calls.

"Oh Maggie, Joyce, you made it, so glad to see you both," Faith says embracing her friends.

"Lovely Party, is this Senator Henley?" Joyce asked, appearing uncomfortable by the large crowd.

"My mom's not very outgoing. She doesn't like being around too many people," Maggie admitted.

"Aww, sweetheart, I don't blame you, I'd avoid them if I could," Faith joked.

Joyce laughed and embraced her senator a second time.

"Have you two seen the ballroom? there's lots of presents with your names on them from me, Liz, Calvin and Gerry. We also have an open kitchen and Bar," Faith said and winks at Maggie. As the women chatted, they were interrupted when Henley joined the conversation.

"Come on mom, let's go mingle," Maggie said leading her mom to the bar.

"How's Lucas and the girls?"

"Having a blast with my assistant. She's never watched kids, but she's doing a great job. She's a natural," he assured.

"Are you sure?"

"Absolutely, they're in the Captain's quarters."

"Well, what can I say other than thank you Senator."

"You've got it. Today I want you to relax and not think about anything at all, okay."

"Okay," she responded.

"Come here," he said, taking her hands leading her up the stairs to the uppermost deck. Henley exhaled a sigh of relief.

"This view," he sighed.

She stood a few feet away from him with her back turned. She could feel his stare. Faith turned around slowly to meet Henley's eyes.

"We should get back to the party, our guests are still arriving," she said as he approaches.

"We are at the party," he said, placing his nose on hers.

"Something about this turquoise bay against a fiery backdrop is unsearchable," she said blushing.

"Do you think that's all it is?" he asked.

"You're shaking," she replied, adjusting his tie.

"Don't you know why?"

She blinked quickly to hide the tears that was filling her eyes.

"*But Henley...*" she whispers, her knees shaking.

"I love you, my darling," he replied.

He then drew her in his arms and kisses her till the fiery sunset disappeared beyond the horizon.

About the Author

Natlie might have seen some of the world's most beautiful horizons. From dawn till dusk, the views from her window have always been the soft yellow ray of the sun as it casts its golden reflection on the bay at sunrise. Then just as faithfully at dusk, displays its multicolored memory of the day's joy-cascading remembrance on the twilight sky at sundown. Natlie is a fascinating Author, American Socialite, and Romance Novelist of four books: A Royal Encounter, Heavenly Pillars, The Little Book of Writing Inspirations and now Sandy Island. She currently resides in Southern California where she is always surrounded by exquisite beauty that instills a fire in her heart to release her most imaginative work.

Made in the USA
Las Vegas, NV
24 August 2022

53918143R00177